"How dare you!"

"Don't you dare presume to run my acquaintances away!" Felicity snapped.

Rafe leaned down and softly touched his lips to hers. "My apologies."

She blinked, realizing she was leaning up toward him, her mouth half open. "What . . . what for?" she stammered.

"For throwing Lord Deerhurst out."

"And the kiss?" she asked boldly, trying to rally indignation, when what she really wanted was for him to kiss her again. Immediately.

Rafe shook his head, running his thumb across the sensitive corner of her mouth. "That wasn't a kiss."

Damnation, she was leaning again. "Then . . . then what, pray tell, was it?"

"Practice. You'll know when I've kissed you."

SUZANNE ENOCH

Taming Rafe

AVON

An Imprint of HarperCollinsPublishers

AVON BOOKS
An Imprint of HarperCollins*Publishers*
10 East 53rd Street
New York, New York 10022-5299

Copyright © 1999 by Suzanne Enoch
ISBN 978-0-380-79886-5
www.avonromance.com

First Avon Books mass market printing: April 1999

Again, for my sister, Nancy,
who makes me be historically accurate
even when I don't want to be

Prologue

"This place is a damned sieve," Rafael Michelangelo Bancroft complained, shaking his wet sleeve and moving his chair for the third time. "It was drier in Africa during the monsoon season."

Half-filled buckets caught a symphony of leaks in the shabby gaming parlor. Thunder rumbled over the rooftops of Covent Garden, the lightning illuminating the damp clientele taking shelter in Jezebel's Harem.

"Then why'd you return to England?" Robert Fields asked as he placed his wager.

Rafe shrugged. "I'd seen the whole country, so there wasn't much point in repeating the experience. I have enough tales of Africa to last awhile."

"Including the one about the bloody Zulus trying to serve you up for breakfast—that's my favorite," the third wagerer broke in.

Rafe took a long swallow of port. "Thank you, Francis," he said dryly.

Francis Henning smiled, his round cheeks flushed from alcohol. "I know how you are. Go off on a grand adventure, and ignore the damned trouble waiting for you there until it tries to run you through or eat you."

1

"What about the trouble waiting for you back home?" Rafe asked, half serious.

"At least that's trouble you know about." Francis tapped his chest. "Take my advice. Grand adventures are fine for stories, but not much else. The way to the good life is patience, Bancroft. Slow, simple, safe patience."

Grinning faintly, Rafe took in Henning's new, well-fitting gray coat and the emerald pin stuck through his cravat. "Patience . . . I thought you looked particularly well-heeled this evening."

Francis's smile widened. "You'll never believe it, Rafe—turns out I was Grandmama's favorite relation, after all. The old girl kicked off last January, and left me two thousand bloody quid!"

"Hope you don't mind sharing some of it with us, Henning," Fields said from across the table, while in the corner Sir William Thornton vomited into one of the rain buckets. "Good God, keep it down, will you, Thornton?"

Rafe chuckled. "I believe that's the problem, Robert."

"What? Oh. Well, blast it, Henning, place your damned wager, will you?"

Rafe's momentary amusement ebbed. His luck at the tables since he'd returned from Africa had been abysmal, though in truth his aim had been more to occupy himself and to avoid his father, than to add to his income. But now his losses had equalled last month's pay, and he realized what a sorry state he'd fallen into.

The fourth member of their quintet placed his own wager on the table and tucked a well-oiled lock of black hair back into place on his head. "All patience ever got me was stuck," he grumbled, glancing uncertainly at Rafe.

Nigel Harrington had been doing that all evening, and it was beginning to wear thin. "A Bancroft," he'd said with awe when Robert introduced them, as though he'd just come face to face with the Colossus of Rhodes. At least their tall, red-haired hostess had been equally impressed. Being the second son of the Duke of Highbarrow was mostly a damned nuisance, but he wasn't a complete idiot about using it to his advantage, either.

He placed ten quid in the redhead's palm. "The seven, if you please," he murmured.

Lydia giggled and placed the wager where he indicated. That done, she settled back onto his lap and resumed nibbling on his earlobe. It had been over two years since he'd last spent an evening at Jezebel's Harem, and if not for the amusement Henning and Fields offered, he would have gone to find plumper game. The Harem had long since ceased to be a gathering place of the ultra wealthy.

Francis leaned sideways. "I hear you sold out your commission, Rafael. The army too tame for you now?"

"You going to clerk for Papa now? Or go about taking tallies of his cattle?" Robert chuckled. "Oh, I know—you could join the priesthood, what? Father Rafael."

Rafe narrowed his eyes. "Very amusing."

Lydia scowled. "Don't listen to him, love. What a waste of a fine man that would be."

She trailed her finger down the long, narrow scar that ran from his left cheekbone to his jaw. Flinching, he curled his fingers around her wrist and returned her hand to where it had been fiddling with the buttons of his waistcoat. "Never fear, my dear. I couldn't possibly do such a thing to myself."

"But what's it to be?" Robert pursued. "His

Grace won't stand for you lounging about in gaming hells much longer."

That was true. But at the same time his return to civilian life after seven years with the Coldstream Guards would please his father no end—no doubt the reason he hadn't yet announced the news to his family. He looked across the table. "Are you in or out, Whiting?"

The thin dandy placed his stack of coins by the seven of hearts, beside Rafe's. "In, of course, Bancroft."

Rafe watched him. He recognized a fellow gambler when he saw one. And Peter Whiting was cheating. He was doing such a fine job of it, in fact, that no one else seemed to have noticed.

But even studying Whiting's technique and having a voluptuous chit wriggling about on his lap couldn't distract him from one annoying fact: He was bored. Again. Leaving Oxford to join the Coldstream Guards had seemed exciting and challenging, and in the beginning it had been. It also had the advantage of being expressly against his father's wishes. Wearing snappy uniforms and leading endless parades, though, had not been nearly as fulfilling as he'd hoped.

Volunteering for Wellington's regiment at Waterloo had been Rafe's solution. He had finally been able to put some of his hard-earned knowledge to use—but then his father had ordered him returned home as soon as the Bancrofts received word that he'd been wounded.

After that he had spent three long years in England before he'd finally argued, cajoled, and connived his way onto a schooner carrying a battalion of lancers to southern Africa. And now his father had managed to get him unvolunteered from that duty, as well. A desk—or worse yet, a pulpit—

would be next, but that would kill him.

He and Whiting won the round of faro, as Rafe had been fairly certain they would. Lydia giggled and did a bit more sliding about on his lap as she raked in his share of the winnings. Though being sluiced over the ivories and Lydia's squirming were pleasant sensations, neither erased the fact that he had poor odds of winning enough blunt to arrange his escape—to anywhere that wasn't London, and anywhere the illustrious fingers of the Bancroft family didn't reach. The duke, of course, would eat coal before he gave Rafe more than ten quid for something so useless. And his older brother, Quin, the illustrious Marquis of Warefield, would require him to write a paper discussing the merits of the various peoples and countries and civilizations he encountered.

Rafe reached around Lydia for his glass and drained it. Because he'd been watching for it, he caught the swift exchange of looks between Peter Whiting and the dealer. Now, that was simply too much. He might have been counting cards himself, but at least he'd been doing it on his own. To enlist the aid of the house was just plain dastardly.

When all bets were placed, the dealer flipped the next card. This time Rafe saw the turn of his wrist, and he nodded as Peter Whiting won the hand. "Well done," he congratulated. "What say we play one more round and then call it a night?"

Rafe leaned forward and caught the dealer a sharp blow across the jaw. With a surprised grunt, the man fell out of his chair and onto the floor.

"What in damnation are you doing, Bancroft?" Nigel Harrington shot to his feet.

"I do believe the fellow wasn't paying the appropriate attention to his duties," Rafe drawled. He lifted a hand and guided Lydia to the dealer's vacated chair. "Now. Everyone will please contribute, oh, one hundred quid, say, into the pot, and then Lydia will turn over the top card."

"This is highly irregular, Bancroft," Harrington protested again, flushing.

Francis chuckled. "Most things about old Rafe are. What's your new scheme, boy?"

"India, I think," Rafe answered, chin in his hand. "Or China. Never been there."

"And we're supposed to fund your travels?" Nigel glanced uncertainly at Whiting.

"Only if you lose. Are you in, or out?" Rafe asked coolly, sliding over his money.

The lad eyed the cash on the table, the unconscious dealer on the floor, the small pile of money remaining before him, and the expression in Rafe's eyes. He licked his lips. "I don't have a hundred quid," he muttered, resuming his seat.

"Then good evening."

Peter Whiting watched his companion over the rim of his glass. "Time to toddle home, eh, Nigel?"

"Blast it, Whiting, stop that." Harrington met Rafe's aloof gaze again. "I've got this," he said, and reached into his breast pocket to produce a heavy, much-folded piece of parchment, which he dropped onto the table.

Whiting laughed. "Good God, Nigel. You *have* got balls!"

"It's worth at least a hundred quid," Harrington said, slumping in his chair and reaching for the port.

For a moment Rafe nearly took pity on him. But despite Harrington's dandified aping of his crony's manner and attire, he had to be twenty-two or twenty-three—old enough to know better than to hang about a snake like Peter Whiting if he didn't want to share the risks.

Rafe dragged the parchment into the center of the table with his fingertips, then poured himself another glass of port and glanced at Lydia. She smiled, running her tongue along her front teeth. "It'll do."

Chapter 1

❦❦❦

"**M**ay?" Felicity Harrington called, anxiety making her voice shake. "May, hurry please!"

Another tremendous gust of wind hit the house, rocking the building. Felicity held on to the banister, fearing the storm would push the house off its foundation and hoping the old place would hold steady until she and May made it safely down to the ground floor.

"Felicity, the rain's coming in my window!"

"I know, sweetling. But there's nothing we can do about it right now. Just bring your blankets and we'll sleep in the morning room. It'll be an adventure."

"All right!"

"Damnation, Nigel Harrington," Felicity muttered through clenched, chattering teeth, "you should be here."

It wasn't that her brother would have been of any use; he never had been before. There were times, like tonight, when she felt a thousand years older than her twenty-two-year-old twin. Though they both had their mother's black hair and dark eyes, as did May, all similarities ended there. Mother had used to say that Nigel had inherited

Father's share of common sense, which was a kind way of saying that he had none at all.

Five weeks ago he'd dismissed Smythe, the last of their servants. True, the butler's absence would save them three pounds a month, but then Nigel had taken it into his head to go to London and win enough money to see their ancestral home repaired. Despite her protests, off he'd gone, taking their carriage, their last horse, and all their ready cash with him—all except what she'd been putting aside in case of emergency. But tonight looked more like a catastrophe.

Wind and torrents of rain battered the old walls, and the attic timbers groaned. Plaster dust fell in a damp cloud around her as thunder boomed again over Forton Hall.

"Felicity!" May screeched.

"I'm coming!" She could only guess what May, only eight and possessed of an excruciatingly vivid imagination, must be going through.

With a curse she heaved her bulky quilt over the railing and let it drop to the foyer floor. It knocked one of their last crystal vases off the hall table as it went, shattering the delicate glass. As Felicity hurried down the hallway toward May a window broke, and she shrieked at the sudden cold blast of wet wind that hit her. Shielding her face with one arm, she made her way into her sister's bedchamber.

Curtains flapping above her head and her dark hair blowing around her face like a mad halo, May was swiftly piling clothes, books, toys, and shoes onto the middle of a blanket. "Felicity, where is Polly?" she asked frantically, her brown eyes wide.

"She's downstairs in the morning room, still having tea with Mr. Bear. Here, let me help you with that."

Kneeling, she pulled the four corners of the blanket together and knotted them. Dragging the bundle out into the hall, she headed for the stairs. May followed close behind her, her favorite pillow held tightly to her chest.

"Everything's getting all wet!" she yelled, ducking her face behind the pillow.

Felicity grabbed her sister's arm and pulled her toward the stairs. "It's all right—it'll dry!" The groaning of the old west wing took on an alarming timbre, and she looked anxiously up at the ceiling. Cracks spread across the rough surface with such speed that she could see them growing. "Oh, no," she whispered, hoping May wouldn't notice and panic.

They reached the bottom of the stairs just as the front door blew in. May screamed. One of the double doors cracked off its hinges and slammed onto the foyer floor, narrowly missing the two of them.

The wind howled like a mad wolf. Felicity grabbed May by the arm and dragged her toward the morning room in the newer east wing. Her hair had come loose from its clips and the wet strands whipped into her face, half blinding her. More glass broke behind them, and the house shuddered again.

A resounding crack echoed through the west wing. With a rumble louder than thunder, the entire wing lurched drunkenly sideways and then collapsed on itself. Plaster and glass and wood and water flew outward. Felicity screamed, but she couldn't even hear the sound in her own throat.

Without realizing it, she'd fallen to the floor. As soon as the house stopped shaking and shuddering, she scrambled to her feet, fighting against the tangle of her sodden skirts. "Come on, May!" she yelled. "We'll be safe in the morning room!"

May shook her head. "No! It'll fall, too!"

"No, it won't! The east wing is much sturdier, May. We'll be fine! I promise."

"I hope so," May wailed, gripping her older sister's hand tightly.

So do I. Felicity glanced up at the dark, lightning-streaked sky where a third of her roof used to be. Damn Nigel for running off. If he didn't return with money soon, there wouldn't even be a Forton Hall for him to return to.

Rafael Bancroft awoke to the sensation of having his chest licked. Reluctantly he opened one eye to see a disheveled head of flaming red hair working its way down toward his abdomen.

"Good morning, Lydia," he murmured, stretching and trying to ignore the pounding in his skull. "Where are we?"

She lifted her head to look at him, then grinned and resumed her downward journey. "My room, upstairs from Jezebel's." Lydia giggled, the sound muffled. "And it ain't morning."

Rafe glanced over at the window. "Damn." Although what she was doing felt very good, he supposed he did have things to do. He stretched once more and started to sit up, but then her nimble fingers joined her mouth. With a happy sigh, Rafe lay back and closed his eyes again. Nothing was worth hurrying over that much.

He shifted, tugging her bare legs up over his chest. Then he noticed Nigel Harrington's parchment on the nightstand. Reaching over, he unfolded it to see just what he'd signed for last night. And then he sat up so quickly he dumped Lydia off the narrow bed.

"Blast it!" Lydia sat, stunned and naked, on the floor for a moment, then scrambled to her feet and slammed him across the head with a pillow.

Rafe grabbed it away from her, barely noticing the blow. "Show some respect, dear. I seem to be a landowner."

"You're a bloody, rotten pig, that's what you are!" she snapped angrily.

He grinned. "But at least I'm a well-to-do one."

"You don't think he was serious about China, do you?"

Victoria Bancroft, the Duchess of Highbarrow, turned from gazing out over gloomy King Street to face her elder son. "*You* seem to think he is, or you wouldn't have bothered telling me."

Quin Bancroft, the Marquis of Warefield, scowled and sipped his glass of Madeira. "It's ludicrous. Even for him."

She studied the marquis as he turned his head yet again to listen down the hallway for his wife. Both her boys had her tawny blond hair and green eyes, though Rafe's were much lighter—almost the color of the sea—with a devilish twinkle that came from knowing he was the absolute delight of his mother's heart. "You sound like your father."

"Well, thank you very much," Quin said indignantly. "I thought you'd be pleased to hear the information that Francis Henning passed on to me."

She smiled. "What's so ludicrous about Rafael wanting to travel?"

"He has a life here. He's a Bancroft, for God's sake."

"I believe he thinks he's already explored that aspect of his life to death, Quinlan."

The butler scratched at the morning room door. "Luncheon is served, Your Grace, my lord."

"Thank you, Beeks."

She rose, and Quin followed her through the

maze of rooms and doors and hallways to the huge dining room. "You're certain he didn't return home last night?" he asked.

"Quin, now you sound like his mother. That's my position, I believe."

"I am merely showing brotherly concern."

"Yes, you are, and it's lovely, but what do you have in mind for Rafe to do here?"

The marquis hesitated. "I'm sure if he'd sit down and talk to me about it, we'd come up with something that would keep his interest."

"You could let him attempt something on his own."

"Not if it involves blasted China. He's been back from Africa less than a damned month; I can't believe he wants to travel again already. Why didn't he mention that to me?"

"Perhaps he thought it might upset you, dear."

Quin narrowed his eyes. "If that stopped him from doing things, I wouldn't be so close to having an apoplexy every time he walked through the door."

Victoria couldn't help laughing. "Please, Quin. Someone has to take risks."

"I've got Maddie for that, thank you very much."

The duchess paused by her chair, then glanced at the other, empty seats. "Beeks, are Maddie and His Grace coming?"

The butler inclined his head. "Yes, my lady. His Grace requested that I inform you they will be along 'in a damned minute,' Your Grace."

Quin chuckled as he held out his mother's chair for her. "Maddie's beating him at whist again. He hates that."

While Quin kept up a stream of amusing banter, avoiding further discussion of his brother's highly disputed future, Victoria glanced at the clock on the mantel. Rafael was in town so rarely, and he'd been avoiding them since he'd returned. An uneasy sensation ran along her bones. He had already helped to defeat Bonaparte, charmed his way into the hearts of London's loveliest ladies, and won and lost himself a small fortune in London's most famous, and infamous, clubs. She had to wonder what would appear next on his shrinking list of challenges.

"Your Grace, hand over Highbarrow Castle and all its lands, and I'll forget that you owe me one hundred and thirty-eight million pounds." Her gray eyes dancing, Madeleine Bancroft swept into the dining room. With Rafe's frequent absences she'd been the force to bring life back into the staid Bancroft family, and Victoria would always adore her for it.

"Absolutely not, girl. You said pence, not pounds."

"I did not, and you know it."

Victoria stifled a smile at the unaccustomed look of good-humored befuddlement on her husband's face. And to think everyone in the world but she and Maddie—and Quin—were terrified of His Grace. Rafe pretended not to be, but he, probably more than anyone else, both craved his father's acceptance and kept himself as far as possible from the duke, as if it didn't matter to him one way or the other. And Lewis Bancroft hadn't a clue about any of it.

Quin stood to kiss Maddie and hold out her chair. "You'd best give in, Your Grace. I've yet to win an argument with her."

"That's because you're always wrong, my love."

"Now just a moment—"

"Good afternoon, everyone."

Rafe entered the dining room, and Victoria's uneasiness deepened. Something had agitated and excited him, though he tried to hide it. Being recalled from Africa had angered him deeply, and Victoria couldn't blame him. Thus far he'd avoided a direct confrontations with His Grace over it, but from Rafe's expression it looked as though today was the day.

Maddie narrowed her eyes. "Good heavens, Rafe, you look like you had to dig your way out of your own grave."

He forced a chuckle. "Got a bit inebriated last night."

The duke's mood blackened at his younger son's appearance. The Highbarrow Thundercloud, Quin called it, more predictable than any storm front. "You might have shaved and changed your clothes before you stumbled in here, boy. For God's sake, we had King George here for luncheon last week."

Victoria cleared her throat. "Rafael, might I—"

"Ah, good afternoon, Father. Didn't recognize you until you scowled. You look completely menacing now, as usual."

"I'd rather be menacing than useless."

"Lewis," the duchess said quietly.

Rafe leaned over her shoulder and kissed her on the cheek. "Not to worry, my sweet. He's about to be very impressed."

"Bah. I doubt that," the duke sneered.

With a flourish, Rafael produced a heavy piece of parchment from his coat pocket. He opened it and set it beside his father's plate. "You see?" he said, folding his arms over his chest. "I am now the owner of Forton Hall. In Cheshire."

Quin reached out to grab the paper, mingled

astonishment and amusement on his face. "You're what?"

Maddie clapped her hands together in delight. "Whom did you kill, Rafe?" She laughed. "Was it a duel, or an assassination?"

Rafe's expression eased a little. "No one died. I used my commission money as a stake, and—"

"You sold out your commission?" the duke bellowed, flushing furiously.

"I thought you'd be pleased." Rafe ran a hand through his disheveled, honey-colored hair and kept his expression aloof.

"First bloody thing you've done that makes any damned sense."

"By God, it's even signed over," Quin mused, handing it to the duke. "It looks completely legitimate. Francis kept mumbling about some piece of paper or other, but I couldn't make any sense of it."

Victoria kept her eyes on her younger son. Unless something as catastrophic as Parliament exploding again had occurred, Rafael had not suddenly become a conventional landowner. "So you bought yourself an estate," she said.

His gaze touched hers and then slid away again. "Not precisely. I won it. This Harrington fellow put the deed on the table and lost it, and said 'glad to be rid of it.' He signed it, I signed it, and Henning and Fields witnessed it, and now it's mine."

"And?" the duchess prompted.

"However he got hold of it, Rafael is finally using his head for something other than a sharpshooter's target," the duke finished. "A landowner. Thank Lucifer. I thought for certain you'd end up on some damned fool expedition or other."

A muscle in Rafe's lean cheek twitched. "Actually, Father, you're not that far off the mark."

Lewis shook his head. "You can't be gadding about to Hades and back when you've an estate to run."

"I'm—"

"Hm. I imagine you'll need me to look over the estate and books, since you don't know the first thing about—"

"I'm not keeping the bloody thing. I intend—"

His Grace surged to his feet, knocking his chair backward. *"You're what?"*

Rafael glared at him, his green eyes glinting with a month's worth of suppressed anger. "I have no intention of sitting about on my fat ass waiting for the wheat to grow every year," he snapped. "Your life is a bloody, stifling bore, and you're welcome to it—you and Quin, both. I'm—"

Quin straightened. "Now just a damned minute—"

"I'm going to sell this blasted place," Rafe growled, ripping the paper out of his father's fingers, "for as much as I can make off it."

"And then what, you idiot? Gamble it or whore it away?"

Rafe stuffed the paper back into his coat pocket. "I'm going to travel," he stated sharply. "You may own half of England, but you don't own the Colonies, or the southern Americas, or the Orient. And you don't by God own me. Mother, Maddie, good day."

His gaze lingered for a moment on Victoria, and then he strode out the door and slammed it behind him so hard the windows rattled.

Victoria sat looking at the door. "My," she muttered faintly.

The door flew open again. "Beeks!"

The startled butler stepped forward. "Yes, Master Rafael?"

"I'm taking my kit with me. Box the rest of my things. I'll send word if I need any of it."

"Very good, sir."

The door slammed again.

"Go stop him, Victoria, before he does something he'll regret," the duke blustered.

She faced her husband, trying to remain calm. It would do no good if she exploded as well, much as she would like to. "You think I could stop him, Lewis? After what you said to him?"

"After what *I* said? Bah. A good riddance to him, then."

Maddie and Quinn looked at each other, cleary dismayed, and Victoria sat back in her chair. She wondered if Lewis realized that, barring a miracle, he'd just lost a son. Apparently Rafe's next challenge was to escape the Bancrofts.

Chapter 2

~~~ᗡᗡ~~~

Rafe arrived in Cheshire three days later. By the time he rode up the muddy, rutted road that led to Forton Hall, he'd decided to begin his travels in India—though Japan still had a definite pull. If the Hall was of decent-enough size and location, he would never have to worry about money or his independence from the duke again.

At the last inn the locals looked at him with obvious curiosity, and then gave him directions. He hoped it wasn't their idea of rural humor to send him into the middle of a bog, or something. Four miles west he came upon Crown Creek and its stone bridge, as they had instructed. If it wasn't the right direction, at least it was picturesque. He crossed the old bridge, then pulled up his bay, Aristotle.

He couldn't recall that he'd ever been to Cheshire before. It was one of the few counties where the Bancrofts didn't have a holding, so according to his father's thinking, it had little to recommend it. A pair of redwing thrushes, a hundred miles south of their usual summer range, fluted at him and vanished into the surrounding woodlands of scattered beech, ash, and maple. It was beautiful country, the fresh green a welcome change from his last two months in southern Africa during the

19

dry season. The hills of neighboring Derbyshire rose dimly blue-gray to the east, and he could almost smell the ocean to the west on the slight, cool breeze.

Rafe smiled, humming a waltz tune, as he sent Aristotle forward again. Pretty, quiet, green country—just the type of land that would fetch the best price from prospective landowners. Sometimes he simply couldn't believe his own good fortune. Nigel Harrington was a complete fool to have parted with Forton Hall for a hundred-quid wager.

An overgrown hedge curved northwest and merged into a chaos of yellow-flowered weeds and tall grass. Rafe's gaze followed the drive up the slight rise, to the doorway of Forton Hall itself. The smile dropped from his face.

"Damnation," he swore. "Damn, damn, damn."

He slowly dismounted, unable to take his gaze from the complete wreck before him.

The entire west wing of the house had caved in on itself, with small sections of rafter and wall still sticking up into the sky like the bleached rib bones of a great whale. Broken shutters lay in tumbled heaps of wood and shrubbery at the foot of the pitted white walls, while the coverings that remained hung at crazy angles from the windows. Broken glass, plaster, wood, stone, and shingles flattened the remains of what might once have been a pretty rose garden.

"Good God," he muttered, leading Aristotle gingerly through the maze of destruction spilling out onto the overgrown lawn. In Belgium he'd helped bring down fortifications, and Forton Hall looked just like a place hit by cannon and a keg or two of blasting powder.

He dropped the gelding's reins, and with a hand

motion ordered Aristotle to stay put. Broken glass crunched beneath his boots as he made his way up through the tattered vines covering the shallow front steps. Only one of the double doors remained on its bronzed hinges, while someone had hammered the other door into position with a pair of awkwardly placed cross supports. The door scraped across the floor and gave an earsplitting squeak as he pushed it cautiously open. He stepped inside, and a small flock of sparrows chirruped at him and flew through a jagged hole that had once been the beginning of the west wing.

The stairs winding up to the east wing's second story were intact, though he was unwilling to vouch for their sturdiness with half the building gone. At least the walls and most of the roof of the other wing remained.

Apparently Nigel Harrington hadn't been the biggest idiot playing faro that night. No one in his right mind would ever purchase such a spectacular wreck. And taxes on the land and the broken windows and whatever pitiful crops remained would still be due.

Swearing at Harrington, himself, and everyone else who hadn't won that last hand of faro, Rafe kicked the remains of a chair into a corner. The best he could hope for was that Harrington had left behind enough valuables to pay off any debts already owing, so he could declare the place abandoned and walk away. Five hundred pounds had seemed a wealth of ready cash when he only needed it for the time it took to sell the estate. Now it was all he had.

"Won't Father be amused," he muttered, entering the dining room. A mishmash of clutter covered the table and the chairs, and lay stacked in every corner. Angrily he shoved the table aside and

pushed on the door that would lead to the first floor
sitting rooms. It wasn't locked, but something held
it closed from the other side. He put his shoulder
against the door and shoved harder. It didn't budge.

"Wonderful. Bloody, bloody wonderful. I've
won a blasted rat's nest," he snarled, backing a few
steps and running at the door. "Ouch! Blast." Rafe
rubbed at his shoulder and glared at the barrier for
a long moment.

"Don't you want this?" a muffled voice said.

The sound came through the half-open door
leading back into the hallway. Not only did he *not*
have a saleable estate, now he had thieves scav-
enging what little remained of it.

"Not for long," he murmured, and slipped out
into the hallway.

Whoever they were, they weren't attempting
stealth. Undoubtedly they thought the owner had
abandoned the estate. A grim smile curved his lips.
They were about to find out differently. *Someone*
deserved a beating for this disaster.

Felicity Harrington set down the armful of
gowns she'd salvaged from the collapsed remains
of her bedchamber. It had rained again yesterday,
and everything was damp. Thankfully, hanging
them in the kitchen around the stove seemed to be
drying them out and keeping them from getting
musty. Before much longer, though, both her and
May's things would be hopelessly mildewed.

"What should we do about Nigel's things?"
May asked, as she set shoes down to dry around
the stove.

"They come last," Felicity stated, putting a finger through a hole in her favorite morning dress.
"If ever."

May chuckled. "He won't be very happy when he sees all his clothes turned green."

Felicity smiled. "Green and fuzzy."

"Green and fuzzy and *smelly*."

The door slammed open. With a gasp, Felicity whipped around just as something tall, hard, and heavy hit her, throwing them both to the floor. She shrieked.

"Damnation!" the brick wall on top of her growled in a deep voice.

She kicked out, and her attacker grunted as she made contact. "May, run!" she yelled, kicking again.

He shifted off her, and as she struggled to her knees she glimpsed tousled blond hair and a scar. Crying out again, she swung her fist into his face as hard as she could.

He grabbed her arm, yanking her off balance again. "Ouch! Don't—"

Felicity rammed his chest with an elbow, and he backed off and raised a hand as though to ward her off.

"Get out!" Flinging her hair out of her face, she shoved at him again. He was kneeling on her skirt, keeping her pinned to the floor. He intercepted her arm as she struck at him again, and twisted it behind her before she could even gasp.

"Look," he panted into her hair. "I'm sor—"

He jerked forward and collapsed on top of her. May stood behind him, a dented copper tea kettle gripped in both hands.

Felicity squirmed out from under her attacker and grabbed a stout stick of firewood as she scrambled to her feet. "I told you to run, May," she managed, her heart hammering madly.

"You wouldn't have," her sister said, boldly tapping the man's head with the tea kettle again. It bonked hollowly. "Do you think I killed him?"

"I shouldn't think so," Felicity answered, looking at him more closely. He'd fallen on his face, and blood trickled from the back of his skull onto the floor. "Good Lord. Help me tie him up, and then we'll send someone for the constable."

"Send who?"

"Whom," she automatically corrected.

"Send whom?" May repeated.

Oh, dear—she had no one *to* send. "Send me, I suppose. Both of us." Felicity glanced up at May. "Run to the stable and get some rope. Hurry."

"All right." May handed over the kettle. "Here. Bash him with this if he moves."

Felicity stifled an entirely inappropriate grin. "Thank you, my dear."

Once May had gone, Felicity studied her attacker. Her first sense had been correct—he was definitely tall, and lean though well-muscled. Golden-blond, disheveled hair hung into his face, so she couldn't see what he looked like. His clothing surprised her. He dressed like a gentleman—one in need of a change of clothes and a shave and bath, but a gentleman, nonetheless.

He groaned and she jumped, instinctively thwacking him across the head again. The man jerked and went still.

Felicity shuddered. Horrified that she might have finished him off, she leaned down closer to his face. After a moment she heard his soft breathing, and sighed in relief. It didn't look as though they'd ever be able to pound the teakettle back into shape again, though.

"Here," May panted, running in with several long coils of rope draped across her slim shoulders. "It's all I could find."

"It'll do nicely." Felicity took a length, then

knelt beside the man. She pulled one arm behind his back, while May did the same with his other. She looped the rope around his wrists and tied it as tightly as she could, then knotted it again for good luck. He wore no rings, and while several of his fingers were callused, neither did they look to be the hands of a farmer.

"I've got his feet done," May said a moment later, sitting back.

Apparently May had studied sailors' knots in her spare time, because Felicity couldn't make heads or tails of where the ropes began or ended. "They look very sturdy," she complimented, eyeing her sister. May seemed to be enjoying this rather too much.

"What now?"

"Well, I suppose we should turn him over and finish the job. I don't want him getting loose while we're gone into Pelford."

She took his shoulders, pulling hard against his weight, while May turned his legs. With another pained groan her attacker slowly rolled onto his back, his head thunking solidly against the floor again. "Oh, dear," she muttered, almost feeling sorry for the poor brute. Felicity looked down at his face for the first time. "Oh, dear," she repeated.

A painful-looking scar ran from the corner of his left eye, deepened across his high cheekbone, and then trailed off at the line of his jaw. Honey-colored hair partially covered one closed eye, but the scar, together with his arched brows and tanned skin, made him look quite piratical. And exceedingly handsome.

"Do you think he's a pirate?" May asked, apparently sharing her assessment. She leaned over her sister's shoulder to get a look at their captive.

"He's a long way from water, if he is," Felicity returned slowly, wrapping the remaining rope around his broad chest and hard, flat stomach as tightly as she could and knotting it.

"Perhaps he's lost, then."

Somehow Felicity didn't think so. "Perhaps."

His eyes fluttered and opened, light green and startled. She gasped and sat backward. "Don't try anything!" she warned harshly, grabbing for the kettle again.

The eyes tried to focus on her, closed, then opened again and rolled back into his head. "Damned female," he muttered in a slurred voice, shutting them again.

"He's drunk," May declared.

"I don't smell liquor on him," Felicity disagreed. "We did hit him rather hard, dear."

"Do you think we broke his head?"

"We might have."

"Cracked my skull, you damned assassin," his deep voice uttered again.

"Watch your language, sir," Felicity ordered. "There's a child present."

The eyes opened again, crossed groggily, then focused on her. "You're no blasted child," he said after a moment's hesitation.

"I am," May stated, leaning over him again. "Are you a pirate?"

"No."

"May, keep away. He's dangerous."

"Am not," he muttered. He made as if to sit up, then raised his head a little to look at his bound chest and legs. "Damn," he repeated, and lay back again, banging his head. "Oh, God! You've killed me, I think."

"We have not. And we're going to get the constable," Felicity warned him.

"Good."

That stopped her. "Why is it a good thing that we should have you arrested?" He was definitely piratical, especially with the thin trickle of blood running past one ear. She swallowed, her mouth dry. Good Lord, she'd captured some sort of splendidly handsome pirate king, and he'd meant to drag her off to the Spanish Main, or somewhere.

"Because I'll have *you* arrested," he managed. "Thief."

"I am not a thief!" she declared indignantly. "You are a . . . a rogue and an attacker of helpless women!"

"Helpless, my ass."

Felicity banged the kettle on the floor beside him. "Your language, sir!" she reminded him.

He flinched. "Fine. I'll watch my language, Miss Helpless."

She attempted to ignore the cynicism dripping from his voice. "That's right. Now what do you think you were doing?"

The pirate blinked fuzzily again. "Is this," he said, enunciating each word as though to be certain he got them out correctly, "is this Forton Hall, in Cheshire?"

For a moment she looked at him. "Yes. Yes, it is."

"Ha! You're a damned—you're a trespasser!"

"*What?* You're the one who broke into my home and attacked me!"

"Thought you were a man. Besides, it's *my* house."

"He's daft," May said.

"Am not. Let me up."

"Absolutely not, sir. For all I know, you're a mad, knife-wielding murderer."

"Listen, Miss Helpless. I am Rafael Bancroft,

and Forton Hall is mine. I can prove it."

Felicity rolled her eyes at his lunacy. "Forton Hall belongs to me, my sister, and my brother."

The light green gaze sharpened. "What's your brother's name?"

"Not that it's any of your business, but Nigel. Nigel Harrington."

For a moment he stared at her. "Good God!" he burst out. "That blasted, bloody, sniveling, cowardly liar! How in hell—"

"Mr. Bancroft!" she interrupted sharply, alarmed at the venom in his voice and the high color flushing his cheeks. "I don't know what you think is going on, but please desist—"

"I know—no damned cursing! *Sweet Lucifer!*"

May giggled.

He closed his mouth again and eyed her younger sister. Finally he returned his attention to Felicity. "What's your name?" he asked in a more even tone.

She scowled. "Felicity Harrington."

"Miss Harrington, will you please look in my left breast pocket? Then everything will be clear."

"Don't do it, Lis. It's a trap."

"Hush, May." Nothing this man said made any sense. Looking at him, she also found it impossible to believe that she and May had overpowered him. If he'd wanted to, he could have done her serious injury. Maybe he wasn't really dangerous. Still . . . "Don't you move an inch," she warned him.

"I won't."

Taking a deep breath, her heart thudding again, she reached out. His coat was strapped tightly to his broad chest by the ropes, and she tugged at the lapel to loosen it a little. He flinched as the motion rocked him, but otherwise made no move.

She gave another tug, then slid her hand inside

his coat, feeling for the pocket. His heart under her fingers beat strong and fast, and Felicity hesitated. It was ridiculous, the way she couldn't breathe, just because she had her hand on a man's chest. Yes, she was single and nearly twenty-three, but she certainly wasn't so desperate for a man's company that she'd prolong touching this particularly handsome, disheveled one—though she couldn't help thinking about it.

"A little farther, Miss Harrington," he murmured.

Her eyes snapped to meet his. Some of her confusion must have shown on her face, because his own expression was leaning toward amusement. Collecting herself, she shifted closer and stretched her hand partway under the taut ropes.

"Do you feel it?"

She scowled, flushing. "Feel what, precisely?"

He had the temerity to grin. "A large, thick piece of paper."

Her fingers touched it. "Yes, I do."

"Well, pull it out, then," he said in a low voice, light green eyes holding hers.

Flustered, she yanked. The paper came free, and his head bounced against the floor again. "Got it. And you're hardly in a position to be flirting, or whatever it was you were doing, sir."

"Sweet . . ." he began, wincing again. "Unfold it if you please, Miss Harrington."

Suspicious, Felicity did as he suggested. She scanned the first paragraph, which was couched in precise, legal terms, and blanched as she realized that it did look and sound very much like the deed to Forton Hall. Quickly she skipped to the bottom of the paper.

"This is not my brother's signature," she stated, her voice shaking with relief. Good Lord, for a moment she'd thought Mr. Bancroft might be telling the truth.

"I assure you it is."

Felicity examined it again. "I might believe it to be a poor forgery," she conceded.

"Would it help to convince you if I admitted that all parties concerned were at full sail?"

"You see, he is a pirate," May put in.

"Poor choice of words," he said hurriedly. "We were inebriated. Extremely inebriated."

Felicity lowered the parchment. "Well, that explains it, Mr. Bancroft. You were duped by some unscrupulous fellow who knew my brother was in London."

"I don't get 'duped,' " he said flatly.

Abruptly more sympathetic toward her inept would-be attacker, Felicity looked at the parchment again. "I'm certain if you've never seen a deed before, it would be difficult to recognize one. This does look somewhat impressive."

"Thank you for your compassion, Miss Harrington, but I assure you that I have seen deeds before. Dozens of them."

Poor man, she and May must have hit him too hard, after all. The way the kettle looked, she could only imagine the damage his skull must have sustained. "Of course you have."

He scowled, opened his mouth, and then shut it again. "Miss Harrington, allow me to inform you that my father is the Duke of Highbarrow," he finally said. "So yes, I have."

Felicity looked at May again. If Rafael Bancroft's confusion was genuine, as good Christians they had an obligation to help him since they had wounded him. After all, he'd gone from grand dreams of owning an estate, to being knocked unconscious by an eight-year-old girl and then learning that he'd been the victim of some scoundrel's heartless scheme. No wonder he needed to believe himself someone important.

"I have a proposal for you," she said before her common sense could return, and still not entirely certain whether it was kindness or simple attraction guiding her decision. She did feel mightily attracted.

"You have me captivated."

She tried to ignore that. "I shall write my brother in London. He will be able to clarify everything. Until then, you . . . you may remain at Forton Hall—as long as you give your solemn oath to do no harm to May, Forton Hall, or myself."

Rafael Bancroft closed his eyes as a slight, bemused smile touched his face. "And the alternative?"

"We send for the constable, have you locked up for assault and trespassing, and write the Duke of Highbarrow to see if he'll come and rescue you."

The smile faded. "I am in a spot, then, aren't I?" he said. "All right, Miss Harrington. I agree to your proposal."

He did have some sense, it seemed. "And?" she prompted.

He opened his eyes once more, serious now. "And I swear to do no harm to May, Forton Hall, or you."

She studied his face, looking for any sign that he might be lying, or irretrievably mad. All she saw was a man who looked a little dazed and lost, both emotions with which she could sympathize. Especially lately. "Agreed. May, you hold the kettle, and I'll untie him."

Chapter 3

By the time she undid the last of the ropes holding him helpless as a stuffed pheasant, Rafael Bancroft was beginning to wish they had killed him instead of merely beating him senseless.

His head throbbed, and he had to clench his jaw against every movement to keep from being ill. It was humiliating enough to have ended up bound and unconscious; he certainly did not want to cast up his accounts in front of her. Being chivalrous could be damned painful.

Freed from his bindings, he sat on the floor in the middle of the kitchen, trying to ignore the two females watching him with such suspicion in their eyes. Gingerly he felt the back of his skull. "Damnation," he muttered under his breath.

"You're not supposed to curse," the little, dark-haired girl reminded him, hefting the tea kettle menacingly.

Rafe looked up at her. "Are you the one who did this?"

She glanced at her sister. "Partly."

"Partly?"

"You started to wake before we had you secured," Felicity said, taking the kettle from her younger sibling. "I had to crown you again."

"Marvelous."

Whether it was an illusion caused by the blow or not, Felicity Harrington had the darkest, most expressive eyes he'd ever seen. And the rest of her, from her loose raven hair to her full, sensuous lips and tall, lithe form, was stunning. He simply wanted to sit in the middle of her—his—kitchen, and look at her. Every inch of her. Rafe blinked, surprised at the sudden intensity of the yearning.

She set the kettle back on the stove. "As long as you keep your word, May and I will refrain from injuring you further, Mr. Bancroft."

"Rafe, please." His fingers were bloody from touching his head, and he wouldn't have been all that surprised if they *had* cracked his skull. Woozy and ill, he tried to slow the wild wobbling of his thoughts. "Might I have my deed back?"

Felicity held the parchment out to him. "I am sorry you had to come all the way here from London just to learn that someone has treated you so poorly."

He pocketed the paper. "I'm sorry to learn that your own brother has treated *you* so poorly." Rafe lifted a hand when she opened her mouth to argue with him. "I would appreciate if you would write him immediately so we can settle this matter face to face."

"I shall."

He gazed at her again, and when a soft blush crept up her cheeks, a responding heat touched his own pulse. Perhaps being left alive did have its merits, after all. "And would you please have your groom stable my horse? My kit is fastened to the saddle. If you would have a footman show me to a room, I would like to lie down for a bit. I have a rather stout headache."

"We are short of servants at the moment, I'm afraid," Felicity said, lifting her chin. "I will be happy to tend your horse, but under no circumstances are you sleeping in this house.''

Annoyance began to push Rafe's woozy infatuation aside. ''Why not? Besides the fact that I own this house, of course.''

''You do not—'' She broke off. ''Rusticated as we may be at Forton Hall, Mr. Bancroft, I will not have a male stranger staying under the same roof with myself and my sister. Especially after the way you introduced yourself to us.''

''You said you'd put me up,'' he reminded her. ''And I'm hardly in a condition to do any further damage to anyone.'' He flashed his charming, rakish smile—the one that generally got him invited to share a bed, let alone a house.

Felicity looked at him calmly. ''You may stay in the stable. It is perfectly warm, and its roof leaks no more than the house does.''

''I am not staying in a damned stable,'' he snapped. Lovely or not, Miss Harrington was being completely unreasonable. Blast it all, *they* had cracked *him* over the head.

''Very well, the Childe of Hale inn is only four miles down the road. I'm sure they will be happy to put you up there. Mr. Davey Ludlow is the proprietor.''

Despite her confident words she hesitated, glancing toward May and then back again. Rafe stopped the hostile retort he had been about to make. Oddly enough, she seemed to want him out of the house, but not gone. Groggily he forced his brain to put together what he'd seen of Forton Hall and the two young ladies before him. Neither of them had called for help, nor looked as though they expected any. ''Who stays here with you?''

''May and I are perfectly capable of looking after ourselves,'' she stated, turning her attention to a stack of damp dresses draped across the kitchen table.

Rafe wondered whom she was trying to convince. "The two of you live here alone?"

She faced him again. "Apparently I've been speaking too quickly for you in your weakened condition. Yes, May and I live here alone. Until my brother's return, that is."

"Good God," he murmured, feeling a twinge of admiration. He'd never heard of such a thing. "What if I'd been some sort of maniac? I hope you have something more substantial than a tea kettle to ward off intruders."

She sniffed. "The tea kettle seems to have worked perfectly well, Mr. Bancroft."

He scowled. "Yes, thank you for reminding me."

"Shall I direct you to the Childe of Hale, then?"

Now she was just baiting him. "Not necessary," he grumbled, wondering why he felt the need to step in and take charge after they had practically murdered him. If anyone didn't need him watching over them, it was these two lethal females. Even so, he wasn't cad enough to toss them out of their home. From the way his head ached, he wasn't going anywhere for the next few days, anyway. Let their damned coward of a brother come and take them away. "Forton Hall is mine, Miss Harrington. And I won't have it defended by a woman and a little girl."

"I don't need—"

"Until your dear brother proves my ownership to our mutual satisfaction, I'll be staying in the blasted stable, nice and close so I can keep an eye on my property."

She looked at him for a moment, something like relief in her gaze. "Just remember," Felicity returned, "I'll be keeping an eye on you, as well."

Rafe staggered to his feet, lurching against the table. "Good."

The retort ideally would have been full of sly innuendo about what part of him in particular she would be eyeing, but all he could manage was a pained grunt. With a final glare in her general direction, he wobbled toward the kitchen door.

"Do you require assistance, Mr. Bancroft?" Miss Harrington asked, resuming her position as hostess and rightful owner, damn it all.

"No."

"Shall I bring your horse?" May offered.

He hesitated, considering the distance he would have to walk between the kitchen, Aristotle, and the stable. He could whistle the gelding to him, of course, but that would split his head wide open. "Yes, that would be fine. Thank you."

This time Felicity didn't even bother covering her amusement. "I'll bring some blankets."

Rafe waved a hand in response and staggered out the back door. Once out of earshot, he let loose with a string of the most descriptive, venomous curses he knew—which was quite a few, considering the seven years he'd spent in the military.

In the stable doorway he paused, leaning against the warped, peeling wood frame. It abruptly occurred to him that he'd missed his chance to rid himself of the entire mess: if he hadn't been so dizzy and ill, he might simply have told the lovely Miss Harrington that she was right—the deed was a forgery, and she was welcome to the wreck of Forton Hall.

On the other hand, this way he'd be able to get his hands around Nigel Harrington's scrawny neck and choke the life out of the coward. And it would keep him around long enough to see whether Felicity Harrington's dark eyes still fascinated him tomorrow. He had the distinct feeling that they would. "In for a penny, in for a pound," he muttered, and fell face forward into a pile of straw.

Felicity looked up from her book as May entered the morning room. "I left some toasted bread for you in the kitchen." She took a sip of her morning tea, grateful for the few minutes of peace she'd had. Reading was well on its way to becoming an unimagined luxury.

May wrinkled her nose. "It was burned," she said distastefully. "I had some marmalade."

"Just marmalade?"

"Yes. It was very good."

Felicity studied the high color of her sister's cheeks with some suspicion. "What've you been up to this morning, dear?"

May plunked herself down on the couch and smoothed at her flowered yellow skirt. "I thought Rafe might be dead, so I went to see. He was snoring, though, so he must be all right."

Alarmed, Felicity set the book aside. "Do not go near that man. Do you understand, May?"

"Well, why not? You said he could stay here."

Felicity stood and picked her way through the clutter of recovered knickknacks to sit beside her sister. "Mr. Bancroft is a poor unfortunate whom someone duped into thinking he could become an important, wealthy man. Judging from his scar, it is entirely possible someone has hit him on the head at least once in the past, and our actions certainly didn't help his . . . mental condition. It is our duty as good Christians to see him well again. After that—"

"But—"

"After that, and when Nigel returns, we will let

him explain the matter to our guest. And then Mr. Bancroft will leave.''

''But—''

''Hello?'' The deep male voice echoed up from the kitchen.

Felicity jumped. Although she tried to blame her speeded heartbeat on trepidation, an odd tingling excitement fluttered along her nerves. ''We're in the morning room, Mr. Bancroft,'' she called.

A moment later he leaned into the room. Seeing him upright and not wobbling about from dizziness, she was struck by the way he filled the doorway—from his mud-dimmed Hessian boots to his dark gray breeches and light gray patterned waistcoat; black, well-fitting coat; hopelessly wilted cravat; and overly long, wavy golden hair. Slowly and deliciously she took him in, and the entire time his light green eyes looked steadily back at her with dancing, lighthearted humor—or madness, she reminded herself—just beneath their surface.

''Good morning. I'm unarmed. May I approach?''

An unexpected grin touched her lips. ''Of course. How are you feeling?''

''Half dead, thank you.'' He turned his attention to her sister. ''Miss May, in the future I would appreciate if you wouldn't poke me with a rake while I'm trying to sleep.''

''May!'' Felicity admonished.

''I told you, I thought he was dead!'' the girl protested. ''I stopped when he snored.''

''It's the first time I've used snoring as self-defense.'' Then Rafael grimaced. ''Well, it's the first time it worked, anyway.'' He faced Felicity again. ''Might I trouble you for something to eat this morning? And please call me Rafe. I have an uncle who is Mr. Bancroft.''

"Is Mr. Bancroft the duke's brother?" May interrupted.

"Yes, he is."

"We don't have any food," the little girl continued. "I ate marmalade."

"May." Felicity flushed, embarrassed. Sometimes May's direct manner of speaking was simply too much. "I must apologize, Mr.—Rafe. We meant to go into town yesterday, but—"

"There's some toast on the table," May contributed again.

Rafe cleared his throat. "Yes, I noticed it on my way in. Did you make it, Miss May?"

Felicity stiffened. "No. I did. I . . . lost track of it." She had no intention of telling him that she'd been daydreaming about a pirate captain who looked suspiciously like her stable guest.

Again he glanced at her. "Ah."

Felicity blushed once more, annoyed at her poor showing. Now she'd have to go into Pelford to purchase food for breakfast—and luncheon and dinner. She'd meant to finish the search for salvageable clothes in the old wing this morning. Going to the village would take two hours away from that, and she'd already lost at least that much time yesterday due to Rafael's arrival.

She eyed their tall guest speculatively. "I don't suppose you feel up to riding into Pelford this morning, Rafe?" She smiled her best smile at him. According to him, he wasn't a guest, anyway.

He stood for a long moment, staring at her. "For supplies?"

"Well, yes."

To her surprise, he grinned, the expression a little lopsided because of his scar. "I suppose so, since I want to eat. Might I have May to accompany me?"

"It's directly down the lane," she pointed out, reluctant to relinquish her sister to this poor, befuddled man, handsome and charming though he might be.

"I know where it is; I passed through it yesterday. It's just that I prefer to have someone capable with me—in case I'm set upon by bandits."

May giggled.

Again Felicity hesitated. "You can't expect me simply to send you off with my sister."

"Oh, Lis . . ."

"Miss Harrington," he said quietly, his smile fading, "you've been trusting me with both your sister and yourself since you untied me."

"I've—"

"And I gave you my word yesterday," he continued. "My recollection may be rather fuzzy, but I do remember that."

She held his gaze for a long moment. He had a very good point. And her instinct told her he would never harm them. "Very well. May, put on your shawl and your bonnet."

Her sister cheered. "Can we gallop?" she asked, jumping up. "What is your horse's name? He's top of the trees, Rafe. How fast is he?"

He gave another slight grin that sent Felicity's pulse skipping. If he had his wits about him, he might very well have been irresistible. Thank goodness for small favors. "No, Aristotle, thank you, and I have no intention of finding out today."

May's face became a comical vision of dejection. "Why not?"

"Because he will be walking. Very slowly."

From behind Rafe's back, Felicity pointed at his head and grimaced. May giggled again, then covered her smile with one hand. "All right."

Rafe motioned May to precede him to the stable.

"Bloodthirsty little chit," he grumbled, and she laughed again.

Felicity smiled as the two of them left the room. In reality, broken head or not, Mr. Bancroft likely had no wish to run his horse after riding the poor thing all the way from London. Of course, she hadn't actually seen this Aristotle, but May was constantly trying to adopt old, broken-down nags—which was lucky, since that was all they'd been able to afford lately.

With a glance at the clock, she put her book back in the pile of tomes drying beneath the window and banked the fire to conserve wood. A stack of paintings in the dining room needed her attention, and she went to work separating the repairable ones from the hopelessly ruined.

A few minutes later, May raced into the room. "Lis, we're going. Rafe said to ask if you had a list."

"Oh, yes, I do. It's in the kitchen." She straightened and led the way down the hall. "You may have to read it for him, sweetling."

"You think he can't read?" her sister whispered.

"Most people can't," Felicity reminded her as she handed over the list. "Ask Mrs. Denwortle to add the expense to our account. Tell her I'll send her a side of mutton on Wednesday." Hopefully that would be enough to repay the shopkeeper. She couldn't spare any more than that.

"All right."

May skipped out the door, while Felicity followed behind her—and started thinking about pirates and heart-pounding adventure again.

Whatever Aristotle was, it was not broken-down. The bay was a big, beautifully proportioned hunter with one white sock on his left foreleg, and a long, lovely mane and arched tail. Part Arabian, at least. He looked faster than the wind.

Her gaze lifted to his rider, and a grain of doubt over his supposedly fractured wits touched her mind. Even if Aristotle had been stolen, there was absolutely no escaping the fact that Rafael Bancroft knew how to ride. He sat relaxed and easy in the saddle, the reins loose in his right hand, and a slight smile on his lean, handsome face. When May reached him he shifted sideways, caught hold of her hand in his, and effortlessly lifted her up in front of him.

"Are you certain we can't gallop?" May asked, patting Aristotle's neck.

"Absolutely." Rafe saluted Felicity. "We'll be back soon, Miss Harrington."

"You . . ." She cleared her throat. "Yes. Be careful."

"We will."

For several minutes after they disappeared down the lane, Felicity stood in the yard looking after them. Other than Nigel and a few distant relations, May was the only family she had. Since their parents had died, she'd barely allowed her little sister out of her sight. Yet there she was, riding off with a perfect stranger they'd pummeled into unconsciousness only the day before.

She folded her arms and leaned against the kitchen door frame. When he'd looked at her and said she could trust him, though, she'd somehow known she could. Although the last days had been extremely trying, she couldn't believe she'd lost the ability to make rational decisions. And his very . . . capable appearance this morning had served to remind her that if his true aim had been to hurt her or May, he could have done it yesterday. Taking a deep breath, she went back inside to finish with the paintings and see if she could salvage anything else from the west wing.

The curious looks Rafe had received on his way through Pelford yesterday increased tenfold as he swung down from Aristotle and then lifted May out of the saddle.

"Do you have the list?" he asked her. People stared at him all the time in London for various reasons, particularly when the Bancrofts made an appearance together. He noted the attention and then ignored it.

She produced the scrap of paper from a pocket of her flowered yellow muslin dress. "Yes. And I shall read it, so you don't have to."

Rafe resisted the urge to rub at the back of his head again. He didn't need to touch it to know he had a knot the size of a peach pit growing out of his skull. "Thank you, my lady."

May took his hand, and together they walked across the cobblestones to Mrs. Denwortle's market shop. Rafe looked down at her as she tried to match her short legs to his long stride. He had very limited experience with children, and had classified them as an entirely different species than adults. The loud, drooly things certainly didn't seem like anything he wanted about.

This one, though, seemed fairly rational. And exceedingly delicate and in desperate need of protection, despite her efficient manner of thwacking intruders on the head. "How old are you, May?"

"Eight and a half." Dark brown eyes twinkled up at him. "How old are you?"

"*Twenty*-eight and a half," he answered.

She laughed. "You're old."

Rafe lifted an eyebrow. "Well, thank you very much. How old are your brother and sister?"

"Nearly twenty-three. Nigel is one hour younger than Lis, but he hates it when she tries to boss him around."

"I can imagine."

In the store's doorway she stopped and pulled on his sleeve. "Rafe, I have to tell you something."

He bent down, despite the resultant pounding of his skull. "What is it?"

"I don't like Mrs. Denwortle very much," she whispered. "She says mean things about Nigel." With a nod she continued into the small shop.

"Can't fathom why," Rafe murmured, following her.

"Why, Miss May," a portly woman in a bright green muslin exclaimed, as she emerged from the shop's back room. "Where is your sister?" Her gaze focused on Rafe. "And who have we here?"

"Felicity is at home. This is Rafe," May announced, as though he were her pet dog.

He stifled a grin. "Good morning."

"I have a list," May continued, lifting it. She cleared her throat. "We need a loaf of bread, two pounds of flour, two pounds of salt, one—"

"I assume you brought payment with you?" Mrs. Denwortle said, her expression skeptical. "Or is that why your sister stayed home?"

Blissfully unaware of the sarcasm in the woman's voice, May shook her head. "Felicity said for you to add it to our account, and she'd send you a side of mutton on Wednesday."

The shopkeeper folded her arms over her chest, which couldn't have been an easy feat considering her ample bosom. "I need to eat too, miss. And with that brother of yours, I may not receive payment until Judgment Day. You tell your sister that when she sends me a whole sheep—including the wool—I'll be pleased as a peach to extend the Harringtons credit again.''

"We don't owe you a whole sheep," the little girl argued.

The sarcasm hadn't escaped Rafe. Technically, he supposed, the Harringtons didn't owe the shopkeeper anything. Forton Hall was his, and its residents had now become his guests—whether he wanted them about, or not. "Excuse me, Mrs. Denwortle, isn't it?"

"Yes"—and she looked pointedly at his well-made, if somewhat wrinkled attire—"sir?"

Damn, he was going to have to send for some of his things. "Precisely how much do the Harringtons owe you?"

She scowled at him. "What business might that be of yours?"

He returned her gaze coolly. "Do you want to be paid, or not?"

Mrs. Denwortle continued to glare at him. With a sniff, she finally pulled a ledger out from under the counter. "Seven pounds eight," she said, consulting it.

Apparently Felicity hadn't been able to pay her account for some time. With a sigh at the further depletion to his stake, Rafe reached into his pocket and produced a ten-pound note. "Get Miss May what she wants," he said, dropping the money onto the counter, "and credit the rest to the Harrington account."

She snatched up the blunt with grasping, pudgy fingers. "As pleases you, sir," she agreed, her tone more respectful.

While May happily recommended reading the list, Rafe took a stroll about the small shop. Everything from candles to bonnets and cloth, eggs, and perfumes adorned the shelves, while several sides of beef hung just outside the door. From the variety, it appeared that she ran the only market shop in the area. And from the prices she charged, she was quite aware of that fact. He paused before a jar of bright-colored hard candies.

"May, do you like sweets?" he asked over his shoulder.

"Oh, yes! Lis loves them, too."

Rafe recognized a plea when he heard one. Grinning, he removed the lid and a dozen candies. "These as well, Mrs. Denwortle."

"Very good, sir."

Finally they loaded everything into two large sacks and tied them over Aristotle's saddle. The bay swung his head around to look at them, clearly disgusted at being reduced to a pack animal.

"Sorry, old boy," Rafe chuckled, patting him on the withers.

"Where did you get thuch a wonderful horth as Arithtotle?" May asked around the piece of candy that puffed out one cheek.

He lifted her into the saddle and swung up behind her. "I purchased him, sight unseen, from the Earl of Montrose. Monty said he was the damnedest—ah, the most stubborn—colt he'd ever had the displeasure to be bitten by." Rafe sent them off at a sedate walk down the lane toward Forton. "My brother, the Marquis of Warefield, had custody of him for a while, but I won him back."

"I'm glad. He's smashing."

Rafe chuckled. "Where did you learn words like 'smashing' and 'top of the trees', anyway?"

"Nigel. Felicity says it sounds knot-headed, but I like it."

"You do it very well, I must say."

She giggled. "Thank you. Rafe, do you really own Forton Hall?"

He looked down into her dark, innocent eyes and hesitated. "We'll wait until your brother returns to decide that," he hedged. "So what do you and Felicity do with yourselves all day?"

"I do my lessons, and Felicity mends our clothes. Then I help her, and we dust and sweep and clean, and feed the chickens. Twice a week we walk out to the far pasture to check on the cattle and sheep to get whatever milk we can chase down, and Lis makes cream and butter. She's been growing cabbages and potatoes, too, but I think the last rain ruined them."

Rafe sat silently for a moment. "That's a great deal of work."

"Felicity says we like hard work. Sitting about all day never got anything accomplished."

"And she cooks for you, as well?"

"Oh, yes. She's very good, except that we have chicken and rabbits a lot."

As the little one continued to chat about the daily routine at Forton, Rafe could only marvel at Miss Harrington. He'd grown up with an army of servants at his beck and call, and even in the military he'd never had to mend his own clothes or cook for himself, unless he wanted to. His disgust for Nigel deepened. Whatever his intentions, going off and leaving his two sisters to manage an estate all on their own, with no funds to speak of, was exceedingly shabby—even if they'd accepted their situation. "And who catches the rabbits?" he asked, though he was fairly certain of the answer.

"Lis. She can do anything."

Rafe smiled. "I'm beginning to believe you."

"Lis," May yelled from the opening gaping in the hallway, "we're back!"

Felicity straightened, nearly lost her balance, and

wiped a dirty hand across her brow. "Don't come over here," she warned.

"I know, I know. It's dangerous. Rafe and I will be in the kitchen."

"All right."

Stumbling again, Felicity grabbed onto a broken roof beam for support. It was strange, standing in the middle of where the drawing room used to be, and seeing her broken bedchamber furniture occupying the same space. She wanted to cry every time she looked at the rubble, but weeping wouldn't help her dig out her jewelry box or the books piled in the wreck of the library.

Something caught her eye, and she bent down to free a glass figurine from the mess. It had been a colorful African parrot, but the head was missing and both feet were broken. She cast it into the corner she'd already picked through. Perhaps she could convince Rafe that the deed was real after all, but only included the west wing.

"When did this happen?"

Felicity jumped and turned around. "Mr. Bancroft, I didn't hear you," she said needlessly, unsettled again at his smooth, deep voice. "Four nights ago."

"Rafe, please," he reminded her. "What was this, the drawing room?"

"Yes." She returned to digging through the mess. "And the remains of my bedchamber."

"Just be glad you weren't in it at the time." Concern touched his sea-green eyes.

"When everything started shuddering and shaking, May and I decided to sleep in the morning room. Even so, it was a close call."

"It looks as though a herd of elephants trampled it." He pushed aside a smashed chair. "Two or three herds."

Felicity put her hands on her hips. "And I suppose you've seen a herd of elephants?"

He squatted down to extricate another parrot. "Just the African ones," he said absently, examining the figurine. "I think this one's survived."

"And where did you see these African elephants?"

"In Africa." He perched the parrot on his shoulder and scrunched his left eye shut. "Excuse me, matey," he drawled in a Cockney accent, "but would ye have some paper and a pen about?"

She chuckled. "Aye, Captain."

Rafe grinned back at her. "Since I'll apparently be stuck here for a time, I need to write my parents' butler to send me some of my clothes." He gestured at his splendid but well-worn attire. "I left London in a bit of a hurry."

No doubt he had, if he'd stolen Aristotle at the same time. Felicity studied his face again as he set the parrot aside and dug for more buried treasures. Good God, he was handsome, and even with his head injury he moved with the grace of a born athlete. She sighed. It had to happen, she supposed, with every other calamity that had already occurred this year. A superbly attractive stranger finally appeared on her doorstep, so of course he had to turn out to be a charming, good-natured imbecile.

If he truly were of sound mind, he certainly wouldn't be in Cheshire County trying to own Forton Hall. A son of the Duke of Highbarrow would have a thousand more interesting places to go. No doubt next he would claim to have fought side by side with Wellington at Waterloo.

"I generally look a good deal more presentable than this," he said unexpectedly.

Realizing she'd been staring, Felicity looked away. "I'm sure that's none of my concern," she said, blushing, and with exaggerated care freed a book and brushed at its water-stained cover.

He chuckled, and the warm, light sound tingled down her spine. "It's just that my pride has been wounded over the past few days. I'm feeling rather . . . unkempt. No doubt you think me a complete fool."

Finally he was making some sense. Felicity smiled. "Not a fool, Rafe. Simply overwhelmed by unexpected circumstances." Poor dear, how humiliating to have been rendered unconscious by an eight-year-old.

"Underwhelmed, perhaps," he conceded, and returned to toeing through the heaps of broken walls and furniture. "I've seen most of Europe, and the sale of this sad heap was supposed to get me either to the Americas or the Far East. Now I'll be lucky to get to Ireland."

The compassionate smile dropped from her face. "This 'sad heap' is my ancestral home," she snapped. "I'll thank you to remember that."

He lifted an eyebrow at her heated expression. "It *was* your ancestral home," he corrected. "At the moment it's your ancestral pile of rubble—and the millstone around my very stupid neck." He tossed a broken tea saucer into the corner, shattering its remains. "And I thought Forton Hall would be *good* luck."

"No one's forcing you to stay here."

Rafe looked at her for a long moment, something she couldn't quite decipher in his eyes. "I suppose not. What keeps *you* here?"

Felicity hesitated, knowing he wasn't looking for a flip, obvious answer. "It's my home. If I weren't here, no one would look after it."

"Forton Hall is luckier than it deserves. So— where might I find that paper?"

"In the morning room, in the wooden box on the desk."

He nodded and turned on his heel.

She spent another hour digging through the wreckage. It was dirty, exhausting work, and every broken object caused a pang in her heart. She'd never been overly sentimental, but this was Forton Hall falling down around her. And it was likely to grow worse, unless Nigel returned home soon, and with plenty of money.

Apparently Rafe intended to stay at least until his clothes arrived. As long as he didn't mind going into Pelford for supplies, she supposed that his presence wasn't such a bad thing. It was one less chore for her. Felicity suddenly paused, straightening. Actually, having an able-bodied, feeble-minded man about might be the best thing that had happened to Forton Hall in a long while!

With that in mind, she climbed the stairs to the leaky attic of the remaining east wing to see if she could find him some temporary clothing. When she returned downstairs, she heard May's laughter coming from the morning room. Rafe Bancroft already *was* of some use, if he had kept her free-spirited sister from running wild all morning. Nigel had never been good with May, referring any questions to Felicity, and constantly chastising her outbreaks of high spirits. Lis carried her bundle to the morning room, and stopped, smiling, in the doorway. Apparently Mr. Bancroft didn't mind high spirits—and she certainly preferred May loud and laughing to quiet and forlorn.

"That's not a word," her sister protested, pointing at the paper Rafael leaned over.

His scowl didn't conceal the twinkle in his eyes. "It is too, a word. 'Posthaste.' "

"It looks like more scribbles to me."

"How old did you say you were, anyway? Four?"

"I'm eight," May said with a giggle. "And I can read. And write."

"Well, so can I." Rafe scrawled something at the bottom of the page and folded it. "Better than you."

"That whole letter is just a bunch of squiggly lines."

He grinned faintly as he addressed the letter. "Is not."

"Is too."

"Is—"

Felicity cleared her throat. "I hate to interrupt the debate, but I found some old clothes of our grandfather's in the attic. None of Nigel's have survived, and you're a bit . . . taller than he is, anyway. While you're waiting for your own things to arrive, I thought you might have some use for them, Rafe."

He stood. "That's very kind of you, Miss Harrington." Stepping forward, he took the bundle from her. Then, taking her fingers in his free hand, he lifted them to his lips and lightly brushed her knuckles, his green eyes holding hers.

This time she was certain he was flirting. And while she'd been flirted with before, she couldn't ever recall excited shivers running down her arms. Suddenly very conscious of the dust and grime covering her dress, her hands, and her face, Felicity flushed and pulled her fingers free. "No need to thank me," she managed briskly, feeling as awkward as a schoolgirl. "They were certainly doing no one any good where they were. And I thought that while we're all waiting for Nigel's return, perhaps you might wish to lend us a hand."

He set the bundle of clothes in a chair. "Lend you a hand with what?"

Playing along with his notion that he was nobility would likely accomplish more than arguing. "I know it's far beneath your station, but with just May and me here, there are some things we have simply been unable to attend to."

His expression surprisingly interested, Rafe folded his arms over his chest. "Such as?"

"The roof leaks in the dining room and the upstairs bedchambers, to begin with." She didn't want to overwhelm him before he'd even begun. For all she knew, the least little thing could be beyond his capability, fit and healthy though he looked.

"You want me to fix your roof," he repeated.

"Well," she said, stepping forward and laying a hand softly on his arm, "according to you, it's *your* roof."

"Hm. So it is." Narrowing one eye, he picked up the clothes again. "I don't suppose you have a ladder?"

She nodded, holding back a triumphant smile. Having a roof that actually kept out the rain would be so pleasant. "Behind the stable."

He sighed. "All right." With a mock scowl he turned to face May. "And you, young miss, can you keep from poking me with a rake while I change into my roof-mending attire?"

"May will be making luncheon with me," Felicity said.

"But Lis—"

"Very well." Rafe brushed past Felicity's shoulder and headed down the hall toward the kitchen and the stable yard beyond.

"But Lis," May repeated, capturing her fluttering attention again, "we already made a luncheon fit for the Prince of Wales."

Chapter 4

Rafe lifted his arms, examining the loose, ivory-colored sleeves. "By God, I feel positively historical."

Grandfather Harrington had apparently followed the fashion of old George III in the days before his madness. Rafe felt as though he were wardrobed for some sort of masquerade ball, but at least the clothes were clean, and fit decently. Foregoing the hat because of the knot on the back of his head, and the shoes because he absolutely refused to wear buckles, he pulled on his Hessian boots and strolled around the back of the stable to find not only a ladder, but a barrel of tar and some weathered-looking shingles.

His head still ached, and he would rather have waited until tomorrow to crawl about on the roof. The gathering clouds in the east, though, didn't look as if they intended to wait for his skull to heal. Besides, sitting around wasn't something he did well. And, as he reminded himself, every repair he made to Forton Hall before he sold it would increase the pitiful price he could ask for the wreck.

He lit a fire in a space apparently cleared for that purpose, and grabbed a bucket to heat the tar in. The ladder looked steady, if a bit ungainly, but no doubt the Harringtons had used it on a regular basis. Or rather, Forton Hall would have been better off if they *had* made more use of it. Whistling a vulgar soldier's ditty, and for once grateful that as a youth he'd enjoyed hanging about the servants and repairmen employed to maintain the grounds and buildings of Highbarrow Castle, Rafe dragged the ladder across the tangled, overgrown lawn and propped it up against the back of the manor house. That done, he went back into the stable to look for a heavy brush or an old broom.

"You weren't supposed to pay for our supplies."

He started. Felicity stood framed in the stable doorway, hands on her hips and the already familiar look of embarrassed frustration on her face. In the sunlight her black hair took on an edging of bronze, and he gazed at her, unable to help himself. In his vague plans for estate sales and world travel, he'd never expected *her*. He was used to pursuing what interested him, and catching what he pursued. Felicity Harrington attracted him mightily, and as far as he was concerned, the chase had begun the moment he set eyes on her.

"I was hungry, and I didn't want to be bashed on the head by Mrs. Denwortle. She's a bad-tempered old bag, isn't she?"

Her lips twitched into a half grin, nearly as compelling as the blinding smile that had convinced him to scale the walls and fortify the roof of the estate. Swiftly she ran her eyes up and down his historically clothed form, and the color in her cheeks deepened. "You are our guest."

So the other party was interested, as well. Good. That would make things easier. "If you'd come in here a few moments earlier, I'd have been your half naked guest. Then whatever would we have done?"

"I . . . Yes, you're right. I apologize."

Finding a broom, he banged it against the wall a few times to remove the dust and cobwebs, then headed back outside to collect the heated bucket of tar and an armload of shingles. "No need. Just pointing out a fact."

She cleared her throat. "Well, yes. But don't pay any more of our bills, if you please."

"I doubt I can," he said, pausing as he absorbed that little bit of information. "So, there are more debts involved?"

"A . . . a few."

He didn't have to look at her to know how difficult that must have been for her to admit. "Miss Harrington, don't begrudge me a loaf of bread or two. I eat more than the two of you combined, no doubt."

"What about the candy, though? I suppose that was to bribe me?" she demanded, following him.

Rafe stopped and turned to face her. She nearly ran into him, and had to put a hand against his chest to keep from stumbling. Dropping the shingles, he caught her elbow and tugged her closer on the pretext of helping her find her balance.

She'd felt damned pleasant when he'd jumped on her yesterday, and however standoffish she pretended to be toward him, she also managed to touch him and converse with him whenever possible. He had no intention of discouraging that. "Bribe you into what? You already said I could stay," he pointed out with a soft smile. "Is there something more I should be asking of you?"

Felicity pulled her arm free and smoothed at her skirt, blushing furiously. "Why did you make luncheon?" she demanded, ignoring his question.

"It was only sandwiches. Not all nobles are completely useless, you know." If the morning's toast was any indication of her cooking ability, he hadn't wanted to risk being poisoned on top of his cracked head. "Besides, your schedule seems to be more than full without me adding to the mix."

"Ah. But how does a nobleman like you learn to make sandwiches? By watching your cook, I suppose?"

"Yes, as a matter of fact." He bent to retrieve the shingles. Felicity seemed so hungry to know about the way the landed gentry lived. Rafe wondered how long she'd had to scratch and scrape to get by at Forton, and how long it had been since someone had waited on her. He'd be more generous with information in his tales of London from now on. "Cook used to make splendid cucumber sandwiches. My brother and I would take them and glasses of lemonade out to go fishing."

Felicity nodded. "Ah, yes, your brother. May mentioned him to me. The Marquis of Warefield, is he not?"

"Yes, he is."

She looked at him curiously. "And I suppose you know the king, as well?"

Rafe grinned and resumed his way to the ladder. "Georgie? He's a fat, witless toad with an absolute gift for planning soirees. My father and Quin— Warefield—are much better acquainted with him than I am, but I can tell you a tale or two, if you'd like."

"Is there anyone in London you don't know?"

He paused on the ladder's second rung and looked down at her, wanting to know all about his so-called grand life when he only wanted to escape it. Dirt smudged across her nose and one cheek, and something odd and breath-stealing ran through his chest. "I don't know *you*," he answered, stepping to the ground again. And abruptly he wanted to, with a strength that surprised him. He wanted to brush her soft, smooth skin with his fingers, and cover her tall, slender body with warm, slow kisses.

Looking flustered, she backed away a step. "I've never been to London."

Rafe shook himself, trying to concentrate on the conversation. "Why not? Your brother's a land-owner. And forgive me, but you are over eighteen, and exceptionally attractive. What about your debut?"

Felicity hesitated again, fiddling with the fraying hem of her sleeve. Apparently the blue and green muslin was her "mucking about the ruins" gown, because she'd worn the same one yesterday. The gesture seemed hesitant and vulnerable, and Rafe caught himself sighing as he gazed at her.

"My parents died five years ago of influenza, just before Nigel and I turned eighteen."

"I'm sorry."

She shrugged. "There was no mon—it would have been inappropriate for me to dance off to London. Besides, May was only three, and Nigel had been accepted at Eton." She stirred and patted him on the arm as though he were some old tea party matron. "So, now you know my life's story. It'll be getting dark soon. Shouldn't you begin on the roof?"

If he'd had more than three fingers free for climbing, he would have saluted. Whatever excuses she made to seek him out, Forton Hall still occupied more of her thoughts than any contemplations of amorous behavior. At the moment. "Yes, Miss Harrington." He started up the ladder again.

"Rafe?"

He looked down at her. "Yes?"

"Have you ever repaired a roof before?"

"No, Miss Harrington." He resumed climbing.

"You're welcome to come up here with me and supervise."

"Oh," she answered hurriedly, "I have complete faith in your abilities. If you'll excuse me, I need to mend some of May's stockings."

She hurried into the house, and with another sigh he hefted the heavy bucket onto the roof. His London cronies would have been laughing at him right now, but he was unperturbed enough to begin humming another tune. Fixing the roof could only benefit him. The pursuit had begun.

Felicity was awakened early by a metallic squeak. She lay in bed, reluctant to leave the warm, soft blankets, especially with no one to light the fireplace for her. Even with the cooking, cleaning, mending, and everything else she faced daily, the morning without a fire was when she most missed having servants.

Then she heard the squeaking again, and she sat up. Like May, she'd taken one of the guest bedchambers in the east wing, and pale sunlight softly lit the curtains.

The squeak sounded once more. Curious, she edged off the bed and pushed aside the window coverings.

"Oh, my."

Rafael Bancroft stood beside the water pump outside the stable. Technically he wasn't naked, she supposed, because he wore a pair of white wool breeches. From the way her pulse skittered and sped at the sight of him, though, and the way she couldn't take her eyes from his lean, strong body, he might as well have been completely undressed.

Wet, dark blond hair nearly touched his shoulders. Streams of water glistened down his smooth, well-muscled chest and flat stomach, and made the wool breeches cling to his muscular thighs. Crouching, he lowered his head beneath the spigot and sent the handle up and down again. It squeaked once more, and a cascade of water poured down his head and bare back.

He straightened again and shook his hair out, the droplets catching the sunlight. Light steam came off his body from the cold water. Felicity abruptly yearned to touch him, to run her hands along his smooth, warm skin.

Without warning, he looked up toward her window. Cursing, she ducked backward, tripped over the corner of the bed, and landed hard on her backside. "Drat!"

It hurt, but at least it jolted her back to reality. She was far too old and had far too many responsibilities to be acting like a moonstruck girl, for heaven's sake. Deliberately avoiding the temptation beyond the curtains, Felicity washed in the handbasin, dressed, put up her hair, and went downstairs to cook a breakfast of eggs and warm bread.

"Good morning, Miss Harrington," her stable guest greeted her a few minutes later, stepping in through the kitchen entry.

"Good morning, Rafe." She concentrated on breakfast, hoping she wasn't blushing. She felt hot inside, just under her skin.

"Do you like eggs?" May asked from the table.

"I do."

"I helped gather them," she said proudly, between mouthfuls.

"It looks like you did a fine job."

Felicity placed a heaping plate on the table, and he sat beside May. Watching them teasing and making faces at each other, she felt distinctly befuddled. How odd, the way they looked like a family, when she and May hardly even knew him. For that matter, how odd that she wanted to run her fingers through his still-damp hair, and feed him his breakfast with her fingers. His lips looked so soft, and when he smiled . . .

Rafe took a bite, and then another. "Delicious, Miss Harrington." He winked at May. "I have to say, I'm a bit relieved after seeing the toast yesterday."

"I told you that was an accident," Felicity retorted. "You didn't complain about dinner last night."

May laughed. "You might have hit him again."

"The mutton was excellent." Rafe chuckled. "And I would have said that even if I weren't in dire fear for my life."

Felicity laughed. "Oh, stop it."

"You should smile more often," he said softly, then wiped his chin with a napkin. "By the way, I thought I might ride into Pelford this morning. Do you need anything?"

I need the roof fixed, she almost said, but didn't. He wasn't a slave or an employee, and much as she could have used the assistance, she was accustomed to doing things on her own. "No, I can't think of anything."

He nodded and went back to his breakfast. "How many chickens do I—you—we own, anyway?"

Felicity had become expert at detecting her brother's attempts to change the subject, and chickens seemed like a definite distraction—though Rafe was a fairly formidable one all on his own. "Twenty-four. What do *you* need in Pelford?"

"I just wanted to take a survey of the countryside, since I own this place now." He shoveled in another mouthful.

She frowned at him. "To avoid any confusion

with the neighbors, please don't tell anyone that until my brother returns and we can determine the true story.''

He sighed. "Don't worry. And I'll be back in time to work on the roof. It looks as though we're in for another storm.''

"Can I go with you?" May asked, springing to her feet.

"No, you may not," Felicity put in, reluctantly looking away from him. "We have cleaning to do, you have reading, and we have a luncheon engagement with Squire Talford.''

Rafe paused with the fork halfway to his mouth. "Who's Squire Talford?''

"A neighbor. The local school is on his land. I'm on the education committee.''

"I'm not surprised." Turning to May, he leaned back in his chair. "So, how old is this squire?''

"He's at least a hundred," May answered wisely.

Felicity's pulse jolted into high speed again. He couldn't possibly be jealous. They barely knew each other, and he was only rowing with half an oar, anyway. "Why do you ask?''

Rafe looked straight at her. "Because you look so lovely this morning. I wanted to be sure someone—besides me, of course—appreciated you.''

With a smile he pushed away from the table and was gone, leaving Felicity to stare at the kitchen door and wonder whether she'd also lost her mind. She had no reason to desire and enjoy the compliments of a lunatic stranger, however compelling and interesting he might be. And she certainly shouldn't go to the trouble of dressing in her best remaining morning gown simply to impress him. She glanced down at the yellow and green muslin with the carefully matched green pelisse. At least he'd noticed, which was gratifying, considering that now she'd have to change out of it again to continue digging through the wreckage.

"He likes you," May whispered, giggling.

"Oh, hush," she answered, settling down to finish her own breakfast.

"Well, are you a solicitor, or aren't you?"

The man seated opposite Rafe in the small, second-floor office fidgeted once more with his ink blotter. "Of course I am. It's just that—"

Rafe leaned forward. "It's just that what?"

"Well, this is highly irregular, Mr. . . . Mr. Bancroft. You must understand, I am a part of this community. I would never—"

"You would never stoop to selling an estate without the owner's permission or knowledge, which would both be illegal and in very poor taste." Rafe tapped the estate title resting on the young man's desk. "I applaud your decency and the rigor with which you defend your fellows. But I *am* the owner of Forton Hall, blast it all."

The dark-haired man began stammering again, and Rafe stood to pace the narrow, cluttered office. It had been difficult enough to explain his presence and his eighteenth-century apparel. Once he'd claimed ownership of Forton Hall, he'd had to tell the whole damned tale all over again. At least young Mr. Gibbs had been to London and knew that the Duke of Highbarrow had two sons, though he apparently hadn't decided whether Rafe was one of them.

"Look. I am not going to sell Forton Hall until Nigel Harrington returns and we can settle this in a reasonable manner. When he does return, though, I want to be able to make a sale posthaste. All I'm asking is that you begin a discreet—and I repeat, *discreet*—search for a buyer.'' He had no wish for Felicity to find out what he was doing, whether it was perfectly within his rights or not.

Somehow, over the past two days, Felicity had become someone he didn't want to upset—and it wasn't out of fear of her tea kettle. When she had smiled that morning, it had stirred something unexpected in him. And selling Forton Hall out from under her and May would take away his opportunity to find out what that something was.

John Gibbs's eyes followed him as he paced back and forth, and he tried to curb his impatience while the solicitor weighed Rafe's statements and his own awe of the titled Bancrofts against whatever monetary and moral responsibility he felt toward the Harringtons.

Finally Gibbs nodded. "Very well. I don't see anything illegal in simply looking about—unless and until I hear differently.''

"Thank you, Mr. Gibbs. I'll be by in a few days to check on your progress.''

That done, he set out from Pelford to ride the borders of Forton Hall. He had a strong desire to see exactly what it was that he'd won.

Half-wild cattle grazed along the banks of Crown Creek and stampeded when he approached. The sheep dotting the field on the far side of the waterway didn't even bother looking up as he and Aristotle passed. That property belonged to another landowner, the Earl of Deerhurst, and Rafe looked upon the well-kept fields and fences with some envy.

A dozen small tenant farms were spread out along either side of the road east of the manor house, all but three of them abandoned to the elements. A splendid crop of weeds rose to his thighs as he rode across two of the fields. Tumbled fences and rotting sheds and barns bespoke a neglect that had begun years, rather than months, ago.

Forton Hall was a mere trifle compared with the sprawling magnificence of Highbarrow Castle or Warefield Park, but it was larger than he had realized. In good condition, the place would have seen him comfortable for the remainder of his life, wherever he chose to spend it. As it was, he'd be lucky to keep the stake with which he'd begun.

"Ho, there!" A sharp voice came from the shrubbery off to his left. Immediately following the shout, the unmistakable sound of a musket being primed brought Rafe up short.

"Ho there, yourself," he said to the bushes, keeping his hands in clear view and wishing he hadn't left his pistol wedged beneath the boards of the stable.

"You have business here?" the gruff voice asked.

Rafe didn't relish the thought of a musket ball piercing his heart. His mother, and scads of London ladies, would be terribly upset. "No, not really. I'm an old friend of the Harringtons. Do you know them?"

"Aye." A moment later the bushes rustled and parted. The barrel of the musket emerged, followed by a short, sturdy-looking man in his mid-forties. "Nice horse."

"My thanks. Nice musket."

The older man chuckled and lowered the weapon. "You're a cool fellow." He stepped forward. "Name's Greetham."

Rafe dismounted and held out his hand. "Bancroft."

Greetham had a firm grip, and with a wince Rafe wondered how many broken bones he'd end up with before he finished his business in Cheshire.

"This your farm?" He gestured at the field of weeds behind them.

"Aye. Damned shame, ain't it? Rain ruined the spring crop, and Mr. Harrington couldn't get new seed for his tenants to put in. I left the weeds in to keep the topsoil from washing down the creek before the fall planting season."

Rafe nodded, impressed. "You like the Harringtons, Greetham?"

The farmer squinted one eye, assessing the stranger. "Like Miss Harrington and little May fine."

That was direct. Rafe looked right back at him. "You know, I think we can make a trade." And perhaps at the same time, impress a lovely, dark-eyed lady who seemed rather uncertain about her houseguest.

"What sort of trade?"

"The Harrington ladies have a roof that needs repairing. You have no crop to tend, and I could use another pair of hands."

Greetham looked at him for a minute. "Miss Harrington would never ask for charity."

"*She's* not asking. And then maybe we can discuss your weed problem."

"Another pair of hands." The farmer held his right one out again. "You've got them, Bancroft."

"Your first instinct was correct. He's obviously deluded, and you should have sent for the constable. In fact, it's not too late to do so."

Felicity looked across her teacup at Squire Talford. She'd decided not to tell anyone about Rafe, mostly because she didn't want to hear any more speculation about her brother's lack of common sense. Nor could she adequately explain why she'd let a complete stranger—and a man, at that—stay on at Forton Hall. Unfortunately, though, Mrs. Denwortle had already seen to it that the entire community knew both that Rafe Bancroft was staying at Forton Hall and that he was paying their grocery bills.

"Actually, Charles," she said, "I feel . . . sorry for him. I'm not entirely certain May and I haven't compounded whatever mental injury he already had." "Sorry" wasn't quite the right word, but it certainly sounded better than "infatuated."

The squire sat back, tapping the underside of his tea saucer with his long, knobby fingers. What hair he had was silver, but his wits were as sharp as ever. Squire Talford had always seemed more of a father to her than her own ever had. Since her parents' death, he had become her dearest companion and confidante. So it surprised her that she was so reluctant to discuss her new houseguest—stable guest—with him.

"No one can fault you for protecting yourself, Felicity. He could be dangerous."

"Rafe's not dangerous." May looked up from the corner of the parlor, where she sat laughing with a mound of foxhound puppies wriggling across her lap. "He's smashing."

Felicity looked down at her tea to hide her smile. "May adores him," she said, glancing at her companion. "And I haven't detected anything menacing about him. In fact, he seems quite willing to be helpful."

"Even so—"

"Even so, I am keeping my eyes open. He's sleeping in the stable, and I've put him to work repairing the roof to keep him out of trouble. When Nigel returns, we'll give him a few quid and see him on his way." She took another sip of tea, then set the cup and saucer aside. "And that will be the end of that. Now, on to a more urgent matter. What was this about Mr. Wenvers needing a new atlas for the school?''

Charles's kind gray eyes studied her for a moment. "All right, handle him as you will. But you needn't do everything on your own, you know."

"I don't need a knight in shining armor," she returned firmly.

He chuckled. "I'm a bit rickety for that, but thank you for the vote of confidence."

"Nonsense." For the first time she realized that the third member of their education committee was missing. "Where is Lord Deerhurst this afternoon?"

"I believe he had business in Chester. He wasn't certain if he'd return in time to join us."

"Oh, that's a shame."

In truth, she was rather relieved that James Burlough was absent today. He was absurdly protective of her, and he would never understand her allowing Rafe to stay.

They made plans to send to London for a more current atlas, which Charles insisted on purchasing himself before she could even worry about the expense. Paying for one-third of Mr. Wenvers's salary was already stretching her funds to the utmost, but educating the children of east Cheshire was one thing she could not, and would not, give up.

As she rose to leave, Squire Talford put a hand on her arm. "You could stay here until Nigel returns. I know I've offered before, but—"

"Charles, please." Fond as she was of him, Felicity was beginning to tire of everyone assuming she needed help. "I am perfectly able to take care of myself. And if I'm here, I can't get Forton back in order."

Gentleman though he was, the squire couldn't

keep a skeptical expression from his face. "All right, all right. I surrender. But at least let my coach take you home."

May scattered puppies off her lap and stood. "It's a lovely day, Charles, and we like to walk," she said.

The squire laughed. "You're going to grow up as stubborn as your sister, aren't you?"

"Oh, yes."

The two-mile walk back to Forton was lovely, though the clouds hanging over the foothills to the east didn't look as though they intended to wait much longer before drenching them all again.

"Lis, look at that."

Felicity followed May's gaze to their house. Rafe stood on the roof, bare-chested, handing shingles to Dennis Greetham. They'd laid out nearly one whole corner of the roof, and piles of old, half-rotted shingles lay scattered on the ground below.

"Hello, Rafe!" May called, waving. "Hello, Mr. Greetham!"

Grinning, Rafe swept a bow to the two ladies, and gave an additional salute to Felicity. She supposed a properly bred London lady would be expected to faint in shock at the sight of a shirtless gentleman, but he looked far too delicious for her to close her eyes.

With supreme effort she tore her gaze from him to look at his companion. "Mr. Greetham, I didn't expect to see you here." In fact, she'd thought that the only reason Dennis Greetham was still on Forton land was that he was too stubborn to be forced off by something as trivial as starvation. Never would she have thought to see him voluntarily helping his landowners.

The stout farmer smiled. "Bancroft and I made a trade."

She lifted one hand to shield her eyes against the sun. "What sort of trade?"

"That's between us bargainers," Rafe interrupted loftily.

For a moment she contemplated pressing one of them for an answer, but the odds were fairly good that it would end up being connected to more of Rafe's nobility nonsense, which would then make her feel obliged to send Mr. Greetham home. And Forton Hall could use the assistance, whatever the source. "Would you care for something to drink, then?"

"Lemonade would be smashing," Rafe returned, wiping at the sweat glistening on his brow.

May giggled. "I'll make it," she called, and skipped into the kitchen.

"Where did you find the new shingles?" Felicity called up to Rafe. "I know we didn't have any lying—"

"Whoa, there!"

She started as a phaeton rounded the corner of the manor at high speed and came to a precise stop beside her. A tall, dark-haired gentleman of impeccable dress smiled at her as he hopped down from the carriage.

"Felicity, I'm so sorry to have missed our meeting," Lord Deerhurst said a little breathlessly, doffing his beaver hat and taking her hand.

She smiled back at him. "The only thing we discussed was an atlas."

He brushed her knuckles with his lips and then released her fingers. "Then I shan't chastise myself for being so late."

"*You're* Squire Talford?"

Felicity jumped again as Rafe's deep voice came from right behind her. Reflexively she turned to look up at him—and was completely unprepared for the rushing tingle of electricity that ran down her arms. Rafe had pulled his shirt back on, but it hung loose and untucked down to his thighs. Damp blond hair clung to his forehead and his neck. He was simply . . . beautiful. She'd seen handsome men before—Lord Deerhurst, for one—but none had ever caused her to tremble merely by their nearness. Swiftly she clasped her hands together before she could do something as absurd as flinging herself upon him.

"No, I'm not Talford. I am James Burlough, the Earl of Deerhurst." The earl's pleasant smile capsized into not-quite-polite puzzlement. "And who might you be, sir?"

Felicity blinked and looked at her neighbor. "Oh. Forgive me. My lord, this is Rafael Bancroft. An . . ." She looked at Rafe again, sidetracked as she wondered if his lips would taste salty with sweat. "Ah, an old, ah . . . family friend."

The earl frowned, though he offered his hand to her stable guest. "That's odd. I've never heard Felicity or Nigel speak of you."

Rafe delayed a moment before he stripped off one of his heavy work gloves to return the handshake. "Never heard of you, either."

The earl hadn't removed his driving glove, and somehow—even though she couldn't quite determine why—that seemed significant. And it spoke in Rafe's favor as a gentleman, if not as a nobleman. "Well," she began, "we haven't—"

May opened the kitchen door. "Rafe, it's too heavy!" she called.

Her stable guest nodded curtly at the earl. "Deerhurst." His sea-green eyes turned to Felicity as he pulled off the other glove and tossed the pair of them into the back of Greetham's wagon. "Lis." Then he strolled away and walked into the kitchen just like—well, just like he owned the place.

The use of her nickname startled her, and a soft blush crept up her cheeks. When she turned back to Deerhurst he was looking at her, his own expression distinctly disapproving.

"Who is this . . . Bancroft?" he asked, wiping his gloved hand against his trouser leg.

"I told you who he is," Felicity answered. Dash it, defending her decision to take Rafe in was becoming a damned nuisance. She wished everyone would just mind their own business—at least until the roof was repaired. "An old friend of Nigel's."

"He isn't staying here, is he?"

"Was there something you wanted, James?"

His face reddening, he sputtered for a moment, then cleared his throat. "Of course I would never question your good sense, but you know I worry about your being here all alone."

Declining to inform him that May had turned out to be quite an efficient bodyguard, Felicity put a hand on his arm. "I know, and I appreciate your concern. But it's really not necessary, my lord. Truly."

"Even so, I would feel so much better if you would—that is, if you and May would stay at Deerhurst until Nigel's return."

Everyone seemed to want her to abandon Forton, as though having Nigel present made any real difference whatsoever. "That isn't necessary, either."

"At least let me help pay for some of the repairs to dear old Forton Hall."

Her eyes narrowed at the second mention of charity that day. "Very kind of you to offer, but again, unnecessary, James. As you can see," and she gestured at Dennis Greetham high up on the roof, "we have matters well in hand."

"Well, yes, but—"

"Lemonade, Lis?" May asked, holding a pair of glasses.

Rafe came behind her carrying a tray laden with a pitcher and two more glasses. Fleetingly she wondered whom they were excluding from the refreshment party. When she glanced over at her stable guest and found his eyes on her, it became rather clear.

"Mr. Bancroft, Lord Deerhurst is Forton's neighbor to the east," she explained, lifting a glass from the tray and handing it to the earl. Was it the heat or Rafe's direct gaze that was making her pulse quicken? "We've all known one another forever." And knowing her for three days did not give the supposed second son of a duke the right to behave rudely—especially toward an actual earl with an actual title and an actual estate.

"Oh, yes," Deerhurst smiled, taking the glass, "we all grew up together. Which is why I was surprised that I've never heard you mentioned before today."

"I've known Rafe forever," May interrupted, and took their stableguest's hand in her small one. "Let's go give Mr. Greetham some lemonade."

Oh, dear, now everyone was behaving atrociously. "May, why don't you ask Mr. Greetham to come down and join us?"

"All right." Scowling, May stomped off toward the ladder.

"And don't you climb up there," Felicity ordered.

"Damnation."

"May!" She turned to Rafe. "Now you see what you've done?"

He grinned and took a long swallow of lemonade, droplets running down his chin.

"How long do you intend to stay here, Bancroft?" the earl asked.

"Just until Nigel's return," Felicity said hurriedly, before Rafe could begin talking about the forged title and dukes and Africa.

"He's selling me the place." Rafe drank again, watching her over the rim of the glass as he emptied it.

"What?" The color draining from his face, Deerhurst stared from her to Rafe and back again.

"Nigel is doing no such thing," she stated, glaring at Rafael. "Mr. Bancroft is only teasing."

Deerhurst looked at the two of them again, then forced a disbelieving laugh. "Well, I must say, it wasn't very amusing."

Felicity took the glass from the earl's hand and propelled him back toward his phaeton. "No, it wasn't. But you needn't worry about losing the Harringtons as neighbors."

The earl smiled as he craned his neck to keep Rafe in view. "I should hope not. You are my dearest friends." He clutched her hand to his chest. "My very dearest friends."

"Of course we are," she soothed.

"I couldn't bear to lose you."

"You don't have to worry about that." Felicity freed her hand, wondering what had upset him so much. Other than his annoying habit lately of offering to lend her large sums of money, which thankfully hadn't begun until after Nigel left, he was unexceptionally pleasant. In addition to that, he was her one and only suitor.

He stepped up onto the phaeton and took his seat. "Are you still going to attend the Wadsworth dinner on Thursday? Because I did want to chat with you."

"I wouldn't miss it. I'll see you there."

Deerhurst snapped the reins, and his gray gelding turned toward the drive. Felicity watched the carriage out of sight, then, furious, turned to find Rafe. He had vanished. "Where is he?" she asked, her teeth clenched.

"He went into the stable," May said, pointing. "Are you mad?"

"No," she said brightly. "I merely need to clear up a little misunderstanding." Hiking up her skirt, she strode toward the stable.

"She's mad," her sister informed Mr. Greetham. "Aye."

"I am not," Felicity called back over her shoulder.

Rafe was brushing down Aristotle when she stormed into the stable and stomped to a halt.

"How dare you!" she snapped, hands on her hips.

He turned to face her. "How dare I what?"

"You promised you wouldn't go about announcing your supposed ownership of my estate!"

"I didn't," he corrected her. "I said I was *going* to be the owner. I thought that was quite decent of me."

"Decent? You practically threw Lord Deerhurst out of the house on his ear."

He dropped the brush into a bucket. "He was practically drooling on you. You should thank me."

Rafe's apparent calmness didn't soothe her own pounding heart in the least. "He's a dear friend," she protested.

"Then he should have offered to climb up on the roof and help us."

"Don't be ridiculous. He's a nobleman!"

"Not much of one."

Felicity wasn't sure why she was so angry, but

she knew for certain that it was his fault. "You know nothing about him, and don't you dare presume to run my few acquaintances away!"

Wishing she had a tea kettle, she stormed past him. He grabbed her arm, and spun her back to face him. As she took a breath to shout at him again, he leaned down and softly touched his lips to hers.

"My apologies," he said, straightening.

She blinked, realizing she was leaning up toward him, her mouth half open. "What . . . what for?" she stammered.

"For running your acquaintances away."

Felicity struggled to remember what they'd been arguing about. "And the kiss?" she demanded, trying to rally her indignation, when what she really wanted was for him to kiss her again—immediately, so this time she could memorize it.

Rafe shook his head, running his thumb across the sensitive corner of her mouth. "That wasn't a kiss."

Damnation, she was leaning again. "Then . . . then what, pray tell, was it?"

"Practice. You'll know when I've kissed you, Lis."

Rafe strolled past her out the door. As he disappeared in the direction of the ladder, Felicity took an abrupt seat on a bale of hay. He intended to kiss her again. Was that a threat—or a promise? Slowly she reached up and traced her lips with one finger. So *that* was a kiss. "My goodness." A shivering thrill went down her spine.

Then she remembered that he was demented. "Dash it all," she whispered. For a moment longer she sat, wishing that Rafe Bancroft could be who and what he claimed, and that for longer than the space of one kiss, she could regard him the least bit seriously. Then she rose, swept hay off her skirt, and went back into the house. She'd learned a long time ago that wishing was a poor substitute for reality.

Chapter 5

ometimes, Rafe decided, he could be an absolute blithering idiot. "Just practice," he muttered, as he secured the last of the available shingles. *"You'll know when it's for real."* Disgusted, he blew out his lips. "Jackass."

"What's that, Bancroft?" Greetham, partway down the ladder, popped his head back up over the eave to eye him curiously.

"Just talking to myself," he said, dropping a hammer and an old, rusty saw down to the ground.

"Miss May said you were a bit soft-headed." Greetham continued his descent.

Rafe leaned over the edge of the roof, torn between affront and amusement. That little chit had a mouth on her, for damned certain. So did her sister. "I am not soft-headed. I had an accident the other day. That's all."

"No need to explain to me. I'm just a simple farmer."

As the farmer reached the ground, Rafe started down the ladder, chuckling as he descended. "Simple farmer, my ass. Do you have any appointments planned for tomorrow?"

" 'Appointments,' is it? Well, I'm having tea with the king and Lady Jersey, but—"

"Good God, why?" Rafe grimaced. "They're dull as mud."

"Rafe."

At the sound of Felicity's voice, he jumped. Her voice was pretty, with a soft, musical lilt quite at odds with her claims of practicality. He found himself wondering if she could sing, until he noticed Greetham staring at him.

Shaking himself out of his daydream, he turned to face his hostess. "Lis?"

She hesitated for a moment, and he could see the censure in her mobile expression at his use of her given name. Now that he'd gotten away with it, though, he wasn't about to give up the privilege. Sweet Lucifer, he'd already kissed her. "Miss Harrington" simply would not do.

"Please don't pester Mr. Greetham," she said. "He has his own responsibilities." Felicity scowled at him for another moment, then turned to her tenant. "How are Mrs. Greetham and Sally and the boys?" she asked with a warm smile.

"Glad to be rid of me for the day, to be sure, Miss Harrington." He smiled. "I'll tell Rosie you asked after her."

"I would be grateful." She put a hand on his arm. "And thank you for all your help today, Mr. Greetham."

The stout farmer actually blushed. "No need, miss. 'Twas my pleasure." He doffed his cap at Rafe. "Good evening, Bancroft."

"Greetham." Rafe watched the farmer hop up to the wagon seat and start down the drive with his mules, then turned to find Felicity. She was gone, vanished back into the house. "Damn," he muttered, not blaming her an ounce for wanting to escape him. He generally wasn't so clumsy with his seductions. He'd been attempting to charm her, for

God's sake, not to drive her and May out of Forton. "Idiot."

Dinner was finely roasted pigeon. Landed gentry or not, she cooked better than Quin's old chef at Whiting House in London. And he'd wager a month's army pay that neither the famous Lady Jersey, nor any of her flighty, fluttering, titled friends, could roast a pigeon if it jumped into the oven for them.

Felicity kept giving him dark glances throughout the meal. Rafe couldn't tell if she was angry with him for kissing her or for calling her by her first name, but he wasn't about to ask.

Over a bottle of brandy Quin had once tried to describe how he felt when he kissed Maddie for the first time, and the resulting jumbled mishmash of fluff from his cool-headed brother had started Rafe laughing so hard he'd nearly tumbled to the floor. To his growing horror, some of the nonsense Quin had spouted suddenly made sense. He kept catching himself watching her, wondering what she might be thinking.

Certainly he didn't regret kissing her. Her presence made his stay in Cheshire very interesting. But he'd kissed women before. He'd had affairs and lovers and several complete disasters before. Never, though, had one damned kiss—and barely a kiss, at that—left him feeling so . . . disjointed.

He was looking at her again, at the graceful curve of her neck as she helped May with some arithmetic problems. Her skin that afternoon had felt so soft, and his fingers twitched with the desire to touch her again. "I think I'll head out to the stable and read Aristotle a bedtime story," he said hurriedly, rising before he could begin composing odes to her earlobes. She'd likely only want to correct his grammar.

"Mr. Greetham says it's going to rain," May said, looking up. "Don't you think you should stay in the house tonight?"

Rafe risked another glance at Felicity, hoping that their kiss would at least have gained him that. He was blasted tired of picking straw out of his ears and nose and eyes, and every other nook and cranny in his body.

"Rafe enjoys spending time with Aristotle," Lis countered. "Now concentrate, May."

He scowled, then quickly wiped the expression from his face as Felicity looked at him again. "Is that thunder I hear?" he asked, trying to change her mind.

She turned toward the window. "I didn't hear anything."

Blast. At least he had her sister as an ally—and he needed to keep it that way. He leaned over May. "The answer is thirty-one," he whispered in her ear.

"Thirty-one, Lis," May piped up.

Her sister clapped. "Excellent, May. Five more, and we'll be finished." She eyed Rafe, and he tried to look pitiful. It didn't work. "Good night, Rafe," she said firmly.

He sighed. "Good night, Felicity, May."

"Night, Rafe. Are you going to work on the roof again tomorrow?"

"Unless it's raining." He strolled over to grab a book from the pile drying by the fire. *Culpepper's Herbal Guide*. He started rooting for a more interesting tome.

Felicity perked up. "You know, I've been thinking. If it *is* raining tomorrow, you might make a go of fixing the main doors." She smiled at him, and he felt his insides melting into goo.

He grinned helplessly back at her like a drooling

idiot, wondering if she knew how her smile lit her eyes and made him think about kissing her sweet lips again—as if he'd been able to think of anything else all evening, anyway. "The doors. Splendid idea."

"Yes, I thought so."

Feeling even more moronic, Rafe collected a lamp and headed off to the stable. The blow to his head must have caused some sort of temporary mental imbalance. He had no other explanation for his own odd behavior. When Deerhurst had arrived, he'd practically vaulted off the roof to get between the earl and Felicity. Generally he wasn't that territorial with women he had a claim to, much less someone it would actually benefit him to be rid of.

The gusting wind kept blowing out the lamp, making reading impossible unless he wanted to risk burning down the stable. Since he'd ended up with the damned herbal guide anyway, he piled on every blanket they'd given him and curled up into a scratchy pile of hay.

The rain began right at dawn, accompanied by a cacophony of thunder and lightning. The wind had picked up as well, and it moaned hauntingly through the rafters. Rafe sat up amid a tangle of blankets, looking up anxiously toward the roof.

"Bloody hell," he muttered, as miniature waterfalls began cascading down into the hay all around him.

With every gust the structure creaked and groaned, and Aristotle nickered uneasily from his stall. With the wreckage of the west wing fresh in his mind, Rafe dressed quickly, put a halter on the bay, and led the horse out of the stable.

The storm had evidently awakened Felicity as well, because when he pushed open the single working door, she was waiting just inside. Clad in her nightgown, a shawl wrapped tightly around her, and her midnight hair loose and curling past her shoulders, she looked like the waking vision of the dream he'd had earlier. At least that was how she'd looked at the beginning of the dream. By the end, she'd been wearing considerably fewer clothes.

"Good morning," he said, smiling as welcome heat ran through him. Kissing her had been one of the more intelligent things he'd done since his arrival. In fact, even with the cold rain, he was still thinking of several other things he'd like to do with her.

"You are not bringing that animal into this house."

His smile dropped. "I most certainly am."

"This is not a stable."

"Your stable's hardly a stable. And I am not going to have it collapse on my horse."

She folded her arms. "No."

Rafe narrowed his eyes. "If you want me to fix these doors," he offered as calmly as he could with rain drenching his backside, "you will let me bring Aristotle into the foyer." He folded his own arms over his chest, mimicking her. "Otherwise, you can do it yourself."

He watched the play of emotions across her delicate features. Finally she sighed and stepped back. "Very well. But he will remain in the foyer, and as soon as the rain stops, I want him out. Is that clear?"

He nodded. "Absolutely."

To his credit, Aristotle entered the house as though he did that sort of thing all the time. He did nibble a little at the vase of daisies beneath the stairs, but after Rafe cuffed him on the nose, he left the posies alone.

"You see?" he said, grinning over the gelding's

back at Felicity's stony expression. "A perfect gentleman."

"Hm. And how—"

Thunder boomed deafeningly overhead, drowning out the rest of her sentence. She jumped, and upstairs May screamed.

"Felicity!"

"Oh, no," she gasped, and ran for the stairs.

Rafe was faster. He bounded up the curving staircase, taking the steps two at a time. As he reached the second floor, a small figure in white flung itself at him.

"The roof's falling!" May cried, wrapping her arms around his waist with surprising strength.

"No, it's not," he said in his calmest voice, putting his hands on her slim, trembling shoulders and not quite certain what to do. Flighty females he could deal with, but terrified little girls were something else entirely. "You're perfectly safe, May."

Unexpectedly, Felicity slid her hand along his shoulder and down his wet back, then knelt on the fraying carpet at his feet. Briskly she rubbed May's shaking back and her sleep-tangled dark hair. "Shh, May. You were just dreaming. The roof won't fall again."

"How do you know?" May mumbled, her voice muffled against Rafe's stomach.

Disturbed by May's shaking, Rafe pulled her away from his waist. He squatted down beside Felicity, and immediately May flung her arms around his neck, attaching herself to him again tighter than a sea limpet to a rock. "Good God, May," he rasped, "you could strangle a hippo."

"No, I couldn't," she quavered against his shoulder. If he hadn't already been soaked to the bone, her tears would have taken care of it.

"I beg to differ." He put his arms around her

back and rocked her slowly from side to side. "But you really are safe. I put Aristotle in the foyer, and you know I wouldn't do that if I thought the house would coll—"

She lifted her tearstained face. "Aristotle is in the foyer?"

"Mm-hm." He nodded. "And I think the thunder's made him a bit edgy. He could probably use some company."

May released his neck from her stranglehold and wiped at her eyes. "Might I give him an apple?"

"I would be grateful if you would."

With a last sniff, May hurried down the stairs. A moment later, Rafe heard her comforting Aristotle. "Don't worry, old Totle. I'll make sure nothing happens to you."

"Thank you."

Felicity was kneeling beside him, still in her nightgown and with her long black hair loose around her shoulders, and the desire to run his fingers through her dark, curling hair, and to kiss her full, soft lips hit him hard. "For what?"

"For calming May down. I was worried this might happen. She was so frightened the other night."

"So were you, no doubt."

She smiled a little, and shrugged. "I'm older. And I don't frighten as easily."

Her brown eyes studied his face, and his pulse leaped and sped. "Here," he said, rising, "let me help you up."

When he extended his hand she slipped her slender fingers into his. He slowly pulled her to her feet, wondering what she would clobber him with if he simply jumped on her again.

"You haven't told me," she said, color creeping into her cheeks as she swiftly freed her hand, "what you had intended to do with Forton Hall—if the deed had turned out to be legitimate, I mean."

"I'll let that go"—he grinned—"because you've let old Totle in the house. Poor lad—with that nickname all the other horses will be laughing at him, now."

She continued looking at him expectantly, and he cleared his throat. Rafe could distract most other women of his acquaintance much more easily than he could Felicity Harrington. "China," he finally said. "I've always wanted to travel, and selling Forton Hall is my chance to see the world."

"Ah. I see. But why don't you simply ask your father or your brother for the money? I would imagine they are fabulously wealthy."

He nodded, following her as she started back down the stairs. "Oh, they are; but it's *their* money. I don't want to have to answer to them for anything—everything—that I do. I'm blasted tired of that."

Felicity paused, turning around to look up at him. For a moment, something vulnerable and uncertain touched her eyes. "Being a second son must be difficult," she finally offered.

In view of the disaster she faced, Rafe felt a bit selfish. "I make do."

"You made it to Africa on your own, didn't you?"

"You went to Africa?" May asked from downstairs. She held an apple up for Aristotle, who snorted at it hopefully.

"He saw elephants," Felicity added, smiling at him before she resumed her way downstairs.

"You didn't shoot any of them, did you?" May demanded. "I like elephants."

"No, I didn't shoot any elephants," Rafe returned. "A few gazelle and a wildebeest, but that was to eat."

"That's all right, then."

Rafe leaned back against the banister and folded his arms across his chest, his rain-soaked clothes clinging unpleasantly to his body. "Thank you."

"What did you do in Africa?" May gave the apple to the gelding, then walked over to lean beside Rafe, copying his stance.

"I tried to look menacing so the settlers wouldn't shoot all of us, or their Dutch neighbors." The little girl looked puzzled, and he grinned. At least she wasn't terrified, any longer. "I was in the army," he explained.

Suddenly Felicity began laughing. "Of course you were," she managed, looking absurdly relieved. "We have several regiments in Africa, don't we?"

He looked at her quizzically. "Yes, we do. Not mine, unfortunately, but I managed it, anyway."

"What regiment were you?" the little girl asked.

"The Coldstream Guards."

"Are they important? They sound bang up to the mark."

Rafe chuckled. "Well, mostly I led troops about for parades, coronations, and funerals and such."

Felicity stopped chuckling. "You *led* troops?"

Perhaps when he'd landed on her, she'd hit her head, as well. "Yes. I was a captain. I only resigned a few weeks ago."

"Did you learn how to fight?"

An unexpected chill rattled Rafe's teeth. The gaping hole where the west wing used to be certainly wasn't helping to keep the house warm. He'd have to see to that after the doors. "I learned seventy-three ways to kill a man."

May straightened and grabbed his arm. "Seventy-three?'' she exclaimed, her eyes wide. "Will you teach me some of them?"

Rafe lifted an eyebrow. "You already know at least one."

Felicity stepped forward and put her hands on May's shoulders. "Yes, the infamous tea kettle maneuver."

"Ooh, is that one of them?" the girl asked excitedly.

Solemnly Rafe nodded. "Number twenty-eight."

Felicity smiled at him over May's head, her eyes dancing. *Thank you*, she mouthed, then tugged her sister toward the hallway. "Come on, let's get you wrapped in a blanket and warmed up."

"Number twenty-eight," May chirped. "You know number twenty-eight, too, Lis."

Rafe watched them go down the hall, then walked over to hunch against Aristotle's warm flank. "Don't worry about me," he muttered. "I'm only the one soaked to the skin and freezing to death."

The horse swung his head around to eye him.

"Oh, be quiet, old Totle."

Felicity chuckled from the doorway. "Which number is freezing to death?" she asked, stepping forward with a blessedly warm-looking blanket in her arms.

"Number seven," Rafe answered promptly, his teeth chattering again.

"Well, we must prevent number seven, then." Felicity hesitated, then lifted the blanket to wrap it about his shoulders.

Rafe closed his eyes as her hands slid over his shoulders, too slowly and gently to be anything but a caress. He felt *much* warmer than he had a moment earlier. And he realized that the acquisition of Forton Hall was becoming very complicated, indeed.

Stop touching him, Felicity chastised herself as she sipped tea in the morning room an hour later. Rafe sat on the hearth before the roaring fire, playing jackstraws with May. *And for heaven's sake, stop looking at him.* Addle-brained though he was, at least he knew enough to come in out of the rain—even if he had waited until he was soaked through, and even if he had insisted on bringing his horse into the house with him.

"You cheated!" May declared, giggling.

"I did not, little Miss Cutthroat."

Felicity smiled. May would be devastated when Rafe left—she'd never seen her precocious sister become so attached to anyone. And she hardly made a habit of letting strangers step into their lives, herself. Since he'd arrived—exploded into their lives, more like—she'd been off balance and befuddled. For the first time since she could remember, she felt as though she was moving forward instead of treading water, or worse yet, slipping backward into further ruin.

"How did you get your scar?" May asked him, reaching out toward his face.

With a grin he gripped her wrist and returned her hand to the game, but not before Felicity saw him flinch. She settled deeper into the couch's soft cushions, studying him over the rim of her teacup.

Rafe shrugged. "Just an accident." He loosened the blanket around his shoulders. "I say, I think I'm beginning to thaw."

May wrinkled her nose at him. "What sort of accident?"

Felicity should have told her to stop prying, but she was supremely interested in hearing the answer herself, and whether it would involve more dukes and elephants and fabulous adventures. May's manners were becoming atrocious, but at least they were useful—and their guest didn't seem to mind a whit.

Rafe sighed. "Fine. My horse stumbled and rolled on me and broke my leg in two places, and a French soldier stuck me in the face with a bayonet."

"Aristotle rolled on you?"

"No. I was in Belgium."

May's eyes widened even further, while Felicity's narrowed. "At Waterloo?"

While her sister mentally congratulated May on her knowledge of geography, Rafe looked ill at ease. "Yes, at Waterloo. Until damned—deuced—old Arthur wrote Prinny and my father that I'd probably lost an eye and a leg, and that they were shipping me home posthaste before I expired."

"Who's Arthur?" May asked.

"Wellington." Rafe smiled, then leaned forward to tap her on the nose. "And you know what?"

"What?"

"He could never beat me at jackstraws, either."

May scowled. "You never played jackstraws with Wellington."

Rafe shrugged the blanket off and stood. "How do you know that?" He sketched them an elegant bow. "Excuse me, ladies, while I check on old Totle and go take a look at that door."

As he left, May scooted around to face her sister. "Do you think he really knows the Duke of Wellington?"

Felicity set aside her tea. "I'm sure Rafe has seen His Grace," she conceded.

"I think he's telling the truth. He knows about elephants, and hippos, and seventy-three ways to kill someone. And he ate a wildebeest."

With a sigh Felicity nodded and patted the cushion beside her. "Come here for a moment, May." When her sister had settled onto the couch, Felicity put her arm around May's shoulders and hugged her. "I need to explain something to you."

May looked at her warily. "All right."

"Remember how Nigel always said his friend Peter Whiting was so wonderful, and when he finally visited we really didn't like him all that much?"

"He was a damned stuffed shirt." May nodded.

"May!"

"All right, deuced. But Rafe's not like him at all. Rafe's top of the trees."

"Yes, he is. But what I mean to say is, he may see things one way, like Nigel did, and really they might not be that way at all."

May thought about that for a long time. "So you mean he might think he's seen a hippopotamus, but it's really a pig," she said finally.

Felicity smiled in relief. "Yes. That is precisely what I mean."

"He's as mad as a Bedlamite."

"We don't know that for certain." She tugged her sister up against her side. "Remember, though, he may be completely smashing, but we really can't rely on him. We must rely on ourselves."

"Can we rely on Nigel?" May asked, looking up with her dark eyes.

"We can rely on what we know about Nigel," Felicity answered.

As May scampered off to help Rafe, Felicity sat on the couch and stared into the fire. Relying on what they knew about Nigel wasn't very comforting.

There were a few things still salvageable in the

west wing, but with the bad weather, anything made of cloth or paper would be lost. And all she could afford to do about it was to board up that end of the hallway so the snow wouldn't come in when winter arrived.

She stood to straighten the room. If Nigel didn't make good on his promises, by the time winter arrived, she and May would be lucky to have any roof at all left over their heads. And given his history of grand schemes that went nowhere, their situation was becoming more tenuous by the moment. Like their father, Nigel had always been full of good intentions, and completely incapable of carrying through on them.

And then there was Rafe. Full of wild fantasies and impossible dreams, at least he knew how to mend a roof. She felt guilty about abusing his kindness and his delusions, but if she turned him away, she could only imagine what sort of trouble he might get himself into. At least here he had a roof—well, part of a roof—over his head, and he could be of some use. Neither she nor May had smiled or laughed so much in ages.

Believing himself to be nobility, though, could get him arrested elsewhere—particularly when he was so bad at it. Nigel, who complained about the deficiencies of rural life and the way his attire must be fading sadly out of fashion, seemed much more a member of the nobility than amusing, easygoing Rafe, who was wearing clothes far older than he was. If Nigel ever attempted to hang a door, he'd be more likely to end up hanging himself by accident.

"Damnation!"

Something heavy thunked and crashed, resonating hollowly through the remains of Forton Hall.

"Oh, my God!" Felicity lurched to her feet and

dashed toward the foyer. She was stupid, *stupid* to let May play about in this wrecked house, especially with a strange man pretending he knew how to fix doors and cook wildebeest. *"May!"*

A vision of her sister crushed beneath the heavy door filled her mind as she ran. She nearly stumbled into Rafe coming toward her, and the somber expression on his face wrenched her anxiety into panic.

"Where's May?" she asked frantically. "What happened?"

His expression immediately softened into surprised concern, and he grabbed onto her shoulders before she could rush past him. "It's all right, Lis. Really."

"But—"

"May is fine," he said firmly. "I broke your vase. I'm sorry." He let go of her and held up a broken-stemmed daisy. "I was trying to make a jest out of it so you wouldn't get mad at me. It was stupid. I should have realized you'd think we'd flattened May, or something."

"I'm all right, Lis!" May called a moment later.

Felicity stood staring up at Rafe, trying to collect her wits and catch her breath. "What do you mean, 'we'?"

He looked sheepish. Suspecting duplicity, Felicity put her hand on his chest and pushed. Reluctantly he moved aside, like a great lion being held at bay by a mouse, and she continued into the foyer. And stopped again.

May did seem perfectly fine. She sat upon Aristotle's bare back, while the bay stood as far from the front door as he could manage. Odd as that sight was, the three men lifting the fallen door of solid oak surprised her even more. As she entered they froze, the heavy, ornately carved plank suspended between them.

"Miss Harrington," Mr. Greetham said. "Sorry for the noise."

"Wood was slippery, Miss Harrington." The second man, Bill Jennings, grimaced apologetically. "Won't happen again, miss."

The third man—or boy, actually, for Felicity knew Ronald Banthe couldn't be older than eighteen—tried to doff his hat and nearly dropped the door on his foot. "Morning, Miss Harrington."

"Good morning, gentlemen." Felicity turned around again, nearly running into Rafe for the second time. "Mr. Bancroft, might I have a word with you?" she asked, moving past him into the shambles of a dining room.

She didn't turn around to look, but when the door softly closed a moment later, she knew he had followed her.

"I really am sorry," he began again. "I didn't mean to frighten you."

"What," she said, turning to face him, "are they doing here?"

"They?" Rafe repeated. "Oh—my troops. They're assisting me. With the door."

"I don't want them doing that," she stated, putting her hands on her hips.

He tossed the broken daisy onto the table. "If you're worried about them sullying your carpet, I hardly think—"

"No!" Felicity flushed, embarrassed that he would think such a thing. "For heaven's sake, that's not it. They—they have their own lives and responsibilities. I . . ." She stopped.

Rafe took a step nearer. "They *want* to help you, Lis. I don't know if you realize it, but you're quite popular here in Cheshire. If you'd asked, they would have been here a month ago.''

"But I can't pay them," she blurted.

"They *want* to help," he repeated. "I barely had time to mention it before they volunteered." He stopped in front of her. "Don't be so stubborn. You can use the assistance."

"I am not being stubborn," she insisted, having difficulty meeting his intensely curious gaze. "It's just . . . It's not right. I am a landowner—or Nigel is, anyway. I'm supposed to help *them*. They are not supposed to help me, or even think that I might need help." Finally she looked up into his light green eyes. "I wish you could understand what that's like."

"I do understand," he murmured. "But you don't have to do everything yourself. Sometimes people just want to do kind things for one another." He reached out and took her hand, tugging her closer. "Sometimes you have to let other people help you."

The back of his fingers brushed across her cheek, and suddenly she couldn't speak. Taking her face in his hands, he leaned closer.

"Has anyone told you how beautiful you are?" he asked softly. Then he kissed her.

Felicity closed her eyes as lightning and hot liquid fire coursed through every part of her at his touch. She slid her hands up his chest and over his broad, strong shoulders.

His mouth, warm and soft and infinitely more knowing than hers, teased at her, kissing and pulling away until she had to pursue. His teeth found her lower lip and gently bit, tugging at it. Felicity gasped, hot sparks tingling down her spine and up her thighs to where they met.

As his hands slid, caressing, down her back to

her hips, she realized the soft, yearning moan she heard came from deep in her own throat. Her eyes flying open, she pulled away, knocking his hands away from her.

"Stop that," she protested. Not even her voice was steady, and she was half surprised her legs didn't collapse and send her to the floor in a molten puddle.

Rafe looked at her for a long moment, something startled in his own eyes. "I'd best get back to the door," he said.

As he moved past her, his fingers brushed and momentarily curled around hers. The brief touch of their hands unsettled her as much as the kiss. They were connected in some way, she and Rafe—and she did not need the additional burden of a madman on her hands. What she did want, though, was much less clear.

Unable to move, Felicity looked sightlessly toward the rain-streaked window. Mad or not, he thought she was beautiful. She'd heard the words before, from Deerhurst and Nigel's nodcock friends. But Rafe had meant them. "Brass hinges."

His footsteps stopped. "Beg pardon?"

Until he reacted, she hadn't actually been certain she'd uttered the words aloud. "I want to use the brass hinges that are on the doors now. My great-grandfather took them from an old ruined castle in Spain."

For a long moment he didn't say anything, and then she heard him sigh. "Brass hinges, it is."

Chapter 6

Felicity Harrington was an absolutely remarkable female, Rafe decided as he flattened his thumb for the third time. "Damn blasted bloody..." He trailed off, glancing at May, still seated aboard Aristotle and watching the proceedings with interest. "My, that was painful," he amended, and she laughed. "Ronald, please hold that board still next time."

Ronald swallowed, his Adam's apple bobbing nervously. "Aye, Mr. Bancroft. On my honor, I won't move it again."

Rafe hammered at the twisted hinge again, trying to flatten the thing out. Mostly, though, his mind was occupied by the incident in the dining room. From his side, that kiss had been quite possibly the most memorable one he could recall.

As for Lis—well, she'd clearly been underwhelmed, if all she could come up with afterward was that she wanted the brass hinges back on the doors. She was so far removed from the pretty, pampered, empty-headed misses of society that he had no idea how to deal with her—which made her two things he couldn't resist: a puzzle, and a beautiful, intelligent woman.

"I think it's going to take a forge to get those back into shape," Greetham commented.

The farmer was right, and Rafe supposed he shouldn't begrudge the five or six shillings it would take to get the job done right. Any estate would be more saleable if it actually had front doors on it. "You're right. Ronald, will you take them by the blacksmith on your way back to the Childe of Hale?"

"Pleased to, my lord."

Rafe narrowed one eye. "I'm not—"

"I know, sir," the boy said, doffing his hat again. "But it was so kind of you to agree to—"

Rafe cleared his throat as Felicity walked through the foyer, a pile of books in her arms. She glanced at him, then continued on her way. "No need to thank me," he said brusquely as she vanished.

"So says you, my l—er, sir, but I've always wanted to be able to ride and jump my horse like a gentleman, like I saw at the Derby that year. It's grand of you to show me how it's done." He grinned and nudged Jennings in the ribs. "Perhaps I'll enter myself in the Derby next year, eh?"

"Don't care about jumping," the tall, lanky farmer said. "Just want my fence mended before Deerhurst's damned cows eat what's left of my potato crop."

"And we'll see to that immediately," Rafe reassured him, hoping Felicity wasn't near enough to overhear just how he had encouraged the locals to "volunteer" their assistance.

All of Forton Hall's neighbors with whom he'd conversed with had expressed their liking for Felicity and May, just as they'd let him know exactly what they thought of sod-headed Nigel Harrington. And apparently Felicity's father hadn't been any more proficient at estate management than his son. Farmers had long memories for maltreatment, and he couldn't blame them for their reservations when it came to lending their assistance at Forton.

He also knew these three men would tell everyone in east Cheshire what was going on at Forton, and how the attitude of the residents had changed. That report would either net him the possibility of more help, or if he couldn't make good on his promises it would make him—and the Harringtons, probably—irretrievably disliked. And even if he were going to sell the place and never set eyes on Cheshire again, he didn't want that to happen.

The men left a little after sunset. The rain had lessened to a miserable but steady drizzle, and Rafe intended to inform Felicity that he was not, by God, going to sleep out in the stable again.

She had made a sweet potato pie for dinner, and the smell had him salivating. Before he could take his first bite, though, Lis folded her hands primly before her on the pitted kitchen table. The fork halfway to his mouth, Rafe paused, steeling himself for an argument and regretting that he hadn't at least gotten to taste the masterpiece.

"Rafe," she began.

Regretfully he set the fork back down. "Yes?"

"I've been thinking," she continued, her attention on the lit candle in the center of the table, "perhaps you should move into one of the spare bedchambers upstairs. Uncertain as the weather has been, you would be risking influenza if you remained in the stable."

Rafe stifled a cheer. "I certainly wouldn't want to make myself ill," he agreed. "I wouldn't be able to continue work on the house, if that happened."

She flushed, a good indication that he'd found her primary concern—and that it wasn't his health. "I didn't—"

He nodded, amused at her transparent motivations. "Yes, I suppose staying inside is for the best, though I will miss the squeaking of the rats all night lo—"

The makeshift barricade they'd put up across the front entry shook and rattled. May jumped, grabbing Felicity's hand, and for a moment Rafe thought Aristotle was attempting an escape.

"I say," a voice called down the hallway as the sound repeated, "how does one get in here?"

"Lord Deerhurst," Felicity said, her expression easing. "I'll see to him."

Damnation, the man had poor timing. Rafe pushed away from the table. "*I'll* see to him," he countered, rising and heading down the long hallway.

The earl had pried one of the outside boards loose, and he stuck his face into the resulting opening as Rafe arrived.

"Ah, Bancroft. I just came by to check on Felicity," he said.

"The Harrington ladies are fine," Rafe answered brusquely, leaning against the barrier and folding his arms across his chest.

"Well, I'd like to see that for myself, if you don't mind."

Rafe did mind, very much. "I'm not stopping you," he said instead.

The earl's face, craned at an awkward angle to view the interior of the foyer, began to grow red. "You *are* stopping me. Please remove this . . . barricade."

Rafe shook his head. "I just got it put up." Actually, they'd made it easy to swing aside to accommodate Aristotle, but he saw no reason to enlighten Deerhurst about that.

"Let me in at once, I say." The earl rattled at the boards again.

"Go around." This was infinitely better than being exiled to the stable.

"I will not."

"Fine by me, Deerhurst. Is it still raining out there?"

"What is going on?" Felicity stomped into the foyer, her annoyed glare directed at Rafe.

He put on his most innocent expression. "Nothing."

"Felicity, thank God," Deerhurst said through the crack in the barricade. "I'd begun to fear this madman had done something foul to you."

Rolling his eyes, Rafe snorted. "Oh, please."

"Rafe!"

With another glower, Felicity elbowed him aside so she could lower her face to the earl's level. Considering that it gave Rafe a spectacular view of her bosom, he didn't mind all that much.

"My lord, please come around to the kitchen entry and share some sweet potato pie with us."

Deerhurst smiled. "I would be delighted. Thank you, Felicity."

When the earl's face had vanished, she straightened again. "Please stop antagonizing James. He's a very nice man."

Rafe held her gaze. "Are you looking to become Lady Deerhurst?" The idea infuriated him, though he wasn't certain why. It would make selling Forton easier, if Lis had a husband and another home to go to.

Felicity flushed. "That is none of your concern," she said, and turned on her heel.

"How do you know what concerns me?" He immediately regretted the words, for it made him sound jealous though he'd only known her a few days. Felicity only squared her shoulders and continued back into the kitchen.

*　　*　　*

The Earl of Deerhurst stood outside the Forton Hall kitchen door, wondering if Felicity was going to make him go through the humiliation of knocking at the servants' entrance before she let him in. Wading through the mud and drizzle in his new boots, fresh from Hoby's in London, had done nothing to improve his fraying temper.

Neither did the presence of that bastard Bancroft. The brute deserved a good flogging, and Deerhurst hoped to be present when it was delivered. Finally the door opened, letting the scent of baked chicken and sweet potato pie escape out to the cluttered yard.

"Welcome, my lord," Felicity said warmly, stepping aside to allow him entry.

"That pie smells delightful." The earl smiled, taking her hand and bringing it to his lips.

"It *is* delightful." Bancroft sat at the tiny kitchen table, half a wedge of pie stuffed into his arrogant mouth.

"Please, have some."

Felicity motioned him toward the table, and so he took the only seat remaining. Apparently they were all to dine in the kitchen. "Good evening, May," he said, nodding at her.

"Do you know how many ways there are to kill a man?" she asked, kneeling in her chair and leaning her elbows on the table.

James frowned. Little girls were so . . . messy. He liked them better after they'd grown. Felicity slid a plate of pie in front of him, and he smiled his thanks. Some of them, he liked *much* better.

"Well, do you know how many?" May insisted.

He waited a moment to give Felicity the opportunity to chastise her sister for her ill manners. When she didn't, he made a show of tapping at his chin as though seriously considering her question. "Hm, well, I would say two."

"Two?" she scoffed.

"Well, yes. Stopping the heart, or stopping the brain."

Felicity sat opposite him. "Can't we please discuss the weather or something a little more pleasant, sweetling?"

James smiled. "Of course. The creek seems—"

"There are seventy-three ways to kill a man."

Annoyed at the continuing interruptions, the earl took a moment to inspect his fork. "I'm sure there can't be seventy-three," he said gently. "Now— little girls are meant to be seen, and not heard. Your sister and I were conversing about—"

"There are too seventy-three! Rafe knows them all!"

The earl turned to glare at Bancroft. "I should have known you would be behind this nonsense."

The rascal pushed his plate away. "Nonsense?"

"It's complete balderdash, and an utterly inappropriate topic for ladies to be subjected to."

"I'll be happy to demonstrate a few of the methods outside for you, then."

"Rafe!"

"I know number twenty-eight!" May piped in.

"May! That's enough!"

"Come on, May," Bancroft said, rising. "Let's go see to Aristotle." With a last glance at Deerhurst, he left the room, the little girl skipping along behind him.

Finally. James looked across at Felicity. "Alone at last."

She smiled again. "I apologize for May's high spirits. There's been an unusual amount of activity here today, and she's been cooped up inside."

He patted her hand. "No need to apologize. I

know how difficult it's been for you. I'm sure if she had a governess she would be much better behaved.''

Felicity took a breath and nodded. ''We do what we can.''

''You know I would be happy to hire a governess for her. And a housekeeper for you, my dear. You shouldn't have to cook for yourself.''

''Thank you, James, but—''

''Whoa, Aristotle! No galloping in the house.''

The earl lifted an eyebrow as May's laughter echoed into the kitchen. ''There is a horse in here?''

She blushed. ''Well, yes. Just for tonight.''

With difficulty he refrained from frowning, instead leaning forward and grasping both of her hands in his. ''Felicity, please. This is too much. You must listen to reason.''

''James—''

''This is no way for you to live. I insist that you and May come and stay with me at Deerhurst. I ask you to come as my wife, but even if you again refuse me, you are still welcome as my guest. Both of you are.''

She pulled her hands free. He wanted to grab her arms, to convince her that he adored her, but he'd begun to realize that patience had a better effect than bold proclamations. He was beginning to run out of patience, though, and having this Bancroft fellow around to distract her from her situation could only make matters more difficult.

''James, I know you want to help, and I thank you for your continuing kindness, and your compassion. But you know that I will not marry you to secure your assistance with Forton Hall.''

''Then marry me because I love you.''

For a long moment she remained silent. ''My

lord, I thank you again for your kind regard. But my duty keeps me here. My brother and my sister need me here, and Forton Hall needs me here. It is my home.''

Hot anger began curling up his spine. ''So you've said before. And I respect that, of course. Eventually, though, Nigel will marry and May will grow up, and then you will have no place or status here at Forton. Wouldn't you rather have a place to live near to your ancestral home and to your brother?''

''That's a cruel thing to say, James.''

''I don't mean to be cruel; I only mean to be honest. And you need to be honest with yourself.''

She nodded, her eyes downcast, and his heart leaped. Finally she'd seen the sense in what he said. And once she became his wife, the first of his troubles would be over.

''Lis, look what I found.''

Bancroft stood in the doorway, and James flushed, wondering how long the bastard had been there, eavesdropping. ''I beg your pardon,'' he snapped. ''Miss Harrington and I are having a private conversation.''

The blond, scarred interloper ignored him, instead holding up a simple silver necklace in his fingers and keeping his attention on Felicity. ''May said it was yours.''

Felicity stood and hurried over to collect the trinket. ''Oh, thank you, Rafe! Where in the world was it? I've been looking everywhere.''

''I was taking Aristotle for a short walk, and he knocked over a chair—which was already broken, by the way—and it fell from behind the seat cushion.''

She actually put her hand on the buffoon's arm

and smiled. "Thank you again. I thought I'd never find it."

He grinned back at her. "My pleasure."

Whoever this arrogant ass was, she knew him well enough to call him by his given name. Unable to stand watching the idiotic tripe any longer, James surged to his feet. "I'd best be going, Felicity."

She turned to look at him. "But James, you haven't even finished your pie."

"I only stopped by to make certain you were well." He strode to the door and stopped. "Good evening."

Belatedly she joined him and pulled open the door. "Good evening, James."

Taking a last opportunity, he leaned forward and kissed her on the lips. "I do hope you will consider my offer." James took a moment to glance at Bancroft, and for a bare moment he paused, startled. The oaf hadn't moved, but his expression seemed almost . . . dangerous.

"I . . . I shall," Felicity answered.

The earl blinked, returning his attention to his prize. "I'll see you at the Wadsworths' tomorrow night."

"Yes. Of course."

Deerhurst stepped out into the dark, muddy yard to collect his carriage. At least he'd made some progress. Damn Bancroft for barging in just when he finally had her listening to reason.

It was critically important that he wed Felicity Harrington. At least he was fortunate enough to find her irresistibly attractive; marriage would have been a much less appealing solution if she'd been a fat old trout. James climbed into his phaeton and sat for a moment, looking at the pitiful ruin of Forton Hall and sneering in disgust. The Harringtons couldn't even manage their own estate. He could only imagine what they would do with Deerhurst.

The earl shuddered as he sent the carriage toward home. His father had been an idiot and a fool. However bad his monetary position, a noble did not sell his land. And certainly not to an untitled simpleton with absolutely no concept of responsibility or honor.

Thank God they'd agreed to keep the sale a secret. If they hadn't, the next five generations of Deerhursts would have been laughed out of the House of Lords. James twisted the leather traces in his hands so tightly they cut into his flesh despite his heavy gloves.

In the five years since the death of the Harringtons' parents and the four since his own father's demise, Deerhurst had flourished, while Forton Hall had slid into rot and ruin. Informing the Harrington offspring that they had an estate worth over a hundred thousand pounds at their disposal would be titular suicide. As long as Felicity lived at Forton, she would never let such a sum go—not when the sale of Deerhurst would save her ancestral rat heap.

It would have been much simpler if Miss Harrington had let him lend her money. Then he could have claimed Deerhurst as repayment whenever he liked. But she was either too stubborn or too clever for that, and Nigel had already left for London before he realized precisely how poor the Harringtons had become.

Marrying Felicity and having her convince brainless Nigel to hand over Deerhurst, her new home, was by far the wisest option. If everything went as he planned, he would be wed to her before Nigel returned from London. From that point, reclaiming the Deerhurst estate would be easy.

One thing had become quite clear this evening, though: Rafael Bancroft was going to have to go.

"May tells us you've spent time in Africa," Mrs. Wadsworth said to Rafe. "Is it as dirty and primitive as they say?"

Felicity glanced at her houseguest across the Wadsworths' dining table and then returned to her venison stew. She'd hoped to avoid discussions of Rafe's dubious past, but that obviously wasn't going to happen.

"It was dirty," Rafe agreed amiably. "At the time I left it hadn't rained for eighty-three days in a row."

On his other side Mrs. Denley touched his sleeve. "But what about the natives? I heard some of the tribes are cannibals."

"Oh, my heavens!" Mrs. Wadsworth exclaimed, flushing.

"Don't be silly, my dear," Mr. Wadsworth broke in. "The cannibals live in northwest Africa, in the jungles. I'm sure our guest was never in any real danger."

"I did see a few shrunken heads on necklaces, but they were all worn by Englishmen." Rafe smiled and took a drink of Madeira. "The Zulus are a fierce and proud tribe, and they seem none too happy to have us about, but I was more worried about getting a spear through the chest than about one of the lads eating me."

The dozen guests at the dinner laughed and toasted that, though Felicity didn't know what was so amusing. They all seemed completely taken with Rafe Bancroft. Next they'd have him doing a Zulu rain dance or something. Deerhurst seemed to be the only other guest more interested in his dinner than in Rafe's tales.

May stood up from the children's table at the far end of the room. "Tell them about the lion."

Rafe's expression turned sheepish. "They don't want to hear about that, my dear."

"Lucinda's Lady foaled yesterday," Lord Deerhurst said into the air. "A colt. I daresay in a few years he'll be a match for his sire at the Chester races."

Mr. Denley nodded and chuckled. "I daresay." He toasted the earl, Mr. William Pender following suit.

"Oh, tell us about the lion," Elizabeth Denley exclaimed, blushing.

"Yes, do," her mother and Mrs. Wadsworth echoed, followed by Betty and Lucy Caster.

Rafe glanced across the table and caught Felicity's gaze, his eyes dancing. "It really isn't all that exciting. The regiment had a herd of goats we'd bought from the local tribesmen, and they began vanishing by ones and twos during the night. We thought it must be goat thieves, and a few of us decided to stand watch and see if we could catch the culprits. I stood the third night. It had been quiet, so we figured perhaps they had seen us and been frightened away. Then, just past midnight I heard rustling in the bushes behind the boma, and the—"

"What in the world is a boma?" Lucy Caster interrupted, tittering.

"Beg pardon. A corral, of sorts, made up of thorn bushes."

"Continue, lad," Mr. Denley urged.

"The goats were becoming agitated, as well. I crept around as close as I could to the blackguard and then jumped up, yelling 'Halt, you thief!' "

"Oh, my," Betty gasped, her hand at her bosom, "and it was a lion?"

Felicity realized she'd been sitting there with her fork halfway between her plate and her mouth. Hurriedly she lowered the utensil and took a swallow of Madeira.

"A very large and very surprised lion," Rafe continued. "It stood up only six feet in front of me and roared. And then it sprang at me." With a hooded, amused glance at Felicity, as though he knew she was as caught up in the tale as the rest of them, he took a bite of stew.

"For God's sake, man," Felix Caster blurted, "what happened?"

Rafe shrugged. "I had to shoot it. Damned shame, though. It was a magnificent beast."

"So you might have ended in some animal's belly after all," Lord Deerhurst said, looking directly at Rafe. "What luck you have."

Something in his eyes and the way he said the words made Felicity uncomfortable, and she took another swallow of wine and forced a laugh. "My goodness, Mr. Bancroft. What a fearsome tale you tell."

Squire Talford, beside her, chuckled as well. "Marvelous, indeed. I don't suppose you kept a souvenir of the encounter?"

An ally, finally. She'd nearly forgotten that he knew of her misgivings about the soundness of Rafe's mind. And being a gentleman, he'd asked for proof in a way that wouldn't embarrass Rafe when he couldn't produce any.

Rafe sat back and reached into his pocket. "It's a bit difficult to tote a lion carcass around the world," he said, and lifted his hand. "But I did keep this." He lowered his fingers to reveal a single, ivory-colored claw as long as his thumb. "More than he would have kept of me, I imagine," Rafe continued, handing it to Mrs. Wadsworth.

Felicity sneaked a look at the squire and saw him eyeing the claw with an intrigued expression as it passed around the table. Rafe could have bought it somewhere, she supposed, but even so, Rafe Bancroft was becoming even more confusing. He'd charmed the local gentry with apparent ease, and whenever he caught her eyes, her heart sped and fireworks exploded into the sky. And she was beginning to find a great deal of satisfaction in the knowledge that at the end of the evening, the ladies fawning over him would have to say good night, and she wouldn't. ·

"Your brother's been gone well over a month, Felicity," Squire Talford noted from the comfort of her couch five days later. "Are you certain he knows what's going on in his absence?"

"Yes, I wrote him to return immediately. I can't imagine why he hasn't arrived yet." Felicity continued patching the hole in what Rafe had dubbed her muck-about dress. It would only get torn again, but she needed it to last as long as possible.

The squire sipped at his tea. Gentleman that he was, he hadn't asked for port, though she knew that to be his favorite afternoon drink. The closest thing to port at Forton Hall was a half-empty bottle of Madeira in the kitchen she'd been using to cook with, and she suspected that Rafe had been sipping from that when she wasn't looking.

"And where is your Mr. Bancroft this afternoon? He made quite an impression at the Wadsworths' dinner. I have to admit that after what you told me, and from Deerhurst's description the other day, I expected him to be frothing at the mouth, hackles raised and teeth bared."

She chuckled. "He's pulling part of the upper

story out of the way so we can do one more search for valuables.''

"He seems to have turned out to be quite helpful,'' the squire noted.

"I told you he was.'' Felicity looked up, then set aside her sewing when he continued to gaze at her. "Are you implying something, Charles?''

The squire took another sip of his tea. "No. Just that you failed to mention—how did Betty Caster put it—his 'strikingly handsome and gentlemanly appearance'.''

She felt the heat rise in her cheeks. "Yes, he is attractive, I suppose, but what does that have to do with anything?''

"Come now, Felicity. If he'd been eighty and toothless, no one would care. As it is . . . well, I know he isn't staying in the stable any longer. Ronald told Mrs. Denwortle as much, and now the entire county knows. You should be more careful with your reputation, my dear.''

She scowled, more disgusted than angry. "I know, but I wouldn't have a horse staying in that wreck of a stable. I couldn't very well have Rafe remain there while it collapsed around his ears. It was a much-considered decision, believe me.''

She could read the curiosity in the squire's gaze, but in truth she had no answer for it. Rafe had been at Forton Hall for a fortnight, and it seemed he'd been there forever. He fit into their routine effortlessly, and he'd done so much for them that she'd almost begun to hope Nigel wouldn't appear for another few weeks. And not just so that Rafe could haul away the remains of the west wing and clean the debris out of the garden. Since he'd come to Forton Hall, she hadn't been lonely.

Rafe now had a brigade—as he and May called them—of ten local farmers, stableboys, and assistant shopkeepers volunteering their services. They came when they could, and they brought their wives and daughters and sisters with them. She couldn't remember ever having so much company—or having so much attention paid to her, in the person of Rafe Bancroft.

But charm alone didn't explain why her pulse raced every time he walked into the room. May clearly adored him, but Felicity wasn't quite ready to define the affection she herself had begun to feel for him, soft-headed and lost or not.

Squire Talford cleared his throat, and she jumped. "Beg pardon?"

He smiled and shook his head. "Nothing."

"Felicity!" May called, running up the hallway, "I fetched him for you!" Panting, she burst through the open doorway.

"Thank you, May," Felicity answered, amused. "Where is he?"

"Right here," Rafe's deep voice said. He stepped around May into the morning room, stripping off his work gloves as he entered.

"I beat you," May said gleefully, following and plunking herself down onto the couch.

"Well, I'm old," he returned with a grin, stopping before the squire. "Squire Talford." He sketched an elegant bow. "I wish we'd had more time to converse last week."

Charles stood and shook Rafe's outstretched hand. "So do I. You tell quite a tale."

Rafe perched in the deep windowsill. "And it was mostly true." He grinned. "Have you heard the one about the tea kettle and my skull?"

Charles laughed. "Yes, I have. Felicity and May can be quite a formidable pair. Be glad you survived."

Rafe glanced at Felicity. "I am grateful every day."

That was how it had gone for the past week. He would say something that sounded perfectly innocent, and then he would look at her. She'd immediately take the words as a compliment and blush. Then she would get mad at herself for blushing, and madder at him for aggravating her so. At least the work kept her distracted, and she was beginning to feel grateful that there remained an unending supply of it.

"How are you progressing today?" she asked.

"Well, you've smiled at me twice—so far, quite well, I'd say."

Felicity blushed again. She was becoming a regular rouge pot. "Rafe," she grumbled, and turned her attention to the squire. "He's a terrible flirt."

"So I see."

"I was asking about the west wing, Mr. Bancroft."

"Oh. Why didn't you say so?" With a completely unrepentant smile, Rafe draped his gloves over one knee. "The west wing is going more slowly than I'd like, but if you have anything still intact under all that rubble, I certainly don't want to crush it now."

"Was that your horse I saw grazing behind the stable?" Charles asked unexpectedly.

"Yes, that's Aristotle," May answered before Rafe could. "He's a right goer."

"He is magnificent," the squire agreed. "What did you pay for him?"

"Fifty quid, about six years ago."

"That's a hefty sum."

Rafe glanced at Felicity again, his expression a little uncomfortable. Perhaps he didn't like being reminded of his absurd dreams of grandeur any more than Felicity did. He shrugged. "It was worth it."

"Aristotle was just a colt, and he bit Lord Montrose," May said conversationally, sitting forward to pour herself a cup of tea and then adding five lumps of sugar to the brew. "Poor old Monty."

"May, that's quite enough of that," Felicity chastised sternly, though she was more annoyed at the squire for bringing reality into the conversation. They'd been doing quite well without it. She had no idea Rafe counted her smiles—she'd only been counting their kisses.

"What did I do now?"

It was getting to the point where she didn't know any longer, but she was certain it couldn't be proper. "Don't waste sugar," she improvised.

"I'm not wasting it; I'm drinking it," May countered.

"Beg pardon. Miss Harrington?"

Dennis Greetham stood in the doorway. "Good afternoon," she greeted him, surprised. "Please join us for tea."

"My thanks, miss, but I've got my team hitched to a pile of rafters. Just wanted to let you know Jarrod's brought the post." He stepped forward and handed Felicity a few letters.

"Thank you, Mr. Greetham." Felicity smiled, and the farmer nodded and backed out of the room. When he'd gone, she looked down at her letters. One of them immediately caught her attention. "Nigel—finally!"

"Does it say when he's coming?" May asked, jumping up and coming to stand at her knee.

"I don't know. Let's see." As she broke the seal and unfolded the paper Rafe was silent, and she wondered what he might be thinking. This could be the end of his charade, unless she—they—he—

could come up with another reason for him to stay.

She smoothed the parchment on her lap. " 'Dear Felicity,' " she read aloud, " 'I received your letter about Bancroft arriving at Forton. Please behave yourself, Lis—his family could ruin me in London.' " Felicity stopped, looking up at Rafe, and something cold and dreadful tightened in her chest.

"Lis?"

"Um, just a moment, May." She blinked hard, and continued reading. Nigel generally took a while to get to the point—but it couldn't possibly be what she'd begun to suspect. " 'Whiting's invited me to go to Madrid after the Season. I think some of his cronies are going on to Paris, and I'm sure they'll let me tag along. Sterling bunch, they are.' "

"Good God," Rafe said almost soundlessly.

Felicity pretended not to hear. " 'I'm sorry' " she continued, her voice beginning to shake, " 'that I couldn't win the blunt to save Forton, but Whiting says it was for the best. My spirit was never meant to be contained in Cheshire. And this is my chance to make my fortune. I know you'll manage, Lis— you always do. Just try not to be so bossy and managing. I'll send May a doll from Spain. Your brother, N. Harrington.' "

He'd done it.

He'd seen his chance and run off, without even bothering to tell her to her face. Feeling as though he had just pulled the floor out from under her feet, Felicity sat staring at the letter, unable to look away. She'd lost Forton Hall, just when she'd begun to think they could save it. Tears ran down her face, but she didn't notice them until they splashed onto the letter, staining and blurring her brother's writing.

"Felicity," Rafe said softly, "I—"

She shot to her feet. "If you'll excuse us, May

and I need to . . . to . . ." Grabbing May by the
hand, she fled from the room. Once they were
safely down the hallway she stopped again. "Damnation," she muttered, wiping at her eyes.

"Nigel really did gamble Forton Hall away to
Rafe?" May asked, her own expression concerned.

"Yes—he did."

"Well, it's all right, Lis, really. I like Rafe.
Don't cry." The little girl squeezed her hand.

Felicity began to cry again, harder. "Oh, May,
you don't understand." She knelt so she could look
her sister in the eye. "This is Rafe's home now.
Not ours. We have to leave."

"But where would we go?" May whispered, real
fear touching her voice.

"I don't know, May." Felicity took a shaky
breath as a tear rolled down her sister's cheek. This
would never do. "Don't worry, though. I have
nearly forty pounds put aside, and I—"

"I don't want to go," May wailed, flinging her
arms around Felicity's neck.

"Shh, May," Felicity said soothingly, glancing
behind her. She absolutely did not want Rafe to
come out and say something stupidly noble. They
were on their own—again—and they would simply
have to make do. "Come help me find the old valises in the attic."

"We have to go *now*?"

"The sooner, the better." Squire Talford would
put them up, of course, and so would Lord Deerhurst, but then she would have to watch Rafe sell
off Forton Hall to the highest bidder. And she
would have to wait and hope he would change his
mind, unable to leave until she knew for certain. It
would be time wasted for no good purpose, especially when she had May depending on her to support them both.

"I know," she exclaimed, wiping at her face and trying to inject some enthusiasm into her voice when she only wanted to lie down and cry, "I can look for work as a governess. I've been your governess for years, haven't I? And then there'll be other children for you to play with."

"I think we should ask Rafe if we can stay," May countered, her lower lip quivering.

For a moment, Felicity wished she were eight years old and could solve the disaster so easily. "We can't, May. He's already allowed us to live here for a fortnight, and he wants to sell Forton. We would have to leave anyway."

"I think you should talk to him," May insisted. "He's very nice."

"I know he's very nice," Felicity agreed. And apparently not at all insane. And he had kissed her, and called her beautiful. "But we can't stay."

"What an ass!" Rafe finally exploded.

"I assume you're referring to Nigel?" the squire asked.

Rafe started. He'd forgotten Talford's presence. "He might have come himself to tell them. Especially after Lis wrote and asked him to return." It wasn't right. Nigel was supposed to come and take his sisters away, and Rafe would know that they would be cared for and have a damned roof over their heads. Nigel Harrington hadn't just abandoned a rundown piece of land; with his letter, he'd abandoned his family. "That damned seedy rip!"

The squire stood. "Please give my excuses to Felicity. She won't want my wise, crusty advice just yet. I'll be at Talford, should they need me."

Rafe looked at him. The morning had begun so well, with them making real progress in hauling away the old west wing. It took a bit of adjustment to realize he'd just become the villain of the piece. "So you abandon them, as well?"

"I'd ask them to stay with me," Talford said, pausing on his way to the door, "but I've asked before. Felicity never would. She's not one to sit about and bemoan her fate."

"Yes, I've noticed that about her."

When the squire had gone, Rafe retrieved Harrington's letter from the floor where Felicity had dropped it. He reread the missive, looking for anything that indicated Nigel intended to return to Forton and collect his sisters. Finally he tossed the thing aside.

"Bastard," he muttered.

Well, he had his undisputed ownership of Forton Hall now, for whatever that was worth. A little more cleaning up, and he might even be able to sell it for enough to give him three or four years of freedom before he had to go crawling back to His Grace and beg for employment. He supposed he should be happy.

All he could think of, though, was that Felicity and May had just lost their past and their future, all in one blow. It wasn't his fault—it really wasn't; counting cards wasn't cheating, precisely.

"Damnation," he swore, and slammed his fist against the window frame. His window frame.

He looked at it for a moment, at the worn couch and the frayed carpet, at the miscellaneous knick-knacks on every available surface. There were cattle in the field, a scattering of sheep, downed fences, no crop—and he didn't know what to do with any of it before he sold it off. Slowly Rafe smiled.

His father had always called him an idiot, while his mother and Quin claimed that he'd simply never had to apply himself. He'd pretended not to hear either one, for they both hurt, and they both meant essentially the same thing: he was either a fool for not knowing how to act, or a fool for not acting. Well, it was time to act.

Rafe went to find Felicity. When he arrived outside her open bedchamber door, he stopped. A valise half filled with clothes lay in the middle of the bed, while Felicity sat at her dressing table engrossed in writing a letter. Rafe scowled. He hadn't expected her to ask to stay, but the abrupt, angry panic that shot through him at the idea that she might actually leave surprised and dismayed him.

"Lis?" he said, rapping at the open door.

She looked up with a start. "I . . . really . . . I'm a bit busy at the moment," she said, and returned to the letter.

"Why would you think I would throw you out?" he asked.

"I don't think you would," she said, not lifting her head. "But you are the . . . the owner of this estate now, and May and I have no right to be here."

Damned remarkable. Tears five minutes ago, and now she was planning her withdrawal and no doubt her next campaign. Wellington could have used her assistance. "Do you think Nigel will remember to send May a doll?"

Felicity looked up again, eyeing him in the reflection of her dressing mirror. "Yes." She stopped, then sighed. "He'll send it here, of course, and it probably won't even occur to him that she won't be here to receive it."

Though she hadn't invited him in, neither had she told him to go away, so he stepped into the room. Little of her personality showed in her bedchamber—but with the destruction of her former room, she likely had few personal things left. The most telling personal item remaining was Forton Hall, itself. Rafe stopped, leaning against the bedpost, as she turned in her chair to face him.

"I wouldn't have taken the wager if I'd known Harrington had family he'd abandoned at Forton," he said quietly.

She shrugged. "If you hadn't, someone else would have." Felicity hesitated again. "And they might not have reacted so well to being cracked over the head. I suppose I should thank you for your tolerance."

Rafe nodded. "I probably do have the hardest head of anyone at that gaming table. How is May?" It wasn't the question he needed, or wanted, to ask, but he'd faced French Old Guard Grenadiers with less brave determination in their eyes, and it was rather off-putting.

"Confused, but she'll be all right. Rafe, we are not your concern. Nigel was never attached to Forton. I simply . . . overestimated his sense of duty and responsibility. I should not have let him go to London."

He gave a half smile. "May informed me that you didn't exactly 'let' him leave. I believe you chased him halfway to Pelford."

She began crying again. "If he hadn't taken the last horse and the phaeton, I might have caught him." She squared her shoulders and wiped at her face. "Even so, that was nearly two months ago. Weeping about what I should have done certainly won't help me today. I am not completely without skills, and my mother saw to it that I received an education. I daresay we shall make do."

Rafe swallowed, his heart pounding. This would be the sticky part, and he tried to pretend that her answer really wasn't that important to him. "Oh,

I'm certain *you* will be fine. It's me that I'm worried about.''

"You?" she said in disbelief.

"Well, yes. As my father has pointed out innumerable times, I have little skill at anything besides drinking, whoring, shooting, and blowing things up. I . . . have no idea how to manage an estate."

She looked at him for a long moment. "You don't need to manage an estate. You only need to sell it, I believe."

"That's true," he agreed, straightening. "But I can't very well sell it like this and expect to get much for it." She only continued to gaze at him coolly. "So, I thought perhaps you might help me out."

"Help you out?" she repeated, her expression growing grimmer by the moment. "I beg your pardon, but helping you out is not—"

"I'd like to hire you," he interrupted.

"You . . . what?"

Taking advantage of her surprise, he continued. "If you see to the daily accounts and what-all, then I can concentrate on making Forton presentable and on finding a buyer."

"I don't want your charity. I'm used to being on my own."

"I know. But this is not charity—I have no idea how to do this. When I came up here, I thought it would be a matter of hiring a solicitor, hanging about for a few days, and then returning to London until my man sent me the proceeds from the sale. I had no idea it was going to be this involved."

"I have several distant relations scattered about England," she said by way of answer. "I am writing them regarding employment as a governess."

He wondered which of them she was trying to convince that she had alternatives to his little plan.

He didn't like *her* little plan. "Splendid," he said instead. "And while you wait for a response, you would be earning . . . five quid a month for aiding me." He had no idea of the correct figure for an estate manager, but five quid seemed a reasonable amount.

"Seven quid," she returned. "And May and I keep our current rooms."

Suddenly she was a parliamentarian. "Agreed."

"And we may leave whenever we wish."

He stifled a grin. "Agreed again."

Felicity stood and thrust out her hand. "All right. I accept."

Before she could change her mind or raise her salary to a figure he could even less afford, Rafe gripped her hand in his and shook it firmly— though he really wanted to kiss her knuckles, her palms, her elbows, her throat . . . When she looked up at his face, he realized he'd been holding her hand for quite a long moment. Reluctantly he released it. "Thank you."

Chapter 7

"So we don't have to leave Forton," May stated, circling the kitchen table while Felicity sliced potatoes.

"Yes, we do have to leave Forton," she corrected, reaching for the salt and wondering why in the world she felt so exuberant this evening. "Just not right away."

"Whom does our house belong to, then?"

"It belongs to Rafe."

May sat and thunked her head down on the table. "I'm confused."

"So am I," Rafe said, as he stomped his boots off and stepped through the kitchen door. "What do you wish to tell the neighbors?"

Everything had upended itself so fast, she hadn't even considered that. "I . . . think that should be up to you. You are the master of Forton Hall."

He looked at her for a moment. "I suppose I am. How about if we say business affairs called your brother away to the Continent for an indefinite period, and given our long acquaintance, he accepted my offer to purchase Forton Hall as he wouldn't be able to see to it properly any longer."

"I thought Nigel lost it at the gaming table." May looked up at her idol.

"Well, let's not spread that about, sweetling."

Rafe made his way around to Felicity's side of the table.

She flushed, embarrassed. "Please don't lie on our behalf. Our neighbors are well aware of Nigel's propensity for doing absurdly stupid things." She knew she sounded bitter, and she cleared her throat and concentrated on slicing potatoes.

Rafe leaned closer, his breath warm against her hair. "Which is no reason for you to feel ashamed," he said quietly.

"I am *not* ashamed," she snapped.

"I am," May offered.

Felicity glared at her sister. "You are not."

"Lis," Rafe continued, his mouth brushing her cheek as he reached past her for a potato, "you've been here your entire life. They'll know me for an eye blink. *You* tell them what *you* wish."

For a moment she wondered what he wanted with a potato, but he picked it up and made a show of examining it for any imperfections. Felicity doubted he'd know a potato eye from a foot, but after a moment he made a noncommital sound of vague approval and set it down again. As he retreated, his fingers slid along her wrist and sleeve. A delighted shiver ran up her spine, taking her anger with it. She shrugged to hide her sudden trembling. "Your story is as good as any, I suppose. And thank you."

"Are you going to live at Forton?" May asked, apparently oblivious to the flirtation going on across the table.

"No. I'm going to sell it."

"Why?"

"So I can see the world."

"Now just a moment," May countered. "You have seen the world. You told me so."

Rafe took the seat beside her. "I've only seen a little bit of it. I want to see all of it."

"May, quit pestering," Felicity ordered. She scooped up the potatoes and dumped them into a pot. "If Rafe wants to go see the world, then he should be able to go see the world."

He looked up at her. "You make it sound daft."

She almost laughed at his comically offended expression. "Far be it from me to judge."

"Hm."

"Do you intend to sell Forton immediately?" Her voice caught as she asked the question, and she knew he heard it. Damnation, she hated being so weepy, no matter how much it hurt to think of losing her home. It belonged to him now—and it didn't matter how well she knew its every inch, or how well she loved the land, or how lovely the garden used to be. None of this was Rafe's fault; someone would have won Forton away from Nigel, because he hadn't wanted to keep it. But that couldn't keep her from wishing Rafe Bancroft wasn't quite so interested in seeing China.

He stretched. "Since I'm right in the middle of things, I think taking another few weeks to tidy the place up would be worth the time and trouble."

Felicity nodded, unable to disguise her sudden relief. She had a few more weeks, anyway.

Rafe stood back and surveyed the absence of the west wing. It was easy to see that something had been there, of course—the foundation still stood, and a few of the sturdiest upright supports still rose into the air like pillars of a forgotten Greek temple. "Hm, Greece," he mused aloud. "Haven't been there, either."

"Full of old buildings in worse shape than this

one, from what I hear.'' Dennis Greetham strolled up beside him.

"Somehow it loses its allure, when you put it that way,'' Rafe said dryly. "What do you think?''

"I think you bloody well might have told us you owned Forton Hall before Ronald went and told everyone and the man in the moon,'' the farmer returned.

"I meant about the west wing, actually, but I suppose you're right. In all fairness, though, I was trying to protect the Harrington ladies. I'm beginning to suspect that Felicity thought I was some sort of escaped lunatic. She didn't want me going about spreading groundless rumors or growling and foaming at the neighbors.''

Greetham folded his arms across his chest. "I think it's a snipe hunt, either way.''

Rafe grinned. "I will assume that you're referring to the building now, and not my sanity.''

"Oh. Aye.''

The farmer was right, again. Either tearing down the rest of the wing or putting up a new one would be a long-term, thankless, and backbreaking project. And he was steadily running out of items and skills to trade for any assistance.

Even so, the part of him that delighted in the intricacies of demolition and construction was definitely stirring. The engineering talent his fellow army officers had raved about had been completely at odds with both his social status and with the dull-minded career his father would eventually push on him, but he had loved it anyway.

No matter what visions and possibilities he saw in the sturdy old foundation, though, he certainly didn't have the blunt to do anything about them. Nor did he have the time to invest in the project. If he couldn't sell Forton by autumn, the weather would stick him with it at least through March. By then, he'd be even more a pauper than Felicity.

"So, Bancroft. What's it to be?"

Rafe sighed. "Let's start clearing the dead growth out of the garden."

"You sure you want to bother with that?"

Yes, he was, because Felicity had twice mentioned how much she used to enjoy reading out in the garden in the mornings. And whether it was out of guilt or because he delighted in seeing her smile, he wanted to please her. "We may as well."

By the time he and three volunteers had cleared out just the tiny north corner of the garden where it sloped down to the lane, Rafe was tired, covered with scratches, and very annoyed. It had been two damned weeks since he'd last seen his solicitor, and now that the news of his ownership was out, he needed to ride into Pelford for another visit with John Gibbs.

"Good afternoon, Miss Harrington."

Rafe turned as the chorus of greetings trailed, along with Felicity, toward him. As had happened every time he'd set eyes on her over the past fortnight, he was seized by the nearly irresistible desire to pull her into his arms and cover her skin with kisses. He felt like a starving man, and she his Christmas feast.

She wore gardening gloves, he noted with delight. "Lis, what do you think of our progress?"

Felicity stopped beside him, the top of her head coming up to his chin. Wisps of her black hair strayed from her prim bun to caress her cheek and her slender neck. Good God, he wanted to make love to her.

"I think you should have seen Forton Hall ten years ago. You would never even consider selling it."

"If I wanted to manage an estate, I have a plentitude to choose from," he returned, taking her smaller hands in his under the pretext of examining her gloves. "His Grace or my brother would have been delighted to hand the bookkeeping of any number of grand holdings over to me. And I'd have turned to stone within a month."

She looked up at him, her dark eyes both curious and serious. "Are you bored here?" she asked.

He smiled. "No. But then, you're here."

Felicity blushed, soft rose stealing up her cheeks. "I daresay I am the least of Forton's attractions."

She was flirting; he could see it in her upturned lips and the tilt of her head. Rafe stepped closer. "If we were alone, I would be happy to show you just how much I disagree with you."

Felicity held his gaze boldly, her color deepening. "Promises, promises," she breathed, then with a grin turned on her heel and fled to help Ronald Banthe clear out a flower bed.

Rafe looked after her. Something very interesting was going on, and he was enjoying it immensely. He began work on her blasted garden with renewed enthusiasm.

"Bancroft! A word with you!"

The Earl of Deerhurst charged up the drive and brought his mount to a weed-flinging halt a few feet short of Rafe.

"Deerhurst. Good morning." He pulled off his dirt-covered gloves. "You've met Miss Harrington, haven't you?"

"Of course I have, you . . ." He trailed off as Felicity strolled up beside the horse. "Felicity, my apologies," he gushed, his annoyed expression vanishing in a heartbeat. "I didn't see you there."

"No need to apologize, my lord. What brings you to Forton in such a hurry?"

"Just a small matter I need to discuss with Bancroft."

"Discuss away," Rafe urged, curious to see whether the earl's foul manners would reappear.

They didn't, which made Rafe dislike him even more, the prissy lout. His pleasantness was an act, put on for Felicity's benefit. He hoped she wasn't naive enough to fall for it.

"It is a matter of some urgency, which I would prefer to discuss with you in private," Deerhurst said mildly.

Rafe stifled a scowl. "I need to find a shovel. Come along."

Deerhurst left his mount standing in the yard, which Rafe decided he had done solely to give himself another excuse to see Miss Harrington before he left. So, it only seemed fair that he take the muddiest route through the yard to the stable. The earl looked like a cat trying to keep its paws out of water as he minced across the yard in his bright new Hobys.

"Bancroft, I heard a very disturbing rumor this morning, that . . . you . . . have purchased Forton Hall." Now that Felicity was out of sight, his annoyed expression—the same one he'd worn the other night at the door barricade—returned.

Rafe nodded, keeping his expression cool and aloof. "My family buys and sells property all the time. What about it do you find so disturbing?"

"The Harringtons are my dearest friends and neighbors," the earl snapped. "I can't like the idea of hordes of solicitors crawling all over their property looking for a profit for you."

"Don't trouble yourself, then. It was a private transaction between Nigel and myself."

Deerhurst scowled again. "Whatever the circumstance, the sale of the Harringtons' home disturbs me.''

''But having it collapse around them doesn't?''

''Don't think I didn't offer my services!'' he shouted, his face growing red. ''They were refused.''

Rafe couldn't resist another dig. ''Well, now your services are unnecessary.''

The earl stopped, but Rafe could feel the pleasant blue eyes boring into the back of his skull. He continued into the stable, hoping Deerhurst would give up on whatever it was he wanted and go home.

''What are your plans for the estate, then?''

''I haven't decided yet.''

''That isn't what I've heard.''

He eyed Deerhurst. ''Then why ask the question?''

Rafe tried to decide why he disliked the earl so vehemently. He'd grown up with Deerhurst's kind all around him in London, and they hadn't bothered him a whit. Some of them, like Robert Fields, he considered cronies. Here, though, there was one key difference—Deerhurst wanted Felicity. That made him a rival, and that made him an enemy. And the seriousness with which Rafe regarded that startled him.

''All right, Bancroft,'' the earl continued from the doorway, ''it's obvious you're not interested in polite conversation. How much do you want for the place?''

Rafe halted in mid-step, surprised. Swiftly wiping the expression from his face, he turned around. ''You want to purchase Forton Hall?''

''Why shouldn't I?''

''Why should you? It's a wreck.''

The earl swiped at a cobweb hanging across one of the empty stalls. ''It borders my land, and it has sentimental value to me—not that my reasons are any of your damned affair. I'll give you fifty thousand pounds for it.''

His mind racing, Rafe went back to rooting for a shovel. Fifty thousand quid would fund his travels for ten years, or more if he were frugal. It was also about twice what Forton was worth right now. That shouldn't matter—as Deerhurst had said, it really wasn't any of his affair—but it did matter. And if he sold right away, it would leave Felicity and May with nowhere to go, and him with no good reason to stay. He turned around again.

''No thank you. I'm not interested.''

''What? How can you not be interested in fifty thousand pounds?''

Rafe shrugged. ''I'm not. And my reasons are none of *your* damned affair.''

''You bastard! Half the county's been talking about how you want to travel to China and God knows where else. You don't want Forton Hall!''

Striding forward, Rafe jabbed a finger in the earl's chest. ''Neither do you. You want Felicity. And you're trying to buy her.''

Deerhurst shoved him backward. ''What if I am? How is that different from you keeping a place you don't want just so you can hang about her? I've seen how you look at her.''

Rafe shoved back, hard enough to send the earl staggering against the wall. ''Don't start something you won't be conscious for at the finish.'' Picking up the shovel, he nodded curtly. ''Good day, Deerhurst. I'm busy.''

He brushed past the earl and strode back out into the sunlight.

''Seventy thousand!'' Deerhurst shouted after him.

Sweet Lucifer, he was the worst kind of fool to

turn down that kind of money, just so he could moon after a black-haired chit. "I'll think about it!" he bellowed over his shoulder, not turning around.

Whatever Rafe and James had been discussing, neither of them seemed very happy about it, Felicity thought. Lord Deerhurst barely nodded at her before he galloped off toward his estate. And Rafe looked more as if he were strangling French foes than pulling weeds. When May emerged from the kitchen toting a pitcher of lemonade, he didn't even stop to take a drink.

"I think this is the best mix you've made yet, lass," Mr. Greetham complimented the dark-haired sprite.

"Thank you. I've been practicing." May glanced over at Rafe halfway down the gentle slope. "He looks angry."

Felicity nodded, though she didn't know how her sister could tell that just from looking at his backside, attractive as it happened to be. "I think he had an argument with Lord Deerhurst."

"Should I bring him some lemonade?"

Felicity filled the remaining glass. "I'll do it."

She had to clear her throat twice before he would even straighten and look up. That was unusual, because he generally paid more attention to her than she was comfortable with. Well . . . that wasn't quite true. She loved the way he seemed to hang on her every word. No one, and certainly no man, had ever done that before. Even the Earl of Deerhurst, polite as he was, seemed more interested in talking than in listening.

"My thanks," he said, and pulled off his gloves. Their fingers brushed as he took the glass, and the familiar tingle jangled down her spine.

She was becoming used to the sensation, and in fact sought it out by touching him. "Are you feeling well?" she asked, trying to be as diplomatic as she could and still discover what in blazes had happened.

"Nothing a pint of whiskey wouldn't cure."

He downed half the glass of lemonade, trickles running down his chin to mingle with the damp sheen of sweat on his throat. Felicity watched, mesmerized. Sweet and salty . . . what would it taste like if she licked it off? She shivered in the heat.

"James . . . can be a bit monotonous, I'll concede. But he means well."

"Is it your intention to marry Deerhurst?" he asked stiffly, as though getting the words out was difficult for him.

"What? Is that what he told you?"

"No. Not . . . precisely."

"Then what did the two of you discuss, pray tell?"

He shook his head. "It really doesn't—"

"Don't you dare tell me it doesn't concern me," she interrupted, lifting her chin. "Clearly it does, or you wouldn't have asked that ridiculous question."

His light green eyes caught hers. "Is it ridiculous?"

She held his gaze, a hundred inappropriate and highly improper responses coming to mind. Flushing, she stammered something incoherent and then turned on her heel and headed up around the vanished wing of the house.

"What?" he called after her.

"I said, 'Everything you say is ridiculous!' " She sped up her retreat, figuring he wouldn't bother following her.

"Lis?"

Damnation. He *had* followed her. She couldn't outrun him, nor did she want to make a spectacle of herself by trying, so she stopped and turned around. ''What?''

''Deerhurst made me an offer for Forton Hall.''

For a moment she couldn't breathe. ''He did?'' she asked almost soundlessly, her hands and feet turning to ice.

''He did.''

It had been bound to happen sooner or later. Forton Hall couldn't go unsold forever. She'd just hoped it would be much later—though the logical part of her kept asking why it made a difference whether Rafe or someone else owned it, and why in some ways it still felt like hers. ''Well, I'm happy for you.'' She turned to escape.

Rafe grabbed her arm and spun her back around. ''He offered me seventy thousand quid.''

Felicity looked at him. ''Seventy thousand pounds?''

He nodded. ''That was after I refused his offer of fifty.''

''Forton Hall isn't worth nearly that any longer!''

''I know.''

''Even so, it's a great deal of money, Rafe! Why didn't you agree, for heaven's sake?''

Rafe hesitated. ''I couldn't help wondering what he thought he was purchasing.''

Abruptly she realized what he was implying. ''James has been asking me to marry him since I turned eighteen. He knows my feelings. Don't be ridiculous.''

Rafe took a step closer. ''So I should accept his offer?''

''You shouldn't use wild speculation as a reason not to.'' In a sense, though, Rafe was right; with no time yet for a reply to any of her queries about work, she and May would be trapped and homeless unless the squire took them in—or unless James did.

"So I should accept his offer," he repeated.

"Rafe, Forton Hall is yours. You—"

"I told him I would think about it," he interrupted, his exasperated expression showing he was tired of her evasiveness.

"Oh. Well. Good, then."

"After all, I can say yes in a month as easily as I can tomorrow. You ... should have yourself fairly well straightened out by then, don't you think?"

He was giving her time. He was willing to sit about decaying old Forton Hall instead of beginning his exciting, dangerous travels, just so she would have time to hear whether she'd found employment. "I ... I don't know what to say," she whispered. "You don't owe me anything."

"I don't know about that." He smiled. "Besides, I'm having fun."

Felicity stepped closer. "Thank you."

"My pleasure."

She leaned toward him, boldly wrapping her fingers into the loose ties at the open neck of his shirt. Tugging herself up against him, she touched her lips to his. Rafe's hands slid around her waist, bringing them closer still. His lips tasted of lemonade and sweat, sweeter and saltier than she had imagined. Her whole body felt warm and tingly. His mouth parted a little, teasing at hers and making her feel as though she were about to melt.

She moaned, and slipped her hands up around his broad shoulders. She wanted to devour him, to feel his hard, slick body all over; to taste his salty chest; to—

"Lis?"

With a gasp Felicity pulled away, just as May pranced around the corner. "What is it, May?" she asked with as much calm as she could, knowing her face must be flushed.

"Mr. Greetham has to drive into Pelford for a new saw blade. Might I go with him and get a pastry?" May looked at the two of them a bit strangely, and for once Felicity wished her sister wasn't so bright and inquisitive.

"Of course, dear." Belatedly she realized Rafe still had one hand about her waist, and she brushed it away. She didn't dare look at him; she could feel his arousing heat just by standing beside him.

"Bring me back one," he said, his voice more controlled than hers, and flipped May a sovereign.

May grinned as she caught it. "Aye, aye, Captain." She saluted and marched back around the corner.

Felicity started after her. Before she'd taken more than a step or two, Rafe grabbed her hand and pulled her back up against his chest.

"Not so fast, Lis," he murmured, and bent his head to capture her mouth again.

After a surprised moment, Felicity kissed him back with renewed hunger. Finally he lifted his head and looked down at her.

"You're absolutely smashing," he said, grinning. "Top of the trees."

Even though she half wished he would stop talking and kiss her again, she had to chuckle. "Let go," she ordered, pushing at his hands. "Someone will see."

He released her waist, sliding his fingers down her arms and taking her hands. "You run an estate and raise your sister, all on your own, and you don't want anyone to see us kissing?"

"Running an estate makes me odd. Kissing you would make me ruined," she said, her voice unsteady. She used to be much more sensible; she was certain of it.

"Haven't you talked to Mrs. Denwortle lately? You and I have been carrying on an illicit love affair since I arrived in Cheshire—and possibly even before that."

She stared into his amusement-filled eyes with horror. "I'll kill her!"

"I hardly think that would help your reputation, my dear. Though it's not a bad idea."

"This is not funny! And it just points up why we can't continue behaving this way. It's not seemly."

"Beg pardon, but didn't *you* just kiss *me*?"

"Well, yes, but—"

"But two minutes later it's unseemly." He pursed his lips. "I'm afraid if you expect me to stop kissing you, you're going to have to come up with a better reason than that." He ran his thumb along her lower lip. "A much better reason."

Felicity really wasn't all that interested in thinking up a better reason. Neither, though, did she want to risk losing her heart to someone she'd known so briefly and who planned to sail off to China and parts unknown for the next ten years.

"Hm. How about if I tell you the taxes are nearly due, and Forton has no money with which to pay them?"

Slowly his hand dropped. "What about your tenants' rent?"

"*Your* tenants, you mean," she corrected gently. "The seed washed out, and . . . Nigel wanted a new phaeton." The memory of her brother's selfish stupidity tightened her throat, so that the words nearly made her choke. "We couldn't provide replacement seed, so to compensate we reduced the rent. Half the remaining tenants have left since then.''

For a long moment he looked at her. "How much do we—I—owe?"

"One hundred and eighteen pounds."

He blinked. "Beg pardon?"

"It could be worse," she hedged, for the first time grateful that Forton's problems were someone else's responsibility.

"And how is that?" Rafe asked skeptically.

She smiled. "You could come from a poor family."

Immediately she realized that she'd said the wrong thing. Rafe's expression hardened, and he turned on his heel. She watched him vanish around the far wing of the Hall. A few moments later he reappeared on Aristotle, and rode off toward the trees. Felicity retrieved the glasses of lemonade and returned them to the kitchen. No doubt Rafe was now regretting having turned down Lord Deerhurst's offer. Seventy thousand pounds would see him a long way from run-down Forton Hall, and from her.

"Blast it," she muttered, sitting at the kitchen table.

Earlier, he'd mentioned some sort of tension between him and his father, and that he didn't like the idea of taking Bancroft family money. And then she'd gone and told him to ask Papa for help. Coming from someone who wouldn't ask for a rope if she fell down a well, her presumption was appallingly thick-witted.

Another, more disturbing thought rattled her. Rafe had ridden toward Deerhurst. What if he'd gone to tell the earl he'd changed his mind?

"Oh, good Lord!" She lurched to her feet, nearly overturning her chair. Halfway out the door, though, she stopped. Forton Hall belonged to Rafe. As much as she loved it and needed it, she had no right to it.

Not any longer.

Chapter 8

Rafe slammed his fist against the desk, and had the satisfaction of seeing his solicitor jump. "You've had no offers?"

John Gibbs cleared his throat. "No, sir. No offers." He shuffled the papers on his desk. "Not even any inquiries."

"I know I asked you to be discreet, but you did put out word, didn't you?"

"Yes, of course, sir. It's just that, well, with the Season and all, no one's—"

"Damn." Rafe sat back in his chair. "Nothing?"

"No, sir."

That offer from Deerhurst was looking better and better. "Advertise in the newspaper," he decided. "Nothing too gaudy, and make Forton sound . . . comfortable. And for God's sake, don't mention my name."

The solicitor looked puzzled. "I don't understand, sir. Your ownership of the estate is no longer in dispute, and to be blunt, given the present condition of Forton Hall, the Bancroft name is your major selling point."

Rafe sighed. "Just use your name as the contact, will you?"

"As you wish. I, ah, will need to pay for the advertisement in advance."

Rafe eyed him. "How much?"

"For a discreet ad, twenty shillings. Per week."

Cursing under his breath, Rafe produced the correct change and dumped it on Mr. Gibbs's desk. "Just remember, Gibbs, I want Forton to sound nice. And pleasant." He stood.

"Yes, sir."

Rafe strolled back out to the cobblestoned street and whistled Aristotle over. The bay stayed close by his left shoulder as he wandered past the scattering of shops and residences toward Mrs. Denwortle's establishment. They were nearly out of fresh peaches, Lis's favorite.

Gibbs was right about the interest the Bancroft name would draw, and using it to sell Forton Hall had been his original plan. Now, though, he had no intention of doing so. He merely wanted to sell the estate to someone who would appreciate it—not to someone attracted to Cheshire by the Bancroft name. Why he'd suddenly become so concerned about the Hall's future well-being, he had no idea. "Like hell, you don't," he muttered to himself, and Aristotle snorted at him. Apparently even his horse knew better.

Ever since he'd arrived, he'd been adding conditions to the sale. Rafe ran a hand through his tawny hair. There was no use denying it: He felt responsible for the Harrington ladies. Their brother's stupidity certainly wasn't his fault. It was just that they had no one to turn to—no one but him.

"Good afternoon, Mr. Bancroft," Mrs. Denwortle said, as he entered her shop.

"Good afternoon. Lovely weather we're having." She aggravated him no end, but at least he seemed to irritate her, as well. He continued to work on refining that aspect of their relationship, but he had to admit that she was a fairly imposing opponent.

"Oh, yes, lovely. Nights are still a bit chilly, though. What brings you into Pelford on such a fine day?"

Rafe shrugged. "A little business, and some supplies."

"Goodness me. What sort of business would the son of the Duke of Highbarrow have in little Pelford?"

"Estate business." He had little liking for gossips, and in London, he would have told the shopkeeper just what he thought of her curiosity. Here, though, he had the standing of the Harrington ladies to consider. So he would be polite—to a point.

"Oh, my. 'Estate business.' That sounds grand."

"Mm-hm. Half a dozen peaches, if you please." He looked at the shelf behind her, and strands of bright colors caught his eye. "Are those new hair ribbons?"

"Oh, yes. They arrived from Paris just this morning. Lovely, aren't they?" She waddled over to collect the fruit.

Rafe scowled at her back. "Yes, they are." He knew full well if he purchased one of the ribbons for May or Lis, Mrs. Denwortle would see that the entire county knew he was providing Miss Harrington with her wardrobe. On the other hand, Lis would like a new hair ribbon, blast it all, as most of hers had perished in the collapse of the west wing.

His army training provided the answer: what he needed was a distraction. He spied a music stand in the corner, and immediately hit on the solution. "Ah, that reminds me. Where might one find musicians to hire? And I'll take two of those ribbons. A blue and a green.''

She froze, mid-step. "Musicians? What sort of musicians?''

Ha. "The sort that play instruments.'' Rafe leaned up against the counter and put his chin in his hand. "Out of doors. And I changed my mind. Yellow and blue ribbons.''

Hurriedly she pulled the ribbons off their peg, wrapped them in paper, and placed them beside the peaches. "Oliver Hastings plays the fiddle at the Childe of Hale when he's short of whiskey money.''

"I had something a little more substantial in mind, but thank you, anyway. What do I owe you?''

"Twelve shillings.''

Rafe handed over the change and lifted the sack of goods. "My thanks.''

"The Denleys had an orchestra at their Christmas soiree last year. I'd be happy to—''

"Good, I shall inquire of them,'' he interrupted, before she could arrange for the London opera's orchestra to come out and bankrupt him. "Thank you again, Mrs. Denwortle.''

"Oh, it just occurred to me. Chester has a church choir.''

"I'll consider that. Thank you.''

Aristotle had become accustomed to toting packages, and he didn't object as they headed back down the road. As they crossed the bridge over Crown Creek, Rafe noticed that an additional section of fence along Forton's western border had collapsed. It wasn't much of a barrier, just two rows of weather-beaten lumber. Even so, it marked the end of his land and the beginning of Deerhurst's, and he decided to repair it first thing in the morning. The more distance between himself and the earl, the better he liked it.

Slowly he drew Aristotle to a stop. *My land*. He'd never really thought of it that way before. The field sloping down from the creek and the scattering of trees to the northeast belonged to him. He owned the cattle and sheep grazing along the near side of the creek. For someone who had depended on a disapproving father for practically every farthing in his possession, it was a very odd feeling. And a comfortable one.

Rafe shook himself and sent Aristotle into a trot again. He was far too young to be succumbing to comfort. He would be comfortable when he was old and gray and had gout. And this land would be his for only another few weeks, until he found a buyer. He didn't have the blunt to be sentimental.

The Hall was in sight again before he remembered that he needed to send one hundred and eighteen quid to King Georgie if he wanted to hold on to the estate long enough to sell it. Out of the five hundred pounds he'd arrived with, only ninety-three would remain after taxes. "Blast it," he muttered, as his crew of gardeners came into view along the north side of the manor house.

Felicity straightened as he neared, and a shiver of anticipation ran down his spine at the sight of her. He wanted her, as he'd wanted her since he'd come to on her kitchen floor and seen those dark, expressive eyes looking at him. He needed to apologize to her for being so curt; it wasn't her fault that he could barely stand to be on the same continent as his father.

"Peaches," he said, lifting the sack as he passed her.

She smiled, and he grinned back, absurdly pleased that she approved his selection. This was

getting ridiculous. Next, he'd be bringing her flowers and . . . Rafe stifled a scowl as he dismounted.
Flowers and hair ribbons, or something.

Rafe seemed in a better temperament as he re-
joined them in the garden. At least he'd gone into
Pelford instead of riding off to be rid of Forton
Hall. And he'd brought back fresh peaches, of all
things. She *loved* peaches. Felicity couldn't figure
him out at all.

"In Africa," he said, strolling up beside her,
"it's the women who tend crops and gather roots."

"And what do the men do?"

"Hunt gazelles and drink fermented cows' milk
mixed with blood."

She wished he could be content with the gazelles
he'd already hunted. "That sounds dreadful."

"Actually, the stuff's so potent that if you can
get that first swallow down your gullet, you don't
care what the rest of it tastes like."

"So you've imbibed?"

He laughed. "Repeatedly."

And she'd tried to fool herself into thinking that
Rafe Bancroft would be content with something as
tame as growing roses. "Oh, dear," she said, turning away so he wouldn't see the disappointment on
her face. "Speaking of taste, I need to get dinner
started."

He touched her shoulder, stopping her. "Lis, I
wanted to apologize."

"There's no need," she said, pulling away. "We
both merely lost our heads for a moment. It won't
happen again, I'm sure."

She fled inside. Once there, though, she puttered
aimlessly about the kitchen, wishing she'd never
given into her silly desires and kissed him like that.
Before, at least she could have blamed it on him.

Of course, if she hadn't liked the way he kissed so much before, she wouldn't have been tempted into doing it again. So maybe it really was his fault. Felicity put her hands on her hips as annoyance replaced her embarrassment. Why had he apologized? He'd kissed her before and apparently hadn't regretted it.

When he stepped through the kitchen door a few minutes later, she rounded on him. "What do you mean, apologizing for kissing me? *I'm* the one who kissed *you*, and *I* apologize."

"I was apologizing for being sharp with you," he said, looking surprised. "And why are you apologizing for kissing me? It was very nice, I thought."

She blushed. "Oh. Well, thank you. But even so, it was stupid, and we shouldn't do it again."

He shook his head and pushed away from the door to join her. "It was not stupid, and we should definitely do it again. It only gets better, believe me."

She shoved firewood into the bottom of the oven and brushed past him to set a pot on the stove to boil. "I think you should go back to selling my home so you can go drink fermented cows' milk with the Zulus again."

"It was the Masai."

"Whatever." Good Lord, she wished he would go away—she couldn't think straight when he was standing so close.

Rafe grabbed her arm and spun her around to face him. "Why don't you want me to kiss you again?"

"Let me go, you big oaf!"

He released her arm but remained standing directly in front of her, willing her to meet his gaze. "Explain, Felicity."

She backed away and hurried to find some turnips. "It's perfectly clear to me. I've already agreed to work for you, and I certainly have nowhere else to go at the moment. You don't need to play at flirting with me."

"Play?" he repeated, snatching the turnips away from her. "What in hell makes you think I had some motive besides simply wanting to kiss you?"

"You did," she answered evenly, trying to keep a rein on her own temper.

"I did?" He held her gaze, his eyes searching hers. "Well, you'll have to forgive me then, after all. I took a blow to the head recently, and it seems to have damaged my ability to fathom nonsense."

"It's not nonsense. Don't be so stupid."

His eyes narrowed. "Beg pard—"

"You're the one who's been to Paris and Africa and everywhere," she interrupted.

He took a step closer. "What does that have to do with anything?"

Felicity wanted to whack him. "You don't know how to run Forton, so you decided you needed me about. That's why you're being so nice to me." She wanted to point out that he'd made it quite clear he had no intention of staying in Cheshire, but she didn't want to remind him if he had by some miracle forgotten.

Rafe glared at her. Abruptly, though, his expression cleared. He glanced down at the turnips in his hands, and tossed one into the air. Catching it deftly, in a moment he had all three vegetables circling with dizzying proficiency. "I'm nice to you because I enjoy your company, Lis. I'd begun to hope you enjoyed mine."

Her pulse jumped. Damn him, he could make her insane just by saying the simplest, most straightforward—if improper—things. But she could play that game, as well. Putting her hand to her heart, she smiled shyly. "Are you asking me to marry you, Rafael?"

The turnips careened into the air and hit the floor.

"Oh, now you've bruised my roots." She clucked her tongue at him. "Do go fetch me some more, dear."

For a moment he stared at her, then burst into laughter. "You are devastating, Lis."

"So I've been told."

May burst into the kitchen. "What are they for?" She ran forward, her cheeks flushed, to tug on Rafe's hands. "What are they for?"

His expression baffled, Rafe looked from Felicity down to May. "What are what for, sweetling?"

"The musicians! Mrs. Denwortle said you're hiring the same orchestra the Denleys used at Christmas! Are we having a party?"

Felicity saw a muscle in his cheek twitch. "Oh, *them*," he said, nodding. "You confused me for a moment. I, ah, wanted it to be a surprise, but yes, we are having a party. Of sorts."

"What sort of party?" Felicity asked, surprised. "We—you—can't afford to have a—"

"It's a working party," he broke in, smiling dazzlingly at her.

She'd seen that sort of smile before. It was the very same one Nigel used when he was embarking on some outlandish scheme. She folded her arms. "Explain, please."

"Well," he said, turning May around so that her excited, delighted expression squarely faced her older sister, "the stable . . . yes, the stable is a complete disaster. I can't afford to hire a crew to pull it down, so—"

"You've managed to have a crew here nearly every day," she noted dryly.

"So I thought, why not provide music and host an al fresco, potluck sort of soiree, the highlight of which would be the razing of the stable?" He looked at her expectantly.

"It sounds reasonable, I suppose," she admitted, still suspicious. "But I don't like the idea of using our neighbors as slave labor."

He grinned. "If I can get them to volunteer, it's not slave labor. Besides," and he dragged May a step closer to her, "with the stable gone, you can hardly banish me to sleep in it again."

"Felicity taught me to waltz," May put in excitedly. "May we have a waltz?"

"Several of them, my dear."

Rafe and May strolled off hand in hand, plotting over whom they would invite and which villager's wife made the best sweet tarts. Felicity leaned back against the table. He was definitely up to something—though destroying the stable in order to keep himself in the house *was* the most likely explanation.

He'd told her he wanted to do more than kiss her, and the idea didn't shock her nearly as much as she'd expected. Whatever prospects for marriage and family she'd once had were speedily diminishing, and as May constantly pointed out, Rafael Bancroft was absolutely smashing. She'd been on her own for so long. Besides, if it kept him here . . .

She shook herself and turned to retrieve the sack of peaches. He'd likely been intimate with enough women that it wouldn't be enough to convince him to remain, and she would be the one to pay any penalty. He was also capable of breaking her heart, for undoubtedly she would do something stupid like fall for him. Felicity dumped out the fruit, and a pair of brightly colored hair ribbons fluttered onto the table.

She lifted one, holding its blue coolness against her cheek. It was entirely too late for wariness. She'd fallen for him already.

"That damned bastard!"

The Earl of Deerhurst slammed the neatly ironed issue of the *London Times* onto his dining room table. He glared at the small, discreet ad up in one corner toward the back of the paper, and then ripped it free. He tore it in half, and continued ripping until nothing remained but the word "quaint," still attached to the rest of the page. He pulled it free and shredded that, as well.

Rafael Bancroft was making the task of regaining Deerhurst more difficult, and reducing any chance of keeping his father's stupid blunder a secret. If Forton Hall exchanged hands in the traditional manner, through damned nosy solicitors, the bookish louts would swiftly discover the amended clause that included ownership of Deerhurst. It was only because that idiot Nigel had made a private sale to his so-called friend that that particular complication had gone unnoticed. Mrs. Denwortle was already clucking to everyone about Bancroft's attention to estate business. And according to the shredded advertisement, he'd already hired at least one solicitor.

"Fitzroy!" he yelled.

A moment later the butler appeared. "Yes, my lord?"

"Clean up this mess. And have Taft meet me in my bedchamber. I've a soiree to dress for."

Bancroft hadn't explicitly invited him to the soiree, but practically everyone else in the county would be attending, and he had no intention of being excluded. Felicity would be there.

She'd always had something of a *tendre* for him, and if he couldn't persuade her to marry him, at least he could convince her that Forton Hall would be better off in his hands than in those of that arrogant London dandy. And if that failed—well, there was always bloodshed. Deerhurst smiled. That would certainly turn everyone's attention away from rotting old Forton Hall and its deed.

Rafe bit into an apple and wiped his chin with his sleeve. "So how many cattle do I have?"

Felicity pulled one of the ledgers from the stack of papers covering the dining room table. He didn't know why she'd chosen today to make him sit and go through the accounts with her, but any time spent with Lis was all right with him. And though he would never have suspected it, some of this twaddle was actually interesting.

"Last year," she said, indicating a line on one of the pages, "we had thirty-six."

"So I have thirty-six." He took another bite of apple. His minstrels should be wandering by anytime now. Pleasant as the morning had been, he needed to get moving.

"Will you pay attention?" Lis snapped, glaring at him. "Cows have calves."

"Thank you for the biology lesson," he said dryly, startled by the venom in her tone. "I'm rather new to this keeping accounts business. You'll have to be patient with me."

With a sigh, Felicity sat in the chair beside him. "I'm sorry," she said in a calmer voice. "My brother absolutely refused to pay any attention to the estate, and you were wearing a rather distracted look just now."

He grinned. "Just thinking of you."

"Do try to concentrate on the cattle, will you?"

Resolutely Rafe returned his attention to the disheveled spread of papers before him. She smelled like lavender, though, and he had to keep fighting the desire to lean toward her to smell her hair. If this kept up, he was never going to learn a thing about estate management—not that it mattered, if he sold the place. Rafe shook himself. *When* he sold the place. He had no choice. And it was what he wanted, anyway.

He jumped when her fingers brushed his temple, moving a strand of his tawny hair aside so she could see his scar. Rafe pretended to keep reading, though he might have been holding a newspaper written in Chinese for all he saw. Gently her fingers traced the length of the old wound. Generally he hated being touched there, but at Lis's caress he only closed his eyes and shivered a little. It would be all right, as long as she didn't begin cooing over his bravery, like the London ladies loved to do.

"Just how did you manage to get stuck in the face with a bayonet?" she asked, her voice slightly unsteady.

A little cooing might have been nice. "I fell on it."

The caress stopped. "You *fell* on it?"

Reluctantly he opened his eyes again and faced her. "Did you want to hear the 'heroic Rafe Bancroft' version known to most of London, or the 'stupid lucky sot' version, as my brother calls it?"

Her lips curved in a slow smile. "The true version, if you please."

He was curiously pleased at her choice. "I was roaring away at full charge in the middle of the cavalry, and neither my horse nor I saw a lovely little troop trench right in front of us. The nag tried to stop, and I was thrown headfirst into it and onto a very startled French soldier, and knocked my skull on his bayonet. The horse fell in on top of both of us, broke my leg, and snapped the poor fellow's neck.''

"Good God," she whispered. "You were more than lucky.''

At least she hadn't laughed. "Yes, I know. I've been reminded of that on a regular basis.''

Hesitantly she traced the scar again. "You could have broken your neck, or lost an eye.''

Rafe swallowed. "I thought I *had* lost it, at first. Had blood in both eyes, in my ear, up my nose, in my mouth . . .'' He stopped talking as her cheeks paled. "Sorry," he murmured. "It does sound rather appalling, doesn't it?''

Lis shook her head. "Not appalling. Terrifying.''

"Others were wounded far more badly, but I was the only one who got carried to Wellington's tent and tended by his personal physician.''

She looked at him. "Would you rather they'd left you in the trench to die? You don't seem the vainglorious, self-destructive sort, Rafe.''

"Oh, no. I was quite happy to be the Duke of Highbarrow's son that day.''

"So what's your complaint?''

If he'd ever thought Felicity some empty-headed society chit, that question would have forever dispelled the notion. "Complaint?''

"I assume you used your father's name to get you to Waterloo, and it was your father's influence that got you tended when you were wounded. It all balances out, I would say.''

For a long moment he stared at her, torn between amusement at her practicality and annoyance at her bluntness. "Ouch," he said finally.

"Oh, please," she said, humor touching her

voice. "You can't tell me someone who appreciates irony as much as you do hasn't considered that."

"Of course I have. But when I'm trying to impress a beautiful lady with my brave feats, she's not supposed to throw the truth back in my face like that."

"Then you shouldn't have told me the truth in the first place." Her expression grew more serious, and her warm fingers brushed his temple again. "Why did you tell me the true version?" she asked softly, her dark eyes meeting his.

"Because you asked me to," he replied in the same tone, unable to deny even her smallest request.

She leaned closer, and he half closed his eyes, anticipating her kiss. Lis hesitated, their lips a breath apart, then turned to face the papers on the table again. "We had eight calves last summer, and two more this spring. On the counter side, I've sold four head over the past year to pay the bills."

"Kiss me," he ordered, trying to decide whether to laugh at her stubborn practicality or drag her under the table and tear all her clothes off.

She smiled, looking at him from beneath her long, black lashes. "Tell me how many cattle you own."

"And then you'll kiss me?"

"Yes."

"Forty-two." He slipped his arm around her waist.

"Yes, but—"

He wasn't about to be tricked out of a kiss, and he pulled her forward and closed her mouth with his. Felicity's arms swept up around his neck, and he thrilled in the knowledge that she couldn't resist him any more than he could resist her.

Now that he'd started kissing her, he didn't want to stop. Slowly he pushed her back, until they were lying across three of the dining room chairs. He shifted to nibble at her earlobe and the line of her jaw, reveling in the taste and scent of her.

As she ran her hands up and down his back, he slipped one of the clips out of her hair, wanting to see it loose again around her shoulders and to bury his face in the cool lavender darkness. Kissing her hungrily, he pulled loose the other clip and let her long hair tumble down.

"Rafe," she murmured silkily against his mouth.

"Hm?" Damn, she felt good. Painfully hard, he swept a hand down to her hips to pull her closer against him.

She took an unsteady breath. "Rafe, don't forget that you have . . . four cows . . . with calf," she managed shakily.

"What?" Fuzzily he lifted his head to look down at her. "I'm trying to make love to you, and you're talking about cows?"

"It's important," she protested, her hands still twisted tightly into the back of his shirt. She lifted herself toward him and flicked her tongue along his jaw.

"Jesus," he muttered, trying to maintain his glare and a shred of his composure. "Do you want to make love, or talk about farm animals?"

Her dark eyes focused on his lips; then she blinked. "Did you hire me for kissing, or for accounting?"

Rafe opened his mouth to answer, though he wasn't certain what to say. Answering "both" would get him cracked on the head again, but it was becoming obvious that that was the truth. "Lis, I—"

"Shh!" She put a hand over his mouth, and

reached up with her other arm to coil her hair up over her shoulder.

At the same time, May's familiar, excited tramping sounded down the hallway. "Rafe?" she called, sticking her head into the dining room. "Rafe? The musicians are here!"

She evidently couldn't see them lying across the high-backed chairs, for a moment later she continued into the foyer, still calling out her news.

"Rafe, get off," Felicity whispered. "You have to go host your silly soiree."

"Silly, is it?" He sat up and pulled her up beside him. Frustrated and annoyed as he was, he also knew that if she were less complicated, he would have been much less interested. "This is my first time hosting an event, so please show a little respect."

"Your first time?" she repeated, her face still flushed. "And your last, I suppose, since you're selling your home."

It was the most pointed barb she'd launched at him about Forton Hall, but he could sympathize—too much, it sometimes seemed. "That is not my fault, Lis. If I'd known—"

Her expression softening, she again put her fingers to his mouth. "I know." Lightly she replaced her fingers with her lips, and kissed him. "I know."

A chasm of wishes and what-ifs opened in his heart. Taking a quick, painful breath, he stood. "Let's go destroy your stable."

"*Your* stable, Rafe."

"My stable."

Chapter 9

Rafe might never have hosted a soiree before, but he certainly had a flair for it. Of course, he also had an advantage in hosting an event the likes of which no one had ever heard.

Felicity scooped a large portion of Mrs. Denley's cook's lemon pie onto a plate and handed it to Bill Jennings. Beside her Mrs. Crandel tended the stewed potatoes, while her daughter Beth sliced bread for sandwiches. There were four tables, all laden with such an abundance of food and confections that she could scarcely believe it.

Even with the assistance they'd already received, part of her had been more ready to credit Rafe's charm than general goodwill. Nigel had done little for anyone but himself, and his lack of interest in Forton Hall and their tenants had been well known and much discussed. As she looked out at the jolly, noisy crowd spread out across the stable yard and the overgrown garden, she was warmed by her neighbors' generosity.

"Lis," May called, running toward her with a half dozen other young girls in tow, "Rafe says the musicians won't play any dances until after the stable is gone. He says dancing is only for the survivors."

"That's very cheery of him. Did he say when

they'll be finished stringing those ropes so they can come and eat?"

"It looks more like a giant spider web than a stable," Mrs. Crandel contributed with a smile. "I've never seen such a complicated-looking thing."

May rose up on her toes. "Rafe studied engineering at Oxford and in the army," she announced loudly. "He said we'd have a better time of it with elephants or a few cannon, but it should be smashingly loud when it comes down."

"Elephants? My goodness." Beth Crandel sent Rafe, standing at the top of a ladder up against the stable, an awed, doe-eyed expression. "He knows everything, doesn't he?"

Felicity only smiled as May piped in with a testimonial of Rafe's near godlike abilities. Just as at the Wadsworth dinner, half the ladies present had been giving him love-struck looks all afternoon, but he didn't seem to notice. Perhaps he was used to the attention. Only the sheer amount of bustling about she'd been doing kept her from her own daydreams. This felt so right, and Rafe's obviously delighted hosting of the event let her imagine for a few moments that she could convince him to stay at Forton. If only he could see how well liked *he* was becoming, and how happy he—they—could be here.

"Your Mr. Bancroft is going to end the day either as a hero or as a complete jackass."

Squire Talford stood beside her, a plate of luncheon in his hands. "Yes, I know." At that moment Rafe looked across the yard at her, and heat crept up her cheeks. She nearly dumped a slice of pie on the squire's boots before she realized what she was doing. "At least it will be exciting, either way."

A growing network of ropes and planks wound

up and down, in and around the stable. Rafe pulled another length of rope around a post in the loft, and dropped the free end down to Mr. Greetham. The other men seemed to think he knew what he was doing, for they arranged everything exactly as he instructed and with almost no argument.

"How much longer does he plan to stay?"

Her dream began to wilt a little at the edges. "I don't know. Until he's sold Forton Hall, I would imagine."

"Have you tried to convince him not to sell it?"

She looked at him sharply, wondering if her old friend had gained the ability to read minds. "Why would I do that?" she asked briskly. "Forton is his, and he is determined to travel the world with the money it will earn him."

"He's doing a great deal of repair work for someone who's only interested in a few fast quid. If he were to continue this way for another year or so, he could make double what he would get today."

Felicity glanced at the women alongside her, but they seemed engrossed in their own conversation. "I don't think he can afford to do any more than he's done," she answered in a low voice.

"Then why doesn't he sell to Deerhurst? I heard there was an offer. In fact, everyone's heard there's been an offer."

"I'm sure that's none of my affair," she answered, unwilling to explain further.

"Hm. Well, I think it has more to do with you than you're willing to admit," the squire said, holding her gaze with his kind, wise eyes.

"Charles, you're imagining things." She looked up to see Rafe and Mr. Greetham strolling toward them across the yard. "So, when do you go to visit Charlotte and the baby?"

"Trying to be rid of me, eh?" he chuckled. "I leave in a fortnight. They've asked me to stay through September, so I'll have Deerhurst look in on Talford for me."

"I would be happy—"

"You've enough to worry about, my dear," he interrupted, turning to greet Rafe and Greetham.

"We loosened the last of the supports," Rafe said as he came to a stop. Elizabeth Denley brought him a glass of lemonade, and he smiled at her. "A good gust of wind could knock the whole thing down, I think."

"You picked a fine day for your affair, Rafe," Miss Denley pointed out, batting her lashes at him. "It's been ages since I've had such a good time."

"My pleasure, Elizabeth."

Just as Felicity was beginning to consider dropping a pie on Elizabeth's gown, Mrs. Denley called her daughter back over to tend the lemonade. "My, Rafe, are you acquainted with everyone in east Cheshire?" she asked, when the squire and Mr. Greetham left to discuss barley.

"Nearly, I think. Why?"

She sliced another wedge of pie. "It just seems a great deal of effort to go to when you've no intention of staying."

Rafe looked at her, then glanced away at May and her gathering of young followers. "Your sister is the belle of our destruction party. I only hope she's not teaching the rest of those girls the tea kettle maneuver."

So—he didn't want to discuss the possibility of staying. She had no right to ask him to do so, however much she craved being in his warm, sure embrace. The longer he stayed, the worse it would be for her and for May, anyway. In six weeks or six months, she wasn't certain she would be able to watch him leave.

"I've been thinking," she said hesitantly. "If you're only prolonging your stay here in order to give me time to find a position, it's not necessary. I can manage." She smiled, trying to keep the expression brave and sincere. "As Nigel says, I always do."

He kicked a stone from under his boot. "Are you suggesting I toddle back to London and leave the two of you alone here—or God knows where—until I return to hand over the estate and forget about you completely?"

She couldn't meet his gaze. "Nigel did."

"I'm not Nigel." He gently tilted her chin up with his long fingers until she had to look him in the eye. "I don't abandon people. And certainly not ladies I regard . . . as fondly as I do you and May."

"But you don't stay anywhere, either, do you?" she whispered, and ducked away from his embrace. Turning, she nearly slammed into James Burlough. "Beg pardon, my lord!"

"No need, Felicity." Deerhurst made a show of leaning close beside her to examine the various pies at her table. "I see the sweetest lady is in charge of the sweetest treats."

"Thank you, James," she said, grateful for the distraction, because from the look on Rafe's face, he was ready for an argument. "Would you care for a slice?"

His blue eyes met hers warmly as he smiled. "Indeed, I would."

"You've arrived just in time for dinner, Deerhurst," Rafe added graciously, though to Felicity his tone sounded like that of a cat inviting a mouse to tea. "You'd best move to the front of the line.

The rest of us have worked up quite an appetite."

The insult was barely veiled, and Felicity sent Rafe a warning glance. She had no intention of allowing a brawl in the stable yard. Rafe was avoiding her gaze, though, and the earl appeared not to notice any abuse as he accepted a generous portion of peach pie.

"Indeed. The stable looks . . . most interesting. I applaud your efforts at whatever it is you're doing."

"My thanks. Perhaps you'll gain a better understanding once you've seen the results." Rafe set down his glass, put two fingers to his mouth, and whistled. Turning to face his guests, he said in a carrying voice, "Since our most illustrious guest has arrived, it's time for the main event: Let's pull down the stable!"

As the crowd cheered and gathered round, Felicity's heart began to pound. "Rafe," she hissed urgently. Men were so stupid sometimes.

He edged closer. "Yes?"

"James will have everyone laughing at you if this doesn't work."

His gaze touched hers. "It *will* work. Thank you for your vote of confidence."

"I—"

He clapped his hands. "Now. Might we have two gentlemen on each of the ropes we've staked out around the stable? And where's Miss May?"

"Here!" she crowed, running up to him.

He moved aside a few of the pies and lifted her up onto the table. "When May counts three, everyone pull—hard and until I say to stop."

"When should I count?" May asked excitedly.

"I'll signal you. Loud and clear, all right?"

She saluted. "Aye, Captain."

Rafe set off with Greetham to one of the ropes

anchored at the near side of the stable. Another dozen ropes fanned out from the stable like a great Maypole. *Please let this work,* Felicity prayed silently as the men took up their ropes and the women tittered excitedly and pulled their children clear of the building.

It took several minutes for everyone to position themselves to Rafe's satisfaction; then he waved at May.

She cupped her hands around her mouth. "One!"

Deerhurst folded his arms. "Ridiculous display."

"Two!"

"Oh, dear," Felicity murmured, fighting the urge to cover her eyes or turn her back.

"Three!"

In near perfect unison the ropes pulled tight around the perimeter of the stable.

And nothing else happened.

With all her might, Felicity willed the structure to fall.

Twenty-six men continued to haul on the thirteen ropes, their muscles straining.

The stable shuddered, groaned, and shuddered again. The sound of lumber creaking echoed from inside. Then, all at once and with a great cracking roar, the building gave a half twist and collapsed on itself. Hay and dust and pieces of lumber rose into the air, billowed outward, and slowly settled again.

"Hurray!" May yelled.

The laughter, yelling, and delighted applause of Forton Hall's neighbors drowned out the rest of her cheer. Davey Ludlow, proprietor of the Childe of Hale inn, produced a keg of ale and honored Rafe with the first frothing mug.

Protecting his drink from the abundance of back-pounding congratulations, Rafe made his way back to the dessert table. "Not as impressive as the fall of Rome, I'll admit," he said, grinning cheekily, "but a fair imitation."

May leaped off the table at him, and he caught her against his chest with his free arm. "That was smashing!" she said at high volume, and planted a sound kiss on his cheek. "What else can we tear down?"

He spun her around in the air and set her on her feet. "I've just retired from demolition, sweetling."

"Well, you've gone out with a bang." Felicity smiled. "Well done."

His eyes danced in the afternoon sunlight. "Thank you, my lady."

Deerhurst nodded. "Congratulations. Didn't think you'd pull it off." He took a bite of pie. "Of course, you've lowered the value of the property by as much as a fifth. Buyers tend to want an estate with a stable, I believe."

Rafe's smile faded again. Clenching his fist, he strode toward the earl. Before they could meet, Felicity moved between them. "Might I?" she asked, gesturing at the mug of ale.

Wordlessly Rafe handed it to her, his eyes reluctantly shifting from Deerhurst to her as she took a long swallow. "Oh, my," she sputtered, handing the drink back. "I have to admit, that rickety old thing is one part of Forton I won't miss. Good riddance to it." She boldly wrapped her fingers around Rafe's arm. "I'd like a closer look," she announced.

"My pleasure."

She practically had to drag him away from the table, but as they neared the pile of rubble, she felt the tensed muscles of his arm relax a little. She leaned closer, reveling in the tall, warm strength of him.

"Not very subtle," he said, glancing down at her. "Which of us were you trying to protect?"

"My pies," she answered promptly, wishing he weren't quite so astute.

"Then you should have escorted them away from that bloated dung heap."

"Rafe! Be fair."

He stopped, turning to face her. Behind him the setting sun turned the windblown ends of his wheat-colored hair to copper. She wanted to curl her fingers into his hair, to be swept into his arms for a hundred breathless kisses.

"Be fair about what?"

"Lord Deerhurst made you a ridiculously generous offer for Forton Hall, and you turned him down. You can't expect him not to be annoyed and frustrated with you."

"He didn't seem annoyed with you, and you've turned him down several times, I believe."

She flushed. "That's different. Men always take business more seriously than romance."

"You obviously haven't been pursued by the right men." He smiled roguishly at her and offered his arm again. "Shall we?"

Felicity stifled a yearning sigh. She'd finally *found* the right man; he simply wasn't asking the right questions. But she wasn't about to begin another argument—not when she had him all to herself for the first time in hours. "Were you really so certain your rope trick would work?"

He nodded. "I've always been fascinated with engineering and architecture." He paused. "Lis, did Nigel ever try to sell Forton to Lord Deerhurst?

Or did his lordship ever offer to purchase it before now?''

She thought about it for a moment. ''Not that I'm aware of,'' she answered. ''Nigel constantly whined about going to London, but I think he liked the prestige of being an estate owner—until it got in the way of his having fun.''

''Hm,'' Rafe said noncommittally, and she liked him even more for not seconding her poor opinion of her brother.

''And James—Lord Deerhurst—has lately offered to lend me funds to repair the house. However, he knew how fond I was of Forton. If he did want it, I think he also realized I'd never stand for Nigel selling it.'' She looked up at him, to find him studying her face with unsettling intensity. ''Why do you ask?''

Rafe shrugged and glanced toward their boisterous guests. ''Just trying to figure out why he's suddenly willing to pay so much for an estate he apparently never had an interest in before.''

''He never *expressed* an interest in it before. For all we know, he might very well have been lusting after Forton for years.''

Rafe's expression darkened. ''Or lusting after something, anyway.''

Warmth crept up Felicity's cheeks, and slid shiveringly down her spine. ''Are you jealous?'' she asked, hardly believing she'd dared to utter the question aloud.

A slight, sensuous smile touched his mouth, and he leaned a little closer to her. ''Insanely,'' he murmured.

''Rafe, stop it,'' she returned, pushing at his chest. ''Everyone will see.''

''See what?''

''See us kissing, you big oaf.''

His smile deepened. "So you do think about kissing me."

These days, she barely thought of anything else. "Among other things," she hedged.

"I think of other things, too. Would you like to hear them?"

"Will they be socially acceptable?"

Rafe chuckled. "No."

"Then I'd best get back to the pies."

"Waltz with me tonight," he said, tugging at the tie of her pelisse as she turned away.

"All right," she whispered, half wishing he would ignore her warning and kiss her right there, in the middle of the stable yard rubble.

"And don't waltz with *him*," Rafe continued.

She looked over her shoulder at him. "Lord Deerhurst? I won't refuse him a dance, if he asks. For heaven's sake, Rafe, he's my neighbor. And he's nobility."

"Dance anything with him, except a waltz," he clarified, the expression in his eyes unreadable. "Don't make me blow up the musicians."

She laughed. "Oh, dear. All right."

Of course, when the Earl of Deerhurst approached her an hour later to ask her for the first waltz of the evening, she couldn't refuse him. Rafe was already gliding about the yard with May, and with his gouty leg, Squire Talford didn't dance.

Felicity looked up at Charles apologetically. "Will you excuse me?"

The squire nodded. "For goodness' sake, enjoy the festivities. You've earned a bit of fun, my dear."

Actually, May looked as though she was having more fun, but Felicity smiled and took the earl's proffered hand. He led them to the middle of the yard, bordered by three great, roaring bonfires, and slipped a hand about her waist.

"You look so enchanting this evening," James commented, turning her about in time to the music.

"Thank you."

"I shall miss you, once you've gone."

"I shall miss you as well, James."

"Are you certain you won't consider staying?"

"James—"

Deerhurst shook her a little, and she started, her gaze snapping back to his face. "I think it is important that I put one more . . . offer . . . on the table, as it were," he said. "You should know all the facts before you make the decision to stay or go. If you were to marry me, and if you could convince Bancroft to sell me Forton Hall, I would give it back to you as a wedding gift. It would remain *yours*, Felicity. Not Nigel's, and not anyone else's. Yours."

Felicity opened her mouth, then closed it again. His words echoed in her head so she wasn't sure what he'd actually said. She could have Forton Hall—not to live in perhaps, but at least to have. Over time she might even be able to repair it, and rent it to someone who would appreciate it. Or keep it, just for herself. "That's too much," she said belatedly.

"It's not too much." He smiled. "I want to prove to you how much I adore you. Giving you Forton would be the merest token of that affection. And my very great pleasure."

The idea tempted her, but she felt compelled to answer him honestly. "You are very, very generous, James. But you know how I . . . I feel about you. I could never be so mercenary. It wouldn't be right—and it wouldn't be fair, to either of us."

For a long moment he looked at her, his lidded

expression for once completely unreadable. It unsettled her a little, until his warm, familiar smile reappeared. "You make me feel like a brigand. Of course I know your feelings. I am merely trying to induce you to understand mine. I don't require that you love me. Only that you not rule out the possibility that you could—eventually—love me."

Unable to stop herself, Felicity gazed over at Rafe, gamely hunched over to dance with May, who insisted that he not lift her to his own height and carry her about like an infant. He'd certainly made no mention of marriage, or love, nor was he ever likely to. Other than finding employment, marriage was her only real alternative. She looked back at the earl, who was watching her closely. "That doesn't seem fair to you, James."

"I know what's fair to me. And in all honesty, Felicity," the earl continued, "who *is* there but me to love you? You will never be presented in London, because you don't have the funds or the sponsorship. And the only other men remotely of your station here are Talford, a good forty years your senior, and a fool who only wants to sell your birthplace as quickly as he is able so he can sail off into the great unknown."

Felicity lowered her eyes so he wouldn't see how much that had hurt. Of course she knew all that already, but to hear it said aloud . . . She'd learned, though, that the truth was frequently painful. "I can't give you an answer tonight," she said stiffly, trying not to give in to sudden, self-pitying tears. "I need to consider things."

Deerhurst's kind smile appeared again. "Of course."

When the music stopped, Deerhurst escorted her to the tables at one end of the yard, where most of the young ladies had gathered to chat and wait for partners. Felicity wished she'd accepted a mug of ale from Davey Ludlow—she could use it right now.

"Lis, did you see me?" May bounded up beside her, Rafe in tow. "I waltzed! And Rafe said I was completely above board for such a little dab of a thing!"

"Yes, you are," she answered, avoiding Rafe's gaze yet still able to sense his annoyance. "You were wonderful."

"Fetch me a punch, girl," Rafe ordered his dance partner. "You've worn me out."

As May skipped away, he turned his attention to Felicity. Before he could say anything about her dancing with Deerhurst, though, she turned her back to speak to Mrs. Wadsworth. He would only begin an argument, and then she would start crying, and begin babbling about how difficult things had truly been the last few months, and how tired she was of having no one to rely on but herself. And then she would admit to being in love with him, and he would turn and run off to the Orient.

After several moments she was able to paste a fairly normal expression on her face, and she turned to look at him. He wasn't there.

"Hey!" May returned to her side, a full glass of punch clasped carefully in both hands. "He said he was tired. Rafe!"

Felicity spied him then, engaged in a country dance with Elizabeth Denley. As she watched he leaned closer, exchanged some comment with the pretty brunette, and then laughed. "May, hush," she chastised her sister. "It's not polite to yell, and certainly not at a grownup."

May looked hurt. "But I fetched his punch."

"You don't own Rafe. He's an adult, and may do as he pleases."

"Then I wish I were an adult."

Felicity knelt and took the glass from her sister. "Sometimes it's not all that wonderful," she said softly. "Enjoy being eight."

May grimaced. "I'd enjoy it more if I were big enough to stomp on Elizabeth Denley's fat foot."

Her sister stifled an understanding smile. "Most unladylike. Go ask Lord Deerhurst if he'll dance with you."

"I'll ask Greetham."

"May," Felicity said warningly.

"*Mr.* Greetham," she amended. Sticking her tongue out at Rafe, she hurried around to the far side of the yard.

It was past midnight before the crowd began thinning. May didn't even object when Felicity sent her up to bed, barely able to keep her eyes open long enough to tell Squire Talford good evening. The musicians continued playing country tunes for the twenty or thirty remaining guests, and Felicity wearily began carrying in the platters and bowls that belonged to Forton.

She hadn't danced with Rafe at all, but if he was going to be so stupid and childish about a simple waltz, she was glad he'd avoided her. She had enough to think about. The squire's half-full mug of ale sat at the edge of the pie table, and with a quick glance around, Felicity drained it. Warmth spread from her throat down to her stomach, and she sighed.

"Let me freshen that for you," Rafe said from behind her. She froze, and he leaned his arm over her shoulder, pouring half of his own full mug into hers. "Cheers."

She turned to face him. "Are you drunk?" she asked, watching his Adam's apple bob as he swallowed.

"I certainly hope so. I've been working hard enough at it." He smiled his charming, roguish smile at her, and tapped her mug with his. "Drink."

Eyeing him, she complied. It was a sweet ale, and tickled going down. Feeling steadier, she set the mug aside. "You hurt May's feelings."

"I know. Come here."

He strolled down to the far end of the line of tables. Curious, and the ale spreading into the tips of her fingers and warming her toes, she followed. The keg of ale sat there, and he turned the spout to pour himself another mug. Rafe downed half of it, then handed it over to her.

"I am not going to let you get me drunk," she stated, handing it back.

He pressed it back into her hands. "I'm not getting you drunk," he retorted, a slight, very sexy drawl touching his cultured voice. "I'm contemplating, and I hate to do it alone."

She smiled and returned it. "I prefer to do my contemplating sober. But what, precisely, are *you* contemplating?"

" 'Night, Bancroft," Mr. Greetham called, as he and Ronald finished loading his dining table onto his wagon.

Rafe waved at him. " 'Night, Greetham. Oh—I want to talk to you tomorrow. About ten?"

"Make it noon. My Tom's reciting in school tomorrow morning. I promised I'd go."

"Noon, then. And bring those . . . " He glanced at Felicity. "Bring those things we talked about."

The farmer looked at him curiously, but nodded as he clucked to his mules. "I'll do that."

"What things?" Felicity asked, eyeing him.

"Are you certain you can contemplate this way? I always come up with much grander ideas when

I'm completely sluiced over the ivories.''

"Yes, I can contemplate this way just fine. What things, Rafe?''

He handed her the mug of ale and wandered off toward the ruined stable. "Number things.''

"Figures?'' she offered, following and hoping he wouldn't fall on his face in the near dark of the dying firelight.

He turned around to look at her, though he continued walking backward with no noticeable difficulty. "All right.'' He smiled slowly. "You have a lovely one.''

She frowned. "A lovely what?''

"Figure.''

Felicity blushed. Rafe's blasted compelling smiles unsettled her so, even when he was completely soused. "Oh. Thank you.''

"Why did you waltz with Lord Dapper?''

She stopped, and so did he. "Because he asked me, and because I've known him since I was two. And you shouldn't call him names.''

Rafe pursed his lips. "I know. Bad form. Waltz with me.''

"That's a country dance your minstrels are playing.''

"Why, yes it is.'' He stepped forward to take her hand. Slowly he moved her in time to the music, while she held up the ale and tried not to spill any.

Rafe knew the steps, and however ridiculous they looked mincing about in the dark, whoever was left by the tables had to be more inebriated even than he was. Giggling as giddily as May, she circled him, while he deftly snagged the ale from her hand, took another swallow, and returned it to her, never missing a step.

"Rafe, I'm tired. We should finish cleaning up and go to bed."

Humming a fine baritone, he spun her up against him. The ale and mug went flying, but he didn't seem to notice. For a long moment he stilled, looking down into her eyes, and then slid his hand down to her waist. His other hand twined into hers, and before she realized it, they were waltzing. He was holding her far too close, but she didn't mind. In fact, his humming was sending a harmony of shivers down her back to her legs, and she wasn't certain she would be able to remain standing without his tall, strong form against her.

She lowered her head against his shoulder, breathing in the scent of ale and wood smoke in his coat. "You dance well," she complimented.

"Bancrofts do," he answered softly into her hair. "You know," he continued almost sleepily, "I've waltzed with women in seven different countries."

Felicity lifted her head. His eyes were half closed, glinting green from the distant firelight. "Which country are you in now?" she whispered, suddenly very tired. He was gone, just as he would go once he sold Forton. And she had herself, and May, to think about.

"I don't think I've ever been here before," he said.

"Rafe, come on. Let go. We have things to do."

His eyes opened again, and he looked down at her. "I like dancing with you."

"And I like dancing with you. But it's very late."

"Is it?" He shifted her in his arms, and bent his head to kiss the curve of her ear. Gasping, she arched her neck, and he took her earlobe between his teeth and very gently bit down. Unable to help herself, Felicity moaned and slipped her hand from his shoulder up around his neck.

"Do you like that?" he murmured.

"Oh, yes."

The tip of his tongue traced her ear. It was the most sensuous thing Felicity had ever felt, and she pulled herself as close up against him as she could. Their slow waltzing had taken them past the back side of the stable, where the ground sloped away to the small creek that wound across Forton's land.

"Rafe," she said dreamily, "look out for the—"

With a startled grunt he lost his balance as one foot stepped into air. Instinctively grabbing his arm to keep him from falling, Felicity toppled as well, and they tumbled in a twining heap down the rise.

Somehow she ended up on top of him, their faces only inches apart. She couldn't have moved if she wanted to, for her skirt was twisted under his legs, and one arm was pinned beneath his back. He smiled, his eyes dancing, and Felicity lowered her head to kiss him.

When she lifted her head to take a breath he pursued her, capturing her mouth again in a rough, wild embrace. His tongue touched her lips and she parted them, her heart pounding, closing her eyes and squirming closer into him.

She could feel the hard warmth of him pressed up against her thighs. She experimentally rocked her hips from side to side and he moaned against her mouth, lacing his fingers into her hair and lifting her head to place light, breathless kisses along her throat.

Her dark hair spilled down around her face, curtaining both of them as he continued his agonizing, delicious trail of kisses. "Rafe," she panted, pushing his distancing arms aside to kiss his mouth again.

His hands swept down her back, loosening the fastenings of her dress with the skill of a maid. She couldn't seem to let go of him, tangling her hands restlessly into his hair, his clothes, the muscles of his arms, wanting somehow to be absolutely inside him, so they were the same person, the same body.

"Lis, shh," he murmured silkily, slipping the gown off one shoulder, then the other, and covering her exposed skin with kisses. "Take your time. I'm not going anywhere."

"I'm sorry," she gasped, yanking open his waistcoat.

"Don't be." He grinned, drawing her fingers into his mouth and sucking gently.

"I want—" she panted, but had to stop, unable to articulate the need she felt.

"So do I. Lift up a little."

"No, Rafe. Just hold me, I think."

He chuckled breathlessly, his eyes dark with desire. "All right, stubborn chit. You lead."

She rocked against him again, feeling him grow still harder. "Oh, my God," she whimpered, arching against him.

He tugged her gown down to her waist. Warm, sure fingers brushed and caressed her exposed nipples, and she gasped again. She sat up, straddling him, and his hands kneaded and molded her breasts. Impatiently she shifted to tug her skirts out from under him, away from her legs, then she sank down again.

"Sweet Lucifer . . . Lis, you're going to have to remove some more clothes," Rafe gasped, rising up to take her left breast into his mouth, sucking and pulling at her nipple while he continued fondling her other breast with his free hand. "Now."

There was no mistaking the urgency in his voice, or in her own trembling wanting. Removing her own underthings was simple, for as soon as she lifted her skirt Rafe twined his fingers into the waist and ripped the flimsy garments free. His trousers were more difficult, though, and she kept fumbling over the buttoned fastenings.

"Sit up," he commanded with a harsh growl, and shoved her hands aside. Shakily she complied and he swiftly freed himself, pushing the garments down past his thighs. "That's better." He ran his hands silkily up her bare thighs, pulling her down toward him.

"Rafe," she said again, laughing breathlessly, "I don't know—"

He kissed her again, chuckling against her mouth. "Shall I?"

"I think so."

Slowly he pulled her down toward him, until she felt the hard maleness of him pressed against her innermost place. This was it—this was where she needed to be, and she moaned again, tugging on the buttons of his waistcoat.

"Rafe, hurry," she demanded.

"I'm trying to be gentle," he returned, laughter and desire in his voice.

"Don't be."

"But it's going to—"

With a wanting growl that surprised her, Felicity sank down on his erect member, taking him deep inside her. At the sudden pain she gasped and tried to raise up again. Rafe moved to hold her firmly against him.

"I tried . . . to tell you, sweetheart. Give it a moment."

She tucked her head down against his chest, the pain already beginning to fade, replaced by the most exotic, intimate sensation she'd ever experienced. "Oh, my," she breathed, astounded at the satisfaction of feeling him inside her.

"Now you can move, Lis." Rafe shifted his hips against hers to demonstrate.

She did, rocking against him and watching the heated anticipation and need on his face. Rocking faster, she ran the tip of her tongue along his scar, and he moaned. Something inside her tightened and coiled deliciously, and she rocked harder—faster— and then exploded. Felicity threw herself down against him again. "Rafe," she gasped.

With a groan he caught her up against him and rolled them over so that she was on her back, looking up at him. He kissed her deeply, open-mouthed, and took her lower lip gently in his teeth. Then he thrust his hips forward, driving deep into her, and she cried out his name again, muffling the sound against his shoulder as he continued to move in and out of her.

Finally he gave a hissing breath and held himself hard against her, then sank his brow down against her neck.

Felicity ran her fingers through his disheveled hair, hearing his harsh breathing and trying to regain her own. He was heavy, but she liked the weight of him on her. It felt safe, and secure, and it had been a long time since she had felt that way.

After a moment he lifted his head and kissed her again, more gently this time. He scooped his arms under her and turned them over again, so that she could rest her head on his chest and hear the steadying beat of his heart.

"Perhaps now I should tell you what I was contemplating earlier," he said, his voice still amused.

"Did I do something wrong?" she demanded, thumping his hard chest.

"Ow. No—absolutely not. I was simply beginning to wonder whether you wanted me as much as I wanted you. Now I know."

Felicity wanted to stay where she was, warm and comfortable and wrapped in his arms, so she wouldn't have to think about how he would be gone soon, and how soon it would be until she never saw Forton Hall again—unless she listened to James Burlough. But not speaking wouldn't keep any of it away. "What were you contemplating, then?"

"Deerhurst was right. A stable would add significant value to the estate."

"That one wouldn't have."

Softly he stroked her hair, twining his fingers through her curls, and she closed her eyes, running her hand up under his shirt along his hard, flat stomach. "I know," he continued. "But a new one would. I'm going to write my brother, and ask him for a loan."

She lifted her head, stunned, and stared at him. "A loan? Why? You said you'd never ask—"

"A small loan, enough to fix Forton up right, will be more than offset by the increased sale price. Don't you think?"

All she could think was that he would be staying longer, that she wouldn't have to say goodbye so soon, and that she wouldn't have to decide so soon. Slowly she settled down against him again, wondering what he would do if she told him how she felt, how much she loved him. "I think you may have something there," she said instead.

"I'm glad you agree. I thought it was a little mad, myself." He started chuckling again, the sound resonating deep in his chest.

"What?" she asked, smiling in response.

"You are extraordinary," he said, hugging her to him.

So are you, she thought.

Chapter 10

Rafe started the letter to Quinlan three times. The first one was a hopeless, rambling disaster, because he couldn't decide how much or how little to tell his calm and cool older brother about Forton Hall, and Felicity, and May. The second letter began well, until he realized he'd been daydreaming and had doodled Felicity's name all over the page.

"Gadzooks," he muttered, horrified, and swiftly crumpled the parchment to toss it into the fireplace.

The third letter he kept short and to the point, merely stating that Forton Hall would benefit from a few minor repairs before he sold it, and suggesting a sum he hoped was small enough that it wouldn't rouse Quin's curiosity.

Footsteps stirred upstairs, and he sat back. At least a dozen times during the night he'd started for Felicity's bedchamber. He'd been her first lover—though why someone as practical and levelheaded as she had chosen him, he had no idea. And Lis had wanted *him*—not the charming, wealthy son of the Duke of Highbarrow, or the heroic, decorated army captain.

He was not used to this, to being unable to banish a woman from his mind. And she'd crept farther inside him than that. When she'd said his name, her voice full of need and yearning, he would have done anything—*anything*—to please her. And the damnedest part of it was that he knew exactly what she wanted—Forton Hall.

"Dash it." Stables and demolished houses had nothing to do with what he wanted for himself. Felicity and traveling to the Orient couldn't possibly be more opposed desires. The problem was, Lis was here, for him to see and hear and touch. The rest of the world was a great distance and a greater deal of money away.

Rafe pulled over another piece of parchment. What he needed was a distraction—something besides Lis and her silky skin to think about. He smiled as he began scrawling across the page. Good old Robert Fields would be able to set him back on course. All he needed was a touch of debauched London cynicism to help him regain his sanity, and Robert possessed a large measure of cynicism. He thought about corresponding with Francis Henning as well, but that puddle-brain would likely take the letter as an invitation to come and holiday at Forton for the duration of the summer. No, a letter or two from Robert, and perhaps one from Quin, would be all he needed to remind him of the freedom ahead of him.

Rafe shut his eyes for a moment, weariness pulling at him. He knew how to seduce a woman, though one wouldn't have thought it from last night. Generally when he made love to a woman, it involved a bed, or at the least, a little romance. They'd been wearing most of their clothes, and he still wanted to see her, touch her, hold her . . .

"Lis?" May stuck her head into the doorway. As she spied him at the writing desk, her pretty face folded into a scowl. "Oh. It's you."

She vanished back into the hallway, and Rafe

sighed, unable to tolerate being in the bad graces of an eight-year-old. "May?"

For a moment she was silent. "What?"

"I'm sorry."

Her head reappeared. "Really?"

He nodded. "Yes. Are we still friends?"

She thought about it for a moment. "All right. But you have to apologize to Lis, too."

"What for?"

"She wanted you to dance with her, and you didn't."

"Ah." Rafe finished the letter, folded it, and addressed the outside. "Well, I danced with her later, after you went to bed." He stood and stretched. Even with yesterday's exertions, he hadn't been able to sleep last night. The realization of just how much he'd begun to care for Felicity Harrington had rather terrified him.

"Whom did you write to?"

He sealed the letters and handed them over. "My brother and a friend of mine in London."

"Robert F . . . Folds," she read.

"Fields, midget," he corrected, putting the stopper back in the bottle of ink. "Want to go into Pelford with me to mail them?"

"May is going to do her arithmetic tables this morning."

Rafe turned, his pulse stirring in elation, as Lis strolled into the room. She looked beautiful, wearing a green patterned muslin gown he'd never seen her in before. She also looked perfectly composed, until her eyes met his. And he wanted her again, right then and there.

"I want to go with Rafe," May complained.

"Good morning," he said.

"Good morning." Lis returned her attention to

her sister. "Arithmetic. Would you please go see if we have any eggs this morning?"

"Oh, blast it all." May reluctantly headed out through the kitchen.

Years as a gambler and a soldier had made Rafe proficient at reading people, and usually Lis's expressive eyes told him what she might be thinking and feeling. This morning, though, he couldn't even guess. "Did you sleep well?" he asked.

She nodded, fiddling with the mismatched knick-knacks on the end table. Then, as the distant kitchen door banged shut, she crossed the room toward him and wrapped both arms around his waist. As she pressed her cheek against his shoulder, he swept his arms up across her back, pulling her to him.

"Good morning," she said again, and tilted her head up invitingly.

He kissed her sweet lips, tasting in her the same passion he felt. "Now that," he said softly, "is more like it."

"Have you been awake all night?" She brushed at the stubble of beard on his chin.

"Yes. When I begin contemplating, it generally takes a while."

Lis chuckled. "Mm. I hope so."

He went hard, wondering if they could barricade the morning room door against May. He kissed her again, and at her hot, wanting response, a weight Rafe hadn't realized was there lifted from his heart. "No regrets then, sweet Lis?"

She searched his gaze for a long moment. "None so far."

It was his turn to chuckle. "Good. Because I'd like to repeat last night, at more leisure. And without pebbles digging into my backside." He ran his hands down to her hips and her rounded buttocks, pulling her against him. "In fact, how about right now?"

She moaned, her fingers kneading into his back. Then, with obvious reluctance, she pushed him away. "Not with May wandering about."

"Is that your only concern?" He pursued her retreat.

"Heavens, no. Only the most obvious one." She turned away and gestured at the letters May had dropped back onto the desk. "To your brother?" she asked.

He let her escape—for the moment. "Yes. I was a bit nasty to him when I left London, but I reminded him how charming and lovable I am, and hopefully he'll send me what I asked for."

The lust-filled humor left her eyes, and then she was gazing away from him, out the window. "Might I ask how much you requested from him?"

"Of course. You are my accountant. Two thousand quid. Not enough to ruffle his feathers, I hope, but enough to give Forton a small, serviceable stable and at least patch up the wall where half the house is missing."

"How long will it take, do you think?"

Rafe looked at her slim backside, the morning sunlight outlining the edges of her gown and making her look like an angel. Though she hadn't moved, it abruptly felt as though she'd gone a hundred miles away. And he wanted her back.

"A month or so, if he sends the blunt fairly quickly. Which he will, if he sends it at all." He walked up behind her, sliding his arms around her waist and pulling her back against him. "What did I do this time?"

She didn't resist his embrace, and in fact relaxed a little in his arms. "Nothing. I'm . . . a bit befuddled this morning."

"Good."

"Good?" She craned her head to look up at him.

"I can think of quite a few words I was hoping you wouldn't use this morning. 'Befuddled' is perfectly acceptable. I feel the same way myself."

She chuckled. "Good."

Rafe could sympathize with her confusion. He had no damned idea what he was doing, either, but at least he had only himself to worry about. "You know," he murmured into her hair, "if you find a position somewhere, you're not obligated to stay and look after me."

"And if you find a buyer, you're not obligated to stay until I find a position."

Rafe closed his eyes, that uncertain chasm of hopes and wishes opening in him again at the thought of her leaving. "Lis—"

She pulled out of his arms and turned to look up at him. "I have no regrets, Rafe," she said firmly. "I want to be with you. But neither am I a fool."

He watched her go out the door to find May. "No, you're not," he said to himself. "I'm beginning to wonder what that makes me, though."

"Oh, I *am* a fool." Felicity absently stirred batter as she leaned in the kitchen doorway, looking out at the yard.

"Well, it's too late now," May said from the table behind her. "Rafe's already gone into Pelford without me."

"You shouldn't get too attached to him, May. He won't be here forever, you know."

She should use the same advice on herself, but it was far too late for that. Despite what she'd told Rafe, she hadn't slept, hoping he would come to her, and wishing she had the courage to go visit him. She'd never been in love before, but she had always told herself that if it ever happened, it would be with someone steady and safe, someone on whom she could rely. Though Rafael Bancroft had more common sense than her father and her brother, and more charm than anyone she'd ever met, steady and safe were not the first two words she would have chosen to describe him.

"I've decided I'm going to travel when I grow up," May said, as she scribbled figures on a piece of parchment. "Rafe says the London Zoo doesn't even have a quarter of the animals he saw in Africa, and I've never even seen the London Zoo."

Felicity glanced at her sister. "If there are eighty-one animals at the London Zoo, and they represent one fourth of what Rafe saw in Africa, how many animals did Rafe see?"

May thunked her head against the table. "Felicity! That's not fair!"

She chuckled. "How many?"

"Pardon me, Miss Harrington."

Felicity jumped. A man liveried in the Earl of Deerhurst's colors stood just behind her in the stable yard, though she hadn't heard him approach. He was big, strong looking, and solemn faced, and she couldn't recall ever seeing him before. "Y-Yes?" she stammered, setting the bowl down on the counter and eyeing the large bouquet of red and white roses he held in his arms.

"Lord Deerhurst requested that I deliver these to you, miss," he said politely, in a low, guttural voice. "With his compliments."

He held out the bouquet, and Felicity hesitantly took it from him. "Please thank him for me," she requested, lifting it to smell the profusion of sweet blooms. "They're lovely."

The servant bowed. "Good day, Miss Harrington, Miss May."

"Good day."

May stood and came over to examine the flowers. "Lord Dapper sent you flowers? Why?"

"May, hush. That is not the proper way to address Lord Deerhurst."

She folded her arms. "That's what Rafe calls him."

"Rafe can afford to be insolent. We cannot."

"Well, why'd he send you flowers?"

"Let's see." Felicity pulled free the note tucked into the flowers. " 'Dearest Felicity, you are a rose among thorns. With my sincere and utmost affection, Deerhurst.' "

May wrinkled her nose. "What's that for?"

Felicity went to fetch one of their intact vases. "He wants to marry me."

Despite the derisive noises May made, and however strongly Felicity felt drawn to Rafe, Lord Deerhurst's favor was not something she could simply dismiss any longer. Too much rested on it. James Burlough was certainly intelligent and handsome, and if he was a little dull, he was also the very epitome of steadiness and reliability. In addition to the gift of Forton Hall, he could give her—and May—a safe, secure future.

"She said *what*?" Rafe straightened too quickly, and banged his head on one of the downed stable supports. "Lucifer's ba . . . big bottom," he amended mid-curse.

May giggled. "I knew you wouldn't like it. And she put the flowers on the table right in the middle of the morning room."

"Did she say anything else?" He finished knotting a rope around the support, then took May's hand to lead her away from the pile of rubble. Once they were clear he whistled, and Dennis Greetham started off his plow horses to tug the section of lumber free.

"She said I shouldn't make fun of him, and then later she said the flowers were a very thoughtful gift."

He didn't like the sound of that at all, but he couldn't very well tell May that he wanted to throttle Deerhurst for sending posies to *his* Felicity— particularly when he had no real claim on her other than the fact that they'd made love, and that he absolutely couldn't get her out of his thoughts for more than two seconds at a time. However, he still had no intention of letting Deerhurst beat him at anything—especially earning Felicity's affections.

"The flowers were thoughtful," he agreed, moving forward to help load the refuse into a wagon. "We should get her something nice, don't you think?"

"Most definitely. Nicer than flowers."

"Any ideas?"

May thought about it while Rafe and his troops piled the wagon as high as they could. It was the only work he'd be able to do on the stable for the next few days—he owed Bill Jennings a new length of fence that he couldn't put off any longer.

"Ooh, I know."

"Enlighten me, sweetling."

"Her favorite color is blue, and she needs a new silk gown. All of the silk ones got water damaged, and she had to throw them out."

"May, *I* can't purchase Felicity a dress. Everyone will think we're . . ." He trailed off, having no clue how to describe the impropriety to a little girl.

"Lovers?" May finished for him.

Uh-oh. Rafe squatted down beside her. "Where did you hear that word?"

"Mrs. Denwortle. I heard her telling Mrs. Wadsworth that you and Felicity are wanted lovers."

He was confused for a moment. "Wanton lovers?"

"Yes."

If Mrs. Denwortle was willing to gossip in the presence of the little sister of one of her victims, his battle with her was about to escalate into a war. "Ah. Do you know what it means?"

She shrugged. "That you love each other, and you kiss. I knew that already, though."

His mother would be laughing right now if she knew he was trying to explain proper behavior to anyone, much less a little girl. Rafe decided to give it a try, anyway. "Your sister and I do kiss sometimes, and I like her very much. I hope she feels the same way about me. But, it's a very . . . irregular situation, with us all living here at Forton, and the most polite—and most correct—thing to do is not to talk about it."

May grimaced at him. "I know that. I'm not a complete sapskull, Rafe."

So much for that. After further discussion, Rafe discovered that Lis's birthday was three weeks hence, and he and May decided that she should be the one to purchase the gown so that the two of them could give it to Felicity as an early birthday present.

In the meantime, all the promises and bribes he'd exchanged for assistance with Forton Hall seemed to come due at once, leaving him so busy and exhausted that for several days he barely had time to exchange two words with Felicity, much less coax her into being with him again. Every day Deerhurst sent her flowers or candy, while Rafe could do nothing but stew and imagine seventy-three ways to kill a damned earl.

*   *   *

Felicity knew something was bothering Rafe, and she could guess what it must be. It had been over a week since he'd sent the letter to the Marquis of Warefield in London, and there'd been no reply. He would want to be rid of Forton by autumn, and with the Season over and August approaching, he was running out of time.

Part of her was hoping the marquis would answer just late enough to keep Rafe in Cheshire for the winter. Maybe spending an additional three or four months at Forton Hall would convince him to stay. She'd received one polite rejection to her application to teach at a girls' school in Bath, and nothing else. Resolutely she sent out another dozen inquiries, worry tugging at her. If she couldn't find a position soon, Deerhurst's proposal would be the only option left to her.

The way Rafe had been galloping about the countryside for the past week, gone from sunrise till after sunset, she couldn't tell what he was up to. Certainly not Forton—he hadn't touched the gardens or the remains of the stable in days. And when he was there, he was so tired he fell asleep in his chair half the time while she and May read in the morning room. Worse, he hadn't even kissed her since the morning after the stable's demolition. And improper as it was, she wanted to be with him again. She wanted him to hold her and touch her and love her, as much as she loved him.

She heard him come into the house, and in surprise glanced up at the clock, stuffed between three vases of flowers and a box of chocolates on the mantel. It wasn't even noon. Her pulse speeding helplessly, she straightened her hair and returned to perusing the estate ledgers, looking for spare change.

"May I carry it?" May whispered from the hallway, and Rafe's low murmur responded. Felicity smiled and continued working.

Rafe cleared his throat from the doorway, and with a pretended start she looked up. "Oh, my, you're back early. Is everything all right?"

"Splendid. Do you have a moment?"

"Well yes, of co—"

"No, you're doing it all wrong," May said, elbowing past him into the morning room, a little dark mouse fearlessly pushing aside a great tawny lion. In her hands she carried a large box tied with a pretty blue ribbon. "Happy birthday!"

"My goodness! But May, you know it's another fortnight until my birthday."

"You see," Rafe said, grinning as he dropped into the chair beside her, "*you* did it wrong. You should have let me explain first."

May set the box in Felicity's lap. "It's just an early gift. From Rafe and me."

Felicity looked at the two conspirators. May was clearly excited, and Rafe, though he looked tired, smiled at her with merry green eyes.

"Thank you, then. But it wasn't necessary."

"Open it," Rafe said, nudging the box with his fingers.

She smiled up at him, then pulled the bow loose and handed it to May, who immediately knotted it into a pirate sash and tied it around Rafe's forehead.

"That's how I imagined you looked at the helm of your pirate ship when we first saw you." Felicity laughed, tugging a lock of his hair over the ribbon. "Doesn't he look rakish, May?"

"Lucifer's big bottom," May snorted, "will you open the blasted present, Lis?"

"That's quite enough, you silly little chit," Rafe drawled. "You're going to get me in trouble."

Felicity was unable to keep from laughing. "Too late."

Steeling herself for whatever oddity her sister and Rafe might have deemed appropriate for a birthday present, she slowly lifted the lid from the box. Paper obscured its contents, and she brushed it aside. And froze. "Oh, my," she breathed.

"It's a gown," May offered into the silence, when Felicity couldn't say anything else.

"Yes . . . yes, I can see that." Her fingers shaking and tears gathering in her eyes, she lifted the deep blue silk gown out of the box.

"We used one of your day muslins for the measurements," Rafe said softly. "I hope it fits."

The neck and short, puffy sleeves were edged in ivory lace, as was the flowing skirt. Tiny white flowers sprinkled the upper part of the gown like glimpses of stars at dusk, while the gathered waist and skirt darkened into solid twilight.

"Do you like it?" her sister asked.

She smiled through her tears. "It's exquisite."

"Rafe and I looked at patterns and catalogs for hours. Mrs. Denwortle said it would be too dark and you wouldn't like it, but Rafe told me to tell her that just by looking at her I could see that she had excessively good taste, but I would stay with my own choice of materials." May giggled. "Mrs. Denwortle stared at me for a whole minute, and then she turned red as a beet and said, 'That Bancroft fellow is a very bad influence on you, young miss.'"

"Lis?"

Felicity looked up at Rafe. "It's too grand," she blurted. "I've never seen anything so beautiful."

He looked puzzled. "But May said you had silk gowns."

"Not like this." Rafael Bancroft had spent his

life among the wealthiest, loftiest families of England. His idea of a proper silk dress was completely different from one she would choose for herself. "I can't accept this, Rafe."

"Felicity, don't be such a pea-goose," May complained.

Rafe stood, his gaze still on Felicity. "May, fetch your sister a handkerchief, will you? Now?"

"Oh, all right." She obviously knew she was being gotten rid of, because she closed the door on her way out.

"You said you liked it," Rafe said, coming forward to kneel at her feet.

"I do. But you have no money, and it's . . . it's too beautiful for words."

"I want to see you in it. And it's *my* blunt—I'll do with it as I please." Gently he took the gown out of her fingers and laid it in the box, then took her hands in his. "And I please to please you, Lis."

A tear ran down her cheek. "I don't know what to say."

"Say thank you and kiss me, before you-know-who comes back."

"Thank you," she whispered, and touched her lips to his.

He sighed, leaning closer to kiss her back. She wanted to melt onto the floor with him, to sink into his warm, sure embrace.

"Rafael! Are you here, m'boy?"

Rafe tore his mouth from hers so quickly she nearly fell out of the chair. As he stood, the morning room door opened.

"Rafael, are you—"

"Quin?"

While Felicity watched, stunned, Rafe strode toward the tall, blond, impeccably dressed man

standing in the doorway. The Marquis of Warefield
had arrived.

"What the devil are you doing here?" Rafe demanded, eyeing him suspiciously.

Warefield raised his eyebrows. "You asked for
help."

"I asked for money."

"It's the same thing."

"No, it's not. You—"

"And who might this be?" The marquis's sharp
green eyes took in the shabby, cluttered room, the
scattering of account ledgers, the gown draped
across the box, and then paused on Felicity.

Hurriedly she stood, smoothing the skirt of her
simple yellow muslin, and curtsied. "Lord Warefield."

"Quin, this is Felicity Harrington. Lis, my
brother."

"Harrington?" the marquis repeated. "Wasn't it
Nigel Harrington you—"

"Yes. It's a very long story. How's Maddie?"

"You can ask her yourself."

"She's here, as well?" Rafe looked even more
discomposed, and absurdly pleased. With a stab of
jealousy, Felicity wondered just who Maddie might
be.

Warefield nodded. "She decided we should provide accompaniment."

Rafe narrowed his eyes. "Accompaniment to
what?"

"I say!" another male voice yelled from the
foyer, "it's an assassin! Get away from me with
that!"

Felicity's eyes locked with Rafe's. "May," they
said at the same time, and bolted past Warefield for
the door.

Chapter 11

Rafe sprinted into the foyer. May, her hair-brush clenched in one hand, had Francis Henning backed into a corner. Before she could wallop Henning, Rafe scooped her up into his arms. Torn between amusement and terror at the sight of the little warrior, he swept her around and set her on the bottommost stair.

"It's all right, sweetling. They're harmless." He glanced over his shoulder as Quin entered the foyer behind Felicity. "Relatively."

"Everyone keeps coming into our house without asking," she complained, reluctantly handing over the hairbrush.

"*Our* house?" Robert Fields looked about for someone to take his greatcoat, then shrugged and folded it over his arm. "I suddenly find myself greatly intrigued, Bancroft."

With a last warning glance at May, Rafe straightened and turned around, belatedly removing the ribbon from around his forehead. Damn, it looked as though half of London had come to Cheshire. "Welcome, everyone, to Forton Hall."

"Or what's left of it." Robert snorted. "You have some sort of frenzied celebration here, lad? Must have been spectacular."

"Oh—ha, ha, I get it." Francis chuckled. "He brought down the house, eh?"

The comments offended Rafe, though he supposed his own words on first viewing Forton Hall had been even less charitable. "You should have seen it a month ago, but no, I'm afraid I can't take credit for it. So, which brave souls have ventured into the wilds of Cheshire with you?"

He knew all of them, of course, but the introductions gave him a moment to collect his wits. Quin and Maddie he could tolerate, though their timing might have been better. As for the rest, whatever homesickness he'd felt for the excitement of London vanished in his consternation at seeing Lady Harriet Mayhew and Jeanette Ockley, hanging on either arm of Stephen Calder. Both ladies knew him more intimately than he wanted Lis to know, and he cursed under his breath. To add to the torture, they'd brought along Rose Pendleton, who could create gossip out of two peoples' placement in a cemetery.

Quin and Maddie made the party eight, though he hardly regarded them as part of Robert's horde. At least his father hadn't decided to visit Cheshire. Rafe shuddered. "How did you know where to find me?"

"Received your letter, my lad. You sounded so glum, we decided to come cheer you up."

Rafe forced a chuckle and edged closer to Robert. "If I'd wanted you to visit, Fields, I would have invited you," he muttered.

"Oh, tosh," his crony drawled. "We're on our way to Lakeford Abbey to spend the rest of the summer with Harriet's parents, but we couldn't resist stopping by to see you."

Rafe knew very well that they hadn't just "stopped by"; they wanted to see what he was up to. It was a game he was familiar with, though it had never been played on him before. He felt like beating Fields senseless. If he remembered anything his father had ever bellowed at him, though, it was never to look out of one's depth, whether that was where one had landed or not. "It's only fair to warn you that we're rather rustic here at the moment."

"I think we'll manage," Quin said dryly. "Might I have a word with you?"

Sooner rather than later, he would have to talk with his brother. Felicity, though, hadn't moved from the doorway, and stood looking from him to his guests as though she'd opened the wrong door and mistakenly walked into hell. "Yes. In just a moment," he said to Quin. "May, will you show my guests to rooms?" Without waiting for an answer he returned to Felicity and took her elbow.

She started and moved away. "May, do as Mr. Bancroft says, please. I'll put some water on for tea." Finally she turned her gaze on him, and his temperature dropped several degrees at the hooded fury in her eyes. "Mr. Bancroft, I believe your guests will have luggage." With that she was gone down the hallway in an angry flurry of yellow muslin.

Though May still looked as if she wanted to begin whacking people, she led the way upstairs. Scowling, Rafe stepped out onto the drive. Five damned coaches waited there, and he had no blasted stable. Drivers, groomsmen, valets, and maids all stood chatting and looking about, obviously waiting for the Forton household staff to appear.

"Where are your servants?" Quin murmured, standing at his elbow.

"I'm selling the place, remember?"

"Ah."

With that the marquis stepped past him and effortlessly organized the drivers and valets into footmen. The mounds of baggage began disappearing into the house. The coaches vanished around to the stable yard, and finally he and Quin stood on the shallow front steps alone.

"Your letter surprised me," the marquis said conversationally, and stepped down to the drive. "I thought for certain you'd have sold Forton Hall by now, and be on your way to China."

They strolled around the side of the house. At the sight of the demolished stable and the horses, including Aristotle, being staked out in the meadow, Quin paused. "I see there have been some complications. Care to enlighten me?"

"Why didn't you just send the blunt?" Rafe asked instead, picking up a stone and tossing it into the pile of lumber. "It was hardly a fortune."

"No, it wasn't. Perhaps I wanted to see you again, before you vanished."

"Look, Quin, if you want me to apologize for being such a boor when I left London, I will."

His brother stopped. "You think I came all this way to demand an apology?"

"I'm a bit rattled right now," Rafe snapped. Quin already knew he was out of his depth, so he didn't see any reason to deny it. "I don't know what to think."

"Who's Felicity Harrington?"

Quin might have been a blasted foxhound, the way he picked up a scent. "Nigel Harrington's sister." He started off again, making for the creek. After a moment Quin caught up to him. "And before you ask, no, she had no idea what her brother was up to. I arrived here to find the house falling apart, and her and May salvaging through the wreckage. That stupid rum puppy gambled away his inheritance with his sisters still living on it.''

"And his sisters are still living on it."

"I couldn't throw them out! Gads, what sort of monster do you think I am?"

"None at all," the marquis answered. "Merely making conversation. Pray continue."

"Not much else to tell," Rafe hedged, unwilling to discuss Felicity until he had her sorted out in his own mind. "I looked for a buyer, then decided I'd get a better price if I did some restoration work. Hence the letter to you."

"And the one to Mr. Robert Fields and company?"

"You sound like a damned solicitor, Warefield. It was just to Fields, and it wasn't a bloody invitation. That was his own idea."

"So why don't you want any of us here?"

Rafe stopped again, remembering why it was he found his brother so blasted annoying. "I don't need the kind of company that stretches you out on the rack and sticks pins into your sensitive parts."

Quin chuckled. "That leaves out nearly everyone."

"What do you mean, 'nearly'?"

The marquis only continued touring the yard and garden. Chafing, and badly wanting to go make things right with Felicity, Rafe stayed at his side. At his brother's casual questions, he found himself explaining every minor detail of work done and planned, while Quin just listened and let him babble.

"So are you going to lend me the two thousand quid, or not?" Rafe finally asked, stopping outside the kitchen entry.

"I don't see any difficulty with that. You've got a sound plan. And as you said, the improved sale value should more than compensate both of us.''

"Thank you, Warefield. I'm sorry I said you were stodgy."

Quin lifted an eyebrow, but before he could reply, the metallic clatter of falling pots echoed out from the kitchen window. Felicity was probably selecting weapons with which to murder him.

"Excuse me a moment," he said, and turned for the house.

"I'll just continue my tour," Quin said to his back. "Don't mind me."

Rafe ignored him and shoved open the door. "You all right, Lis?" he asked, stepping inside.

Impatiently she pushed a lock of hair out of her face. "You *invited* these people?" she snapped. "And you didn't tell me?"

"I did *not* invite them. They just came."

"Well, send them away!"

He frowned. "I can't do that; it would look very ill. And they're friends of mine."

Felicity flung a pan onto the table. "All right. Did you happen to consider, though, who is supposed to clean the bedchambers, light the fires, and prepare their meals? Or do you expect me to do it?"

He loved her stubborn practicality—most of the time. "Don't blame me! It's not my fault!"

"That does not answer my question!"

"Lis—"

"If you feel so glum," she interrupted, "then why stay?" A single tear coursed down her cheek, and she impatiently brushed it away.

"So *that's* why you're angry."

"No, it's not!"

Her voice faltered, and he realized just how hurt and abused she must feel. "Actually," he said, walking up to her as she turned her back, "I'm not at all glum."

"Then why would you write your friends to tell them how unhappy you are?"

He looked at her slender shoulders, shaking with either anger or tears. Or both. "I didn't, Lis. Truly. Robert made that up as an excuse, probably because he can't conceive of anyone enjoying themselves without him about."

"Oh, really?" She kept her back squarely to him. Running out of ammunition, he slid his hands around her waist to pull her against him. Felicity elbowed him in the ribs and moved away.

"Oh, no, you don't. You are not going to seduce me into not being angry with you, Rafe. How do you think it feels, to have the best of London here with Forton so . . . dismal?"

"They're hardly the best, Lis," he protested.

"I don't care! It's humiliating."

That stopped him.

She slammed another pot onto the stove. "I will make them tea, and I will prepare dinner for them this evening. After that, you are on your own, Bancroft. As you said, you hired me to keep your accounts—not to be your servant." She stalked up to him and shook a ladle at his chest. "And don't touch me again." With that she scooped up a tray holding a teapot and half a dozen mismatched cups, and stalked out toward the main part of the house.

"Damnation," Rafe muttered, and squatted down to gather the kitchen implements she'd flung about. Then he straightened. Quin had promised the two thousand quid—which left him his remaining sixty to do with as he pleased. And regardless of whose fault this mess was, he had a great deal to make up for.

*   *   *

Felicity thought she'd begun to know Rafe Bancroft—that he was kind and thoughtful, and that he
cared for her. Then he had to go and invite his
London friends to visit, so she could see how un-
cultured and shabby she looked in comparison.
And whether he'd actually tendered the invitation
or not, it was still his fault they were here.

All the women were lovely, especially the petite
redhead who'd stood watching Rafe so intently
while he welcomed everyone to Forton Hall. She
reached the top of the stairs with the tea tray, and
paused as she heard May's voice.

"Oh, my goodness," a woman's voice replied.
"You and your sister must have been terrified."

"I was, but Felicity said we would have an adventure and sleep in the morning room."

The closest bedchamber door stood open, and
Felicity leaned forward to peek inside. May sat at
the dressing table trying on a riding hat, while the
red-haired woman she'd noticed earlier helped a
maid put clothes into the chest of drawers.

"Your sister sounds very brave."

"Oh, she is. When Rafe jumped on her, she kept
yelling at me to run away."

Felicity flushed as the woman's hands stilled.
She wanted to run in and drag May out, but the
damage to her reputation had already been done.
She could hardly blame May for that, anyway.

"Mary, please excuse us," the lady said to her
servant. Felicity ducked back into the corner as the
maid left the room and went downstairs. "May,
why in the world did Rafe jump on your sister?"
she continued when the two of them were alone.

"He thought we were burglars."

"And did you run away, then?"

May took the hat off and set it aside. "Oh, no.

I hit him on the head with the tea kettle. That's the twenty-eighth way to kill a man.''

The woman grinned. "I'm thankful it didn't work.''

"Me, too. Rafe's top of the trees.''

"Yes, he is. And you're quite brave yourself.''

Felicity cleared her throat and stepped into the doorway. "Beg pardon, but I thought you might like some tea after your journey.''

The lady smiled at her, though her gaze remained speculative. "That sounds wonderful.''

May stood. "Maddie, have you met Felicity?'' she asked grandly. "Lis, this is Maddie, the Marchioness of Warefield.''

Rafe's sister-in-law. Hiding her sudden relief in a curtsy, Felicity then set the tray on the nightstand and poured a cup for the marchioness. "Sugar? I hope my sister hasn't been pestering you, Lady Warefield. She's notoriously curious.''

"Yes, please. But May's not bothering me at all. And call me Maddie, if you like. All my friends do.''

"May!''

The marchioness jumped as Rafe's voice carried up the staircase, and Felicity flinched. In the big, empty house they shouted for one another all the time, but now they had guests, for heaven's sake. Or rather, *he* had guests—but they would judge her, as well. She could see it, in Maddie Bancroft's face.

"I'm up here!'' May yelled back.

"May, behave!'' Felicity said sharply.

"He started it.''

Felicity gave Lady Warefield her tea and an apologetic look. "I beg your pardon, my lady— Maddie. I've been a little lax with May's behavior, I'm afraid.''

"Don't worry. Rafe tends to have a rather boisterous effect on people."

The marchioness grinned, and Felicity couldn't
help smiling in response. "He does that," she
agreed.

As if on cue, Rafe stepped into the doorway.
"Now *you* I am happy to see," he said, and strode
forward to kiss his sister-in-law. "Did you miss me
in London?"

"Not that we get to see you that frequently, but
yes." She chuckled again, and put a hand to her
heart. "A gray pall hangs over the entire town
when you're away."

"Glad to hear it."

"Your mother sends her regards, and asked me
to tell you that she's sending you a gift. And I
believe she and His Grace are going to Spain for
the remainder of the summer."

He nodded as he released her. "That's gift
enough. Better Spain than Cheshire." Spying May,
he lifted her in his arms and threw her over one
shoulder. "Excuse us." While May shrieked with
laughter, he gave Felicity a quick, innocent look
and then headed back downstairs with his burden.

"They seem to get along well," Lady Warefield
noted after a moment.

"Too well. I have a difficult time figuring out
who's responsible for most of the pranks." With
an exasperated chuckle, and feeling that she had at
least half an ally in Maddie Bancroft, Felicity collected the teapot and tray. "I'll leave you to finish
sorting your things out."

She went to find the rest of Forton Hall's guests,
but it proved to be a difficult task. None of them
were in their rooms, though numerous maids and
valets scurried about. She hadn't had a maid for
three years, and she looked enviously at the small

horde of servants. Her brother probably would have felt at home finally, and in all likelihood Rafe did, as well. She simply felt overwhelmed.

Finally she found the visitors, walking along the overgrown garden path toward the former west wing. "Good afternoon," she said, wishing again that Rafe was there so she could bash him on the head with something. "May I offer you some tea?"

"Ah, good afternoon, Miss Harrington, isn't it?" The fashionably dressed, dark-haired man Rafe had introduced as Robert Fields sketched her an elegant bow. "Leave it to Rafael to find the fairest treasure of Cheshire County." His amused, knowing gaze took in the other females present. "Until today, of course. The countryside is fairly bursting with beauty."

Lady Harriet Mayhew cuffed him on the shoulder with her fan. "Too little, too late. Here, my dear. Let me take that from you." She lifted the tray away from Felicity and put it on the cracked stone bench sitting to one side of the path. "You must tell us all about yourself, Miss Harrington. Or may we call you Felicity?"

"Please do." Felicity tried to hide her sudden nervousness in a smile. "There isn't much to tell, really. I grew up here, and when Mr. Bancroft—"

"You grew up here, at Forton Hall?"

"I told you, Rose," Mr. Fields put in, "Nigel Harrington was the lad from whom Rafe won the estate. Didn't realize it till the next morning, though, from what I hear." He pursed his lips, glancing at Felicity again.

"Neither would I have, if that Harem girl had been sitting on *my* lap." Francis Henning, a rotund man with an open grin and the beginnings of a balding pate, slapped the third man on the back.

"Nigel was gambling in a harem?" Felicity

blurted, then blushed. She must sound like an idiot. And they all seemed to know the true story of her brother's foolishness. If they spoke of it to anyone locally, she'd never be able to show her face in public again.

"Jezebel's Harem, I believe it's called," Lady Harriet explained with a condescending smile. "A men's club, of sorts."

"Like White's, only with ladies and shabby red carpet."

"Francis," Robert Fields chastised. "Not the ideal topic of conversation for gentler folk."

"So, Felicity." Another of the ladies, a striking brunette—Jeanette something—strolled forward to take her other arm. "You were living here when Rafe arrived to take over ownership, *n'est-ce pas*?"

"May and I were, yes. But—"

"*Mon dieu*, such close quarters for complete strangers. And yet, you seem to have managed, yes?"

Rose Pendleton giggled behind the curve of her parasol. "Jeanette, you wicked thing, y—"

"Actually, Mr. Bancroft took up residence in the stable," Felicity interrupted, trying to stop the complete wreck of her reputation.

Robert winked at the third man in their company, Mr. Calder, as she recalled. "Where is the stable, by the way?"

Felicity forced a laugh. "We had to tear it down. I did agree to allow him into the Hall when that happened."

Jeanette leaned closer, her short curls scratching at Felicity's ear. "So, do you still serve as mistress of the house?" she murmured in her faint French accent.

"Mr. Bancroft hired me to keep the estate accounts while he looks for a buyer."

"He's kept you on? How . . . unusual for him."

She couldn't tell if they were being deliberately malicious, or just intently curious. Before she could return fire, though, the group began chattering about some woman named Daphne, and how Rafe had worn her down over several weeks the summer before last, and then completely lost interest when her Spanish cousin had arrived in London.

"What do you expect? A dark-eyed Spanish girl arrives on the scene, and Rapunzel had already let down her hair, so to speak."

"Ah, Fields, that's brilliant," Mr. Henning chortled. "I'll have to remember that one. 'Let down her hair.' "

"Yes, Harriet, be thankful you got that bracelet after you let down your hair." Rose smiled slyly.

"Ah, dear Rafe," Jeanette mused. "I got a horse. Best mount I ever had, too, *mes amis*."

Everyone laughed, while Felicity felt ill. She knew she hadn't been Rafe's first lover, but they were all talking as though sexual intimacy—sexual intimacy with *Rafael*—was some sort of game.

"What does one do for excitement here?" Stephen Calder asked.

Grateful for the change of subject, Felicity said, "Pelford is just a few miles to the east."

"Yes, we drove through there. Quaint "

"And the Childe of Hale inn is just beyond that."

"What an unusual name," Lady Harriet said. "It must have a fascinating history."

"It's our greatest claim to notoriety," Felicity said, badly wanting to flee. "John Middleton grew up here some two hundred years ago. He was nearly eight feet tall, and even wrestled the champion of King James I. Our hale child, so to speak."

"Did he win?" Robert asked, his expression vaguely interested.

"Yes, he did."

"And then what happened?" Rose asked.

"I don't know—he never came back to Cheshire again." Felicity gathered up the remains of the tea. By the time she reached the haven of the kitchen, she felt as though she'd run a marathon. Never had she experienced such a tangle of innuendo and supposition. She couldn't even imagine what they would have been like if they weren't friends of Rafe's. If those were the sort of friendships London had to offer, she was glad she'd never been there.

Thanks to Rafe's last supply trip to Pelford, she managed to scrape together the makings of a meal, and for once she was grateful to have been forced to learn to cook. It wouldn't be a meal fit for kings by any stretch of the imagination, but it should be palatable.

She couldn't imagine Rafe living among such nonsense, but he did, and he was apparently quite popular in society's highest circles. With every word and every look so closely scrutinized, though, no wonder he wanted to escape to China. By the time May appeared to help slice vegetables, Felicity was nearly ready to make a dash for the Orient herself. "Where did you and Rafe vanish to?"

"I didn't go anywhere; I helped Maddie unpack. I like her. She's funny."

"Where did Rafe vanish to, then?" The oven was hot, and she swiped a wilting strand of hair back behind her ear.

"To hire mercenaries."

Felicity eyed her sister. "Beg pardon?"

May was nodding. "Rafe says you recruit volunteers, and you hire mercenaries. And you were so angry, he needed mercenaries."

"I was merely very surprised," Felicity retorted. "He might have told me he'd invited half of London to come calling." She paused. "*You* didn't know they were coming, did you?"

"No. And Rafe didn't invite them. They invaded."

Someone scratched at the kitchen door. "Come in," she called.

The door opened. "Excuse me, Miss Harrington, Miss May." Sally Greetham, Dennis's daughter, stepped timidly into the kitchen and curtsied.

"Hello, Sally. Is something wrong?"

"Oh, no, miss. Mr. Rafe said I should come and help you cook for your fine guests."

Anger flared through Felicity. "Sally, your family has been more than generous already. You don't have to—"

"Mr. Rafe said I was to let you know that . . ." She paused, closing her eyes in concentration, ". . . that I am being well compensated." The girl smiled and curtsied again. "He gave me a whole sovereign."

Grudging amusement at Rafe's audacity warred with Felicity's frustration. "Well, in that case, here." She handed over the bowl she'd been mixing.

Rafe himself skidded into the kitchen a few moments later, Ronald Banthe in tow. "Ah, you've met our cook, I see," he said jovially, flashing Lis one of his devastating smiles. "This is our footman. The butler will be here as soon as he finishes feeding his chickens."

Felicity knew him well enough by now to see the discomfort beneath his light banter. He glanced at her sideways, then guided Ronald through the kitchen.

"I think I have a coat and cravat that you can

wear, my boy. Remember, serve from the left and remove from the right."

"Rafe," she said, before he could escape.

He flinched. "Did I get it backward? I can never remem—"

"You got it right. Might I have a word with you? In private?"

"Of course. Ronald, wait here a moment."

Felicity led the way out the kitchen door to the stable yard. The trees already obscured the setting sun, and this evening the air had a definite chill. She wondered if they were in for another storm, and hoped it would pass them by. Though Forton wasn't hers any longer, she certainly didn't want it collapsing on a bunch of nobles.

A moment later Rafe stepped outside and shut the door behind him. "Lis, I know what you're going to say, and I'm truly, truly sor—"

"How much is this costing you?" she interrupted, folding her arms.

"With food and servants and whatever else I can't think of at the moment, I figured about twenty quid a week." He grinned briefly. "If they stay longer than three weeks, they'll starve to death."

She kept a serious expression on her face. "You can't afford this."

"Quin agreed to lend me the two thousand quid. So actually, yes, I can."

"And Sally, Ronald, and your butler?"

"Bill will only be available this evening, but Sally and Ronald are here for as long as you are." He reached out, as though to take her hand, and then stopped himself. "Lis, I am sorry. I never meant to embarrass or hurt you. As my father would say, it was typically idiotic of me."

Felicity looked at him. However poorly her brother's frequent schemes had gone, she couldn't ever remember him apologizing for the embarrassment or for the loss of funds. And his usual way of making amends was to buy her candy, or May a gift—he never did anything to actually set things right again. "It's all right," she said finally. "I'm not angry any longer."

"Then . . . " He cleared his throat, looking like a nervous schoolboy. "You told me not to touch you," he stated. "Is that still the way you feel?"

I want you to stay here with me forever, she wanted to say, but didn't dare. Instead she leaned up and kissed him, savoring the delicious shiver that ran through her at the long, soft touch. "Ask me again after you've become reacquainted with your lady friends," she murmured, and returned to the warm kitchen. Let him consider that, for a while.

Chapter 12

Now that London had arrived in Cheshire County, Rafe only wanted it to leave again.

His cronies would have been a welcome distraction to the Rafe Bancroft they'd last seen in London. To his surprise, he didn't seem to be that same Rafe Bancroft any longer.

It was a damned conundrum. He'd sought excitement all his life, yet he couldn't help thinking about the work that wasn't getting done with guests hanging about. And he had so much to do already, without leading tours and fishing trips, and coming up with other nonsensical amusements for people unable to keep themselves entertained long enough for him to fix a blasted fence.

"Are you daydreaming?" Robert Fields called, beckoning to him from beside the pond. "Come, lad, you promised to join me."

Rafe shook himself and approached. "Catch anything?"

"I don't think there's anything here to catch. You're just trying to keep us occupied so you can go knock down more buildings."

"You wouldn't be complaining, my boy, if you'd caught anything." Rafe sat on the grassy shore beside Fields. "The water level's down a little," he noted absently. "Not bad though, considering we haven't had rain in a fortnight."

Robert snorted. "You sound like a farmer. Tell me about Miss Harrington, Rafe. You've been doing some fishing yourself, I'll wager. Caught anything yet?"

Rafe looked at him coldly. "Miss Harrington is in my employ."

"Ah. Didn't think you had, or you wouldn't still be here."

That obviously wasn't true. But neither was it anyone else's damned business. They could gossip about him all they liked, but Felicity didn't need their London nastiness. "I'm only here to sell Forton Hall."

"I wagered Francis you'd head for the Orient first," Fields continued, waving his pole about in a fashion that would frighten off any fish that did happen to be in the area. "Fifty quid. So do me a favor and wherever you go, send a note saying you're in China."

Rafe nodded, fiddling with a blade of grass. Fifty quid would buy him enough shingles to finish the east wing roof. "So what's the consensus about Forton?"

"That it's a wreck," Robert answered. "Jeanette says it looks like the Bastille after the riots, only smaller and worse off." He chuckled. "That Harrington fellow wasn't as daft as he made out, was he?"

"Since he's the one who's traveling and I'm sitting here in Cheshire, I'd have to agree with you."

A small cart and driver passed down the road, just visible from where they sat, headed for Forton Hall. Red rose petals showed over the wooden lip of the cart.

"More guests?" Robert asked, noticing Rafe's

sour expression before he could cover it. "Sam the farmer, perhaps?"

"Flowers for Lis."

"And you say you're not in pursuit, Bancroft?"

"They're not from me. The Earl of Deerhurst down the lane sends them."

"The tale grows more and more interesting."

Rafe looked at him sideways. "How long did you say you were staying?"

"We haven't even gone hunting, yet. And the ladies were so looking forward to a country soiree."

"I hope they won't be too disappointed," Rafe said dryly. "A picnic's about all I can manage."

"Why should you care about our disappointment? You've all the entertainment you want. And if I'd known Miss Felicity Harrington was here all by herself, I might have come up with you in the first place. She's stunning."

She's mine. Rafe climbed to his feet and brushed off his breeches. "Leave her alone, Fields," he said.

"She *is* less helpless than your usual paramours, I must say. But she's a female, and she's lovely. Leaving her alone is out of the question. And who is this Deerhurst? Have we met?"

Rafe started back to the manor. "Go visit him and see for yourself. I imagine he'll be delighted to have civilized company."

Fields looked from the fishing pole to the still water and shrugged. "I'll just do that." Setting aside the pole, he stood. "Henning! Calder! I found someone for us to gossip with!"

Francis and Stephen emerged from behind the rubble of the stable, where they'd apparently been hunting rats with slingshots.

Rafe shook his head. As long as they were killing vermin and not his livestock, he had no complaints. That reminded him, though, that he had three cows near to calving. "Damnation."

"Something wrong?" Quin leaned against the wall beside the kitchen door and snacked on a peach.

"No. What are you doing out here?"

"Keeping an eye on Henning and Calder. They could kill someone with those slingshots."

"Hopefully each other." Rafe pushed open the kitchen door and leaned in. "May!" he called.

Felicity, standing at the table with Sally and trying to put together a menu for the evening, looked up long enough to glare at him. "I'll have our footman fetch her for you," she enunciated, her jaw clenched.

He grinned at her sudden propriety, then had to duck when she lobbed a potato at his head. "A tea kettle works better," he said, and backed out the door before she could grab one.

"I see you've upended things into your usual state of chaos," his brother noted, eyeing the potato as it rolled to a stop beside his highly polished Hessian boot.

"*You* try managing an estate with no servants, no money, a stubborn chit who makes you sleep out in the stable, and a little girl who wants to learn how to kill people."

The marquis brushed a speck of dust from his sleeve. "So now you're managing Forton Hall. I thought you were selling it."

Rafe stared at Quin for a long moment before he caught himself and turned away. "It's enough of a wreck already, don't you think?" he forced out. "I certainly don't want to make it any worse."

Quin seemed to accept the answer, for he only nodded and turned to watch the drivers hitching up a coach for Robert and company. Rafe barely noticed his cronies as they rolled off down the lane toward Deerhurst. Quin was right—and the realization of just how far he'd wandered off the path stunned him.

He was making far more progress in repairing Forton Hall than in getting rid of it. He hadn't even contacted his solicitor in the past ten days. "Quin," he asked slowly, knowing he'd be far wiser to keep his mouth shut, "if Forton Hall was in perfect condition, both wings intact, roof patched, stable restored, fences mended, and irrigation channels cleared, with tenants occupying all of the farmhouses and lands, how much would you say it would be worth?"

The Marquis of Warefield glanced at him, then turned a slow circle, surveying the land and surroundings with the experience of a lifetime's training. "It would only be a rough estimate," he said thoughtfully, coming to a stop, "but I would wager somewhere between seventy and eighty thousand pounds."

Rafe blinked. "That much?"

Quin shrugged. "It's small, but the land and location are prime. The owner would be wiser to concentrate on barley and wheat than livestock, but either or both would make him a decent income."

"Do tell." Deerhurst's offer hadn't been that far off the mark—but that didn't make Rafe feel any better. Forton was worth nothing near that at the moment.

"Mm-hm. Of course, bringing it up to prime condition would cost a good twenty thousand pounds. Earning that back would take years. You'll need a buyer who wants to occupy, rather than one looking for a short-term ownership and a mound of profits. Because they won't find it here."

Rafe's mouth went dry at the mention of the sum—not because it was so high and would represent virtual enslavement to repay it, but because he actually wanted to consider it. His brother was watching him and making no secret of it, which made him even more uneasy. Quin was warning him, and wanted him to know it.

Everything should have been so easy, and it wasn't. And he knew exactly why it had become so complicated: Felicity Harrington.

May came running up to him, a grin on her pretty face. She'd be as much a beauty as her sister in a few years. God help the bachelors then. "Where've you been, sweetling?" he asked.

"I was showing Maddie where my bedchamber used to be. She said it seemed a bit drafty now." May laughed.

Rafe grinned at her. At least one of the Harrington ladies was enjoying having guests. "I'm going to take a look at our cattle. Want to—"

"Yes. I'll fetch old Totle." She pranced off to where the bay stood staked out in the center of the meadow, grazing and ignoring the lowly coach horses around him.

"Old Totle?" Quin echoed, lifting an eyebrow.

"He's been reduced to child's pull toy. And I think he likes it." Rafe took a deep breath, his eyes still on May and Aristotle. "So, do you think anyone would consider making a loan of twenty thousand quid to fix up a rundown old place like this?"

"That would entail finding two fools—one to make the loan, and one to take it. And thankfully, neither one of us is a fool." With a last, meaningful glance, Quin strolled back toward the house.

Rafe looked after him. "Speak for yourself," he muttered.

*   *   *

Felicity closed her bedchamber door, and leaned her flimsy dressing table chair beneath the handle. It wasn't a very effective barrier, but at least it would keep May from barging into the room as she generally did.

"Oh, this is so foolish."

It was just a dress, for heaven's sake, and just another of Rafe's silly ideas. She had no idea why he'd announced at breakfast that this evening's dinner was to be formal, but she suspected it was because he wanted to see her in her new gown, knowing full well that she had nothing else formal to wear. Luckily for him, she wanted to see herself in it as well, and had been waiting all day for this. The dress lay on the bed, and she ran her fingers over the cool, soft silk.

She quickly shed her plain day gown and pelisse. Then, still listening for May's footsteps or, even worse, for Rafe's, she gathered the skirt in her hands and pulled it on over her head. The dark blue silk slid down to her ankles with a soft slithering whisper. Unwilling still to look into her dressing mirror, she awkwardly reached around to fasten the buttons running up the back.

With a silent prayer that she wouldn't look like a gawky harlot, she turned to face the mirror. And stopped. "Oh, my goodness."

The gown emphasized her slender waist and full, round bosom, and clung to her hips in a way that felt almost shamefully erotic. It shimmered a little as she moved, the fine material reflecting the lamplight. The sensual feel of it on her body reminded her of how she felt when she was with Rafe.

She brushed out her hair and put it up again into a loose bun. Curling black tendrils escaped to frame her face and caress her neck. Rafe had picked the perfect color for her, for skin that had seen a little too much sun for a proper lady, and the blue darkened her eyes almost to black.

Felicity gazed at herself. She didn't look like the self she saw most often—calm, cool, and tired. The dark eyes looking back at her knew far more than the former Felicity had, and the blush touching her cheeks had more to do with anticipation and excitement than with any makeup. Slowly she turned in a circle, wondering what Rafe would say when he saw her.

When she removed the barricade from her door and exited the bedchamber, ready for dinner, she could barely keep in the giddiness bubbling just under her skin. At the stair landing, though, her smile faded.

"So you simply pined away the Season, waiting for my return?" Rafe asked, lounging against the foyer wall below.

Jeanette ran her hand along the lapel of his magnificent dark gray coat. "How could I do anything else, when you didn't even say goodbye to me?"

"I said goodbye to you."

Her pretty, full lips lowered into a pout. "You gave me a horse, *mon amour*, last Season. A very poor substitute."

He grinned. "You manage to make that sound immodest."

She leaned up and kissed his chin. "With you, Rafael, everything is immodest. I left my door unlatched last night. I will do so again tonight. Come and visit me."

"Thank you for the invitation."

Jeanette backed off a little, eyeing him. "One day, I think you will grow tired of breaking hearts. Or you will run out of hearts to break. Who will you find to pursue then?"

"I'm all a-tremble," he murmured. "But don't

worry yourself. There's always a new pursuit.''

"And then the capture, and then the gift, and then you go to Africa or somewhere and forget the ladies you leave behind.''

"Ah, Jeanette, you almost make me feel home-sick.''

She smiled. "Good.''

The clocked chimed, off-key and wobbly since the last rain, and he looked up. He caught sight of Felicity before she could escape, and his easy smile froze. "Lis,'' he exclaimed, straightening.

Felicity nodded politely and continued down the stairs. *He never said he loved me*, she reminded herself as he came forward to meet her. He'd never said he intended whatever was between them to last. Just the opposite. And she'd told him to get reacquainted with his past lovers. *Stupid, stupid, stupid.* "Good evening.''

"Good evening.'' He stopped several feet from the foot of the stairs and ran his gaze up and down the length of her. "You are . . . absolutely stunning,'' he said, as his eyes returned to her face. "Do you like it?''

"Yes, it's very fine.'' She hesitated, then moved past him. "Excuse me. I must go see to May.''

A moment later she heard his footsteps following her, and she had to keep herself from breaking into a run. She was such a fool where Rafe Bancroft was concerned.

"Lis?''

She kept walking.

"Lis? Felicity?''

His hand touched her shoulder, then slid down her arm to close around her wrist. Gently but firmly, he pulled her around to face him. Despite her anger at him and disappointment in herself, the touch of his fingers against the sensitive inside of her wrist began a cascade of delicious shivers inside her.

"Is something wrong?" he asked.

Even if she couldn't help the way her body reacted to him, she could control what she did about it. "No," she answered. "I'm just trying to keep May from making a nuisance of herself."

His eyes searched hers. "She's in the kitchen with Sally. I tried to tie the bow on her dress, but I'm afraid I didn't do it very well. She said I have no concept of how to be a lady."

"I suppose that's a bit much for her to expect, even of you."

That stopped him, and the uncertain expression she found so blasted disarming touched his face again. "Are you angry with me again?"

"No."

"You truly are . . . extraordinarily lovely," he said.

"Does it make you feel homesick?" she asked hotly. The remainder of his guests clattered into the foyer behind them.

He blinked. "You heard that, did you?"

"I couldn't help it. Don't mind me, though. I know I have no claims on you, or on anything el—"

"I don't know how I feel when I look at you," he whispered. "But you . . . arouse every part of me. And that frightens me a little." He sketched a quick bow and strode off to escort his guests into the formal dining room.

That unsettled her, and she sat like a little mouse at the table, unable to summon a thought coherent enough to speak aloud. She was almost relieved when, halfway through the meal, the Earl of Deerhurst strolled into the room. "James," she exclaimed.

"Ah, Felicity." He bypassed the other glittering guests to take her hand and lift it to his lips. "You look radiant beyond words."

"Thank you."

Rafe stood. "What are you doing here?"

"Oh, my faux pas, Bancroft," Robert Fields contributed around a mouthful of chicken. "I invited him. We hit it off quite smashingly this afternoon, and I didn't think you'd mind."

Rafe looked from one to the other of them, all humor gone from his light eyes. Rolling his shoulders as though trying to release the tension there, he gestured at his brother. "Quin, the Earl of Deerhurst. Deerhurst, the Marquis of Warefield."

Quin gestured at an empty chair. "Deerhurst. Your land borders Forton Hall to the east, does it not?"

"Yes, it does, Lord Warefield." The earl sat and nodded politely to the other guests, while the ladies glanced at one another and twittered. Whether it was because he was handsome or because they sensed Rafe's frustration, Felicity didn't know. "And I find Deerhurst's location to be a most happy circumstance for two reasons."

"And what two reasons might those be?" Quin sent his brother a warning glance and resumed eating.

Out of the corner of her eye, Felicity watched Rafe hesitate and then slowly retake his seat. He looked annoyed in the extreme, and even the expression of polite interest he affixed to his face couldn't hide it. She glanced at Robert Fields, who'd spent most of the meal flirting with Jeanette Ockley within clear earshot of their host. Rafe had barely given the pair of them a second glance. If he was jealous, it wasn't over these other ladies. Suddenly she felt a little better about things.

"Well, I'm afraid the first reason is rather obvious." With a warm smile the earl gestured at Felicity.

Francis Henning laughed. "Have to be a demmed turtle not to see that attraction." He toasted her with his glass of wine.

"Thank you, Mr. Henning."

Felicity smiled at his jovial obtuseness as he insisted she call him Francis. Rafe had told her that Francis considered himself a complete wit, while his cronies gave him credit for being half of one.

"And what is the second happy circumstance you mentioned, my lord?" the Marchioness of Warefield asked.

"I don't know whether Bancroft has mentioned it or not, but I have made him what I consider to be a rather generous offer for Forton Hall."

"Bravo!" Stephen applauded, the gesture echoed by Francis and Lady Harriet. "Our traveler may begin traveling."

Felicity looked at Rafe again. He'd dropped the pretense of looking polite, and glared with clear fury at Deerhurst. Before he could rise, though, Lord Warefield did so. Firmly he placed a hand on his brother's shoulder.

"A toast then," he said, lifting a glass in his other hand, "to interesting possibilities."

"To interesting possibilities," Felicity repeated in unison with the others, though she wasn't certain either she or Forton Hall would survive if things became much more interesting than they already were.

Except for Deerhurst's smug, intolerable presence, the evening went fairly well. After the guests retired to the morning room for pie and charades, Rafe helped Sally and Ronald clear the table. One of the mismatched chairs hadn't quite made it through the evening, though unfortunately it had been Francis's rather than the earl's. Since the noise indicated his guests were enjoying themselves without his assistance, he sat cross-legged on the dining room floor to hammer the errant leg back into place in time for breakfast.

"You used to spend your evenings in a more exciting manner."

Rafe glanced up as Quin leaned into the doorway, then went back to his hammering. "So did you. Slightly, anyway."

"Hm. *I'm* happily married. What's your excuse?"

"The chair's broken."

"Why didn't you mention that Deerhurst had offered for the estate?"

With an irritated sigh Rafe set aside the hammer. "Because I don't want to sell it to him." He stood and righted the chair, rocking it to test its stability.

"Forgive my abject stupidity, but why not?"

"Because I don't want to."

"Because of Miss Harrington, you mean." The marquis closed the door and took a seat at the table.

"Miss—Felicity? She's written looking for a position elsewhere, and is just waiting for an answer. She has nothing to do with this."

Quin eyed him. "Which is why you looked like a mad wolf when Deerhurst joined us."

"He's a clod, and I don't like him."

"Does Felicity?"

In the past, Quin would have left off pestering when he grew tired of Rafe's flippancy and well-honed evasiveness. Apparently tonight he was feeling up to a challenge. "When did you get to be such a blasted gossip?"

"I'm merely curious about my brother."

"Then ask about me, and not every other damned inhabitant of Cheshire."

"Very well." The marquis looked him in the eye. "What are you still doing here?"

Rafe rocked the chair so hard it fell over. "Bugger off, Warefield."

His brother looked undaunted. "Interesting way to speak to someone lending you money."

With a scowl Rafe righted the chair again and sat on it. "I don't know why I'm still here. All right? And I'd just like to figure it out before I go." He rubbed at his cheek. His scar was itching, which it hadn't done for years. But then, he hadn't been this tense for a long time, either. "Quin, if I asked, would you lend me twenty thousand pounds?"

For a moment his brother was silent. "No, I wouldn't."

He shot to his feet again. "Why in God's name not? You said I could sell this wreck for seventy thousand if it was in prime condition."

The marquis leaned forward. "Two thousand pounds will keep you at Forton for a month or so. That's enough time for you to figure out what it is you're doing here."

"Twenty thousand would see us both with more profit," Rafe argued against the knowing cynicism in his brother's voice. He needed to know whether he had Quin's support—whatever idiotic course he ended up taking.

"Twenty thousand would mean repairing every last piece of damage to the property. You'd be trapped here for over a year before you could even begin to look for a buyer. If you want to run an estate, run one of mine, where at least the ceiling won't cave in on you."

Rafe strode to the window and back again. "I

don't want one of your damned estates. I want to repair this one.''

"It's a poor investment. No.''

"Twenty thousand pounds is nothing to you! What do you care if you make a profit off it in one year or in ten years, if at all?''

Quin folded his hands on the table, clearly angry, and just as clearly unwilling to be pulled into a shouting match. "Have you ever considered that Miss Harrington would benefit from having you stay and support her and repair her home?''

Rafe stopped. "What?''

"She has every reason to encourage you to stay here. Have you considered that?''

"You're insane! I told you, she's already written looking for a position!''

"And how is her search going?''

"I . . . I don't know. Not well.'' He hadn't thought to ask. He hadn't wanted to ask, because he didn't want her going anywhere.

"Do you care for her?''

Rafe slammed his fist on the table. "Yes, I care for her. She's been through a great deal, and I admire her courage.''

"And she's lovely.''

"Yes, damn it, I'd noticed that, too. Leave off.''

Slowly Quin pushed to his feet. "Before you tie yourself to Forton Hall for ten more minutes, little brother, you'd best figure out whether she genuinely cares for you, or if she simply wants to keep a roof over her head. Because from what I've seen, Rafael, you're not exactly acting like yourself.''

Rafe stood where he was for a long moment after his brother left the dining room. He knew precisely what Quin was implying: that he was in love with Felicity, and that she was using his infatuation to hold on to Forton Hall.

He sat down again. Yes, Lis was beautiful and bright and charming and compassionate and very, very practical. And he absolutely did not want to be in love with her. He'd been half in love with Maddie when he met her, but he'd known she loved Quin, and he'd had no trouble accepting that. This was different. This was jealous rages and yearning and endless thoughts and daydreams—and he didn't want it.

"Damnation," he snarled, slamming his fist against the oak table.

He was insane. That was the only logical explanation. And it was certainly the only reason he could come up with for asking his brother for a loan of twenty thousand bloody quid, for God's sake.

The door creaked open, and he started and looked up. He was both relieved and disappointed that it was Robert Fields and not Felicity who entered the room. When she was about, things just made more sense. And he needed some of that.

"Robert," he said brusquely, standing. He was moping like a damned sick dog. "I was just about to join you."

Fields waved a hand at him. "Don't really care. You have any cigars?"

"No, and why don't you care?"

"You've become a damned dull pot, Rafe. Cattle this, roof that. What a bore. Come with us to Lakeford Abbey before you turn into a farmer. Or worse, a Parliamentarian."

Rafe looked at him. "Ha, ha."

"What's so amusing? I'm bloody serious, lad. You're wasting away here. Even Jeanette says you're halfway to being a cold fish, and from what I hear, you helped her find religion."

Rafe scowled. "Beg pardon?"

Fields wandered over to contemplate the stack of water-damaged paintings leaning against the wall. "You know, 'oh God, yes, yes, God.'" He turned around. "Although I suppose it was actually '*mon dieu*,' considering." He grinned and took a snuff box from his coat pocket. "Which deity does Miss Harrington invoke? Demeter is the goddess of farming, isn't she?"

Rafe eyed Fields darkly. "You go too far."

"Oh, come now, Bancroft, she's stunning. No one blames you for doing a little planting while you're in the country. But Cheshire? Come, come. I imagine some of those Caribbean native girls could have *you* finding religion. And American chits are known for their independence, are they not?"

No one compared his Felicity to a meaningless string of whores, high flyers, and flighty, bored nobles' daughters. "Robert," Rafe said in a quiet, controlled voice, "get out of my house."

Fields took snuff and returned the box to his pocket. "You see what I mean? In another month you'll be as stodgy as your brother. In fact, you're lucky you still have the energy to plow Miss Harrington. Though if you don't, I certainly do."

Rafe punched him. Fields rocked backward and stumbled over a chair, going down hard. Angrier than he could ever remember being, Rafe watched Robert climb to his feet. Fields swung at him, and Rafe ducked to avoid the blow. His left fist shot out again at Robert's face, followed by a flashing right. Fields doubled over and collapsed, clutching his stomach.

"Get out of my house," Rafe repeated coldly, and left the room.

Chapter 13

Felicity chuckled as Francis Henning and Rose Pendleton performed a scene between Oberon and Titania from *A Midsummer Night's Dream*. She wasn't certain whether they meant the reading to be amusing or not, but even the Marchioness of Warefield was laughing helplessly.

She would have enjoyed it even more if Rafe hadn't abandoned his guests and left the hosting to her, and she added another black mark against him to her mental tally board. Lately he'd earned a considerable number of those. And when Lord Warefield walked in a moment later and took the seat beside his wife, she had the distinct impression that Rafe had been earning black marks from his brother, as well.

The marquis gave her a serious, somber look, then murmured something to his wife. Maddie answered him in the same tone, and glanced at Felicity as well. Even though neither of them looked in her direction again, their discussion continued for several minutes. She drummed her fingers restlessly on the arm of her chair, wondering what in the world their discussion had to do with her.

Everything had been so much simpler before Rafe had appeared. She and May would still have lost Forton Hall, but she wouldn't have lost her heart as well. When the time came to leave, there would have been no clinging to hopes and dreams, because there would have been no one to kindle them.

It wouldn't have been so painful if Rafe Bancroft had been someone she could trust, someone on whom she could rely. Looking at his silly friends and former lovers, and his own ramshackle dreams for the future, though, it was obvious that she couldn't—and that she would be worse than a fool if she did.

The drawing room door burst open. Robert Fields, his lip and nose swollen and bloody, staggered into the room.

"Henning? Calder? Fetch my pistol!" he bellowed.

"Fields," the Marquis of Warefield snapped, coming to his feet, "what in hell happened to you?"

"Your damned mad brother! That's what happened to me. And I'm going to blow the bastard's head off!"

"You are not!" May shrieked, running at him.

Felicity grabbed her sister by the ribbon ties and hauled her back into her chair. "Sit still," she hissed.

May took one look at her face and closed her mouth. Rose fainted into Francis Henning's arms and Jeanette dropped her teacup, inconveniently breaking one of the two matching cups that Felicity had remaining.

Scowling at the chaos, Felicity stood and smoothed her skirt. This nonsense was not going to happen in her home—her former home. "Perhaps you should continue this elsewhere," she said in her calmest voice.

Fields turned on her. "You're the bloody reason for this, you scabby wh—"

The marquis stepped between them, blocking her from his furious view. "That's enough, Fields," he said sternly.

Rose miraculously recovered in time to gasp at Fields's language.

The Earl of Deerhurst materialized at Felicity's arm, though she had forgotten his presence. "This is no place for a lady," he said. "Allow me to escort you from here. I knew Bancroft wasn't fit to run Forton Hall. Look how he and his friends disgrace it—and you."

The other ladies, with the exception of Maddie, stood with their hands over their mouths in shock, while they glanced at one another in delight. Felicity could hear the rumors beginning already. Thank God she would never have the chance to show her face in London. She wouldn't be able to, now.

"Fields, calm down," Francis Henning urged uneasily. "We're all a bit bored here. No reason to go about blowing people's heads off, though."

"Felicity, please. You don't need to see this," the earl urged again, taking her elbow.

She shrugged out of his grip. "You should be more concerned about May," she snapped, keeping her attention on Fields. Everyone was always trying to offer her assistance where she didn't need it, and no one was going to shoot Rafe Bancroft if she had anything to say about it.

He sputtered and backed away. "I . . . you . . . well, of course. Come along, Miss May."

"I'm staying."

Rafe appeared in the doorway. "I told you to leave, Fields," he said blackly, and Felicity was shocked at the fury in his face. "I won't say it again."

The two men glared at each another. Finally
Fields pulled out of Stephen Calder's tentative grip.
"I wouldn't stay here for another minute to save
my life," he snarled, and wiped blood from his
chin. "Come on—I've had more than my fill of
Cheshire, and Forton Hall."

He stalked past Rafe, going out of his way to
avoid his broad-shouldered former host in the doorway. The rest of the guests followed him in silence.
Francis came last, and he stopped just out of range
of Rafe's fists. "He'll spread this all about London,
you know."

Rafe nodded stiffly. "I know."

"This isn't at all the thing," Henning muttered,
heading down the hallway. "Blasted hot-blooded
bucks. You never listen to me."

A flurry of valets and maids hurried upstairs to
pack, but Felicity barely noticed the loud activity.
Rafe continued to stand in the doorway, looking as
though he would like to pummel Fields—or anyone
else who dared speak to him.

She'd never seen him like this. Abruptly she remembered that he had been a soldier. He was so
easygoing, she forgot he could be deadly. And startling as his anger was, it gave her another key to
understanding him. She watched him closely for
any sign of what had set him off. He clenched and
unclenched his fists several times before he took a
deep breath. "Well? Anyone else?" He glanced
pointedly at the Earl of Deerhurst, still posed uncertainly between her and May.

James stirred, avoiding Rafe's angry gaze. "I
shall take my leave as well." He bowed. "Lord
and Lady Warefield, I am delighted to have made
your acquaintance."

"Deerhurst."

The earl hesitated beside Felicity. "You should

leave here, my dear, before he does the same thing to you," he murmured in her ear.

"Oh, please, James," she scoffed. However angry Rafe might be, he wouldn't hurt her or May. He'd had plenty of opportunity when they'd first met, if that had been his aim or his nature.

The earl blinked, obviously surprised by her ire. "Very well, but I don't think you're seeing things clearly. At the least, though, you should convince him to sell Forton to me, so we can get him out of Cheshire posthaste."

"James, go." She nodded curtly, worried that the earl would send Rafe into another rage. He didn't appear to need much provocation. "Thank you for the advice. I shall consider it."

When Deerhurst had left, Rafe rubbed his knuckles and glanced at his brother. "Don't look at me that way," he grumbled. "He deserved worse."

"Whatever he deserved," the marquis returned sharply, "your actions reflect on all of us. Robert Fields is well liked at court. With all the new laws restricting the rights of the nobility, we can't afford—"

"Bugger off, Warefield," Rafe snapped. "No one—*no one*—insults my friends or my family."

"I thought Robert was your friend," Maddie said quietly.

He glanced at her. "I just found out differently." Rafe caught Felicity's eyes and held her gaze for the space of several heartbeats before he left the room.

The marquis said something else to Maddie, but she shook her head. "Leave me out of this nonsense," she said, and held her hand out to May. "Come introduce me to Polly Doll and Mr. Bear."

A moment later Felicity stood alone in the drawing room with Lord Warefield. He strolled over to close the door. Felicity swallowed, wondering what could possibly happen next, and whether he was going to warn her about Rafe now, as well.

"Rafe says you've applied for a position as a governess," he began conversationally, facing her. "Have you had any positive response?"

"No. I've had two rejections so far, but I haven't heard yet from a distant cousin in York. She liked me as a child, and I think she will take me on."

"You don't wish to stay at Forton Hall?"

She had the feeling he was aiming the conversation toward something specific, but she was willing to play along—for Rafe's sake. "What I wish for doesn't signify, my lord. Your brother has been kind enough to allow my sister and me to remain here until we find residence elsewhere."

He paused, as though assessing her answer. "What do you think of Lord Deerhurst's offer to purchase Forton Hall?"

"I think it's far too generous." She shrugged. "Rafe doesn't like James, though, and I think he's enjoying puttering about here. No doubt he'll sell when he gets tired of it."

Another pause. "Have you mentioned this theory to him?"

"More than once."

"Would he tell me the same thing if I asked him the same question?"

Felicity narrowed her eyes, annoyance beginning to outweigh her desire to be polite. "Are you calling me a liar, my lord?"

"My brother is rather . . . impetuous," he said slowly. "He frequently jumps into the middle of things, and—"

"And you and your father appoint yourselves his guardians, throwing him a rope to pull him out of whatever mess he's fallen into," she interrupted.

"I wonder whether you have ever considered that he wouldn't leap from one adventure to another if you ever allowed him to feel that what he was doing had any significance."

Warefield lifted an eyebrow, but otherwise her rude directness didn't appear to have affected him in the least. "And do you feel that this particular adventure has significance?"

Felicity stepped past him for the door. "I think, my lord, that you should be asking that question of Rafe. Not of me."

"You know," he said to her back as she exited, "you remind me of my wife."

Surprised, Felicity turned again to face him. "I shall take that as a compliment, Lord Warefield."

He smiled, the enticing expression reminding her of Rafael. "We'll see about that."

"Rafe?" Maddie inquired.

He jumped, dropping his notepaper and measuring stick. "I really don't feel like having my innards ripped out for display and commentary at the moment."

She folded her arms. "Then you should have found a better hiding place."

Rafe recovered his measuring stick and returned his attention to the gap in the wall left by the collapse of the west wing. "Warefield send you?"

"You know better than that. He's interrogating Miss Harrington right now."

"He's *what*?" All he needed to complete his day was Quin sending Lis fleeing into the wilds of England.

"I didn't think you'd like that."

"Why can't he content himself with torturing me? Lis hasn't done anything wrong." Well, nothing that he hadn't led her to, anyway.

"He's being protective."

"I wish he'd stay out of my blasted affairs for once. He needs to remember that I can beat the hell out of *him*, too."

"Ah, brotherly love," Quin said, as he strolled into view. "I assume you're threatening me now, as well?"

Rafe scowled. "Will the two of you leave me alone, for Lucifer's sake?"

They both ignored him, which didn't improve his temperament. Everything had been so damned simple before he'd written to London. He wouldn't miss Robert Fields's friendship all that much, but he had meant to make amends to Quin. After this evening, that wasn't likely to happen. And by acting like a mad bull, he'd probably frightened Lis off, as well.

"Well?" Maddie murmured, wrapping her arm around her husband's and leaning against his shoulder.

The marquis shrugged. "It's all a blasted muddle, as usual."

"Now what?" Rafe snapped, jealous of their easy affection and completely out of patience.

"We're going as well," Quin informed him.

"In the middle of the evening?"

"That seems to be the custom in Cheshire." His brother smiled to take the sting out of his words. "We promised Uncle Malcolm a visit on our way to Warefield Park, and I really don't think you need us about complicating things any further."

Rafe supposed he shouldn't have expected anything else. Despite his refusal ever to admit it, though, he'd always admired Quin's tact and calm intelligence. And it hurt to know that his brother had finally given up on him. "I'll write you before I leave the country, then."

"Yes, at least let us know which continent you'll be on," Maddie said softly.

Rafe looked from one to the other of them, the chasm of uncertainty opening deep inside him again. "I will." He took a few steps away. "I'll leave you to pack."

"Twenty thousand pounds at a reasonable rate of interest," Quin said abruptly, stopping him in his tracks. "And I will expect regular reports on the progress of renovations and repairs."

Rafe slowly turned to face his brother. "I . . . I thought Forton was a poor investment," he said, torn between pure elation and stark terror at the thought that Quin might actually be serious.

"It *is* a poor investment," his brother agreed.

"Then why—"

"*It* is," the marquis repeated. "*You're* not. I'll have the papers drawn up and get you a line of credit. Just keep in mind, the less of the principal you use, the easier time you'll have paying it back when you change your mind about the whole damned thing."

For a long moment Rafe looked at him. "Thank you."

Quin shook his head. "You'll be hating me, and this place, inside a week. I know you, Rafe."

He shrugged. "I'm not so sure I know myself anymore, Quin."

"You truly want to do this?"

"Yes."

An hour later Rafe sat on the shallow front steps to watch the Warefield coach disappear into the darkness. With them gone, Forton Hall seemed lonely and quiet and shabby. Quin was right. He had no idea what he was doing.

He knew why he was doing it—at least he thought he did. But taking on a twenty thousand quid debt to see Felicity's smile was too absurd, even for him. There was more to it. There was a part of him that wanted to know whether he could restore Forton Hall, whether he could see through what he'd begun. He hadn't much of a record for that, and it didn't take his brother's or his father's digs to point it out to him.

"Well, I don't know much of London customs," Lis said, coming out to sit beside him, "but I believe your friends may have set a record for the briefest visit ever."

It was the friendliest she'd been toward him since they'd been invaded. Loath to risk angering her again, he settled for nodding. "They were a herd of complete sapskulls. I don't know how I ever tolerated them before."

Felicity glanced at him, then looked out toward the lane again. "Why did you hit Mr. Fields?"

That was a question he preferred not to answer until he'd thought his motivations over more thoroughly—yet he was familiar enough with Lis to know she'd insist on an answer. "He . . . insinuated some things I didn't appreciate."

"Some things that were true, perhaps?"

He looked sideways at her, and rubbed his hands restlessly along his thighs. It was easier being interrogated by Quin. "Yes."

"Then why—"

"If he knew me, or cared in the least, he wouldn't have said them. Quin didn't."

"But your brother left here, too."

He smiled a little. "Yes, but for a different reason." She waited expectantly, and he sighed. "I think for once he's decided to give me enough rope to hang myself with."

Lis gave him a surprised, almost suspicious look. A moment later, her lips relaxed into the smile that made him feel like a schoolboy mooning after his first love. "And this is a good thing?" she asked.

He shrugged. At least she still seemed to like him. He didn't think it was solely because he held the keys to Forton Hall, but neither was he foolish enough to completely ignore his brother's words. Warefield had a great deal of common sense. "Quin's lending me the money," he said.

"Yes, you told me. Two thousand pounds. I'm glad."

"*Twenty* thousand pounds," Rafe corrected. "For a complete renovation and restoration."

"Twenty . . ." she began, then trailed off. Suddenly she threw her arms around his neck and kissed him. "Twenty thousand pounds!"

Rafe wanted to kiss her back, to pull her into his arms, and to make love to her. And given her sudden elation, he wanted to make one thing absolutely clear. "I'm still going to sell Forton," he said, tension making him sound harsher than he intended.

Felicity slipped her arms from around him and folded her hands in her lap. "At least it will be put back as it should be." Her voice shook a little, despite the calmness of her words.

He wanted to ask her if she loved him at least a little, even if she loved Forton more. But then he would have to confess that he loved her, and that he didn't have the tiniest damned clue what to do about it, or her, or himself. "And will you be here long enough to see it?" he asked instead.

"I don't know," she whispered, tears filling her eyes. "I hope so."

Slowly he ran his finger along her cheek, brushing a tear away. Then, unable to resist, he kissed her softly. "So do I."

*   *   *

The Earl of Deerhurst watched the Marquis of Warefield's magnificent coach roll by, and moved his gelding a little further into the trees. Thank God they were gone. Having polite society come calling was a pleasant change, but their timing had been atrocious. The only positive note had been witnessing Bancroft doing such a splendid job of showing his foul side to Felicity.

He could hardly believe that barbarian was related to Highbarrow and Warefield. Striking a guest was so rare as to be practically unheard of. Felicity had been shocked at the sight, and luckily he had been there to take advantage of the situation. She weakened more toward him every day. He could sense it.

Bancroft sat on his crumbling front steps, illuminated only by the dim candlelight shining out from the foyer. James could almost feel sorry for him. Poor fellow, he had little choice now but to sell Forton Hall to the one person who'd made him an offer, and under whatever conditions of secrecy he required. Then Felicity joined Bancroft. Deerhurst scowled, his sympathy vanishing. When Miss Harrington kissed the bastard, James bit down on his lip so hard it bled.

"Twenty thousand pounds!" she cried, and kissed Bancroft again, and then the lout put his hands on her lovely, unblemished skin and kissed her.

The earl watched for another moment, then turned his mount down along the stream that ran behind the old stable. Something had happened; something that involved a great deal of money. And, given Felicity's reaction, it involved Forton Hall as well.

If Bancroft intended on bringing more attention to the tiny estate, it looked as though his choice of actions had narrowed once again. He smiled in the dim moonlight. That suited him just fine.

Chapter 14

◦───∽◦C∾───◦

"That's number seventy-four!" May
shrieked, laughing.

Felicity finished putting May's clothes into her
makeshift dresser and paused to look out the window. A dozen workers loaded lumber into the three
carts positioned around the rapidly shrinking pile
of stable rubble out in the middle of the yard. Now
that he had funding, Rafe hadn't wasted any time
in starting on the project in earnest.

She sat in the deep windowsill to watch as Rafe
and May practiced fencing maneuvers with scraps
of lumber. May seemed content with shouting and
hacking the air in a haphazard manner while she
invented new methods to kill her foes, but Rafe's
moves were spare, precise, and graceful. It reminded her that he could be dangerous—a lesson
Robert Fields had learned several days ago.

In the five days since his guests' departure Rafe
had been busy, scheduling repairs and sending for
materials. He'd sketched out drawings of the new
stable, and even to her untrained eye the improve-
ments between the old building and the planned
new one were obvious. He made a point of including her in all the decisions, as though she still had
some say in all this business.

Yet she couldn't shake the feeling that something had changed between them. Any compliment or flirtation was always followed by some news about the construction, as though he was testing to see whether she was paying attention. Since she couldn't help but hang on every word he uttered, practically purring, it seemed a rather useless exercise.

She tried to think of the Earl of Deerhurst in the same way she thought of Rafe, tried to remember his infrequent kisses with the same tingling arousal with which she remembered each touch from Rafe. The exercise was unsuccessful, but since she couldn't expect any sort of future with Rafael Bancroft, trading passion for stability, however unsatisfactory, was eminently more practical than daydreams.

She watched the fencing practice for another few minutes, then went downstairs to help prepare luncheon. As usual, Ronald had made himself at home in the kitchen, and sat chatting with Sally. Felicity smiled as she strolled into the room.

"Ronald," she said, watching him jump and flush a bright red, "if you have a moment this afternoon, I'd like to move those end tables out of the foyer before any work begins on the west wing."

He sprang to his feet. "I'll see to it right now, Miss Harrington."

Sally giggled as he fled the room, then with a self-conscious look at Felicity, went back to molding her pie crust. "I thought a peach pie would be nice for dinner," she said.

"It would be more than nice." Felicity reached for a loaf of fresh-baked bread. "You know, Sally, I think you have an admirer."

The girl blushed to the roots of her blond hair. "Oh, Miss Felicity, he says I'm pretty as roses."

It sounded as though Rafe had been giving young Mr. Banthe lessons in charm and seduction. "Well, you are."

"Excuse me, miss."

At the sound of the strange, masculine voice, Felicity turned around. A tall, thin, extremely dignified-looking man, his dark hair just going to silver at the temples, stood in the kitchen doorway, a large valise in each hand.

"I beg your pardon," he continued in the same polite, aloof tone, "but are you aware that a rather ungainly young man is dragging end tables across an unprotected wood floor? And against the grain, I might add."

She looked at him for a moment, uselessly trying to figure out who in the world he might be. "Yes, I am," she said slowly. "The floor is to be replaced."

He nodded crisply and set down both valises. "Ah. Very well, then. Would you be kind enough to direct me to Master Rafael Bancroft?"

Curious, and somewhat amused at his utter, perfect politeness, Felicity pointed at the kitchen entry. "He's out in the stable yard."

"My thanks, miss."

With another slight nod he scooted his luggage into the corner, walked through the kitchen, and pulled open the door. Exchanging a glance with Sally, who looked equally bewildered, Felicity followed him. His black coattails flapping in the slight morning breeze, he made his way through the yard toward where Rafe lunged and wove, showing May some sort of disemboweling maneuver. As their visitor reached the halfway point, Rafe spied the man. His face went white, and her baffled amusement instantly changed to dread.

"Are they here?" Rafe barked, dropping his

makeshift weapon and striding toward the well-dressed gentleman. "Damn it all, no one informed me."

The gentleman stopped. "The duke and duchess are in Spain, Master Rafael." He reached into his pocket and pulled out a folded paper. "I was instructed to give you this."

Rafe took the parchment and opened it. A moment later he looked up, his eyes sparkling. "You're my gift?"

"I'm on loan, sir."

"And whose idea was this?" Color returning to his face, Rafe grinned, and Felicity relaxed. Whatever the disaster was, it had been averted.

"Her Grace's."

As he finished reading the note, Rafe began laughing. "Oh, Beeks, you certainly are going to regret this."

"I do already, Master Rafael."

Rafe gestured Felicity to approach and held out the letter. "My present," he said, indicating their visitor.

Felicity opened the missive. " 'Rafe,' " she read, " 'Beeks needed a change of scenery, and I hope he will be of some use to you while you straighten out your situation. Please return him to us in good condition, and don't torture him overly much. Mother.' "

Felicity smiled, immediately liking the Duchess of Highbarrow. Evidently she knew her son quite well. For a brief moment she was jealous. She'd had a mother like that once, too.

"Lis, May, this is Beeks, butler extraordinaire to the Duke and Duchess of Highbarrow. Beeks, Miss Harrington and Miss May Harrington."

"We had a butler," May said, and solemnly

shook his hand. "His name was Smythe, and he was always cranky."

"May," Felicity chastised, though she could hardly argue with her sister. If she'd been the butler with Nigel in residence, she would have been cranky, too.

Rafe chuckled again. "Beeks is never cranky—are you, Beeks?"

"Not even when I find myself living out my worst nightmare, Master Rafael."

"Are you insulting us?" May asked suspiciously.

"Never, Miss May."

"Far too gauche," Rafe agreed.

The butler bowed. "If you'll allow me to get started? I don't believe I have any time to waste."

With another crisp movement Beeks turned on his heel and headed back to the manor. Felicity looked after him. "May, help Sally with luncheon," she instructed, and the girl skipped off behind the butler.

Rafe eyed her. "What did I do now?"

"No one said—"

"I didn't send for him," he interrupted, taking the note back. "I'm completely and utterly innocent."

"I've encountered evidence to the contrary," she said dryly.

Rafe chuckled. She smiled back at him, wondering whether he knew how handsome he looked in the warm sunlight, with the breeze lifting a lock of tawny gold hair off his forehead. As he met her eyes, his own expression softened. Her pulse skittered, and for a moment she thought he was going to kiss her, right in front of everyone.

"I'd be more than happy to prove that to you all over again," he murmured.

"Rafe, don't change the subject."

"You changed it first."

"Do you really want the Duke and Duchess of Highbarrow's butler seeing..." She trailed off, not wanting to insult her—his—home, but its shabbiness spoke for itself. "Seeing this?" She gestured at the house and yard.

"You mean you don't think it's up to his standards."

Men were so obtuse sometimes. "Of course it's not up to his standards."

Rafe grinned. "That's the beauty of acquiring the butler of the loftiest household in England. *Nothing's* up to his standards."

She flung her arms out. "Wonderful. I feel much better now."

"Glad I could help." For a long moment he was silent, his smile fading as he looked at her.

"What?" she asked finally.

"I was just thinking how much I want to kiss you again. Right now."

Felicity blushed. "Don't you dare! Everyone can see us," she warned.

"Somewhere private, then."

"Oh, stop teasing."

"Who says I'm teasing?" he asked, stepping closer.

She put a hand on his chest to halt his advance, and looked up at him. "I do."

"Only because you won't let me do anything more."

"Hush!"

He leaned closer. "We did once. Is there any reason we shouldn't repeat the deed?"

She'd been asking herself the same question. She knew the answer, and he needed to know that she knew. "Jeanette Ockley," she answered.

Rafe lifted an eyebrow. "Jeanette? That's the second time you've brought her up. There's nothing between Jeanette and me."

Felicity swallowed. "I know. Was there ever?"

She started to turn away, but he caught her arm. "You are nothing like Jeanette. Don't compare the two situations."

"But you're still Rafael Bancroft, on your way to somewhere, aren't you?"

"If," he began hotly, then glanced at the workers climbing through the stable ruins and started again in a quieter voice. "If I knew what the hell I was doing, I would tell you. Believe me." He released her elbow, and with another look returned to the stable.

At times, she thought they'd all be better off if someone would just club Rafe Bancroft over the head again. Tied up, dazed, and helpless, he was much easier to deal with, if no less desirable. In fact, even before she'd made love with him, she'd dreamed of that—of seeing him again for the first time, bound on her kitchen floor, and simply throwing herself on him. At least if he was tied up, he wouldn't be able to leave.

Halfway to the kitchen, May came out to meet her. "Beeks said I'm not supposed to help with luncheon," she announced.

"Oh, he did, did he? And did you inform him that circumstances beyond our control have forced us to lay some traditions by the wayside?"

"No, I just said you'd get mad at him."

Felicity took her sister's hand and marched toward the house. "Very insightful of you."

"Thank you."

Rafe watched Lis and May go into the house, then resumed tossing lumber into a cart. With the money Quin had lent him he no longer needed to do any of the manual labor himself, but he was used to being out-of-doors, and as he'd already discovered, he enjoyed the work. Besides, if he had nothing to do all day but hover about the manor, he'd only get himself into more trouble with Felicity. As it was, he couldn't stop thinking about her.

Dennis Greetham drove up in his cart, and Rafe went over to greet him. "Any word on the lumber?" he asked.

"Aye. Beginning of next week, if the weather holds. And I did like you said and left word at the Childe of Hale that you were hiring workers. You'll likely get a few more this afternoon."

"Amazing what a difference having a few quid makes."

"It's you that's made the difference," the farmer disagreed, pulling on his work gloves. "Folks in Cheshire ain't used to a nobleman offering to help mend their fence if they'll pitch in a day or two's work for him."

Rafe glanced back toward the manor. "I'm no Robin Hood; desperation and poverty breed odd offspring. Money's easier—though I'll probably change my mind as soon as I have to start paying the loan back." And the sooner that began, the better. He barely trusted himself with twenty thousand pounds. Why Quin would do so, he had no idea.

"I've been thinking," the farmer said. "With all the other mess going on I don't know if you want the extra trouble, but if you want to put in a fall crop, there's plenty of work to be done first with some of the fields."

Rafe nodded. "I was thinking the same thing. If you and Felicity could give me some figures, and if you'd be willing to supervise, I'd love to have a crop in the ground."

"You want *me* to supervise?"

"I may know how to demolish a stable, but you know a great deal more about farming than I do." And reluctant as he was to spend any more funds than he absolutely had to, a healthy crop would both make Forton Hall look impressive and give him an actual source of income for the first time. Just the thought made him feel giddy.

"I would be honored, Bancroft."

They discussed the merits of various grains and soils for twenty minutes, and by then Rafe was beginning to wish he hadn't teased Quin so much about the subject every time his brother had tried to bring it up. He could certainly use advice from a landowner's point of view now. He hated going to Felicity for information on yet another subject he knew nothing about, and Quin and Maddie would be in Somerset with Uncle Malcolm by now. And even if he'd been the least bit tempted to query his father, the duke and duchess were in Spain. Aside from that, he wasn't entirely certain which questions needed asking.

He straightened, stretching his tired back. The only other landowners he knew here were the Earl of Deerhurst and Squire Talford, and he wouldn't ask Deerhurst for a rope if he were drowning— which made the choice an easy one.

The squire was just setting out for a midday ride when Rafe and Aristotle arrived, and Talford graciously invited them to come along.

"I heard your London guests have departed," the squire said, as they cantered along the hedge bordering the front drive. "Interesting method of hosting."

Rafe eyed him. "Deerhurst informed you, I presume?"

"One of his footmen informed Mrs. Denwortle."

So the whole county knew. It was time he and Mrs. Denwortle had a little talk. "It was just a misunderstanding," he offered.

The squire pursed his lips as they turned out along the lane. "Seems to me your friend caught your meaning fairly well."

As they rode along, Rafe noted that the design of Talford's garden, while pretty enough, made the main house seem even smaller than it was. He intended to open Forton's garden up in the front, similar to what Quin had done several years ago with Warefield Park. The pond definitely needed expanding, and as far as he could tell, it hadn't been stocked for years. It also needed a name; all good fishing ponds had names. Perhaps he would suggest May Pond. May would like that.

"I don't mean to be rude," Talford said, startling him out of his unexpected daydream, "but did you have a purpose in coming by? You've been rather quiet."

"My apologies, sir. I wanted to ask you about crops."

"Crops?"

Rafe frowned. "Yes, crops. Dennis Greetham is going to help me plant, but I'm beginning to feel like a complete idiot whenever anyone brings up the subject."

"Seems a boring topic for a fellow on his way to China."

Rafe smiled a bit grimly. "I know." With a twenty thousand quid loan to repay, China seemed even further away than before. He had his work cut out for himself, that was for damned certain. "Would you care to assist me anyway?"

"Interesting. Does Felicity know about this?"

"That I'm completely ignorant about grain? I'm sure she's figured it out by now."

The squire smiled and looked away. "I meant about the crops."

"No, but she will. I just want to make the approach from high ground."

By the time he took his leave, it was nearly dark. Aristotle was loaded down with all three volumes of Storchey's *Planting in Western England*, and Rafe had enough information stuffed into his head to give him a fair start on writing volume four. Actually, he felt gratified by how much he'd remembered of the subject—apparently he'd paid closer attention to Quin and His Grace than he'd realized.

Even though it was out of his way, he sent Aristotle off toward Pelford. Mrs. Denwortle was still there, though there were no customers and it looked like she was in the process of closing for the evening. Rafe swung down from the bay and strolled inside. The bell on the door jingled, and she looked up.

"Mr. Bancroft. What can I do for you this evening?"

That was friendlier than she usually was, but she had cause to be glad to see him—he seemed to have become the community's most prolific source of gossip. "Mrs. Denwortle. You don't happen to carry Virginia cigars, do you?"

"From the Colonies? I should say not. Not much call for them in Cheshire."

Rafe tapped the counter with his fingertips. "Hm. That *is* a problem. I suppose I can send to London for a box. They should arrive in time."

She looked at him, curiosity written all over her round face, but he only looked innocently back at her. Mrs. Denwortle wiped halfheartedly at the countertop. "I do have a nice local selection," she ventured.

"Hm? Oh, no thank you. His Grace is very particular."

"His Grace?"

"My father." Rafe straightened. "Well, good evening."

He grinned as he retrieved Aristotle. That should keep her occupied for a while. Let the gossip begin: A whiff that the Duke of Highbarrow would be visiting Cheshire was bound to be more interesting than anything he or May or Felicity did. And that was just the beginning of the celebrity visits he had planned.

Back at Forton, he brushed down Aristotle and staked out the gelding for the evening. Then, mainly out of curiosity, he went around the front of Forton Hall to the main entrance. Beeks had to have the sharpest ears in England, for he had yet to hear of anyone who had actually touched a front door handle where the butler was on duty.

Four steps from the door, or three at the utmost, and Beeks would pull it open with a formal, "Good evening, Master Rafael." Tonight, though, he nearly smashed his face into the hard oak before he brought himself to a halt. No Beeks. "Good God," he muttered, turning the handle and entering the foyer. Now they were driving off people who were actually useful.

"Lis?" he called, striding down the hall for the kitchen, "what did you do with Beeks?"

"Nothing," she answered, meeting him in the doorway.

The butler stood before the table, an apron across the front of his fine shirt, sleeves rolled up and his arms white with flour up to the elbow. At Rafe's entrance he turned and sketched a bow before returning to kneading a pile of dough. "I shall be with you in a moment if you require assistance in changing into your evening attire, sir," he said in his calm, aloof voice.

"Ah, no. No thank you. I'll manage."

"Very good, Master Rafael. Miss Harrington has set dinner for seven, if that is acceptable to you."

Rafe nodded, his eyes darting from Beeks to Felicity, who looked very much as if she wanted to burst into laughter. Whether it was at him or at the butler, he wasn't certain. "Yes, that's fine."

Felicity motioned for him to shoo away, but he grabbed her hand and pulled her after him as he retreated to the morning room.

"Let go," she whispered, tugging her fingers free from his grip.

"What in damnation did you do to Beeks? I don't—"

"Rafe, you—"

"You've turned him into a kitchen maid—my parents will murder me! Don't you know how difficult it is to find a butler of Beeks' qualifi—"

She put her hand over his lips and closed the door. "Shut up, will you? He's butling."

"No, he's not; he's making bread!"

"Your parents' dear butler has been reciting to me all day long the proper duties of butlers in households of varying sizes," she said, exasperation touching her voice. "We apparently qualify as England's smallest noble household, which behooves the butler, as head servant, to assume any duties not covered by our existing staff—in this case our cook and our footman."

"But—"

Chuckling, she covered his mouth with both hands, nearly cutting off his air. "By the by, Beeks has twice attempted to dismiss Ronald for gross incompetence. I tried to explain that he was a stable boy and not a footman by trade, but he didn't seem to wish to listen to me.''

Wrapping his fingers around her slender wrists, Rafe pulled her hands away from his face. "By God. Beeks is making bread," he mused.

"Mm-hm. And since Sally pointed him in the right direction, he's been doing quite well at it."

She was obviously in high spirits. And though he loved seeing her smile, it also bothered him— because the thing that made her happiest was still Forton Hall. "May said you had a letter today," he commented, watching her closely.

Felicity nodded and backed away from him. "Yes."

Alarmed, he pursued her. "Anything interesting?"

"In a manner of speaking." She met his eyes again, obviously trying to read him as much as he was trying to read her. "I was offered the post of governess at a house with two young children in Hampstead."

His heart stopped, and then began a fierce pounding. It took him two tries to utter a word in a fairly normal manner. "And?"

"They don't want the sibling of a governess mingling with their little darlings. If I can find a home for May, the position is mine."

He relaxed. "More likely they don't want our little Leonardo da Vinci showing up their milksop halfwits." She was staying, at least for a bit longer. "May I kiss you?" he asked. "No one will see."

A soft flush crept up her cheeks. "I don't think that's very wise."

She was right, because he wanted to do far more than kiss her. "Come, come, Lis," he murmured, taking her hands and pulling her toward him again, "what does wisdom have to do with anything? Kiss me."

"And then what?"

He grinned slyly. "Use your imagination."

"Lend the man a butler, and he thinks he's king of the world."

"Now you're just teasing." Rafe leaned down and kissed the base of her throat all the way up to her chin, feeling her hammering pulse against his lips. Sweet Lucifer, he wanted her. Right there, and right then. "Kiss me," he demanded.

With an unsteady breath, Felicity rose on her tip-toes and kissed him hungrily.

He kissed her back, opening to her as she teased his mouth with her tongue. They should have picked a more private place than the morning room, damn it all. He was most definitely aroused, and if May burst in, he'd have to leap out the window. "What say we go upstairs?" he murmured, running kisses along her jaw and throat again until she moaned and arched against him.

"You're like my favorite chocolate, Rafe," she said, running her hands down his back to pull at his hips.

Rafe chuckled. "You mean you can't get enough of me, I hope?"

She kissed him again, open-mouthed. Gads, he'd be lucky if they made it to the couch. Nuzzling her neck, he slipped his hands down her back, undoing buttons as he went.

"Yes. And you taste so good."

"Mm. So do you." The gown slipped from her shoulders at his tug, and he sidestepped, reaching out with his free hand until he found the back of a chair. Still kissing her desperately, he shoved the chair beneath the door handle.

Her fingers trembling, Lis pulled his shirt free

from his breeches and ran her warm hands up his abdomen and chest. "And I know you can't be good for me."

"No, I'm not," he agreed, pushing her shift down to her waist and pulling her up against him. He took a breast into his mouth, suckling greedily, and she gasped. "So tell me to stop."

"I can't," she breathed.

"Good." He swept her up and half fell back onto the couch, sitting her on his lap. "You look so beautiful in daylight, Lis." This was what he'd wanted—to see her, to take the time to know her body, to know what gave her pleasure.

She unfastened his waistcoat and pushed it down his arms, then pulled his shirt over his head so hard she nearly took his ears off.

"Careful, my love." He chuckled, then couldn't talk as she ran her lips across his chest and abdomen in a trail of feather-light kisses.

In a moment he had the rest of her clothes off, and she nestled naked in his lap. He endured her fumbling as she unfastened his breeches with pained anticipation, and then shoved them down around his ankles. Immediately she began kissing him again, pressing her body against his, but he held her away.

"This time I am taking off my boots," he managed.

"Rafe," she said, looking at their surroundings for the first time, "what if May or Beeks—"

He silenced her with a kiss. "I've blocked the door," he whispered. He leaned down to yank off his boots and kick out of his breeches.

"You're beautiful in daylight, too," Felicity breathed, taking him in.

Smiling, he pushed her backward along the length of the couch, and settled himself alongside her. With his hands and his mouth he stroked her lithe, slender body until she was practically purring. He'd always enjoyed sex, and had been told numerous times that he was quite proficient at it. This time, though, he felt hesitant, almost unsure, wanting to be certain she wasn't disappointed.

"Rafe, please," she whispered, putting her hands around his shoulders and pulling his face down to hers.

"Please what?" he asked, shifting so that he lay atop her, feeling her body mold itself to him.

"Make love to me," she said, arching her hips against him.

"As you wish, my lady." He pushed inside her, reveling in her tight warmth. She moaned again, throwing her head back. Rafe placed kisses along her throat, holding as still as he could despite the overwhelming need to take her at once. Finally he began to move, slowly at first and then faster and faster, watching the heated ecstasy on her face with intense satisfaction. Apparently his sweet, practical Felicity didn't require romantic murmurings or long, delicate seductions.

"Ah, Rafe," she said roughly, pulling him in closer and lifting her ankles around his hips.

He exploded at the same time she did, holding himself hard against her and not wanting to let go. "Jesus," he muttered finally, his head sinking down beside her.

She tangled her fingers through his hair. "I could become very used to this," she murmured breathlessly.

He chuckled. "I'll remember that."

Knowing he must be heavy, Rafe started to shift off her, but Felicity wrapped her arms around his waist, kneading her fingers into his back. "Stay here."

"All right." Slowly he kissed her again.

"May I ask you something?"

"Of course."

She hesitated, and his heart jumped. He didn't know precisely what he was afraid of, except that he absolutely didn't want to think about her leaving him. He'd been trying to accustom himself to the idea of Felicity and May not being at Forton, and he couldn't do it. And when he tried to imagine exotic spices in faraway lands, the scent that his mind conjured was the lavender of Felicity's hair.

"If . . . if I asked you to, would you sell Forton to Lord Deerhurst?"

Forton Hall again. Perhaps Quin was right, after all. Though with what he offered her, he could hardly blame her for looking elsewhere. "Why?"

Felicity swallowed. "I don't want to tell you. Would you sell it to him for seventy thousand pounds, if I asked you to?"

"You'd marry him to keep Forton Hall, wouldn't you?" he asked abruptly, shifting off her and sitting up. "Damnation, Lis! Why?"

She sat up beside him. Her dark eyes serious, she reached up and ran her thumb along his scarred cheek. "I have no other prospects, Rafe. And I have never had the luxury of choosing someone . . . someone I love."

"What about your applications for employment?" he snapped, grabbing for his breeches, and surprised at the sudden fury coursing through him.

"It's been a month. I haven't heard anything positive."

"You still have time. Another month or two, at least. Or you could wait until spring."

She looked at him, catching and holding his gaze. "Why?"

He stared at her for a long moment, then shot to

his feet. "Bloody hell!" he growled, snatching up his shirt and boots. "If you want to go marry Deerhurst, then do it. If you want to leave, then go! But I will never—*never*—sell him Forton Hall. You're worth more than this damned pile of stone and wood, and I won't let him buy you for it!"

Felicity opened her mouth, closed it, and then knelt to pick up her shift. "Then I have to leave."

"Why, damnit?"

"Ask me to stay, then!" she shot back, yanking the shift over her dark hair. "Would you? Can you even ask the question?"

Oh, God, looking at her right now, he wanted to just hold her forever. For a moment, he thought about it—about living at Forton Hall, and raising cattle and planting crops—and then he remembered the twenty thousand pounds he already owed Quin, and the promise he'd made never to live like his father. "Lis—"

She put her fingers over his lips. "No. I already know the answer. I shouldn't have asked." She gathered up her gown and stepped into it. "Goodness—I can hardly offer the same attractions as China."

Rafe swallowed, trying to slow the pounding of his heart. "I don't know about that, Lis. I rather like your peaks and valleys."

"Yes, but not enough," she said quietly, and pushed aside the chair that blocked the door.

"Lis—"

"I'll see you at dinner," she said and left the room, softly closing the door behind her.

He sank back down onto the couch and pulled on his boots. "Damn," he muttered. "Damn, damn, damn."

Chapter 15

Felicity lay awake for most of the night.

She longed to be in Rafe's arms again, to hear him say that he loved her and that he would stay at Forton Hall forever. But she'd told him she knew he wouldn't stay; and when he tried to make a joke out of it, she'd walked away.

At first she'd felt righteous and indignant, until she'd realized that he was likely to remain at Forton only as long as he could continue to convince himself it wasn't permanent. If she forced him to make a choice, he would leave. So if he fled for China in the morning, she would have only herself to blame. Nigel was right: sometimes she was simply too bossy and managing.

At breakfast, though, Rafe acted as if nothing had happened. At least she didn't have to say goodbye just yet. Every day, she became less certain that she could do it at all.

She welcomed the distraction of visiting Squire Talford for luncheon, but at the same time she couldn't help thinking this might be the last afternoon she and May ever spent with their neighbor. Everyone and everything she held precious was on the verge of slipping through her fingers, and she had no idea what to do about it.

"We'll be certain to write you once I've found

a position," she said, fighting to keep a game smile on her face.

"I won't be gone to my daughter's for more than a few weeks, Felicity. I imagine you'll still be here when I return."

"Rafe said it'll take a good month just to finish the framework for the wing," May concurred. "He's going to let me choose the colors for my new bedchamber."

"May, it's not your bedchamber," Felicity snapped. Immediately she regretted the outburst, and reached over to pull her sister away from the puppies and up against her knee. "I'm sorry, sweetling. I didn't sleep well last night."

"And you had a fight with Rafe. He's cranky, too."

Felicity flushed as Charles looked in her direction. "It was just a little disagreement."

"May," the squire said, "I believe Cook has a plate of table scraps for those beasties, if you'd like to fetch it."

May scampered off, and Felicity gazed suspiciously at her neighbor. "What?" she asked.

He set aside his tea. "My dear, I have no intention of leaving you alone with Bancroft if you still have reservations about his sanity."

"Mr. Bancroft's mind is perfectly sound," she answered. "And we're hardly alone, anyway. James is but two miles away, and Mr. Greetham less than that." She leaned forward to pat his hand. "Besides, we have a cook, a footman, and a butler, now."

"Oh, heavens. Forgive me for worrying about you, then."

She smiled. "I thank you for worrying about us. But please don't. We can manage."

She did accept the offer of his coach to take them

back to Forton. But when she and May stepped to the ground in the stable yard, Felicity felt ready to change her mind about her ability to manage on her own. "Oh, no."

Lord Deerhurst's phaeton stood by the kitchen door, though there was no sign of the earl among the carts and workers and growing stacks of lumber. A moment later Rafe hopped down from one of the wagons and approached her. She stifled a sigh of relief—at least he wasn't somewhere brawling with James.

"Deerhurst is in the morning room," he said in his normal, easy tone, though he avoided looking her in the eye.

"Thank you."

He nodded, and reached for May's hand. "Come help me measure lumber, midget."

Feeling distinctly abandoned, and growing warm and melty at the sight of May teaching Rafe one of her silly, made-up songs, Felicity went to find James Burlough.

He sat on the very edge of the green overstuffed chair by the window, as though he worried over dirtying his breeches. They were exceptionally fine, dark blue with a matching coat and a light blue and gray vest. Compared to Rafe in her grandfather's sweat-stained old shirt, which he still used as work clothes, he looked marvelous—but not nearly as appetizing.

"Good afternoon, James."

He stood. "Good afternoon, Felicity. How did you find the squire?"

"Quite well, and looking forward to visiting his daughter."

"Splendid." James took her hand and brought it to his lips. "And how does today find you?"

She smiled as she retrieved her hand and took a

seat. At least he seemed to have forgiven her for snapping at him during the Robert Fields incident. "It finds me well, thank you. What brings you to Forton Hall?"

The earl sat beside her. "You do, Felicity, as always. I need to drive into Chester tomorrow, and wondered if you would care to accompany me."

That was what she needed—a distraction. "That would be delightful, James. May has been wanting to go to the candy shop there all summer."

His smile faltered a little and then formed anew. "Yes, May should come, too. Of course."

Felicity blinked, immediately realizing her faux pas. "Oh, I'm sorry. I am simply used to having May with me everywhere."

" Having her along will be delightful. Yes. Delightful."

They sat in silence for a long moment before Felicity remembered she could ring for tea. These days, servants seemed such a luxury that she always wanted to laugh when the door opened at her summons.

The butler scratched at the door and then entered. "Yes, Miss Harrington?"

"Would you please bring tea for Lord Deerhurst and myself, Beeks?"

He nodded. "With pleasure, miss."

"Impressive," the earl said as the door closed. "Your Beeks showed me in here. Very correct manners. Wherever did you find him?"

"Actually, he belongs to the Duke and Duchess of Highbarrow. We have him on loan."

"On loan—of course. I couldn't see Bancroft bothering to acquire such a proficient servant when he intends to vacate Forton Hall at the earliest possible moment."

Beeks silently brought in the tea tray and left

again, while Felicity could hear May outside shouting with laughter at something. She wished she were out there, and that she was the one Rafe was attempting to amuse—and touching, and tickling.

James cleared his throat. "I don't mean to pressure you, but have you considered what we discussed before? My proposal, I mean."

Felicity blinked. "I have," she said, "but I do ask you for a little more time, to put things in order." And to be certain that she had exhausted all her other options.

He smiled and took her hand. "Of course. Though I must tell you, I do take this as a positive step." The earl clenched her fingers tightly, then leaned forward and touched his lips to hers.

"Please remember, though, this is *not* an answer," she said, freeing her fingers before he could bruise them. "I won't be guilty of misleading you."

"I know you would not. You have still made me very happy."

Felicity looked at him, keeping the pleasant expression on her face and wondering whether she would have hesitated if Rafe had agreed to sell the earl Forton Hall. It made her feel dirty—as though, as Rafe had said, she was selling herself for the price of her home. Yet with or without Forton, she remained responsible for her and May's well-being.

"There is still the matter of my wedding gift to you. Have you spoken to Bancroft about selling Forton?"

Felicity nodded. She could be straightforward about this, at least, and then go through the rest of the mess with a clear conscience. "Mr. Bancroft, I'm sorry to say, declines to sell Forton Hall to you. You know the two of you met badly, and I'm afraid he won't—"

"He won't sell to me?" Deerhurst interrupted, surging to his feet. "You explained to him that the property would remain in your hands?"

James didn't need to know Rafe's exact answer. "Yes, but as I said—"

"This is preposterous!" The earl strode to the window and glared out across the front drive. For a long moment he was silent, the muscles of his jaw clenched and angry. Then he turned to face her again. "I cannot believe even a man of such poor morals would treat you so cruelly."

Felicity shrugged, trying to hide her alarm at his sudden temper. Good heavens, she'd practically said she would marry him, even without the addition of Forton. If it was only a gift for her, he was taking its loss far too seriously. "He owes me nothing."

"I cannot accept this! I offered him seventy thousand pounds for this . . ." He stopped himself. "For this land. He's practically a pauper! How can he turn that down?"

"My lord," she said, putting out a hand to try to calm him down, "although I cherish Forton Hall, my decision does not rest on it, I assure you."

He looked at her, his expression confused. A moment later he blinked and shook himself. "No, of course not. The workers outside—does he intend to rebuild?"

"Yes. His brother is helping to finance the restoration. I believe they both hope to make a profit from the ultimate sale."

"I've offered him a generous profit, already."

"James, please. Have some more tea."

James shook his head. "No, I cannot stay. I . . . have some things to attend to before tomorrow. I shall come by for you and May at nine."

"We'll be ready."

The earl strode from the room, and a moment later the front door slammed. He hadn't even waited for Beeks to show him out. Felicity sipped at her tea. Deerhurst's elation at her response to his proposal seemed to have been forgotten. Men were such clods, sometimes, fighting over territory neither one wanted, just so the other couldn't have it. It would almost be a relief to have the whole business over and done with. Almost—if it didn't mean losing both Forton Hall and Rafael Bancroft.

Well. That was that, then. The Earl of Deerhurst surveyed the clutter surrounding Forton Hall and sneered. He'd been patient for five years, courting Felicity, watching the estate decay, and waiting for the Harringtons to come to their nearest, dearest friend for help. They hadn't.

Instead, the shining son of the Duke of Highbarrow had appeared, taking everything for himself. Slowly Deerhurst climbed onto the high seat of his phaeton. Since Bancroft refused to sell Forton off quietly, only one option remained open. According to Mrs. Denwortle, the Duke of Highbarrow himself was on his way to visit. The deed would never keep its secrets from a veteran landowner. Therefore, attention had to be turned elsewhere. Rafael Michelangelo Bancroft had to die. And then James could approach the duke with the kind offer to quickly and quietly purchase Forton and any unfortunate memories connected with it.

He smiled as he clucked to his mare. Now all that remained was to decide how to do it. An accident, perhaps. On the trip to Chester, he would find whatever assistance he might need. Bancroft was a fool thrice over. He wouldn't have Felicity, and he was about to lose Forton Hall—and his life.

*   *   *

While woman was by far God's greatest creation, jealousy had to be Lucifer's. Rafe leaned on his shovel to watch Deerhurst hand Felicity and May into his barouche. May waved at him as they started off for Chester, but Felicity didn't even turn around.

Cursing under his breath, he went back to digging out the grass that covered the area they'd marked for the new stable. She hadn't said much about Deerhurst's visit yesterday, and the earl looked more smug than either elated or angry— none of which gave him a clue about what they'd discussed.

Telling himself it was none of his affair didn't do any good, either. He loved Felicity, and whatever happened, he would continue to love her. Falling in love wouldn't have been such a disaster if she'd been curious or even willing to travel. But no, he'd fallen for a woman with roots so deep into an estate that she was willing to stay on even when she no longer had any claim to it.

Beeks approached with a glass of lemonade, Ronald following behind laden with a pitcher and glasses for the rest of the workers. "Thanks, Beeks."

"My pleasure, sir."

The butler stood by patiently, waiting for him to finish. The lemonade was fine and sweet, but Rafe preferred May's with its seeds and clumps of lemon pulp. It brought a certain element of danger to drinking. "Beeks," he asked, handing the empty glass back, "what do you think of this place?"

"It is hardly my position to critique a country estate, Master Rafael. As you are aware, I have been stationed at Bancroft House in London since I began my term of employment with His Grace."

"And you've known me since I was two," Rafe said, unimpressed. "What do you think of Forton Hall?"

The butler looked at him for a long moment. "May I speak frankly?" he finally asked.

"Please do." Rafe steeled himself for a long diatribe on the miserable state of Forton. It was what he wanted to hear: that he would be an idiot even to consider occupying the place on a . . . more than temporary basis. Damnation, he couldn't even *think* the word "permanent" without cringing.

"It's been sadly neglected," the butler stated.

"Yes, it has."

Beeks cleared his throat. "At the risk of jeopardizing the future worth of my opinion, Master Rafael, I . . . like it."

Rafe blinked. "Beg pardon?"

Beeks looked embarrassed by the admission, but at Rafe's skeptical look he continued. "It's dreadfully cluttered, and the green curtains in the dining room are painful to view, but—and I beg your pardon, sir—it has an admirable, if not quite dignified, warmth."

"Warmth," Rafe repeated.

"Yes, sir."

"But what of the buildings, the garden, the—" He stopped, because the complete list of inefficiencies would take all day.

"As I said, all have been sadly neglected."

"And?" Rafe prompted, desperation making his voice crack.

"I'm no architect, sir, but what remains of Forton Hall seems sound enough. Every window has a pleasant view, the rooms are large and comfortable and within easy walking distance from the kitchen and the servants' area . . . and the air is particularly fresh in comparison to London."

Rafe stared at him. "By God, Beeks, you astound me."

"I am sorry, sir. If you wish me to recant, I will of course do so."

Rafe waved a hand at him. "No, no. I asked for your honest opinion. I just didn't expect it to be a positive one."

"My apologies again." The butler nodded and turned back for the manor.

"Beeks? Would you consider accepting . . . long-term employment here, then?"

Beeks faced him again. "Employment with you, sir?"

Rafe cleared his throat. "Well, yes."

For just a moment something very like humor touched the butler's gaze. "No, sir."

"Ah. Thank you."

He watched the butler and the footman return to the kitchen. Beeks's confession would take a little time to digest. Hands on his hips, Rafe turned a slow circle. Two dozen workers, half a ton of bricks, stacks of lumber, carts, horses, and mules cluttered the yard—all because of him, and because he couldn't stand the thought of leaving Felicity, and May.

"What the hell am I doing?" he muttered, and went back to work.

Seven hours later, his back hurt, his hands were blistered even through his gloves, and the stable had a foundation. Rafe walked the perimeter. He liked where he'd placed the building—well above the creek's highest flood mark, and below the lowest part of the manor so that no stable refuse would flow toward the house even in the heaviest rain. It was large enough to be useful with Forton at full production, and small enough that none of the space would be wasted.

"All it needs is some walls and a roof."

He started. "Lis. I didn't know you'd returned."

She untied her blue bonnet and lifted it off her hair. "We just arrived a moment ago."

"How was Chester?"

"Bustling with activity. A little tame compared to London, no doubt, but large enough to keep us occupied."

She sounded melancholy, and he looked at her. "Are you all right?"

Felicity's shoulders rose and fell with the deep breath she took. "Yes. I was just wishing Nigel had put half as much effort into Forton Hall as you do."

"You know, Lis, I meant to ask you something," he said, though it would likely cause another argument. Better to be angry with her, though, than to do too much wishing of his own.

"What is it?"

"Forton Hall."

She turned away. "Rafe, don't."

"No. I want to know. You implied that I didn't care for you enough because I wouldn't somehow conjure ownership of Forton for you. But if it wasn't mine it would be your brother's, or Deerhurst's, or your father's. So why is it me you're angry with?"

"I'm not . . ." Lis stopped. "Because I thought you would be different. I *hoped* you would be different."

He lifted an eyebrow. "Different from what, pray tell?"

She glared at him for a moment, then threw her arms up in exasperation and stalked off to the house. "From everyone else," she snapped.

"That's a rather broad brushstroke," he said to her back, annoyed with both her and himself.

"It's a big canvas," Felicity said, not turning around.

"I don't want to learn French," May stated. "I want to learn Zulu."

Felicity looked up from writing out May's daily lesson. "There isn't much use for Zulu in England, sweetling."

"But there is in Africa."

"May, we've been through this before." Felicity rubbed at her temple. Outside the incessant sawing and hammering continued unabated. She'd tried to detach herself from it and from Forton, since obviously she would not be able to reside here much longer. But it was so difficult. And forgetting how she felt about Rafe was completely impossible.

"Can't I do my lessons tonight? I want to go help build the stable. Rafe said I could."

"May, please."

Her younger sister scowled. "I think you should kiss him again so you won't be mad at each other anymore."

Felicity set aside her pencil. "We're not mad at each other. There's just a great deal going on right now."

May looked at her, then sighed heavily. "And Lord Deerhurst is calling on you for luncheon again today, I suppose."

"As a matter of fact, he is. Do you have something to say about that?"

Her sister shrugged. "I don't like him very much. He doesn't laugh."

Beeks scratched at the door and carried in the post on a dented silver salver, which was considerably better polished than it had been a few days ago. Rafe had received a letter from his brother, and some correspondence from his solicitor in Pelford. Curious about that particular missive, she returned both to the tray, keeping the one addressed to herself. "Will you see that Rafe gets these?"

"Of course, miss." The butler slipped back out the door.

"May, Lord Deerhurst does laugh. He's just a little more ... reserved than Rafe. Most people are." Felicity turned over her letter curiously. "'Mrs. Lawrence Dailey,'" she read, and her pulse jumped.

"Who's that?"

"A distant relation in York," she answered, distracted. Mrs. Dailey was the most promising prospect among all the inquiry letters she'd sent out. "May, please remind Sally that the earl particularly likes apple tarts."

Eager as she was to escape her lessons, May didn't seem to mind that she was being gotten rid of. She dashed off to the kitchen, and Felicity sat back and opened the letter.

It contained most of the words of the previous dozen responses: charity, bother, additional burden of a young, parentless girl. This one, though, ended with a nonnegotiable figure of five pounds per month plus room and board, if she and May could be in York by the twenty-fifth. Three young, headstrong boys had apparently "outgrown" their last governess, and a suitable replacement couldn't be found.

For a long time Felicity simply looked at the letter. She had her way out—her way to remain independent of everyone else's whims and desires. Sixty pounds a year for her and May together was a frightful pittance, but she knew of servants with families who survived on that, or even less. Besides, in York they wouldn't have much need for pretty things, and May could learn to do without her chocolates and hard candies.

Slowly she folded the letter again and put it in her pocket. When she'd written looking for employment, she'd expected that when she finally received an offer, the hardest blow would be the knowledge that she truly had to leave Forton Hall. But the image in her mind as she went to change for luncheon wasn't her ancestral home: it was a rakishly handsome adventurer who liked to buy her hair ribbons and peaches.

She was just pulling on her shoes when she heard a loud crash and shouting. Felicity dashed to her window. Outside, workers hurried toward a tumbled-over stack of lumber. And she didn't see Rafe anywhere.

Her throat so tight she couldn't breathe, Felicity rushed down the stairs, through the hallway, and into the kitchen. May, Ronald, Beeks, and Sally were already out the door, and she ran after them.

"Rafe!" May yelled, and started a sprint for the jumbled pile of lumber.

Beeks grabbed her and pushed her at Sally with a stern, "Stay here."

Felicity and the butler reached the crowd of men at the same time. Frantic, she shoved them aside until she reached the center of the mess. With a shudder, her heart started beating again.

Rafe sat against the remains of the pile, shoving lumber off his legs and cursing. He had a cut on one arm and another on his cheek, but from the strength and potency of the obscenities, he otherwise seemed to be unhurt. Felicity stood frozen with relief, able to comprehend nothing but the fact that he was all right. A moment later he looked up at her, and snapped his mouth shut mid-curse.

"Damn. Oops. Excuse my language."

Shaking with giddy relief, she knelt beside him, wanting to touch him and make certain he really was intact. "We'll make an exception this time. What happened?"

"Half the stable fell on me," he said, kicking free of the last board. "Luckily I ducked most of it."

"Can you stand?"

"Most assuredly."

Mr. Greetham, his own expression relieved, stuck out a hand, and Rafe grabbed hold to haul himself to his feet. He cautiously flexed one knee and then the other, and Lis remembered with dismay that he'd once broken his leg. "Rafe?"

He grinned down at her. "Everything's still attached."

Glancing at the gathered crowd, Rafe leaned down to offer his hand to Felicity. Suddenly feeling rather absurd kneeling in the middle of the circle of gawking men, she wrapped her fingers around his and let him pull her to her feet. "Thank goodness."

"Worried, were you?"

He seemed ridiculously pleased to ask the question, and she scowled. "Of course I was."

A small form hurtled through the workers and attached itself to Rafe's waist. "You're not dead! Sally said you were crushed!"

With a tender smile that made Felicity want to wrap herself around him as well, Rafe stroked May's cheek, wiping away a tear. "The only thing crushed was my pride, sweetling. Don't fret."

"All right, my boys," Mr. Greetham said, clapping his hands together as he stepped forward, "let's straighten up this mess and get back to work."

As the crowd of workers moved away, Felicity

saw Rafe gazing at her with an arrested expression. "What is it?" she asked, her pulse speeding again, this time with the tingling excitement he always aroused in her.

"You're only wearing one shoe, Lis," he said quietly.

She started and looked down. Beyond the hem of her gown, her left foot, with one toe beginning to peep out through a hole in her stocking, slowly sank into the soft, damp grass. "Oh, my. So I am."

Rafe detached May from his waist. "No more tears, sweetling?"

She shook her head.

"Excellent. Go tell Sally I'm not crushed, and that I request a peach pie for supper in return for her lack of faith."

May bounded away. "Sally!"

He returned his attention to Felicity. "Shall I carry you back to the house, to prevent any further damage?"

That would be very nice. "Don't be silly," she said. "It's only a stocking. If that's the worst casualty of the day, I shall be very thankful."

"As you wish, my practical one."

How long they might have stood there, she had no idea, because just then Lord Deerhurst's carriage came rattling up the pitted drive. Rafe's eyes darted to the phaeton and back to her again.

"Your luncheon guest has arrived," he said shortly, and turned away to help restack the lumber.

As she returned to the house, she remembered Mrs. Dailey's letter, sitting now on her dressing table. She had a little time before she needed to answer it, and she decided to delay her response for at least a few days. She also decided to keep the missive to herself. Because at the moment, she

hadn't the slightest idea how to tell Rafe about it—
or how to tell him goodbye.

The earl met her halfway to the kitchen door.
"Good morning, Felicity," he said warmly.

She looked up at him, distracted. "Good morning, James. I hadn't realized it was so late. I wasn't
expecting you yet."

"The fault is mine, my dear. I'm frightfully
early, I fear, but I did so miss you."

"We only parted last evening." Much as she
tried to appreciate it, whimsy just didn't fit their
relationship. She wished he would realize that, because at times it was very tiresome.

He glanced over her shoulder toward the stable
yard. "Is something amiss?"

"No. A slight mishap; nothing to worry about."
With the excitement over, her left foot was becoming cold, and it was already quite wet. She flexed
her toes and started for the kitchen door again.

"No one was hurt, I pray," he said, continuing
to look toward the jumbled yard.

"A few scratches, is all. Please come in. I'll
have Beeks bring you some tea, if you'd care to
wait a few moments in the morning room."

"Hm?" He started and looked back at her. "Oh,
yes. Splendid."

Felicity left him in the butler's care and hurried
back up to her bedchamber for her shoe and to
finish putting up her hair. Her eyes kept straying to
the blasted letter, though, and she finally put it into
her water-damaged jewelry box and snapped the lid
shut.

She felt guilty just having it in her possession,
yet she knew she was being absurd. Given Rafe's
dislike of Deerhurst, he would no doubt prefer that
she leave rather than stay to marry the earl.

She wandered over to the window. Rafe stood at

a makeshift table, Mr. Greetham and two other men with him. He pointed at a detailed drawing he'd made of the proposed stable, then gestured at the various piles of material. One of the men said something and Rafe laughed, the scar on his cheek rendering the expression a little lopsided and rakish.

She wished he would see himself as she saw him: passionate and compassionate, a warm and natural father, and a man who perhaps claimed to want to wander because he'd never had the chance to settle down. He fit so well here—in Cheshire, at Forton Hall, and with May and her.

"Damnation," she whispered, resting her head against the cool glass. It was so selfish, to want him to be what he wasn't, to even think of asking him to stay when she knew how much he wanted to go. If only he hadn't been the one to win Forton Hall. If only she hadn't fallen in love with him.

She looked down at him again, heat rushing through her at the mere sight of him. He consulted with one of his workers, measured something on his drawing, and made a notation on the paper. Sighing, she closed her eyes.

It didn't make any difference. Even blind, she could see him smiling as he worked, enjoying himself more than he would probably ever realize, until it was much too late. For a moment this morning she thought she'd lost him. And she wasn't certain she could go through that again. If only, just for a moment, he could be practical, and she could be absurd.

"I love you, Rafe Bancroft," she said, just to hear the words aloud, and opened her eyes again.

He was looking up at her, his face white and a half smile frozen on his lips. His eyes, emerald-green in the sunlight, locked with hers. He'd seen it. She knew instantly. He'd seen what she'd said, and he'd read the words on her lips.

Trembling, the blood draining from her face, Felicity ran from the window and sank onto her bed, where she covered her face with her hands. "Stupid, stupid, stupid," she moaned.

He wasn't supposed to know. It would only make things worse. Now he would pretend that he hadn't seen anything, and she would be embarrassed and humiliated every time they set eyes on each other, because she would know that *he knew*, and that he was going away to China anyway.

Her door burst open.

"What did you say?" Rafe demanded, slamming it shut and striding up to her.

She stared at him, out of breath and with a bloody scratch still across his right cheek. Her pirate king. "N-nothing," she managed. "I didn't say anything. Just forget it. Oh, *please*, forget it."

He grabbed her hands and yanked her to her feet. "Say it," he repeated, shaking her.

"I . . ." Felicity shook her head. "No."

"Lis," he said, anger and frustration lining his voice, and shook her again. "Say it, damn it!"

She wanted to—that was the worst part. "I . . . I said I love you." Tears filled her eyes. "It's stupid. I'm an idiot. Just ignore—"

"I love *you*, Lis," he whispered, his voice shaking.

He captured her mouth with his own, pulling her up against him with fierce possessiveness. Felicity kissed him back, never wanting to let him go. Finally he sighed, burying his face in her hair. His arms around her waist held her warm and close against him.

"Now what?" she murmured, twisting her hands into his shirt, relishing the tall strength of him.

"Say it again," he whispered, lifting his head to look at her.

"I love you." The words came much easier this time, and she smiled.

Rafe kissed her again, slowly and deliciously, then with a gasp Felicity pushed him away with such force that he nearly stumbled. "Ouch. What is it?"

"Lord Deerhurst is downstairs waiting for luncheon!" she exclaimed, heading for the mirror. "I forgot."

For once, Rafe didn't even mind hearing the earl's name. He moved behind her, wrapping his arms across her waist and nibbling at her ear. "Let him wait. Or I'd be happy to send him away."

She sagged against him, obviously trying to decide whether to give in to him or start another argument. As usual, arguing won. "I can't do that. Let go, Rafael."

Reluctantly he let her escape from his arms. "So you're still going to marry him?"

"I haven't decided yet."

He handed her one of the clips that had fallen from her hair, hiding his hurt behind the motion. "But you love me." She looked at him, her expression frustrated, but he continued anyway. "And I love you. And damned Deerhurst doesn't deserve you."

Felicity faced the dressing mirror and finished repairing her hair. "Love has nothing to do with James," she said slowly. "I have May and myself to think about."

"I hadn't realized you were so mercenary."

"Oh, stop it. You seem to have no difficulty putting yourself first, so don't *you*"—she jabbed a finger into his chest—"cast the first stone."

She opened the door and stalked out, leaving him

standing in the middle of the room. She was right, as she usually was. It wasn't that he thought proclaiming his love would solve everything, but he'd hoped it might make a little difference. He should have known better, by now. "Blast."

It would have made him feel better to at least set Deerhurst out of Forton on his ass. But continuing to share a roof with Lis was going to be difficult enough without his making things worse—though that did seem to be the one thing at which he excelled.

He noticed her broken-hinged, water-stained jewelry box on her dressing table. Maybe this was one small thing he could make better. The oak lid was still pretty, carved with intricate ivy leaves and cherubs, and he flipped it open, wondering if he could salvage the top and replace the bottom. The letter inside immediately caught his attention, and with a guilty look over his shoulder he picked it up.

"York," he muttered, looking at the address. Lis had applied for a position in York.

He had no business reading her correspondence, and he acknowledged that he was being a cad and a snoop as he unfolded it. He read it once, then a second time. "Damn," he swore, breath-stealing panic tightening his chest.

Swiftly he returned the missive to its place and closed the lid. She could leave. Suddenly the worry over whether she was using him to keep Forton seemed small and stupid. If he pushed her again, if he messed up whatever the hell it was he was doing, she could go. If it wasn't to York, it could be to Deerhurst. And he didn't think he'd be able to stand either one.

He headed back outside and concentrated on finishing the wall frames and lifting them into position. With nearly twenty men helping now, the work went much more quickly than before. His leg ached from the accident earlier, but he counted himself lucky to have escaped and ignored it.

Beeks and Ronald brought luncheon out for everyone, and they continued work until nearly sunset. Rafe sent everyone home for the day after they had secured the frame on all four sides to keep the evening breezes from knocking it down.

He stood back, looking at the new skeleton of the stable. Tomorrow would be more difficult, and he was not looking forward to hauling the heavy roof supports up to the top of the walls. Once that was done, though, he would split his crew. He hadn't planned on it originally, but today things had changed. Half his workers would continue work on the stable, while the other half finished cleaning out and replanting the garden. Lis still hadn't had her morning tea amid the roses, and by God he was going to see that it happened for her.

"When can Aristotle move back in?" May asked, slipping her small hand into his.

"I'd give it another week or so."

"I would like to help."

He grinned down at her. "What about your studies?" he asked.

"I'll do them in the evenings. Felicity can't help me during the day anyway, with Lord Deerhurst always coming to visit."

"I'll mention it to your sister, then."

"Thank you." May tugged on his hand, and he obediently returned with her to the house. "You know, Rafe, I've been thinking."

Felicity wasn't the only part of Forton that had stolen into his heart. May was as close as he was likely to get to a child of his own. It was the first time he'd thought of missing fatherhood with regret rather than with cynical relief. Rafe gently squeezed her fingers. "About what, sweetling?"

"About my travels."

"Yes, Lis told me you were going to be an adventurer."

"Right. I think I'll go to Africa first, because I would like to see all the animals that you talked about."

"That sounds wise," he agreed.

"But then I'm not certain where I should go next. All the foreign places are so far from each other, you know. What do *you* most want to see?"

"I haven't really decided yet. The world is a rather large—"

She stopped and frowned up at him. "But I'm going to travel where *you* travel. Plans have to be made, Rafe. I must have servants, and the proper clothes, and it has to be done at the right time of year."

He gazed at her for a moment. "You have been thinking about this, haven't you?"

"Of course I have. It's important."

Rafe glanced back at the stable. "I'll tell you what, then. As soon as the stable is finished, we'll plot out our travels. All right?"

"All right."

He paused with her in the doorway. "May, did Deerhurst come calling when Nigel was still here?"

"No, not really. He came for tea sometimes, and he and Nigel would go riding. After Nigel had to sell Felicity's mare and then let Smythe go, he came by, but Nigel had already left for London. After that, he kept trying to lend Felicity money."

That was fairly close to what Felicity had told him. "Has anyone else ever come calling on Felicity?"

"Squire Talford," she answered promptly.

"Well, of course. Anyone else?"

She scrunched up her face, as though trying to remember. "When Nigel came back from Eton, he brought some friends with him. Lis said they were all cork-brained jack-a-dandies, and finally they left. Nigel said she drove them away, but I was little and I don't remember."

"Would you want to live at Deerhurst, if you could?"

"Lis just asked me that." May pulled her hand free and opened the kitchen door. "I'm going to Africa."

Rafe slowly followed her inside, and went up to change for dinner. With Nigel's cronies and Deerhurst as her only suitors, no wonder Lis had managed to separate the ideas of love and marriage in her mind.

He pulled off his dirty, sweat-stained shirt and breeches, and stepped into the bathtub Beeks had filled for him. On the rare occasions when he had thought of marriage for himself, love was part of it. Quin and Maddie were certainly in love, and he knew His Grace adored the duchess.

Rafe sank down into the tub, letting his tired and bruised muscles relax in the welcome warmth. With all the women he'd known, he'd begun to think that perhaps he wasn't meant to fall in love and marry. But then, he'd never met anyone like Felicity Harrington before.

And he never would again. Nor could he expect her to wait about, fluttering helplessly, while he debated the course of his life. And suddenly he *was* debating that very thing. For Lucifer's sake, eight-year-old May had more concrete traveling plans than he did.

Beeks scratched at his door. "Master Rafael,

dinner will be served in twenty minutes.''

"Thank you, Beeks.''

One thing was becoming clear, anyway. The reprieve Forton Hall had given him wouldn't last forever. Soon, very soon, he was going to have to decide: a free, unencumbered life roaming the world; or chains tying him to one piece of land, and one woman, for the remainder of his life. And for once, he didn't have the liberty of being able to make the wrong decision.

Rafe sighed and stood up in the cool evening air. Perhaps he should have become a clerk for His Grace, after all. Then, at least, he would have someone else to blame for any unhappiness.

Chapter 16

A few days later, Rafe was beginning to wonder whether his wish for someone to blame at Forton Hall had manifested itself as an evil spirit.

First an errant rope became tangled between a cart and the ladder Bill Jennings was balancing on, sending the farmer crashing to the ground and badly bruising his shoulder. The next afternoon, one of the stable's new roof beams snapped while Greetham was working beneath it. If he hadn't dived out of the way, it might have killed him.

"Maybe we're prone to accidents," May suggested. She squatted beside him, pulling weeds from a raised, rock-lined flower bed. With the stable trying to kill someone, he'd banished May to the garden. And she'd banished him there today, as well.

"We are not prone to accidents," he retorted, ignoring Felicity's stifled chuckle on his other side.

"Well, blast it then, Rafe, I don't know what it is."

He lifted an eyebrow. "Ladies say 'dash it all.' "

May scowled at him. "Don't be such a stuffed shirt. I'm not a lady. I'm eight."

"Hm." He glanced up at Lis, a grin pulling at his lips. "She makes a good point, you know."

"Don't encourage her. She can't keep swearing like a sailor forever."

"Lucifer's big bottom," May proclaimed, undaunted. It was by far her favorite curse, and Rafe was continually thankful he'd amended it before the chit heard the undiluted version.

"May," Lis chastised.

Her sister pulled another weed. "Oh, all right. Anyway, I was looking through a book last night, and I found another place for us to go."

"Not another Arctic journey, I hope," Rafe said dryly. "I still don't think we're going to survive the one you planned yesterday."

"Excuse me," Felicity said, standing and brushing off her skirt. "I'm going riding with James in a short while. I need to change."

Rafe looked up as she stepped past him. He knew she was leaving because they were talking about adventures again, but blast it, if she was going to bring up damned James Burlough every two minutes, then he could bloody well talk about the East Indies.

"Madagascar," May enunciated.

He blinked. "Beg pardon?"

"We should go to Madagascar. Or you should, and then write and tell me whether you would recommend that I visit there or not."

"So now I'm reduced to being your holiday guide, midget?"

"Well, I don't want to go anywhere dull, of course."

"Of course not. And what would you consider dull?"

"I wouldn't want to go anywhere terribly hot." She looked down at the plant she'd just pulled from the ground. "Is this a weed?"

Rafe shrugged. "Haven't a clue. Dump it into

the bucket before your sister comes back.''

"Right. I do want to see the pyramids, though. And the Sphinx.''

"Bonaparte's soldiers shot half its face off, you know,'' he commented.

"They did? That's barbaric.''

"I'm sure the Sphinx thought so.'' He looked up as another wagon turned into the drive. More sacks of sand and piles of rocks would be arriving tomorrow, so they could mix concrete to patch the west wing foundation and the front steps. "Africa, especially in the west and south, is very hot.''

"Do they have lots of animals in the . . . north and east, then?''

He grinned and shifted farther down the planter. "Bushels of them.''

"Look out!''

Rafe whipped around. Two work horses pulling a half-loaded wagon careened around the side of the house directly toward the garden. As May stood up to see what was going on, Rafe grabbed her around the waist and vaulted over to the far side of the planter. Pushing May down against the rock barrier, he flung himself over her.

The left rear wagon wheel slammed into the planter only inches from where May had been weeding. Rock chips shot into the air with the force of musket shot. The rear of the wagon careened upward and the whole thing flipped over on its side, dumping lumber and grinding into the grass a few yards beyond the planter. A gardener ran up to grab the traces of the foundering horses, now wheeling the tipped cart around in a circle.

"You all right?'' Greetham yelled, bounding around the side of the house from the stable yard.

Quickly Rafe sat up, pulling May with him. "All

in one piece, sweetling?'' he asked, feeling her arms and legs for broken bones.

She nodded, her eyes wide. Relieved, Rafe rested his forehead against hers. These accidents were becoming almost predictable in their frequency. And now they were involving little girls.

"May?"

Felicity hurried down the front steps, Beeks on her heels. As he and May climbed to their feet, Rafe took a moment to consider that poor Beeks hadn't run so much since he and Quin had been children.

"We're all right," May said, brushing dirt and bits of leaves from her dress. "My goodness."

Felicity pulled her sister into her arms. "And you, Rafe?"

"Annoyed." He turned to face the gathering workers. "Whose wagon is this?"

A big, burly man, one of the group who had come out from Chester, doffed his hat and stepped forward. "It's mine, sir. A hornet stung old Juliet. She hates hornets."

Rafe strode up to him furiously. "Look after your animals better. And next time make sure your damned brake is set, or I'll test it by dragging you around behind it."

"Aye, sir."

"All right. Back to work!"

When he turned around, Lis was fixing one of May's dark braids, and he took the moment to gather his scattered wits. None of the other accidents had affected him like this, and he knew why. His precious ones had been in danger this time.

"That was rather . . . strict, don't you think?" Felicity asked as her sister returned to the house with the butler.

"That's too many damned accidents," he

snapped. "May—or you—might have been hurt."

She came forward and touched his arm. "You're cut."

He looked down at it. Blood oozed from a long scratch on his forearm. "It's all right."

"No, it's not. Come and let me clean it." She glanced sideways at his face. "I don't know how to amputate limbs, and I'd hate to have to learn on you."

Rafe relaxed a little, though frightened anger still pulled at him. "Well, if you're worried about me."

She led him into the kitchen and sat him at the table. "Sally, some hot water and a cloth, if you please."

"Yes, ma'am."

Felicity looked at the wound again. "You'd best take off your shirt."

He lifted an eyebrow. "For a cut on the arm?"

She blushed. "I want to make certain you're not injured elsewhere."

Sally had left the kitchen to find a clean cloth, so with a grin Rafe tugged Felicity down across his lap. "Shouldn't we remove my breeches as well, then?" he murmured, kissing her.

Lis pushed against his chest to right herself. "Are you hurt anywhere else?" she demanded, straightening her hair and then folding her arms across her delightful bosom.

She wasn't angry, though. By now he knew that expression well enough when he saw it. "I seem to be experiencing some swelling, now that you mention it."

The cook hurried back into the room. "Some swelling, Mr. Rafe? Oh, my goodness, where?"

Felicity stood with a choked laugh, and flung the cloth at his face. "His fat head," she managed.

"You're a cold-hearted lady, Miss Harrington," he stated, amused at her good humor.

She took the cloth back from him. "Here, let's get that cleaned up." She wet the cloth and carefully wiped it down the length of the scratch.

"Ouch! Blast it, that stings," Rafe protested.

"I'm sure you've had worse," Lis returned matter-of-factly.

"Clean it out good, Miss Felicity," Sally seconded. "We don't want it turning to gangrene."

"Ouch! Don't worry, Sally. She'll make sure I'm well enough to finish repairing the house." The scratch was deeper than he'd realized; as she cleaned the dirt out, blood began flowing down his hand.

"Will you be quiet about the damned house?" Felicity snapped, paling. "I think this will need stitches. Sally, fetch your father."

"Right away, Miss Felicity."

Rafe gritted his teeth as a sizeable rock splinter came free from the cut. "Do you realize you just cursed Forton?"

"Rafe, you keep getting hurt, trying to help me." A tear rolled down her cheek.

"I'm helping myself, Lis. Remember?"

"No. Oh, I need another cloth."

The fright and concern in her dark eyes shook him. She truly did care about him that much. He put his hand over hers as she wiped the wound. "Don't try to clean it. Just hold the cloth tight against it and it'll stop bleeding."

"Like this?"

He chuckled a little breathlessly. "Not quite that tight. Damn, Lis, I should have you out there lifting those supports."

"Oh, hush. You can't distract me like you do

May.'' She knelt beside him, pressing the blood-soaked cloth firmly against the cut.

Rafe brushed a lock of hair out of her eyes. "I know."

Greetham hurried through the kitchen door, Sally behind him. "Sally says you need sewing up. I've done a dog and a few horses, but never a man. This should be interesting."

"Marvelous." Sally went to fetch Beeks and Felicity's sewing kit, while Felicity kept her attention on his wound. "Greetham," Rafe said, twining Lis's stray curl around his fingers, "before you kill me, what kind of landowner do you think I'd make?"

"What, lad?"

Felicity's face lost what little color was left in it. "What?" she repeated soundlessly, staring up at him.

"Well," he continued softly, meeting her eyes and shifting to caress her cheek, "I've been thinking I'd like to make a go of Forton, but I don't have much experience at it. I'd hate to knock the rest of the place down by accident."

"You're the fastest damned learner I ever met, excuse my language," the farmer said as he rolled up his sleeves.

"What . . . what about China and everywhere?" Felicity asked, staring at his face as though she was afraid to look away.

He shrugged his free arm. "They can wait."

"Rafe—"

"Shh," he interrupted. He knew the arguments; they were still raging about in his skull. Right now he wanted to make certain she wouldn't slip away from him, that he wouldn't have to go through the rest of his life wondering where she and May were, what they were doing, how they were, whether they were safe—and happy. "Lis," he said softly, leaning closer to her, "will you stay here at Forton with me? Will you marry me, Felicity?"

"I don't understand," she said. "When—why—did you change your mind?"

Rafe gave a half smile, wondering who would laugh harder at him—Quin or his father. He was about to become an estate manager, after all. "When I realized I didn't know how to say goodbye to you."

She looked at him for such a long time that he began to fear she would turn him down. Finally, tears filling her eyes again, she nodded. "Yes. Yes, I will marry you, Rafe Bancroft."

He grinned in relief, tugging her closer so he could kiss her sweet, soft lips. "I love you, Lis."

"And I love you," she returned fiercely. "Are you certain—"

"Yes, I am. You are far more important than China."

"By God," Greetham exclaimed, slapping Rafe briskly on the back. "Forton Hall has a new master."

Rafe winced at the blow. He must be in love—because otherwise he'd simply lost his mind.

Felicity watched as Mr. Greetham finished wrapping Rafe's arm in a bandage. Half of her was convinced that she was asleep and dreaming. She'd had enough of these dreams over the past few weeks almost to believe this was just another. Rafe wanted to marry her, and he wanted to stay at Forton Hall!

May banged against the closed kitchen door. "Can I come in yet?"

Greetham nodded, and Sally opened the door. May had a small scratch on one cheek, but otherwise she seemed perfectly fine. They'd all been exceedingly lucky today.

"That should do it, Bancroft," the farmer said, tying a last knot in the bandage.

"My thanks," Rafe said, cautiously flexing his arm.

May stepped up to examine the wrapping. "Are you certain you're all right?" she asked, touching his hand.

He tugged on one of her braids. "I'm fine, midget. No worries."

Felicity roused herself, trying to wipe the silly, delighted grin off her face. It would never do if May heard the news from Sally or someone else, and the cook looked to be fairly bursting already. "Mr. Greetham, Sally, will you excuse us for a moment?" she asked.

"Of course," the farmer said. "No sense wasting daylight." Sally looked content to sit and watch the rest of the play unfold, but Greetham took her by the hand and pulled her out the kitchen door.

May looked at her sister suspiciously. "Am I in trouble?"

Rafe shook his head. "No. I need to ask your permission for something."

"*My* permission?"

"Yes, your permission."

Rafe glanced up at Felicity, and she couldn't help smiling again. Nothing would win May over faster than including her in the decision. Not that May hadn't fallen for Rafe nearly the instant she saw him.

"All right."

He cleared his throat. "May, I would like your permission to marry your sister. Do you have any object—"

May vaulted onto his lap and flung her arms

around his neck before he could finish. "Hurray!" she screamed.

"Good God," he muttered, wincing.

Laughing, Felicity came forward and pulled her sister away. "Don't kill him, dear."

"I *knew* you would!" She climbed down from Rafe and threw her arms around Felicity. "I can't wait to tell Mrs. Denwortle that you are not wanton lovers."

"What?" Felicity had no idea her reputation was being spoken of in such unfavorable terms—or that it was so widely discussed that even May knew of it.

Rafe stood. "I'll tell you later." He drew her into his arms and kissed her again.

Absurdly enough, she wanted to thank him—for being her anchor and her rock, and for loving her enough to give up his plans for a lifetime of adventure. Felicity pulled away a little to look into his light green eyes. When she'd first encountered him, Rafe had been anything but an anchor. And even now she had to wonder whether her wind-tossed pirate king had really thought this through, and really meant to stay.

"What is it?" he murmured, meeting her gaze.

"I'm just happy."

He smiled. "Then kiss me again."

She slid her arms around his strong, broad shoulders and met his eager mouth with hers. If she was dreaming, she never wanted to wake up.

"Miss Harrington, the Earl of Deer—"

"Unhand her!" James Burlough pushed past the startled Beeks and shoved Rafe away from Felicity. "You bastard! How dare you assault a lady, and in front of a child!"

Alarmed, Felicity started between them. "My lord, it's not—"

Rafe's hand shot out. Before Felicity could even gasp, he had Deerhurst by the throat and was pushing him backward into the hallway. "Don't you presume to assault me in my own house," he snapped, in a dark, cold voice Felicity had never heard him use before. "Miss Harrington and May no longer need your protection, or your interference."

They continued down the hallway toward the foyer, and Felicity hurried after them, afraid that Rafe might actually kill the earl. Deerhurst clawed at Rafe's iron grip, making angry, choked noises that might have been curses, but with Rafe keeping him off balance he could do little else.

"The Harringtons apparently consider you a friend," Rafe went on in the same level voice. "If you wish to continue to call on them, you will do so in a proper, respectful manner, as befits a guest. Beeks!"

Without a word the butler stepped around the two men to yank open the front door.

"Otherwise," Rafe continued, "your attentions are no longer welcome. Miss Harrington has agreed to be *my* wife." With that he released his grip on the earl's throat. "Is that clear?" he asked in an even quieter voice.

The earl stumbled backward, colliding with the closed half of the door. "I am a member of the House of Lords," he snarled, red-faced. "I will *not* be treated in this manner."

"Is that clear?" Rafe repeated coldly.

The earl slipped sideways toward the open doorway. "Felicity, is this true? You're actually going to *marry* this . . . man?"

Felicity managed a nod. "Yes." Even so, she didn't want to make an enemy of James. She'd known him forever, and he had even offered to marry her. "James, please understand—"

"Is . . . is he forcing you to—"

"Get out of my house," Rafe growled, moving forward.

Felicity grabbed him by the arm before he could throttle the earl again. "I think you should go, James," she said urgently. She'd try to explain later, once things had calmed down a little.

"Now," Rafe seconded, his eyes never leaving the earl's face.

With another sputtered curse, Deerhurst backed out the front door. As soon as he was clear, Beeks slammed it firmly shut.

"Will there be anything else, Master Rafael?" the butler asked calmly.

"No. That should do it."

"Rafe?" Felicity looked up at him. His anger at Robert Fields had been nothing compared to this.

He shook himself and turned to face her. "Damned fop."

May put her hands to her own throat, her eyes wide with apprehensive excitement. "Oh, my."

"My apologies, May," he muttered. "I got a bit upset."

"It was magnificent. Which number to kill a man was that?"

"Thirteen," he said shortly.

"May, give us a moment, will you?"

Beeks moved forward again. "Come, Miss May, if you please. I believe the gentlemen outside will be looking for their afternoon refreshment."

After they left, Felicity took a short breath. "Lord Deerhurst is going to be your neighbor now," she said quietly. "You haven't made a friend."

"I should hope not." He lifted her hand and kissed her fingers. "It felt very satisfying, though."

"You've been wanting to hit him since the first day you met him."

"Yes, I have. But that's not why I booted him out of our house."

Our house. She liked the sound of that. "Why, then?"

He narrowed his eyes, looking back toward the door as though he wished Deerhurst had stayed for more mistreatment. "That's the second time he's suggested I might hurt you or May." Rafe returned his gaze to her. "And I would never—*never*—hurt either one of you, damnit."

"I know that."

"He'd best figure it out, as well."

"Rafe, are you certain you—"

He cut her off with a kiss. "Don't. Just tell me what day you'd like to marry—but make it soon."

"I have no one to inform," she said, "but what about your family? Your father will certainly want to know."

His expression became grim for a moment. "I'll marry whom I choose, Lis. He can come congratulate us once Forton Hall is repaired."

"You mean he'll object, so you don't want to tell them."

Rafe shrugged. "It's something of a tradition in my family, anyway. So what day do you prefer?"

She blushed. He truly meant to marry her. And as soon as they were married, being intimate would not only be acceptable, it would be her wifely duty. "Tomorrow?" she whispered. "No, that's too quickly."

He smiled softly. "They'll have to read the banns in church over the next three Sundays. I'm afraid I didn't have the foresight to procure a special marriage license before I came to Cheshire."

She put a hand on his injured arm. "Publishing

the banns is a tradition here, anyway.''

"What about the afternoon of the third Sunday, then?''

It seemed like forever. "Yes,'' she whispered, and kissed him again.

The Earl of Deerhurst stalked back and forth across his library floor. That damned coward had nearly strangled him. He needed to be dealt with. He might be a highborn, bloody Bancroft, but this far from London and Staffordshire, the name didn't carry that much weight.

He had at least three weeks to make his move. Though publishing the banns was disdained by the *ton*, it was popular in Cheshire. And as well liked as Bancroft seemed intent on becoming, he would no doubt go that route.

James paused by the bay window that looked out over his garden. If he'd ever had any second thoughts about killing Bancroft to keep the bastard from finding out he also owned Deerhurst, he didn't any longer. He'd be tempted even if he didn't have anything to gain from it. But now it had to be done soon. If Bancroft died after the wedding, Felicity would be in deep mourning for six months, and Deerhurst didn't want to give her that much time to make an escape. He wanted her, along with what already belonged to him. He'd bloody well worked hard enough for it.

Little May was an annoyance, too. He sighed. Well, there was always boarding school, if she didn't accidentally expire along with Bancroft. Slowly James smiled. He'd have to mention that tonight to the men he'd sent to work for Bancroft. That would be lovely—but whatever else happened, Rafael Bancroft was going to die. And the sooner, the better.

* * *

Felicity woke up. She sat straight up in bed, blankets flying and her heart pounding. Outside everything was dark and quiet, except for the crickets and the frogs by the pond. Inside her head, though, everything was in an uproar. She knew it had been too good to be true, and too good to last.

She flung off her covers, pulled her old dressing robe on over her nightgown, opened her door, and headed down the hall. She stopped at the corner room and rapped on the door, then pushed it open without waiting for an answer.

Rafe sat up in bed, his hair tousled. "What is it?" he asked, the covers sliding down his bare chest to his waist.

That shook her resolve a little. Good Lord, he was beautiful. She took a breath. "Why do you want to marry me?" she demanded, closing his door and folding her arms across her chest.

"What?" he repeated more sharply, running a hand through his hair. "Felicity, it's . . . it's too damned dark to see the clock."

Rafe evidently was not a morning person. Trying to steady herself from the frantic nightmare that had awakened her, and from the rousing sight of a very attractive half-naked man sitting in bed, she walked over to light the candle on the bed stand. "There. It's three o'clock in the morning. Feel better?"

He studied her face in the flickering yellow light. "You're shaking," he said. "Come sit down." Sitting back against the headboard, the covers lowering even more provocatively, he reached for her hand and tugged her down to sit beside him.

"I had a dream," she said.

"Tell me." Softly he stroked his fingers through her long, loose hair.

"Nigel came back."

He was silent for a moment. "And?"

"And he offered to sail with you to China, and you jumped up on Aristotle and rode off with him so fast you didn't even take your coat." A tear ran down her cheek at the memory. "And May stood there waving, and you said you'd send her a doll."

"It was just a dream, Lis." His strong, warm arms slipped around her and pulled her back to lean against his side.

"I know." Another tear followed the first. "But it's happened before."

"You've been married before?"

"Oh, hush. You know what I mean. Nigel, my father, they were full of such grand ideas."

Putting his hand on her shoulder, he turned her slowly to face him. "I'm not Nigel, and I'm damned well not your father," he said, meeting her gaze.

She laid her head against his shoulder. "I know, I know. But I also know how much you want to travel and see exciting places, and I know that hasn't just gone away."

"You're exciting," he murmured. "What do you want me to tell you, Lis? I love you. This is a new experience for me."

"Just tell me everything will be all right, and I don't need to worry anymore."

To her surprise, he chuckled. "Good God, I've never had anyone rely on me for anything before, either." Rafe wrapped his arms around her again and held her close. "Everything *will* be all right, Lis. You don't need to worry anymore," he whispered into her hair.

"Are you sure?" she asked, relaxing against him. She couldn't imagine sitting like this with James and telling him of her nightmares. Rafe was so easy to talk to—he had been, from the moment they'd met. Fleetingly she wondered if that was when she'd fallen in love with him.

He laughed again, softly. "Yes, I'm sure. I'll worry enough for all of us. Are you still marrying me?"

Felicity turned and kissed the line of his jaw. "Yes."

"Will you stay with me for the rest of the night?"

Slowly and reluctantly she pulled away from him. "No. It's only three weeks, Rafe."

"That's easy for you to say."

She laughed. "No, it's not."

With a last kiss, she returned to her bedchamber and climbed back under the covers. She still had questions, of course, and she might still worry. But she knew one thing. He loved her.

"Master Rafael," Beeks said in a low, urgent voice, "I must repeat my suggestion that you inform the duke and duchess of your intention to wed Miss Harrington."

Rafe glanced at the butler and then resumed sawing. "An unsolicited opinion, Beeks? What would His Grace say?"

"That is precisely what worries me, sir."

"If you're concerned they'll cut me off, don't worry. His Grace isn't likely to leave me anything, anyway. Hold that end of the board, will you?"

Beeks grabbed the free end of the board. "Actually, sir, it is more *my* continued employment I am concerned about."

With a stifled chuckle Rafe wiped sweat from his forehead and went back to sizing boards for stable stalls. "I already told you there's a position for you here. And I believe you have a standing offer of employment from Quin."

The butler cleared his throat. "As comforting as that is, I am rather accustomed to my position at Bancroft House."

With a last pull on the saw, the board parted, and Rafe tossed the longer section onto the growing stack beside him. "No worries, then. I'll be sure to tell my parents of your strenuous objections."

Beeks threw the leftover piece of board aside. "Don't misunderstand me, Master Rafael. My objection is only to the route you are taking. Not to the match."

Rafe straightened. "By God, Beeks, you surprise me again. Thank you." He'd actually begun to feel he was making the right decision. And Beeks's additional support at least indicated that he hadn't gone completely insane.

"Very good." With a rare half smile the butler turned on his heel.

"Beeks?"

"Yes, sir?"

"How handy are you with a hammer?"

The butler sighed and stopped his retreat. "Proficient enough, I suppose. What of my household duties?"

Rafe grinned. "That reminds me—before you join the construction crew, we need to take care of something. As I'll be staying at Forton, I think it's time I had an actual household staff."

"An excellent idea, sir."

"I would appreciate if you would hire a maid for Felicity and May, a groom, and a downstairs maid. At a reasonable rate of pay." He hated adding that last part, but his debt to Quin already reached well into the thousands. And until Forton actually began making money, things would only get worse.

A gleam of anticipation entered the butler's normally impassive expression. "I shall see to it at once, Master Rafael. Might I suggest a replacement for Ronald, as well?"

"No, you may not. Don't be such a snob, Beeks."

"Yes, sir."

As the butler departed, Rafe took a moment to stretch his back and look over the work they'd accomplished so far. The outside of the stable was nearly completed, lacking only doors and a few coats of paint. Inside, half the stalls and the loft were finished. All it needed was hay and horses.

He leaned back against the pile of bricks he'd been using as a worktable. Time and necessity had stripped Forton well past the bare essentials needed to run an estate. Providing enough to enable it to function again was expensive, tiring, frightening, and confusing—especially when he'd never had any experience remotely similar. And even with all the components in place, he still had a better chance for bankruptcy than turning a profit.

Even so, he couldn't deny that the new stable looked good: practical, efficient, and even picturesque. And he'd designed it. He'd planned it, and built it. It belonged to him, perhaps more than anything else he'd ever done or owned.

"It's beautiful."

He grinned and turned around. "You think so?"

Felicity stopped beside him. "Compared to what used to stand there, it's the Aphrodite of stables."

"Thank you, my lady." He swept a bow.

The idea of marrying had also begun to sit much more easily, especially after she'd stormed into his bedchamber the night before last. Felicity would belong to him, too, even more than Forton—though it seemed more accurate to say that he was earning the opportunity to hang about Forton and stay in her life. That wasn't so bad, either.

"If we can finish the stalls today, I think we can begin on your west wing tomorrow."

"*Your* west wing, Rafe. Stop doing that."

"Doing what?"

She glanced around them, and then stepped closer. "You said you wouldn't let Deerhurst buy me for the price of Forton," she explained, lowering her voice. "Is that what you think you've done?"

"No," he retorted, though he wasn't all that certain he'd answered truthfully. He couldn't seem to think of one without the other. He wrapped his fingers around her wrist. "Just wait until I ask you to join May and me on our expedition to the Arctic."

Her expression tensed, and then she smiled. "At least plan it for the summer, won't you?"

"Of course." He studied her face for a moment. "Now, what were you *going* to say, Lis?"

"Nothing. I don't—"

"None of that."

She made a face at him. "I was just going to say that we won't be able to afford a journey to the Arctic, but then I decided I didn't need to beat you over the head with the obvious."

So she was worried, too, over whether he would stay. Somehow he found that reassuring. "Better the obvious than a tea kettle, my practical one." In truth, though, they hurt about the same. He didn't need to be reminded of what he was giving up, or of what he was getting himself into. He'd never been much of a worrier—but he was beginning to appreciate the finer points.

Some of his reservations must have shown on

his face, because she suddenly leaned forward and kissed him on the cheek. "I love you, Rafael," she whispered, blushing.

"Who would have thought," he said slowly, swinging her hand in his, "that wagering at Jezebel's Harem would have led me to you?"

"Would you have wagered if you had known?"

He wondered if he should mention that he'd been helping the odds a little that night, but decided it wouldn't be very wise. "Yes." Rafe straightened. "Will you look at the new floor plan with me one more time? It's your last chance to change the size of the library."

"I only suggested enlarging it that one time," she protested.

He held up three fingers and cleared his throat.

Lis batted his hand away. "I like books."

"Well, you'll have a great deal of space for a collection, now."

"*You're* putting in a billiards room."

"I like billiards. And May said she does, as well."

Felicity laughed. "She's never played billiards."

At least she was smiling again. "That does explain her thinking it had something to do with running."

Beeks emerged from the kitchen again, the mail salver in his hand. "You have a visitor, Master Rafael," he announced.

Rafe lifted the calling card off the tray. "John Gibbs," he read, and glanced at Felicity. "My solicitor."

"What could it be?"

He shrugged. "I suppose he wants to know why I didn't tell him to stop advertising Forton for sale. I'd best take care of that. Excuse me for a moment."

John Gibbs sat at one end of the morning room couch, a satchel across his knees. As soon as Rafe entered the room he stood, dropped his satchel, and bent to pick it up again.

"Good afternoon, Gibbs," Rafe said, shaking the younger man's hand.

"Mr. Bancroft. I . . . I apologize for barging in on you like this, but I know you've been quite busy."

Rafe motioned him back into his seat. "I'm glad you came by. I need to discuss something with you."

"I also have something rather interesting to impart."

That sounded intriguing, but first things first. "I have decided to remain at Forton Hall."

The solicitor nodded. "I thought that might be the case, sir."

"Oh, really? Elaborate, please."

Gibbs shifted again. "Well, I was purchasing a ledger book at Mrs. Denwortle's establishment, and I . . . happened to overhear her, ah, discussing your upcoming marriage to Miss Harrington. And a visit by the Duke of Highbarrow to give his blessing to the match."

That couldn't be much farther from the truth. He'd have to make another visit and continue the confusion. "Mrs. Denwortle does save one the trouble of writing letters, doesn't she?"

"Yes, sir."

"So, Gibbs, I would appreciate if you would arrange to cancel all advertisements regarding the sale of the estate."

The solicitor nodded. "And may I be among the first to wish you and Miss Harrington well, Mr. Bancroft?"

"Thank you." Rafe sat back. "Now, what was

the 'interesting' matter you mentioned?''

''Ah, yes.'' Mr. Gibbs shuffled through the satchel on his lap, and finally extracted a piece of paper. ''During my search for a buyer for Forton Hall, I wrote Mr. Harrington's old solicitor in London. Thomas Metcalfe was forced to resign his position some dozen years ago because the Harringtons could no longer afford his services, but he apparently harbored some affection for young Miss Harrington.''

''Then he has good taste,'' Rafe commented with a slight smile.

''Yes, sir. In response to my inquiry regarding any possible historic significance for Forton, he—''

'' 'Historic significance'?'' Rafe repeated, lifting an eyebrow.

''I'd hoped to find something to increase the value of the estate. Unfortunately, other than the advanced age of its former west wing, Forton Hall has very little to recommend it to posterity.''

''What a surprise.''

The solicitor looked at him as though he wasn't certain whether Rafe was jesting, or not. ''At any rate,'' he resumed after a moment, ''Mr. Metcalfe did have some information about a loan,'' and he lifted the piece of paper to read it, '''of an undisclosed amount made by Harrington to Robert Burlough, the Earl of Deerhurst.' '' He looked up.

''Harrington lent *Deerhurst* blunt?''

''The present earl's father. Yes, apparently so. Mr. Metcalfe claims not to know any of the particulars, and evidently only mentioned it in his letter because it quite annoyed him at the time.''

''But he doesn't say when or how much or whether it was ever repaid?''

Gibbs scanned the missive again. ''No, sir.''

Rafe sighed. "Hm. Interesting, yes. Helpful, no."

"I'd be happy to do a bit more investigating, if you'd like."

"As part of your retainer, or would there be an additional fee involved?"

The solicitor actually grinned. "If I find something, we can discuss an additional fee."

"Fair enough."

Chapter 17

"**A** loan?" Felicity repeated, frowning. "I've never heard of any such thing."

May swung her legs energetically back and forth under the dining room table. "I haven't, either."

Rafe finished his mouthful of ham and grinned at her. "It would have been before you were born, midget."

"It doesn't make any sense, whenever it supposedly took place," Felicity resumed, with a fond look at the two of them. For someone who'd never spent time around children, Rafe had slipped effortlessly into his dual role of older brother and surrogate father. She wondered if he even realized what a handful most people found May to be.

"Why not?"

"As a child I remember servants and horses and house parties here at Forton, so we did have money once, but Deerhurst has always been that way, too. Even if my father had the money to lend, I can't conceive that the earl would ever have needed it."

"This Metcalfe fellow seemed certain of it, even if he didn't know any of the details."

"Mr. Metcalfe must be a very old man by now. Perhaps he's confusing my father with someone else."

Rafe shrugged. "Perhaps. Wouldn't it be nice,

though, to discover that Deerhurst owed you a few hundred quid?''

''A few hundred quid would be exceptionally nice, but dreaming about an unexpected fortune won't make it happen. James has offered me money innumerable times. I'm certain he would have repaid any outstanding loans.''

From Rafe's skeptical expression he didn't agree with her, but he apparently realized that he wasn't going to change her mind, either. He shrugged and pushed away from the table.

''Forgive me for not seconding your sterling characterization of his lordship.''

''Me, too.''

He winked at May. ''Gibbs has volunteered to look further for any records. Your father might have lent someone money, even if it wasn't Deerhurst. Wishful thinking or not, we could use the blunt.''

She watched as he pulled on the coat he'd left hanging across the back of his chair. He was dressed to go out, she realized. Curiosity blazed through her, but even as she opened her mouth to ask where in the world he might be going after dark in tame old east Cheshire, she stopped the question. He'd been devoting nearly every waking hour to Forton Hall. She had no right to demand to know his whereabouts every given moment.

''Lucifer's big bottom, Rafe, where are you going?''

Thank goodness for inquisitive younger siblings. ''May, that's none of our affair,'' she chastised for show.

''Greetham and some of his cronies are going down to the Childe of Hale. Not exactly White's, but I haven't smoked a cigar or played hazard in awhile. Don't want to get rusty, you know. It'll ruin my chances of winning other estates and valuable properties.''

The color drained from Felicity's face. "You're going wagering?" she asked, more sharply than she intended.

His surprised gaze touched hers. "For a bit. I won't be too late." Rafe continued to look at her when she didn't respond. "What is it, Lis?"

With effort she returned her attention to her nearly empty plate. "Nothing, of course."

"She doesn't like wagering," May supplied in her usual matter-of-fact tone.

Rafe sat at the table again. "No?" he asked, his attention still on Felicity. "Do tell."

She could feel his cool gaze on her, even with her eyes lowered. "I never said any such thing."

"Yes, you did. After Nigel lost your mare, you said if you ever found out he'd been wagering again, you'd break his head."

"Well," Rafe said quietly, "I'm sure Lis remembers that I'm not Nigel, and that I would never be so careless as to wager more than I could afford to lose."

Torn between saying that she trusted him and pointing out that he couldn't afford to lose anything, Felicity bit her tongue and nodded. "Of course not."

Rafe blew out his breath and stood. "I won't be long," he said, and left the room. A moment later the main door opened and closed.

"You made him mad," May complained.

"*I* didn't say anything. *You* made him mad."

"I was only telling him what you said."

"Well, May," Felicity returned, dropping her napkin onto the table and standing, "you don't always need to repeat everything you hear. Don't be such a parrot, for heaven's sake."

"I am not a parrot!" May yelled, but Felicity left her sister in the dining room. "Felicity, you're mean!"

"Wonderful," she muttered, speeding her escape down the hall toward the foyer and the stairs. "Now everyone's angry with me."

All she wanted was a little peace and quiet. After five years of growing silence, having three servants now—four, counting the groom Beeks had hired that morning—made the Hall astoundingly loud. She wasn't used to it any longer: polite nods and not having to cook, fires and lamps lit in her bedchamber when she retired for the evening. It was too perfect, too wonderful, and something would happen to make it all go away again. And she would probably be the one to ruin it, because she couldn't relax and trust.

She entered the foyer and bumped into Rafe coming back into the house. "Oh! I'm sorry!"

He caught her arms, pulling her up against his chest while she regained her balance. As soon as she had her feet under her, Rafe tilted her chin up and closed his mouth over hers. Her pulse skittering, she wrapped her hands into his lapels and kissed him back.

A moment later he lifted his head to look at her. "I am not Nigel," he said fiercely.

She shook her head. "Nigel wouldn't have come back." Felicity leaned against his strong body to kiss him again. "I'm sorry," she repeated. "I just worry, sometimes."

"You worry all the time," he amended, and to her great relief, smiled. "What say I teach you and May to play hazard? Beeks can make us a foursome."

"What about Mr. Greetham and the Childe of Hale?"

"You smell better," he said, dipping his head to run his lips along her shoulders and her neck. "And I find you infinitely more appealing."

Trembling, she brushed her fingers along his scarred cheek. "I'm not trying to keep you prisoner here."

Rafe intercepted her hand and led her back toward the dining room. "The damned inn isn't going anywhere. And neither am I."

Still, Felicity watched him all evening, looking for any sign of restlessness or regret. Forton Hall was still new to him, but she had to wonder how he would feel about being in Cheshire a year from now, or two years from now. For a man who'd spent most of his adult life traveling, staying in one place had to be difficult. And that was assuming he was comfortable with the choice he'd made.

In the morning Rafe rose early to ride Aristotle around the perimeter of Forton land, as he'd done for the past week or so. Felicity watched for him, sitting at her dressing table and gazing out the window. He seemed so much a part of this place, and she hoped he felt it, as well. He'd put part of himself into Forton, as she had.

When he and Aristotle cantered back into the stable yard, Felicity smiled helplessly. She loved May dearly, but nothing made her heart so glad as Rafael Bancroft. Even though he'd ruined her friendship with the Earl of Deerhurst, at least temporarily, she couldn't muster much concern over it. James was generally an understanding man, and she hoped that eventually she'd be able to make amends. But if she couldn't, that was all right, too. She could never condone the unkind things he'd said to Rafael.

May emerged from the kitchen with an apple for Aristotle, and at some secret twitch of the reins both Rafe and the gelding bowed to her. She laughed and curtsied back, and Felicity chuckled. They certainly had the makings of an odd little household. As Rafe dismounted and handed Aristotle over to Tom Milton's care, wagons began rolling noisily up the rutted drive. A completely different kind of excitement touched her. Today, work on the west wing would begin. Soon her home would be a home again.

Rafe caught sight of Felicity watching him out her window, but he pretended not to notice. The first morning he'd bathed beneath the water pump he'd noticed her interest; but since he liked it when she looked at him, he'd said nothing. No sense spoiling a good thing.

He and May had a quick breakfast, then he went out to begin erecting the skeleton of the west wing. By now his crew seemed to consider him just another worker, for the amount of cursing and lewd jests had increased daily, until he could almost think he was back in the army again. Later in the morning Beeks and Ronald carried chairs outside into the shade, and Felicity and May emerged from the house.

Rafe strolled over. "Good morning, ladies."

"Good morning," Felicity returned. "The day looked so pleasant, we decided to do May's lessons outside."

"Or I can help, if you need me," May put in hopefully.

"I'm sure I will," he said dutifully. "I have Beeks held in reserve, as well."

"Will it look the same as it did before?"

Rafe glanced back at the bare beginnings of a shape. "From the outside, as nearly as possible. The old wing suited the surroundings as well as the east wing does.'' He'd noticed that as he'd begun sketching various layouts for the replacement wing.

He'd dug up old drawings to work from and had made numerous changes to the interior, including Felicity's gargantuan library. The exterior design, however, continued to revert to something so similar to the original that after a few days of frustration, he simply gave up trying to alter it. Whoever had originally built Forton had felt genuine affection both for the countryside and for the site of the Hall.

Whether they truly intended to work on May's lessons or were merely looking for an excuse to be outside and watch the proceedings, by noon both May and Felicity were carrying boards and hammering. Felicity seemed fascinated by the whole process, and Rafe was more than happy to answer her multitude of questions about crossbeams and supports and how to keep the wing from collapsing as it had before.

By afternoon, Beeks and Ronald had been pulled into the chaos, as well. Rafe grinned as he finished securing one of the ground level crossbeams. Hard, hot work or not, this was damned entertaining.

''Ouch! Blast it!''

Rafe whipped around as Felicity jumped back and grabbed her left thumb. Immediately half the workers swarmed around her, all curses forgotten, as they clamored to lend advice and assistance. Rafe pushed through the noisy gaggle to reach her side.

''You all right, Lis?''

She scrunched her eyes shut, pained tears squeezing past her long, dark lashes. ''I'm fine. I just hammered my thumb.''

May patted her arm. ''You can cry, Lis. Ronald did, when he hammered his thumb.''

"Ye need to wrap it in a damp compress, miss, to stop the swelling," one of the crew offered, the rest of them echoing the advice like a flock of parrots.

"Let me take a look at it," Rafe said with a faint grin, taking her wrist and pulling her away from the crowd and around the corner of the house.

She reluctantly released the grip on her flattened thumb and held it out to him. "It's not broken, I'm sure."

"Let me see about that." Rafe gently examined the appendage. It was red and hot to the touch, and the skin on her knuckle was scraped and bruised. "Does it hurt to bend it?" he asked, glancing up at her face.

She flinched. "No."

Still holding her gaze, Rafe lifted her hand and slipped her thumb into his mouth.

"Rafe . . ." she began to protest, then stopped. "This is not what they meant by a damp compress."

He continued suckling her thumb. Though he'd seen his share of smashed fingers, he'd never been remotely tempted to perform such a service before. Then again, he'd never had the urge to lie down in the sweet grass with one of his fellow workers to run his hands over her body before, either.

Felicity licked her lips. "Stop that," she finally whispered, though she made no move to pull away. "It makes me want to . . ."

Slowly he removed her thumb from between his lips. "Makes you want to what?" he asked, still tenderly rubbing it.

She flushed. "To throw myself on you and kiss you all over."

Thank God it wasn't just him. "I am at your mercy."

"Not here," she protested.

"Ah. And is kissing all you wish to do?"

"You know it's not." She ran her fingers along the collar of his shirt. "You make me feel so . . . shivery."

Rafe chuckled. "I think that's the best compliment I've ever received. You do the same thing to me."

She leaned closer, passion and amusement dancing in her eyes. "Do I, Rafael?"

He sighed. Sometimes, just looking at her was enough. "Yes, you do."

Feather-light, she touched her lips to his. "Good."

Before he could slip his arms around her and pull her to him, she danced away and vanished around the corner. Rafe looked after her for a long moment. "Good Lord," he muttered, trying to slow the pounding of his heart. If Lis ever regained her senses and decided she didn't want him, God help them both.

"I think we'll have it finished in a week!" May announced. She leaned her elbows on the edge of the building plans to examine the sketches.

"I appreciate your confidence, midget, but it will take a bit longer than that." Rafe continued making notations along one side of the drawing, keeping painstaking track of the supplies they'd used so far. Even with the mishaps they'd encountered while erecting the stable, they were still within the budget he and Felicity had estimated.

"Lis, look!" May pointed at the drawing. "I helped hammer that board right there!"

Chuckling, Felicity set aside her mending and rose. "Oh, yes. I recognize it." She indicated another section. "And this is where I smashed my thumb."

"We'll install a plaque on the wall to commemorate your battle wound." Rafe ran his finger over her thumb. The knuckle was still red and bruised, but the swelling had gone down substantially—unlike his own desire for the blasted practical chit.

"Did you get a plaque?"

For a moment he didn't know what May was talking about, until she reached over to touch his scarred cheek. He waited for the sensation of discomfort and uneasiness to creep up his spine in response. When it didn't, he shook his head. "I got a shiny new medal instead."

"Can I see it?"

"*May* I see it," Felicity corrected.

"Where?" May looked around excitedly.

"Good God." Rafe grinned at Felicity's amused, exasperated expression. "Didn't your parents consider this problem when they named her?"

"Apparently not."

May's confused look cleared. "Oh. I understand. *May* I see your medal?"

He shook his head again. "I gave it to my mother. I think she had it put on a hat."

May laughed. "On a hat?"

Felicity met his gaze, her expression intrigued. "So it was only your father who didn't approve."

"I wouldn't exactly say my mother was pleased with my actions, but she was something of an adventurer herself when she was younger. At any rate, she understood what I was doing." Better than he had, probably.

"That's what I'm going to be, too. An adventurer."

From Felicity's expression, she wished he hadn't mentioned that. And after her panic the other night, the last thing he wanted to do was make her mad at him again. Rafe cleared his throat. "Yes. Well, you see, May, it came about because my mother had been quite well educated—extensively educated—and she wanted to view some of the places she'd studied."

May noisily blew out her breath. "You're bamming me."

"I am not."

She jabbed a finger at him. "You never studied all the places you say you want to go."

Rafe lifted an eyebrow. "And how do you know that, pray tell?"

"Because you want to go places you don't even know about yet."

Blast the uncanny logic of eight-year-olds. "I will study about them before I go," he countered.

"Oh, no you—"

"May," Felicity interrupted, "you'd best go get ready for bed."

Damn it, he should have kept his blasted mouth shut. Whether he still wanted to travel or not, Felicity didn't need something else to worry over. Rafe sat back as he realized that over the past few weeks, something had changed. He didn't think about traveling nearly as much as he had when he'd lived in London. And after today's progress, staying to see his project finished seemed more exciting than tromping about some desert.

"I'm going to dream about elephants," May decided, heading for the door. "What are you going to dream about, Rafe?"

He glanced up from his drawing again to catch Felicity gazing at him. "Your sister," he drawled, and went back to work.

"That's dull."

"Well, thank you very much," Felicity protested

with a laugh, blushing and throwing a darned stocking at her sister.

As May pulled open the door, something very big and very loud rumbled and crashed outside. "Good God," Rafe cursed, shooting to his feet and knowing instantly what it must be. "Damn!"

"Rafe?" May, white-faced and wide-eyed, stopped in the doorway.

"Stay here, sweetling," he said, grabbing up a lamp.

Beeks emerged from the hall leading from the kitchen and the servants' rooms. "Master Rafael?"

"Keep an eye on May," Rafe barked.

"Yes, sir."

Felicity hurried behind him down the hallway. He yanked open the front door, and took the steps in one leap. Rafe rounded the near corner of the house at top speed, and then stopped short.

The skeleton of the new building looked more like an old shipwreck, listing to one side and definitely unseaworthy. "Bloody hell," he muttered, stepping gingerly forward.

"Rafe, be careful."

"Not much more collapsing it can do." Still cursing, he lifted the lamp to survey the damage.

He'd certainly seen his share of disasters before, but this one hurt. He knew which piece of lumber he'd sawed, and which one he'd hammered, and the death of the structure—he couldn't help but think of it as a living entity—was personal, and painful.

"Accidents happen," Lis said in a soothing voice from behind him.

He glanced back at her. "This one shouldn't have. *Damnit.* We're going to have to start all over again."

"At least it's only one day's work."

Rafe lowered the lantern and faced her. "Except now I have to go back and figure out what in hell I did wrong. It shouldn't have fallen. It should have stood up under a volcanic eruption." He slammed his fist against one of the remaining supports. It didn't even rock.

Felicity tugged on his arm. "Come on. Glowering at it all night won't help anything."

With a last scowl at the mess, he turned and followed her back inside. They'd lost more than a day; they'd lost a hundred quid worth of supplies and labor. And he'd be damned if he'd let it happen again.

Felicity sat on the hard, smooth wood of the pew and kept her eyes on her prayer book. Beside her May kicked out her legs and fashioned her fingers into horses leaping from one knee to the other. Beyond her, Rafe leaned back and watched the vicar through half-closed eyes, looking like nothing so much as a great tawny lion sizing up a gazelle.

The parable of Daniel and the Lion's Den dragged on and on. And it wasn't only her own impatience that made the tale seem long beyond bearing. Two rows behind them, Mr. Jarrod snored softly.

"When will he read the banns?" May whispered.

"Hush," Felicity chastised. "Soon enough."

"Do you think anyone will object?"

"May, be quiet."

Rafe stirred. "No one will object," he murmured.

He glanced at the Earl of Deerhurst, seated across the aisle from them, and then settled back again. James had barely acknowledged their presence in the parish church, a far cry from his usual friendly conversation.

Finally the lions spared Daniel, and her own lion straightened a little. The parishioners sang a hymn, and then Reverend Laskey pulled a piece of parchment from beneath his Bible and smoothed it flat. Felicity drew a nervous breath and held it. They might have purchased a license for a few guineas and avoided the public pronouncements, but she knew Rafe still had his doubts about being accepted by the local residents. So, rather than tiptoe around the issue, he chose to confront it head on.

"Three weeks hence," Mr. Laskey announced in his carrying voice, "on the twenty-third of August, Mr. Rafael Bancroft will wed Miss Harrington. Are there any objections to this union?"

A surprised murmur ran through the sections of the church which hadn't already heard the news. No one stood, or shouted, or fainted, and a moment later the vicar continued with his regular announcements.

Felicity closed her eyes in relief. Only two more weeks of this torture, and she could marry Rafe. She glanced over at him, settling back into his half-asleep pose again. His green eyes glinted beneath his shuttered lids, and she wondered whether he'd been hoping Deerhurst would object.

As the service ended, the parishioners trailed out of the church. With the first public announcement of their pending nuptials now made, a crowd of noisy well-wishers surrounded her and Rafe. The Earl of Deerhurst walked by without a glance, climbed up into his curricle, and drove away.

"Your perfect gentleman seems to have a chink in his armor," Rafe noted as they finally escaped the congratulations.

"You tried to pummel him," Felicity retorted.

She watched the married couples who left the churchyard hand in hand, and reminded herself that she wouldn't have to pretend she didn't long to hold Rafe's hand or be in his arms for much longer.

Rafe lifted May onto Aristotle's back and freed the reins. Silently he held his arm out to Felicity, and with a skipping of her pulse she slipped her hand around it. Aristotle and May in tow, they headed down the lane back to Forton.

"Rafe, am I your best man?" May asked from her high perch.

"You certainly are," he answered, and looked sideways at Felicity.

"May, I'd hoped you would be my maid of honor," she said, leaning a little closer against his tall strength.

"Oh, all right."

Felicity stifled a smile at her sister's blatant lack of enthusiasm. "Thank you, sweetling."

"You're welcome. Are the mercenaries coming today?"

Rafe glanced over his shoulder at her. "Just a few, to clear off the foundation so we can begin again tomorrow."

Despite his prompt answer his mind seemed a little distant, and Felicity wondered whether he was thinking about the construction work ahead, or whether he'd mentally traveled to some exotic city where perfume and spices filled the air.

"It will go more smoothly from now on," she stated firmly. "I'm certain of it."

He shrugged. "It's a war now: me against the west wing. And I don't intend to lose."

"The Coldstream Guards never lose," May seconded, leaning forward along Aristotle's neck. "Do we have a motto?"

Rafe chuckled, returning from wherever it was

that he'd been. "Of course we do. *Nulli secundus*."

" 'Second to none,' " Felicity translated.

May looked at him skeptically. "It's not very exciting."

"Just be glad we're not the Royal Scots Regiment."

"What's their motto?"

He cleared his throat. "*Nemo me impune lacessit.*"

"Goodness," Felicity exclaimed. "That's quite beyond me."

"What is it?" May demanded.

Rafe turned on his heel to give May an elegant, precise salute. " 'No one provokes me with impunity.' "

"Oh, yuck. I could never shout that while charging into battle."

Felicity grinned as she took Rafe's arm again and they resumed their walk. "Let's hope you never have to, dear."

Sunday might have been a day of rest, but anyone passing by Forton Hall would have had to assume it was a weekday. Along with Rafe, still cursing under his breath with every piece of wood he had to cast aside, Mr. Greetham arrived to help, along with his two young sons. Three of the workers from Chester, eager to earn a bit of extra blunt, appeared as well.

May insisted on helping, and Felicity decided it would be more useful to help Rafe than to sit in the house and daydream about him all day. Though it was Ronald's day off, he appeared an hour or so later. And when Beeks, wearing an old shirt, floppy hat, and work gloves, emerged from the house a short time later, Felicity could only marvel at the lot of them.

By late afternoon only the scaffolding around the

construction area remained, and she was tired, sore, and dirty. Rafe spent a long time examining the boards, joints, nails, and beams, and making notations on various scraps of paper. Felicity wished he could accept the collapse as a simple accident, but he seemed determined to pursue the cause to the most minute detail. The next version of Forton's new wing would stand for ten thousand years, if he had anything to say about it.

In the morning the entire crew arrived, and they started all over again. Felicity didn't think Rafe had slept at all, because she fell asleep watching him work at the dining room table, and when she awoke, stiff and cramped, he was still altering his drawings.

"You're allowed to rest once in awhile," she finally said, coming up behind him as he helped haul one of the heavy crossbeams aloft at the end of a sturdy rope.

"It keeps me out of trouble," he grunted, flashing her a quick grin.

The word "trouble" inspired a sudden, unladylike urge to run her hands along his sweat-slicked body. Giving in to a delicious shudder and then removing herself from temptation, Felicity retreated to the far end of the construction site until Rafe called a halt to the day's work just before sunset. She'd begun to think he intended them to work straight through the night, and stretched her tired back in relief as he whistled for the men up on the scaffolds to descend.

"Bancroft, look out!"

Alarmed, Felicity spun around as a stack of lumber tumbled off the scaffolding. Rafe stood directly beneath the framework, and she screamed as he dove sideways.

"Rafe!"

"I'm all right," he said, standing again as she reached him. He looked up, his expression dark and angry. "What in damnation happened this time?"

One of the Chester workers, Lawrence Gillingham, squatted down at the edge of the platform. "My fault, Bancroft. I tripped. You all right?"

Rafe scowled. "Another accident and you're fired. We have little ones running about."

"Aye, sir. Won't happen again. You have my word."

Rafe dusted off his shirt and turned to Felicity. "I'm beginning to think I was not meant to be an architect. Or a carpenter."

"Don't be silly. You're grand at it."

"You're only saying that because you want the rest of a roof over your head."

She put her hands on her hips. "I am not," she stated. "I'm saying it because it's true. And that was a spectacular dive. It's a shame May missed it."

He put his arm around her shoulders. "Be thankful. She'd be diving under the furniture, and we'd never be able to find her."

"She already disemboweled Ronald twice this morning with the kitchen broom."

"My protegee should be completely lethal by the time she turns ten."

Felicity laughed, grateful that his good spirits remained intact. "I'll be so proud of her."

Chapter 18

"It's actually beginning to look like something." Rafe folded his arms across his chest and looked up at the new wing from the vantage point of the pond's shoreline.

"You sound surprised," Felicity commented, admiring the view from beside him.

He looked over at her, admiring that view even more. "I didn't expect it to be so pleasant looking."

Felicity tilted her head, obviously trying to decipher his expression. "Why not? You've worked hard enough on it."

Rafe shrugged. "Because I did it, I suppose."

"That sounds like something your father might say."

"Oh, so you've met him," he said dryly, unable to explain that the work toward a goal had always interested and occupied him. The goal itself had never been of much importance, and he rarely stayed around to do more than acknowledge it.

This, though, was different. The further the west wing progressed, the more he liked and enjoyed it. He wanted to see it finished, to know that he had made it, and to live within its walls and windows.

"I'd like to meet His Grace. He sounds as

though he might benefit from number twenty-eight."

"You'd need something harder than a tea kettle. Besides, it would ruin our streak of good luck. No accidents for a week." He took her hand, and lifting it to his lips, gently kissed her knuckles. "And only one more Sunday of publishing the banns."

She blushed. "How much longer will we have Beeks in residence?"

"I should think another few weeks at most. His Grace will want to return to Bancroft House to finish up his affairs for the year before they winter at Highbarrow Castle."

"I'll miss him." She smiled, turning her hand to twine her fingers with his. "I almost think he's beginning to grow fond of the place."

"He still refuses to accept a position here, though; he says I'm too unpredictable."

Lis brushed a lock of hair off his forehead. "I'm beginning to appreciate that about you."

The sun began to sink below the trees, and the edges of the few clouds to the west turned pink and then crimson. They watched the turning colors of the sky until they faded to gray.

"Are the sunsets in Africa as beautiful?" Felicity asked.

He stirred. "Hm? Oh. They're different. The heat rises from the ground in waves." He motioned with his hand. "The lower the sun gets, the more the horizon seems to ripple and move, like it's alive. It's mesmerizing."

She freed her fingers and started back toward the house. "I'm sorry all Cheshire sunsets have to offer are pretty colors."

Rafe watched her retreating backside, tired of the tension between them, and tired of the way he couldn't mention anything farther away than Pel-

ford without upsetting her—even when she lured
him into the conversation, as though to test his interest. "Lis, stop that."

She turned and looked at him. "Then stop pre-
ferring everywhere else in the world above Forton
Hall."

He narrowed his eyes. "I will, if you'll stop pre-
ferring Forton Hall above all the rest of damned
creation."

Felicity opened her mouth, shut it again, and
with a swish of her green skirt continued toward
the house. For a long moment Rafe glared after her,
torn between wanting to shake some sense into her
and wanting to kiss her until all her worries vanished. He wished again that he'd paid more attention when Quin had tried to explain about love. He
didn't seem to be very good at it himself.

He knew that he did love Felicity; even the
thought of not seeing her again was enough to send
him into a near panic. But he had come to love
Forton Hall, too—which at least made standing in
its shadow tolerable. By now he felt as though he
knew every stone and piece of wood and layer of
paint in the manor. Forton Hall already belonged
to him; inexorably, Forton Hall was becoming part
of him.

Rafe sighed and strolled toward the west wing,
to take one more look for the night. Since the collapse he'd been jittery, even with the accidents and
any bad luck they'd conjured apparently gone.

Something moved at the edge of his vision, and
he stopped in the deep shadows of the main house.
A moment later he caught it again, moving among
the uprights of the skeletal wing. It might have
been a deer or a fox, but given the noise the construction created every day, he didn't think a wild
animal would venture so close.

Then his eyes caught the orange glow. With a silent curse he sprinted forward. Felicity and May were inside. If the house burned, so would they.

The saboteur didn't even hear him approaching until Rafe had already launched himself at the man. Gillingham from Chester, Rafe registered as he threw himself forward. He hit hard, and they rolled, colliding with one of the main upright supports. A bucket of lamp oil spilled, splashing the nearest beams.

Gillingham lashed out. Rafe ducked beneath the blow and smashed his fist into the man's stomach, and he crumpled with a breathless wheeze. Panting, and angrier than he could ever remember being in his life, Rafe grabbed Gillingham by the collar and shoved him backward.

"Why?" he snarled.

Gillingham spat at him.

Rafe hit him again, knocking him into the dirt. "Why?" he repeated.

"The blunt," the man rasped.

"The blunt?" Rafe stared at him. "Whose blunt?"

"Go to hell."

"I'll see you hanged for this, so help me God."

Gillingham glanced past him, and Rafe tensed, readying for a second attack. At the smell of burning wood he whipped around. The fire had caught onto one of the side beams, and was eating its way upward. If it spread across the top beams, or if flames touched the spreading lamp oil, the whole structure—and in all likelihood the rest of the house—would be lost. Yanking off his coat, Rafe wrapped it around the beam, slapping and smothering the flames.

When he finally stepped back, breathing hard and smoke stinging his eyes, Gillingham was gone.

To be certain the fire was out, Rafe filled buckets
with water from the stable pump and doused all the
surrounding lumber.

His anger, though, continued to seethe. Someone
had paid to have Forton burned. And now that he
thought about it, most of the accidents had centered
around the workers from Chester. He could think
of only one man who both wanted him gone from
Cheshire, and had the money to hire help to see it
done.

"Deerhurst," he snarled.

Rafe burst into the morning room. Felicity delayed looking up, steeling herself for another argument. If only he would understand that Forton
was in her blood, that she'd been looking after it
for her entire life and couldn't stop now, no matter
how much and how desperately she loved him.

"Rafe, what happened?" May asked, her voice
alarmed.

Felicity looked at him, and gasped. "Rafe!"

Soot and ashes blackened his face, and the rest
of him was filthy and wet. He smelled of smoke
and lamp oil. His coat was completely missing, and
so was the lower half of his right shirt sleeve. And
the fury in his light green eyes chilled her.

"Someone just tried to burn us out," he snarled.

Felicity shot to her feet. "Forton is on fire?"

He looked at her. "No. I put it out."

"Thank God," she exclaimed. "Are you all
right?"

"Yes," he said shortly.

If he hadn't looked so angry, she would have
flung herself on him. She badly wanted to touch
him, to be certain he really was all right, but at the
moment he looked as though he would only push
her away.

"Did you see who did it?" May asked, wide-eyed.

"I did. Gillingham."

"One of our own workers? Why?"

"I didn't like him," May declared. "He would never let me help him."

Rafe's eyes remained steadily on Felicity, even as he paced to the window and back. "He said he did it for the blunt."

"The blunt? Whose?"

"I can guess," Rafe answered coldly, coming to a stop before her. "Can't you?"

She stared at him. "You're mad! Where is this Gillingham? We'll take him to the constable in Chester and find out what's going on."

"He got away from me," Rafe growled. "Think about it, Lis. How many of our accidents involved workers from Chester? And who went into Chester to tell anyone we were hiring?"

"No! May and I were with him. He did no such thing."

Rafe took a step closer. "You were never apart? Not for one moment?"

"Lord Deerhurst went to buy cigars while we were in the candy shop," May piped in.

"Ha! You see? And then the accidents started."

"You're accusing the Earl of Deerhurst of trying to sabotage Forton Hall? That's absurd! They were just accidents!"

He narrowed his eyes. "And the fire? Gillingham *accidentally* brought a lantern and lamp oil and set the building on fire?"

"I don't know. I didn't like Gillingham, either. Perhaps he's simply mad."

"Damnit, Lis, why won't you—"

"Or perhaps you misunderstood him," she said frantically. "You said yourself, nothing exciting has happened for better than a week.''

Rafe glared at her, open-mouthed. "*You think I'm making this up?* Look at me!''

''I think it's absurd to accuse my lifelong friend and neighbor of something so dreadful with only one stranger's mutterings for proof!''

''You're so blind that you can't even consider that that snake might wish us harm?''

''He is our neighbor! Don't call him that.''

''He *is* a snake!'' May seconded.

''May, go to your room!'' Felicity ordered angrily.

''No!''

''Why can't you believe me?'' Rafe snarled. ''Why can't you trust me for one damned minute?''

She hesitated at the deep hurt in his voice. ''Rafe—''

''Forget it!'' Rafe turned on his heel and left the room.

''Rafe?'' May called, but he didn't answer. A moment later the kitchen door slammed. The little girl turned on Felicity, her small fists clenched. ''You ruined it! He'll never want to stay with us now!'' With a choked sob, she ran out of the morning room and slammed the door closed behind her.

Felicity sank back into her chair and covered her face with her hands. ''Oh, no,'' she cried, and sobs began ripping out of her throat. ''Oh, no. Rafe, don't go.''

She'd done it. She'd pushed him too far, and he would leave her and her heart would die without him. Tears ran down her face. She should have burned the stupid place down herself. It had caused her nothing but grief and trouble her whole life. And now it had cost her Rafael.

*　　*　　*

"My lord," Fitzroy said, stopping in the library doorway, "Mr. Rafael Bancroft is here to see you."

"How nice." James Burlough looked up from his book in mild surprise. Evidently his helpers had either succeeded, or failed very badly. "Send him in, Fitzroy."

"Yes, my lord."

Even when Bancroft strode into the library, the earl remained undecided concerning the outcome of his latest venture. "Given your . . . filthy appearance," he said dryly, "I will assume this is not a social call, and I will not ask you to take a seat."

Bancroft remained silent as he approached, only stopping when he stood directly before Deerhurst.

The earl didn't move. He knew Bancroft's type. He considered himself a gentleman, and unless provoked, he wouldn't strike first. So James waited to hear whatever threats and suppositions he'd come up with.

"I intercepted your messenger this evening," Bancroft said in a low, quiet voice, "and I want to give you a bit of advice."

"Ah, how kind. What sort of advice?" Damn that Gillingham; if he'd confessed, things were going to become sticky very quickly.

"If you do anything—*anything*—ever again to harm May or Felicity or one piece of Forton, I will kill you. Is that clear?"

Ah, he didn't have any proof, then. Just supposition. "My dear Bancroft, I am quite fond of the Misses Harrington, as I believe you are well aware. I assure you, they would be much wiser to be wary of you than of me."

Bancroft nodded, his cold expression unchanged. "Say whatever you like. Just stay away from me and mine. Is that clear?"

"Well, yes, of course. And quite unnecessary. Whatever eases your mind."

"It would ease my mind more if I beat you senseless for what you've tried to do. You apparently have more intelligence, though, than I gave you credit for."

The insolent bastard was going too far, but Deerhurst kept himself in check. Bancroft would pay. Very soon. And this moment would be all the more delicious if the fool began to doubt himself a little in the meantime. "My thanks. And despite your unbecoming behavior, if you are ever in need of assistance, monetary or otherwise, for Felicity's sake I will do what I can."

"Felicity's sake is the only reason you're still breathing," Bancroft spat. "Don't make me regret leaving you alive." With one last, angry look, he turned around and left.

As soon as Fitzroy shut the front door, the earl hurried to his second floor study. He quickly grabbed his musket off the wall beside his hunting trophies, primed and loaded it, and strode to the window.

Bancroft, mounted on his big bay, was headed across the meadow toward the shallow creek crossing north of the bridge, taking the most direct route back to Forton Hall. James leaned against the side of the open window and waited. A moment later the gelding reached the thick stand of trees bordering the creek.

The earl aimed carefully, squarely at the middle of Bancroft's back. As if by divine providence the moon broke from behind its cloud cover, filling the meadow with its silvery light. With a slight smile, the earl took a breath, held it, and pulled the trigger.

The sound of the shot echoed into the trees and

died out into the night. Bancroft lurched sideways, his head snapping back as the ball struck him. The bay vanished into the shadows of the trees and Deerhurst straightened. "Damned fine shot," he murmured, lowering the weapon.

He took a deep, cleansing breath. Since Bancroft was the first man he'd killed, he'd thought it would have affected him more. How odd. He simply should have killed Bancroft weeks ago. With one shot he'd deflected any attention from the Forton-Bancroft deed, once more become Felicity's only suitor, and rid himself of a damned annoying nuisance. Now he only needed to wait for Highbarrow's arrival so he could purchase the deed.

"My lord?" Fitzroy said from the doorway. "Do you require assistance?"

The earl put the musket aside. "No, thank you. Do remind me to send someone out to the creek tomorrow to have a look about. I fear there may have been an accident."

The butler nodded. "Very good, my lord."

"And in the meantime, send Vincent out to make certain there will be something to find in the morning. I won't take any chances at this point."

"Yes, my lord. And if I may be so bold, congratulations."

James smiled as he headed back downstairs to his book. "Thank you, Fitzroy."

Beeks scratched at the morning room door. Felicity started, hurriedly wiping her eyes. "Come in."

"Miss Harrington, dinner is served."

"Oh. Thank you." She looked at the mantel clock, surprised so much time had passed since her life and her future had ended. "Will you please inform May, as well?"

"Of course, miss."

Three places had been set at the dining room table; obviously, someone had forgotten to inform the servants that the master of the house was no longer in residence. Trying not to start crying all over again, Felicity took her seat.

A few moments later, as Ronald brought out the soup, Beeks reappeared. "Miss Harrington, I knocked at Miss May's door several times, but she has declined to answer. Neither have I been able to locate Master Rafael. Aristotle is gone, as well. Mr. Milton informs me that he went out riding."

Felicity nodded and stood. "Rafe . . . will not be dining with us this evening." *Or ever again.* She'd destroyed what she had with him, but perhaps it wasn't too late to explain things to May. Her sister was all she had left in the world now.

She went upstairs and stopped outside May's bedchamber. "May?" she called, rapping on the closed door.

Her sister didn't answer.

"May?" she repeated, louder. "I know you're mad, but I need to speak to you, sweetling. It's important."

When May still made no answer, Felicity turned the handle and pushed open the door. Her sister's room was as dark as the night outside—the night she could see through the open window and the curtains fluttering in the chill evening breeze.

"Oh, no," she breathed, hurrying to the window.

An old, half-rotted rose trellis still climbed the wall, within easy reach of a stubborn eight-year-old. And knowing May, Felicity realized she had decided to follow Rafe, on foot, all the way back to London—if that was even where he had gone.

"Beeks!" she yelled, only to jump as the butler materialized at her shoulder. "May was very upset earlier. I . . . Oh, my God. I fear she may have run off. Please, check every room here first, to be certain she's not hiding somewhere.''

"Immediately, Miss Harrington.'' He headed promptly for the doorway, then paused. ''Do you wish me to send word to Mr. Greetham or Lord Deerhurst?''

''Mr. Greetham, yes.'' She nodded, wringing her hands. ''I'll go see James myself. He can muster a dozen men to help us search.''

She grabbed her shawl and flung it over her shoulders. Downstairs in the kitchen, though, she paused. Rafe had a great deal of common sense. And someone *had* tried to set fire to the new wing. Resolutely she snatched up one of the big kitchen knives and tucked it into her skirt. Then she ran out into the night, heading west along the lane for Deerhurst's estate.

''Ah, Vincent,'' Lord Deerhurst said, sipping his port. ''Please tell me your news.''

The big-boned footman remained in the doorway. He was a natural shadow lurker—and very handy to have about from time to time. It was a pity not every household could afford one of him.

''Rode up and down the creek for a mile,'' the footman said in his guttural voice. ''Found blood sign, and where he fell into the water, but no body.''

The earl sat up, setting aside his glass. ''No body?''

Vincent shrugged. ''Might've washed downstream. Creek's high. Or with the clouds I might've missed him in the dark. Don't think so, though.''

Deerhurst tended to agree with that assessment. ''Your thoroughness is one of your most endearing qualities, Vincent.'' He tapped his chin. ''Still, this is troubling. I suppose we should go find him. What of his horse?"

"No horse, either. Must've run off. Did find this, though, crossing the bridge." He stepped forward, yanking something in from the hallway behind him. "Thought you might have some use for it, my lord."

With the footman holding onto her by the scruff of the neck, little May Harrington stumbled into the room. For a long moment Deerhurst gazed at her, while she looked back at him with angry, frightened eyes. For the past few years he'd thought of her as little more than a loud, messy nuisance. As the footman had said, though, tonight she might actually be of some use.

"Miss May. Surely you know better than to wander about by yourself at night."

"I'm looking for Rafe," she burst out. "You should let me go, or he'll be mad."

"Hm. I don't think so, little one." He leaned closer to her. "Does Felicity know where you are?"

"Yes." A tear rolled down one cheek, and she sniffed.

This was becoming very interesting. "Well, perhaps she'll come calling, as well. Vincent, show Miss May to one of the spare bedchambers upstairs. See that she stays quietly in one place."

As the footman hauled the girl out of the room, James stood and rang for Fitzroy. When the butler appeared, he seated himself again to finish his drink. "Fitzroy, have the dinner table set for two. I shall be dining in company this evening."

"Very good, my lord."

James smiled. Events were progressing even more favorably than he had anticipated. His bride-to-be would be coming to call.

*   *   *

Rafe put a hand across Aristotle's muzzle so the
bay would know to be silent. Creek water flowed
coldly around his thighs as he stood, listening.
Nothing save the owls and water and crickets came
to his ears, and after a long moment he sagged
against the bay's flank.

His left shoulder burned and throbbed, but the
wound didn't seem to be too serious. Whoever had
been looking for him had headed back downstream,
so they likely thought him dead or too badly
wounded to fight the current. He didn't have any
more time to waste with evading them. He needed
to get back to Forton—before Deerhurst turned his
attention on the Harrington ladies.

Whatever was going on, the earl was obviously
deadly serious about it. If the shot had been an inch
or two to the right, Rafe would be dead right now.
Hanging on to the stirrup and urging Aristotle forward, he made it up the steep, muddy bank. On the
grass he stopped, trying to catch his breath.

"Here goes nothing," he muttered, and with a
pained grunt hauled himself up into the saddle.
"Damn, that hurts."

The bay swung his head around and nickered at
him. Too late Rafe realized the reins were still
hanging. He couldn't climb down again to retrieve
them. Rafe started to give Aristotle a verbal com-
mand, then realized he'd never taught the gelding
to respond to the word "home." There had never
been a place that was truly his—until now.

"Aristotle, go find May," he ordered, hoping
that would be clear enough. "Go home." He whistled the order to trot, and the gelding hesitated a
moment, then moved off.

With a pained grunt he grabbed on to the cantle

of the saddle with his good hand, and held on. If Deerhurst touched his Lis, the earl was a dead man.

Felicity pulled her shawl more tightly around her shoulders as the earl's butler gestured her into the library. Lord Deerhurst sat gazing at the fire, a closed book across his lap and a glass of port in one hand.

"James," she blurted, not waiting to be introduced, "I'm sorry to call on you like this, but—"

The earl started and came to his feet. "Felicity. Please don't apologize for anything. What can I do for you?"

She held tightly to the remains of her common sense, the only thing keeping her from slipping into complete hysteria. "May seems to have run off. I'm afraid—"

James nodded. "I know."

"I was—" She broke off, staring at him. "You know?"

"Mm-hm. She's upstairs, as a matter of fact, in one of my guest bedchambers."

Her heart began beating again. "Thank goodness! Is she all right?" Felicity started for the door, but a very large man wearing the earl's livery, the same one who had delivered that first bouquet of roses, blocked her path. "Excuse me," she said, but he didn't budge.

"A minute of your time, Felicity, if you please."

She turned around. "In just a moment, James. May and I had a bit of an argument; I need to talk to her."

"They're just setting the table for dinner," the earl continued, as if she hadn't spoken. "Join me."

A whisper of uneasiness ran just under Felicity's skin. James was acting very odd, and whether she could ever believe Rafe or not, he had accused the earl of some rather ghastly things. "I'm afraid I can't stay, but thank you. Please show me where May is."

"May is quite well," the earl returned, the slightest edge of impatience touching his voice. "Don't trouble yourself. Come—my cook has made a splendid venison stew."

Felicity backed away ever so slightly, the whisper of uneasiness becoming a shout. "I must decline, my lord." She cleared her throat. The big footman still blocked her way out, and she had no chance of moving him aside if he chose not to go. "Rafe . . . Rafe was looking for May with Mr. Greetham. He'll be back at Forton by now, and he is expecting me."

"No, he isn't."

Felicity didn't even have a name for the sudden dread that hit her. *How could he know Rafe had gone? May surely wouldn't have told him.* "I assure you he is, my lord."

Deerhurst sighed. "Rafael Bancroft, my dear Felicity, is not anywhere waiting for you. Please save your lies for something more plausible."

"How—"

"Stop talking about him," he interrupted sharply. "He doesn't signify."

Felicity stared at the earl for a moment. "James, I think we should leave this for another time. I know you and Rafe don't deal well, and so I asked him to remain behind. May and I need to return to Forton before he is forced to come here and find us." It was the most boldfaced lie she'd ever told, and the reasonable tone she managed surprised her.

Deerhurst slammed his book down on the end table. "Stop it!"

She jumped. "James, I—"

"Don't you presume to threaten me with that bastard!"

"My lord, I understand your anger," Felicity said soothingly, trying to calm him down and becoming very worried about May, "but Rafael is my betrothed. I do wish the two of you might—"

"He is *not* your betrothed!"

Felicity backed away a step. May must have told him something, after all. "I would like to see my sister now, if you please." This time her voice shook.

"Not until you tell me that you will marry me."

She fingered the handle of the knife in her pocket. "James, I'm truly sorry if I've hurt you, but I have never lied to you about my feelings. I love Rafael, and—"

"Rafael Bancroft is dead!"

"Wha-*what*?"

"He had an accident. Someone shot and killed him not an hour ago."

Felicity stared at the earl for a moment, her mind refusing to comprehend what her ears had heard. "Rafe is . . . not dead," she managed, her voice coming out as a barely audible croak.

"I assure you, Miss Harrington," Deerhurst said, "that he is. Terrible tragedy."

Her legs gave way. She would have fallen to the floor if the footman hadn't moved forward to catch her beneath the arms and haul her back upright. "No," she whispered. "No."

She couldn't breathe; suddenly she had forgotten how. Her heart still beat, because she felt it pounding in her chest. Rafe could leave—that was acceptable, because he could come back. She could convince him that she was simply a fool and that she loved him so much it would kill her to lose him.

A ragged sob ripped from her throat. Rafe was dead. Rafe was dead, and she was alone, *again*, and she couldn't die, too, because May needed her. She clung to the thought of her sister to keep her sanity. This bastard, looking at her with that mildly amused smile on his handsome face, had tried to burn down her home, and had murdered her love. He would pay. She would see to it.

"Do stop whining," the earl commented. "Our stew will be getting cold."

Felicity pulled the knife from her gown and ran at him. "No!"

Deerhurst stumbled backward, falling over his footstool. Before she could reach him, though, the big footman grabbed her from behind, lifting her off the floor.

"Let go!" she shrieked.

Without a word he wrenched her arm. Pain shot up from her wrist, and the knife dropped to the floor.

The earl grabbed the weapon and tossed it into the fireplace. "That was abysmally stupid, Felicity. Don't make me angry." He took her chin between his fingers. "I have May. And you most definitely need me now, if you want to keep Forton Hall."

Felicity sagged. She didn't give a damn about Forton Hall, but she needed to know what was going on. And he was right: First things first. She needed to get May out of there and summon the constable. Then she could mourn.

"Why?" she asked in a stronger voice, wrenching free of the footman's grasp. "Why would you do this, James? I trusted you! We are—we were—friends." Saying the word almost choked her, for all she wanted to do was hurt him, as he had hurt her.

"It's a very long story, Felicity. I'll explain it to

you over dinner." His expression changed. "Don't
make me invite you to stay again."

She swallowed, unable to keep her hands from
shaking. "Then we should eat."

Chapter 19

Beeks sat at the kitchen table and glared at young Ronald Banthe. "Did either Master Rafael or Miss Harrington instruct you to clear away the dining room table?"

The footman flushed. "No, sir."

"Beeks," Beeks corrected.

"No, Beeks."

"Did *I* ask you to clear the table?"

"No, sir—Beeks. But I thought—"

The butler raised a finger, and Ronald swallowed and subsided. "Do not think," he stated. "Anticipate."

Ronald's embarrassed look became blank and confused. "Anticipate?"

Beeks sighed. Being relegated to the country was one thing; being placed in the employ of Rafael Bancroft was another. Being surrounded by complete disarray and incompetence, though, was too much to bear. He watched the footman shift uneasily. Tonight, however, looked to be stressful enough without adding more wood to the proverbial fire. "Yes. Anticipate. But that is a lesson for another evening, I think."

The footman sagged in relief. "Thank goodness."

"We'll see about that. Simply because Master

Rafael is a hopeless eccentric doesn't mean his servants may have the same luxury.''

''Come again, Beeks?''

The butler stood. ''Never mind. Please find Mr. Greetham and see if he needs your assistance in locating Miss May.''

The speed with which the footman fled the room was gratifying. At least he knew enough to be nervous. Instilling fear was half the battle.

Beeks paced down the hallway to the foyer and back again. Whatever tale Miss Harrington chose to tell about this evening's fiasco was fine with him, and he would defend its veracity to the death. However, he had overheard a great deal of the argument between his employer and the young lady.

Knowing the youngest Bancroft's temperament as he did, he thought Rafael should have been back by now—especially with the nefarious explanation for the recent construction ''accidents.'' And with the delightful Miss May gone missing, Rafael's continued absence was becoming rather troubling.

A loud knock shook the front door, as if someone had beaten it with a club. ''For heaven's sake,'' he muttered, returning to the foyer, ''don't go breaking the house again.''

The loud thud repeated, curiously low on the door. Either Miss May had returned, or violent midgets were coming to call at Forton Hall now.

Coming to attention, Beeks pulled open the door. ''Good evening . . .''

Aristotle nickered nervously and stepped halfway into the foyer.

For a moment Beeks stared at the animal, wondering how he had managed to survive more than twenty years' worth of Rafael's games and pranks. Then the horse took another step forward, and he saw Rafael hunched over the saddle.

"Good God!" Beeks stepped forward and pulled Rafe over sideways, taking his employer's weight with a grunt. "Master Rafael?" he said urgently. "Rafe?"

Rafe opened his eyes as the butler yanked him out of the saddle. "Beeks?" he grunted, gritting his teeth and working to get his legs back under him.

"Rafael. You're injured." Beeks put an arm around Rafe's shoulders to steady him.

"Are Felicity and May all right?" Rafe asked, pulling free as the foyer stopped its nauseating rolling about and righted itself.

"I'm . . . not entirely certain."

"What?" Rafe stopped.

"Let's get you into the kitchen and patched up. I'll explain there." The butler frowned. "You've been shot, haven't you?"

"Yes, by damned Deerhurst."

Beeks's normally stoic face went white. "*Lord Deerhurst* shot you?" he demanded.

Rafe, one arm outstretched for balance, strode toward the morning room. "Lis? May?" he called, glaring back at the butler when no one answered. "Wasn't anyone listening when I said he was a bloody Bedlamite?"

"Apparently Miss Harrington should have paid more attention. I believe she was rather angry at the time, though."

He stopped again. At the butler's words and grim expression, dread tightened his chest. "What happened?"

Beeks took hold of his arm again, and began walking him at a brisk pace toward the kitchen. "Miss May apparently left in search of you, and—"

"May ran away?" he interrupted. "Damnation, I'm an idiot. I should have explai—"

"And Miss Felicity went to get help to look for her." Beeks speeded his pace even further. "At Deerhurst."

"*What?*"

"We didn't know he had shot you, Master Raf—"

Clenching his teeth, Rafe tried to yank free again. "Let go, Beeks," he snapped.

The butler shook his head and kept walking, his grip tightening. "I will not."

Anger laced with terrible fear for Lis pulled at him. "Damn it, Beeks! He tried to shoot me in the back! What's to keep him from—"

"I am aware of the situation," the butler returned with uncharacteristic heat. "Your running off to the rescue won't be very effective if you drop dead on the earl's doorstep."

Rafe subsided and let the butler guide him down the hallway. He wasn't quite up to a full speed charge tonight. What he needed was a plan. "All right," he muttered, cursing again. "But make it quick."

When they reached the kitchen, Sally was there, pacing anxiously. As Beeks cleaned out his wound, the butler filled Rafe in on the chaos.

"So where's Greetham?" Rafe asked impatiently.

"Well, sir, thinking that Lord Deerhurst and his men would be searching in the direction of Pelford, Greetham and his fellows headed south and east through the woods."

"Should I fetch them?" Sally asked as the butler wrapped a bandage firmly across Rafe's shoulder.

"No," he grunted, wincing. "For all we know, May did head that way. I want her found, Beeks."

If anything had happened to her, he would never forgive himself.

"I know."

"Damn. A little looser, if you please. I need to be able to move my arm."

"And you also need the bleeding to stop. The ball went right through your shoulder, and—"

"I know. It missed the bone, though, so I'll worry about it later." Anything that would delay him from going to find Felicity would have to wait.

"You cannot go after Miss Harrington alone."

Rafe glanced up at the butler's worried countenance. "I need you to stay here, in case either of them returns. Send Tom for the constable, if Greetham hasn't done it already. And if I don't return by dawn, send to Warefield Park for Quin."

"I'll fetch the constable, Mr. Rafe," Sally broke in.

"I've already sent Tom after your brother, sir," the butler said.

"You . . ." Rafe stopped. "Damn. All right."

He gingerly pulled on the spare shirt Sally had gotten for him, and the old dark coat that had belonged to Felicity's grandfather. Taking a deep breath, he stood. Through the burning pain, a deep, frightened anger grew. He needed Felicity back. Now. He pocketed the pistol Sally had also retrieved from his bedchamber and returned to the foyer.

"Best of luck, Master Rafe," the butler said from behind him.

Rafe smiled grimly. "I'll need it."

Aristotle nuzzled him in the chest. He patted the bay on the withers and led him down the steps. Then he hauled himself up into the saddle again.

"Let's go, boy," he murmured. "We have another visit to make tonight."

He kept an eye out for May as they galloped across the fields back toward Deerhurst. Ordinarily he knew Lis could take care of herself, and he would have joined the search for the little sprite— but James Burlough was a lunatic, and fond as the earl had seemed of Felicity, Rafe wouldn't put anything past him tonight.

They paused at the edge of the trees. Though it felt like hours had passed since he'd last called on Deerhurst, from the position of the moon it couldn't be much past nine. He circled around the back of the manor. No one seemed to be keeping watch. It was likely, then, that they thought him dead. They were about to find out differently.

Light shone through the windows of only one of the second floor bedchambers of the east wing. Lis had told him that, like Forton, Deerhurst kept the west wing for himself, and the east one for guests. On the slight chance that Felicity was the guest inhabiting that room this evening, he coaxed Aristotle up to the wall, awkwardly stood in the saddle, and with the help of a drainpipe climbed up to the neighboring window. His shoulder throbbing, he leaned over and pushed against the window. It was locked.

Cursing, he climbed a little higher along the wall and leaned sideways again, then kicked out hard. His right boot went through the glass, the sound loud in the quiet night. For several long minutes he stayed where he was, listening. When no sound came from the house or the grounds below, he descended, swearing again as the motion wrenched his shoulder.

By stretching across the long drop between the drainpipe and the broken window, he was able to reach the latch and flip it open. With a last hard push against the drainpipe, he half jumped and half fell through the dark opening.

"Damn," he hissed, cradling his shoulder as he sat back against the wall to catch his breath.

He was making a blasted lot of noise, which shortened the time he had to find Felicity. With a grimace he stood. Checking his pistol, he stood and made his way to the door. The hallway beyond was dimly lit, and again no servants seemed to be about. For the moment he would count that as lucky, and worry about what it meant later.

The next door down wasn't locked, and a tremor of uneasiness ran through him. If Felicity was inside, he didn't like the reasons that would allow Deerhurst to leave the door unlocked and unattended. Slowly he eased it open and leaned inside.

May sat in a chair in the middle of the room, her arms and legs secured to it by an absurdly intricate knotting of ropes. When she saw him a tear ran down her cheek, to be caught in the scarf they had used to gag her.

"Sweet Lucifer," he muttered, closing the door and hurrying forward. Swiftly he loosened the scarf and pulled it down from her mouth. "Are you all right, sweetling?" he whispered, stroking her cheek.

"Yes," she quavered. "I want to go home."

He hugged her, then went to work on the ropes. "We'll have you there in no time," he murmured, each knot he untangled multiplying his fury at Deerhurst. This was *his family*, by God, and no one did this to them. No one.

As he freed her from the last knot, May surged to her feet and threw her arms around him. "I knew you wouldn't leave."

Rafe winced as she wrenched his shoulder, but held on to her tightly. "Of course I wouldn't." He

set her a little away from him. "Now—I need you
to wait in the next room for just a few minutes
while I find your sister. Can you do that?"

Her eyes widened. "Felicity is here, too?"

He nodded. "I believe so. You haven't seen
her?"

"No. Rafe, we have to rescue her—right away.
Lord Deerhurst still wants to marry her, I think.
And then she wouldn't be able to marry you."

Rafe stifled an unexpected smile. "Don't worry,
midget. She's not going to marry anyone but me."

"Good."

"Do you know if Deerhurst has anyone helping
him?"

"I saw four or five footmen. One of them is very
mean. He pulled my hair."

Too many for anything bold and straightforward.
That suited him just fine, though. He knew plenty
of other ways to do damage. "All right. Let's get
you hidden."

"I can help," May insisted. "I know number
twenty-eight."

"We'll hold that in reserve. For now, just be
quiet. I need to do a bit of scouting."

He bundled up the rope for future use and led
her next door, hiding her in the corner behind a
wardrobe. Rafe slipped out again, then paused.
Number twenty-eight gave him an idea—and an
opportunity for May to assist in the rescue. It was
time to make a little more noise.

Felicity picked at her stew. Deerhurst's appetite,
though, didn't seem to have suffered at all from the
night's events. Just watching him eat across from
her made her want to gag. She'd always thought
him a bit dull and pretentious; never had she suspected him of being a monster. Obviously, though,

he was the worst sort of beast—eating calmly when he'd killed and kidnapped and God knew what else. And given what he'd already done this evening, she wouldn't put anything past him now.

"You're not eating," he noted.

"You can't expect me to have much of an appetite."

"No, I suppose not." He devoured another mouthful. "You know, all of this is really your fault. But don't fret. I shall forgive you."

Felicity tried to keep her attention on him and away from the dark, empty chasm in her heart. She couldn't fall into it yet—not until May was safe. "How is this my fault?"

"I asked you repeatedly to have Bancroft sell Forton to me. You couldn't manage it. So I had no choice but to kill him."

Her insides jolted all over again at the words. "But you still don't have Forton. It's gone to his brother, or his father."

He shook his head. "It doesn't matter. I will have the deed. And you'll keep quiet about tonight for Forton Hall and May's sakes, won't you?"

"You're insane! Deerhurst is . . . perfectly lovely," she returned, though she hated every stick of it. "Why do you want Forton Hall?"

"I don't want that rotting, ramshackle hole," he said indignantly, looking at her as though she were an idiot. "I only want the deed."

"For God's sake, why?" she burst out.

The earl eyed her. "Because it includes ownership of Deerhurst."

Felicity blinked. *"What?"*

"Oh, it's a long story. We can discuss it later. Suffice it to say that everything is now very close to how it should have been all along. At the moment I'd rather discuss our wedding plans. None of that damned publishing of the banns. I'll secure a license from the vicar, and we can be married by Thursday.''

"I am not going to marry you," she spat.

He took a sip of port. "Yes, you are, or your sister will pay for your stupidity.'' The earl leaned across the table and grasped her fingers before she could pull away. "I won't have you testifying against me in court. And I want an heir, Felicity.''

That sounded even more ghastly than marrying the madman. "Go to hell.'' She flung her glass of wine into his face and rushed to her feet.

In a flash he was on her, slapping her hard across the face and knocking her to the floor. "Naughty, naughty,'' he said with a leering grin, and knelt beside her.

Something very loud and very heavy crashed to the floor upstairs. Deerhurst jumped, and Felicity used the moment to scramble to the other side of the table. Eyeing him warily, she seated herself again.

The earl gazed at her. "Fitzroy!'' he called.

"My lord?'' the butler answered, appearing in the doorway a moment later.

"What was that?''

"I don't know, my lord. I've sent Peters to see to it.''

"Have him make certain little May is still secure.''

"Yes, my lord.''

Deerhurst resumed his seat, as well. "So now you wish to behave?''

"I wish to kill you,'' she said flatly. "But I will behave.''

"But perhaps I shall not.''

Another crash, louder than the first, echoed through the upper rooms of the manor.

"Fitzroy!"

The butler reappeared. "I know, my lord. We are investigating."

"Do it at once."

Felicity listened. One crash she could call an accident. A second disturbance, in a completely different location from the first, was something to pay attention to.

"Now. Where were we?" The earl rose and moved around the table to take the seat beside her. "I feel like celebrating tonight," he murmured, running his fingers down her sleeve. "And you are my prize, after all."

Talking she could tolerate—barely—but being touched by him made her skin crawl. Only Rafe was allowed to touch her. Felicity balled her fist and hit him as hard as she could in the face.

He reeled backward, and then grabbed her and pulled her up against his wine-soaked chest. Before she could gasp, he met her mouth with a hard, wet, kiss.

"You bastard!" she hissed, trying to hit him again.

He yanked her hands behind her back and kissed her again, his tongue plying at her lips.

Deerhurst's prized grandfather clock tumbled down the stairs and landed with a clanging, off-key thud just outside the dining room door.

"Fitzroy!" he yelled. "What in damnation is going on?"

There was no answer.

"Fitzroy! Peters!"

His voice echoed hollowly through the quiet house, and a burst of impossible hope touched Felicity's heart. May was too small to dislodge something so big, and she knew few people who could be so very aggravating.

"Vincent!"

Felicity jumped as the hulking footman materialized in the doorway. "My lord?"

"Go put a stop to that!"

"With pleasure." The servant vanished again.

"At this rate, my lord," Felicity said, grim humor touching her voice, "you'll be out of servants by midnight. Except we won't know when that is now, will we?" She gestured at the heap of wrecked clock.

With an inarticulate growl, Deerhurst hauled her over to the doorway. "Then let's go see for ourselves," he muttered. Pushing her up against the wall, he yanked open a cabinet drawer and removed a pistol. Taking her arm again, he half dragged her toward the stairs. "And then we will celebrate our betrothal. I want to feel your hands on me."

"They'll be right around your neck," she returned, fighting against him and nearly going over the railing.

"Stop that," he ordered, shaking her. "You need to learn some manners."

"You'd best put down that pistol, my lord," she said in a carrying voice, trying to ignore what he was saying to her. And to think she'd imagined Rafe to be the mad one when they'd first met.

All the lamps upstairs had been put out, and only pale pools of moonlight illuminated the long, dark stretches of hallway. Vincent, a darker shadow in the gloom, glided forward a few yards in front of them.

"Check on the girl," Deerhurst snapped. His fingers tightened around her arm, and he kept her close beside him.

The footman slipped through one of the doors to the right, then emerged again a moment later. "The girl's gone. Peters's in there, out cold."

Felicity sagged with relief. Whomever their guardian angel was, May had escaped. "You'd best let me go," she said, tugging against the earl's bruising grip. "They'll be fetching the constable by now."

A door slammed shut behind them. Felicity gasped, and Deerhurst whipped around, his pistol raised. The hallway remained empty and dark. "Vincent," he ordered, "find whoever is in my house and kill him."

"Yes, my lo—"

With a cut-off grunt the footman fell silent. Felicity turned in time to see his legs vanishing through a doorway, and she cupped her free hand over her mouth, torn between surprise, delight, and horror. "Perhaps you have ghosts," she suggested darkly.

"Shut up," Deerhurst snapped. "Whoever you are, I have a pistol aimed at Miss Harrington's head. Show yourself!"

"Don't do it!" Felicity countered. "Take May and get out!"

The earl cuffed her across the face, and she staggered. "One more word and I'll send you to join Bancroft," he snarled.

"That would be fine with me."

Felicity held her breath as a tall, dark form entered the hallway and stepped forward into the moonlight. "Rafe," she sobbed, trying to pull free and go to him. "Rafe!"

"Are you all right?" he asked.

"Now I am. May?"

"Fine. Just remember to watch your step around here."

"You're dead," Deerhurst said wildly, his face white.

She was being warned about something. "I will."

"You're dead!" the earl repeated, and fired his pistol.

Felicity screamed. Rafe dove to the floor. She didn't know whether Deerhurst had hit him or not, and she swung out wildly. Her blow connected, and with a grunt Deerhurst loosened his grip. She wrenched free and ran.

With a roar the earl took off after her. "Damn you!"

"Lis, jump!"

Dimly she saw a rope stretched low across the hallway. Without thinking, Felicity sprang over it. Behind her the earl tripped, pulling a hallway table laden with porcelain figurines down on top of himself.

Rafe jerked her through a doorway. She tripped over something in the dark, and he shoved her toward a chair. She fell into it heavily as the earl reached the entry and stumbled into the room.

No one stopped his fall, and he landed hard on his knees. In a heartbeat Rafe was on him, slamming Deerhurst's head against the floor. The earl managed to throw him off, and they tumbled against a bookcase.

"Lis, get out!" Rafe rasped, rolling sideways.

He was hurt, she realized with horror, and fighting a man who was determined to see him dead. Instead of fleeing, she snatched up one of the fallen books and hurled it at Deerhurst.

It hit him on the thigh and bounced off, but he seemed to have forgotten her completely as he went after Rafe again. Seeing her chance, she grabbed another book and edged forward. Rafe saw her and frowned, but she lifted the book over her head and slammed it down.

Her feet jerked out from under her. Instead of braining the earl, her blow merely clipped his shoulder. Felicity hit the floor hard.

The grip on her ankle tightened and dragged her backward, out of reach of Deerhurst. She twisted as Vincent grabbed for her arm, and she gasped and wrenched sideways, swiping the book at his head. It caught him on the temple, and he half fell across her legs. "Damn," he grunted. "You bloody—"

She whacked him again. The footman grabbed her wrist, sending the book flying as he clawed his way up her body. Kicking and punching, she tried to squirm free of him, but he was too blasted strong. And then it would be the two men against Rafe, and he wouldn't have a chance, and James really would kill him.

"Let go!" she shrieked, kicking him as hard as she could with both feet. She must have hit a tender spot, because he gasped and doubled over.

Moving fast, Felicity scrambled away from him. At the last moment he tangled his hand into her skirt and pulled her down again. Then with a sudden hard jerk, he subsided.

Felicity sat up. May stood over the collapsed footman, the discarded book in her hands. As she saw Felicity, she dropped it and threw herself forward.

"Felicity, I'm sorry I yelled at you," she cried, wrapping her arms tightly around her sister's neck.

"It's all right, May," Felicity managed shakily. "Watch that one," she instructed, gesturing at Vincent and putting the book back into her sister's hands. "If he moves at all, hit him again. I have to help Rafe."

"I'll hit him hard," May said grimly, nodding.

The earl had her love down on the floor and

punched into the back of his shoulder. Rafe gasped, convulsing in pain, and Deerhurst did it again.

"No!" she shrieked, and flung herself forward. Grabbing the earl by the hair, she yanked him backward, all her fury and weight behind her. Cursing, he grabbed for her, but she kept her hold. "You leave him alone!"

"You'll pay for this!" he snarled, swiping at her again, but then Rafe was there, slamming his fist full into Deerhurst's face.

She let go as he flung his right arm hard around the earl's throat. "You will *never* hurt my family again," he grunted, tightening his grip with each word.

Deerhurst flailed wildly, trying to break Rafe's grip. His blue eyes rolled into the back of his head as Rafe choked the air out of him. Suddenly Felicity remembered that Rafe knew nothing about why Deerhurst had tried to kill him—and he needed to hear it from the source, or she would have no proof at all.

"Rafe, stop!"

He glanced up at her, black fury in his eyes. "No."

"I won't be the reason he dies," she said as calmly and clearly as she could. "We know enough to see him in prison for life."

"Lis—"

"Please, Rafe."

He looked at her for the space of several heartbeats, then let go. The earl slumped to the floor, gasping weakly for breath. Worried that one or the other of them would pass out, she yanked the earl's hair again.

"Get away from me," he rasped.

"Who owns Deerhurst?" she demanded. She met Rafe's gaze again, to see the sudden interest tempering the rage and exhaustion in his eyes. "Who owns Deerhurst?" she repeated, jerking James's hair again.

"You bloody . . . whore," he wheezed. "I'll kill . . . you both."

Rafe leaned stiffly closer. "Answer the damned question."

"No!"

"Lis?"

She let James go, and his head thunked back to the carpet. "I think you own it, Rafe. I think Nigel did, and now you do. That's why he wanted you dead."

"Master Rafael!"

"We're up here, Beeks!" May yelled, still holding her book menacingly over the prone Vincent.

"Thank God," Rafe muttered, holding her gaze. "I didn't leave you, Lis." He swayed. "I never would."

"I love you," she whispered, but she wasn't certain he heard her as his eyes closed and he collapsed into her arms. She looked up as Beeks and Mr. Greetham burst into the room and tripped over the rope Rafe had placed there. "My adventurer."

Rafe opened his eyes. Sunlight flooded into his bedchamber through half-open curtains, and outside the rattle of construction had already begun.

He started to stretch, then stopped when the movement pulled his shoulder. With a slight smile, he relaxed again. Since he'd arrived there, he'd never simply listened to the sounds of Forton Hall. It sounded surprisingly like home.

Someone stirred beside him. Startled, he turned his head. With one hand twisted into his nightshirt, Felicity slept beside him. She looked as tired as he still felt, but he couldn't help reaching over to stroke his finger along the smooth skin of her cheek.

Her eyelids fluttered and opened. For a moment she gazed at him sleepily, then she sat up with a start. "You're awake! How do you feel?"

He chuckled. "Good morning." She still wore the blue gown he'd seen her in yesterday, now garnished with a ripped sleeve and missing three buttons. "You've been here all night."

Felicity nodded. "I couldn't leave. How does your shoulder feel?"

"It hurts. But I've had worse."

"Rafe? I've been thinking."

"That doesn't sound good," he said dubiously. Good Lord, he just wanted to lie here with her and hold her forever. If only she would let him. "Thinking about what?"

"About Forton Hall."

He should have let Gillingham burn the damned place down. Being jealous of a building was something he'd never even imagined, and he had no idea how to deal with it. "And?"

She ran her fingers across his chest, under his nightshirt. "And . . . I think you should sell it. If you want to."

Rafe blinked. "Beg pardon?"

"I know you've been doing all of these repairs for me and for May," she blurted. "But I . . . I thought I lost you last night, Rafe."

He clasped her hand over his heart. "You didn't. And sacrificing your home isn't—"

"No, no. It's just wood and bricks and glass, for heaven's sake." She tightened her grip. "And James would have killed you for the deed." A tear ran down her cheek. "And you don't even want to be here."

Hoping mightily that he wasn't dreaming, Rafe awkwardly sat up. "Ouch. Damn."

"Lie down," she ordered, pushing on his chest.

He caught her hand again, and gripped her fingers tightly. "So if I wanted to go to China, you would go with me?"

Felicity nodded. "If you wanted me to. But if . . . you don't want me, you don't have to worry. My second cousin in York has offered me a position. May and I will have a place to go, so you shouldn't feel guilty about any of—"

"You're bloody well not going to York, Felicity," he snapped, panic rising in his heart at the thought of losing her now. "Is that clear?"

"Rafe—"

"And while we're at it—"

Beeks scratched at the door, then cautiously stuck his head in. "Ah, you're awake. You have a caller, Master Rafael. John Gibbs."

"Now what?" he muttered. "Show him in."

Felicity tried to scramble off the bed, but when he wouldn't let go of her hand, she settled for blushing and whacking him across his good shoulder. "You're going to ruin me."

"I already did," he whispered back, grinning.

"Shut up."

"Twice."

"Rafe—"

"Mr. Bancroft," the solicitor said as he entered the room. "And Miss Harrington. Good morning to you both."

"Out with it, Gibbs."

"Yes, ah. Very well." John glanced about the room. "May I sit down?"

"By all means."

"You've, ah, stirred things up a bit in Pelford, Mr. Bancroft."

Rafe lifted an eyebrow. "I should hope so. What does Mrs. Denwortle say?"

The solicitor cleared his throat. "I'd prefer not to answer that at the moment, sir."

"And I didn't even get a chance to tell her about the Duke of Wellington and King Georgie."

"Rafe, let him talk," Felicity murmured, surreptitiously twining her fingers through his.

"Tell us your news, Gibbs," Rafe said obligingly, feeling oddly like singing at the top of his lungs.

"Since the events of last night, I have managed to put several facts I recently discovered into better order. It seems that some fifteen years ago, the Earl of Deerhurst amassed some rather excessive gambling debts. Enough that he would have lost his estate." The solicitor glanced at Felicity. "To shorten a very long tale, Mr. Harrington purchased Deerhurst for twice the amount of the debt in order to provide the earl with enough money to repay his losses and keep the estate solvent."

"So it's true?" Felicity gasped. "All this time, Nigel owned Deerhurst?"

"Yes. It was supposed to be repaid, and the whole thing kept secret to prevent any embarrassment, but unfortunately your father died, Miss Harrington. From there things become rather ... hazy."

She shook her head. "I appreciate your discretion, Mr. Gibbs, but it's not necessary. Once my father died, his own debts came to light. Obviously the old earl and James both feared that we would sacrifice Deerhurst to put Forton back on its feet."

Rafe closed his eyes for a moment, a thousand possibilities running through his head. "So I own Deerhurst."

"Yes, Mr. Bancroft."

"And how much is it worth?"

"Approximately one hundred and fifty thousand pounds."

"Good God. And where is James Burlough?"

"In custody. Given the gravity of his crimes, the constable has sent for Bow Street Runners to take him to London."

"They'll try him before the House, then," Rafe murmured. "My father should enjoy that. For once, I'm grateful he's a vindictive son of a bitch."

"Pleasant thing to say about your own sire."

Rafe looked toward the doorway, and abruptly hoped that he was dreaming. "Your Grace?" he managed. "What in damnation are you doing here?"

The Duke of Highbarrow stood there taking in the shabby room, the young solicitor, Rafe with his shoulder swathed in bandages, and Felicity, white-faced, seated on the bed beside him.

"It's my fault, I'm afraid," a second voice said, and Quin brushed past his father. "If you'll excuse us, sir," he said to Gibbs.

"Of . . . of course, my lord. Your Grace." Fumbling with his satchel, the solicitor fled the room.

"Are you all right, Rafe?" Quin stepped forward to examine the bandages. "Beeks told us what happened."

"I'll live," Rafe said, tightening his grip around Felicity's hand. She was not going to escape now. "What are you doing here?"

Finally the duke stirred, taking the seat Gibbs had vacated. "Quinlan wrote me as we were leaving for Spain. Said you were in another damned tangle and mooning after some chit." Highbarrow returned his gaze to Lis. "You, I presume?"

"Yes, Your Grace," she answered calmly. "I

am Felicity Harrington. Rafe has often spoken of you."

Rafe glanced at her face. She was more diplomatic than he would have been. "We're to be married Sunday," he declared, and took a breath to prepare for the thundercloud to burst.

"You will not."

"Yes we will, by God!"

"Your mother and Maddie won't be here until Sunday."

Rafe blinked. "Beg pardon?"

The duke gestured at Quin. "Your brother says you designed that stable. And the new wing. Is that true?"

"Yes."

"Fine work."

How long he might have sat there, staring at his father, he would never know, because Felicity nudged him in the shoulder. "Say thank you, Rafe."

"Thank you."

"Hm. She's got common sense. You can damned well use that."

Perhaps he was still asleep, after all. Rafe looked from his brother, watching with hooded amusement in his eyes, to his father, sitting straight in the chair and looking for all the world like some medieval judge. "So you approve of the match."

"What the hell do you care whether I approve it or not?"

"I don't. Just curious."

"Ah." Highbarrow stood. "Who's marrying you?"

"Reverend Laskey," Felicity replied, the slightest bafflement touching her own voice. "The local vicar."

"I'll go look him up."

Rafe straightened. This, he was ready for. "You will not do any such—"

"You'll be married on Tuesday, after your mother has a chance to arrive and settle herself." With that, the duke turned on his heel and left the room.

"Quin, I believe His Grace has suffered an apoplexy," Rafe announced.

His brother chuckled and walked over to pull the curtains open. "When your groom arrived last night, Mother questioned him about you and Forton for half an hour before we left. She informed His Grace that if he said one negative word to you about Forton or about Miss Harrington, she would be *very* unhappy." He leaned back against the windowsill. "Though in truth, I don't think he needed the warning. It scared him when you left London the last time. I believe he finally realized that you weren't coming back."

"This is all quite a bit too much for me this morning," Rafe finally muttered, and lay back again.

"We're not supposed to tire you out, so I'll leave you alone. One more question, though. What are you going to do with Deerhurst?"

"Sell it," Rafe murmured, closing his eyes.

"Congratulations then, Rafael. You're a wealthy man."

Rafe opened one eye to watch Quin leave the room, then he struggled upright again.

Felicity looked over at him, her eyes serious. "He's right. You're rich."

"*We're* rich," he corrected, sliding his arm around her waist.

"Rafe—"

"Will you be quiet for a damned minute?"

Lis stared at him. "All right."

He took a breath. "I want you to know something. I love you. More than anything. Whatever I thought I would find in China or Peru, I found here. I realized that last night. I think I've known it for a while, though."

"Rafe—"

"I want to wake up beside you every morning like this, in my bed, and in my home," he pressed on. "With you. Here—at Forton Hall. Can you live with that?"

She began crying. "When James said he killed you last night, I thought I would die, too. I'll be happy with you anywhere, Rafe." Felicity smiled and wiped her eyes. "If it happens to be here, then so be it."

"Oh. So you can tolerate staying at Forton."

"I think so, yes."

Chuckling, Rafe tilted her chin up with his fingers and kissed her. "Good. I rather like the place."

Felicity slipped her arms around him to lean against his good shoulder. This was precisely what he wanted. He could have saved them a great deal of grief and confusion if he'd only realized it before. Rafe brushed his lips against her disheveled hair. Only one thing was missing now.

The door rattled and opened again. "Felicity?" May whispered, peering around the door. "Oh, you're awake. There's a duke downstairs. Ronald spilled tea on him."

"Oh, dear," Felicity muttered. "Poor Ronald."

With a grin, May strolled into the room and climbed up onto the bed. "Did you tell Rafe?"

"Tell me what, midget?" he asked, wiggling his toes at her. *Now* he had everything—except perhaps for one or two of his own, just like the sparkling-eyed sprite gazing at him.

"I did number twenty-eight again. With a book, this time."

"You did?"

Felicity chuckled, nodding. "She did. For a great war hero, Rafael Michelangelo Bancroft, you've been bested and rescued quite a few times by an eight-year-old girl."

Rafe searched her dark eyes, seeing only weariness, humor, and a reflection of his own love for her. "I am completely and utterly humiliated. I'll never be able to go to any of the Coldstream Guards' reunions."

"*Nulle secundis!*" May crowed, giggling. "That's our motto, now."

"Hm." Rafe grinned. "Better than 'number twenty-eight!' "

Felicity laughed and kissed him on the ear. "I love you," she whispered.

"And I love you, my practical one."

New York Times bestselling author

SUZANNE ENOCH

*At Avon Books, we know your passion
for romance—once you finish one of our
novels, you find yourself wanting more.*

May we tempt you with . . .

- **Excerpts** from our upcoming releases.

- Entertaining **extras**, including authors'
  personal photo albums and book lists.

- Behind-the-scenes **scoop** on your favorite
  characters and series.

- **Sweepstakes** for the chance to win free books,
  romantic getaways, and other fun prizes.

- Writing **tips** from our authors and editors.

- **Blog** with our authors and find out why they
  love to write romance.

- **Exclusive content** that's not contained
  within the pages of our novels.

Join us at
www.avonbooks.com

AVON

An Imprint of HarperCollins*Publishers*
www.avonromance.com

FTH 1111